Ten Years After

AMY ROWLINGS MYSTERIES: BOOK 5

T. A. BELSHAW

For Catherine

Best Wishes

First Published 2024 by SpellBound Books
Copyright © 2024 by T. A. Belshaw

The moral right of the author to be identified as the owner of this Work has been asserted by them in accordance with the Copyright, Designs and Patents Act, 1988.

All rights reserved. No part of this publication may be reproduced, stored in a retrieval system, or transmitted, in any form or by any means, electronic, mechanical, photocopying, recording or otherwise, without the prior permission of the publisher.

For readers from my hometown of Ilkeston in Derbyshire. Especially: Angela, David, Tracey, Heather, Gaynor, Ann, Carol, Carol and Carol.
Thank You.

Chapter One

The storm broke mid-afternoon, finally bringing an end to the oppressive humidity. The heavy, lead coloured clouds that had hung over the town for days, holding in the heat like a vast, iron, saucepan lid, swirled and churned, lit up here and there by flashes of lightning as if announcing the appearance of the Valkyrie from Wagner's opera.

Torrents of water ran down the hill from High Street onto Middle Street, washing away the accumulated dust and cigarette ends that had lain undisturbed for weeks. At the Ironworks, sweaty, grime covered men stepped out into the rain, removed their shirts and raised their hands in the air to welcome the downpour.

In Witchy Wood, a four acre mass of holm oaks, lindens, sycamores and aspens, interspersed with thick tangles of blackthorn and hawthorn, a lightning strike hit the eaves of a long abandoned cottage causing the eastern end to collapse, opening up an old storeroom that had been hidden away behind a crumbling stone wall and a thick covering of wisteria for decades.

'Thank goodness!' Amy Rowlings exclaimed as a deafening thunderclap sounded overhead. Even with every available window open inside the London Connection fashion shop, the customers and staff mopped their brows with already sodden handkerchiefs. The atmosphere had been oppressive since the doors opened at nine o'clock that morning. The humid air enveloped her like a heavy shroud as the strategically placed electric fans whined and strained, only moving the sultry air from one place to another.

Amy resisted the urge to wring out her sopping handkerchief and dropped it instead into the waste bin at the side of the counter. She still had a clean one in her bag after buying two new ones from Jimmy Cousins' market stall earlier in the day.

Amy worked two and a half days a week at the shop where her keen eye for fashion and her sympathetic manner when quietly explaining to a customer that the particular tight fitting dress she had her heart set on buying wasn't quite the dress for her, was greatly appreciated. The rest of the week was spent behind her sewing machine at Handsley's Garments, a clothing factory known locally as 'The Mill' because it was once a cotton mill driven by a long-dismantled water wheel that had powered the factory in the late eighteenth century.

Amy wasn't a clock watcher by any means and thoroughly enjoyed both of her jobs, but today had been stressful, with a stream of bad tempered customers, all intent on finding someone to complain to about the conditions inside the shop.

At five-thirty, Amy breathed a big sigh of relief and after ushering the last grumbling, sweating, middle-aged lady of the day out of the front door, she hurried through to the staff room, where she half-filled the sink with lukewarm water from the tap and plunged her face into it.

'Move over,' Jill, the trainee seamstress said, nudging Amy aside in her hurry to get her own face into the water.

Amy put her head back, looked up at the ceiling and allowed the refreshing water to run onto her neck. After reaching for a towel, she dried her face and stuck her head out of the open window, relishing the cooling breeze that had replaced the stagnant heat. 'If it's your turn to lock up tonight, Jill, don't forget to close all the windows or Josie will arrive to find she has no stock left on Saturday morning.'

Jill pulled her head out of the sink and reached out for the towel that Amy was offering. 'You're so lucky getting every Saturday off, Amy. I'd like just one Saturday a month to myself.'

'Ah, but you get every Wednesday afternoon off,' Amy replied. 'When I leave here at one, I have to get the bus straight to The Mill. I have to be at my machine for half past. I don't even have time for lunch.'

'It's still better than working on Saturdays.' Jill patted at her damp hair as she looked forlornly at Amy. 'Everywhere closes for half a day on Wednesdays. There's nothing to do except walk around the blooming market. My young man, Sidney, works through the week, but he gets Saturday afternoons off. Not that he can see me until the evenings. He has to spend his half day watching Spinton United playing blooming football.' She sighed. 'He'd much rather be spending that time with me.'

Amy shook her head and smiled to herself. 'I bet the poor lad has to go to the pub at lunchtime too, just to pass the time.'

Jill sniffed. 'Yes, but I know he'd much rather be spending time with me than with his mates. He gets to see them all week at work.'

'Who has the keys tonight?' Josie, the manager said as she walked through from the shop.

'Me, madam,' Jill said, holding out her hand for the large bunch of keys.

'Make sure you close all the windows. Don't forget what happened when Jenny Harris forgot to lock up properly. We found a tramp on the floor of the fitting room when we opened up the next morning.'

'I'll make sure everything is safe and secure,' Jill replied, giving the Guides salute. She dropped her hand to her side quickly as Josie gave her a stern eye.

'Make sure you do.'

At the front of the shop, Amy waited as Josie used her spare set of keys to unlock the half glass doors, then stepped smartly outside as the manager prepared to lock them again.

'I'm tempted to wait across the road and check that she has locked up properly,' Josie said as Amy hung her bag over her arm and turned towards the street. 'She's meeting her young man later tonight, so she'll be in a hurry to get away.'

'She'll do a proper job, Josie,' Amy said with a quick nod of her head. 'She knows she's lucky to be working here.'

'You're right, of course,' Josie replied. 'I still haven't forgotten that tramp though. I had to get Elsie the cleaner to disinfect the entire shop. I almost convinced myself that I'd picked up head lice.'

Amy laughed. 'Right, I'll get off then. See you next Wednesday.'

Josie put her hand on Amy's arm. 'I really wish I could convince you to work here full time, Amy. You know how much the customers love you.'

'You wouldn't think so today. I took the worst of the flak from ill-tempered so and sos.'

'The customer is always right. Isn't that our motto?'

'It is,' Amy replied flatly. 'Even when they insist they can fit their size eighteen frames into a size twelve dress.'

Josie grinned. 'Ah, but you explain why it isn't possible so inventively.'

Amy smiled back and turned to walk across the street to get her bus. 'Oops, sorry,' she said as she bumped into a tall, dark-haired man, wearing a shiny suit and an extremely crumpled shirt.

'Just the lady I was hoping to find,' the man said. His eyes lit up as he smiled at her.

'Bodkin? What are you doing here? I didn't think I was seeing you until tomorrow.'

'That was the plan, but things can change quickly,' Bodkin replied. 'Especially when there's an unexplained death to investigate.' He paused, nodded to Josie, then took Amy by the arm. 'You know your way around the Witchy Wood, I take it?'

'Of course. Alice and I spent a lot of our summers in there when we were young.'

Bodkin grinned. 'Good, you'll know that long abandoned cottage on the west side of the wood, then?'

Amy nodded. 'We used to call it the Creepy Cottage. No one's lived there in my lifetime. It's pretty much a ruin.'

'It's even more of a ruin now,' Bodkin said. 'An end wall has fallen in during the big storm this afternoon. When it was over, a dog walker and his pooch discovered something very interesting.'

Bodkin was silent as he led Amy towards his Morris car that he'd parked just around the corner.

Amy dug him in the ribs. 'Come on, Bodkin, stop teasing. What did they find?'

'A skeleton,' the inspector replied. 'A skeleton that may have suffered a brutal attack while it was still attached to a living body... or at least, that's how it appears. There is severe skull damage.'

''How it appears?' Couldn't the wall have done the damage when it collapsed?'

'I doubt it,' Bodkin said as he unlocked the passenger side of the car and opened the door to allow Amy to climb in. 'There's a rusty old pickaxe buried in it.'

Chapter Two

Amy was about to open the passenger side door when Bodkin put his hand gently on her arm. 'Don't you want to drive?'

Amy almost snatched the keys from the policeman's hand. Bodkin had been teaching her to drive since the investigation into young Effie Watkins' murder during the factory fortnight holidays at the end of July. She had been an enthusiastic learner and Bodkin thought she might be ready to take the statutory driving test sometime during the autumn, if the government tests were still being offered. The political situation was very unstable. War was on the horizon and if the worst happened, he was sure that many of the government departments would shut down or merge with other, more important sectors of the civil service. No one would worry about driving tests when the bombs were falling, and the enemy was preparing to invade.

'Another dog walker finds a body,' she said as she went through her start up routine. 'That's three that I know of in Kent in the last few weeks. There were two mentioned in the papers recently. One in Maidstone and one in Sittingbourne.'

'I know,' Bodkin said as he looked over his shoulder to double check that the road was clear before Amy pulled out. 'Dog walkers should be at the top of our suspects list. They're always sniffing out corpses. One of these days the dog walker will be proved to be the murderer and then a whole raft of previously unsolved cases will have to be investigated again.'

Amy looked at him quizzically. 'Are you being serious? I never know with you half the time.'

Bodkin grinned. 'Semi-serious. I honestly do think we ought to investigate them more than we do. We seem to take their word for it that they just happened across the body, every time.'

'I'd love a dog,' Amy said wistfully. 'But Dad won't have one... or a cat... or a blooming telephone,' she added with a frown.

'Your mum would end up looking after it with you and your father at work all week and I'm sure she's got enough on her plate without having to find time to walk a dog.' He glanced over his shoulder again, then back to Amy who was looking through the back window of the Morris.

'She'd find the time. She loves animals. It's just Dad being... Dad.'

Amy started up the Morris and after one last look over her shoulder, pulled out onto Middle Street and drove smoothly down the hill towards the police station.

'Pull over for a minute, Amy. I need to get Ferris's report from my office.'

'Ferris's report? Haven't you been to the cottage yet?'

Bodkin shook his head. 'Nope. Chief Inspector Laws and Ferris were first on the scene. I was out on a burglary investigation... At least I think it can be classed as burglary.'

'So, why has Ferris put a report on your desk and not Laws'?'

Bodkin ran his fingers through his mop of unruly, dark hair. 'According to Ferris, Laws took one look at the scene of the crime and decided that it was going to be someone else's investigation. That body could have been there for decades.'

'So he passed the buck?'

Bodkin nodded. 'Laws doesn't want anything other than open and shut cases on his desk these days.'

He opened the passenger door as Amy pulled up. 'Won't be a tick. I'll just pick up the file and find Ferris. It's a good job he was with Laws today or we wouldn't have a report at all.'

Bodkin was as good as his word and was soon climbing back into the car as the new appointment to his CID team, Constable Ferris slid onto the bench seat at the back. Ferris was a young man with piercing blue eyes, a handsome, clean-shaven face with neatly parted light brown, almost blond hair. He was a smart-looking man of about five feet ten and wore a freshly pressed navy pinstriped suit. Ferris was a talented singer with a rich baritone voice, who appeared fortnightly at the swish Milton Club with the house jazz band.

As Amy pulled away from the kerb, Bodkin opened up the buff folder and ran his eyes over the three-page report, while running his free hand over the dark stubble on his chin. Bodkin was the polar opposite of Ferris. He could look untidy in a freshly laundered, made to measure designer suit. It made no difference if he wore a belt or elastic braces. His trousers would crumple over his shoes as though they were three inches too long for his legs. Amy had made alterations to two pairs herself using her mother's sewing machine, but within an hour of pulling them on, they were lying in crumpled layers over the top of his shoes.

'This is good work, Ferris,' he said, scratching at his chest. 'Were you alone when you bagged up all this stuff?'

'No, sir, I had a couple of uniforms with me. PC Smedley, and Forrester, the new lad. He did well to say it's the first skeleton he's ever seen.'

'Whereas you've seen scores of them.' Bodkin grinned as he looked into the back seat.

'I saw one at the British museum when I was a kid,' Ferris said.

'Did that have the head of a pickaxe buried in it too?'

'No... but it was still a skeleton. When you've seen one, you've seen them all. They all look the same to me.' The constable grinned to himself as he sang, 'your toe bone's connected to your foot bone...'

Bodkin shook his head and went through the report again. 'You say here you found a decomposed skirt, a belt, one complete shoe and one with a missing heel?'

'Yes, sir, the skirt isn't too bad considering it's been there for so long. I didn't find the missing heel, but it could be under the fallen masonry, I suppose.'

Bodkin nodded. 'There was a handbag too. What was in it?'

'I don't know, sir. I just bagged up the items we found. Chief Inspector Laws told me not to go messing with the evidence; he said, leave it to someone who knows what they're doing.'

'Where is it all? There was nothing in my office apart from this.' Bodkin waved the report in the air.

'I left it all in Chief Inspector Laws' office. There were only a few bits and pieces and they easily fitted into two bags. I wasn't sure what to do with it. He just said, make sure the report is on Inspector Bodkin's desk for when he gets back.'

Bodkin sighed. 'Laws has gone home for the day. He and Mrs Laws are going to a posh dinner do in Gillingham tonight. I hope he didn't lock his office door. I'd like to get an early look at the evidence.'

Amy listened to the conversation intently as she steered the car off the main Gillingham road and onto what was little more than a dirt track. With the trees getting thicker on either side and the path getting narrower, she parked the car on top of a recent set of tyre tracks, applied the handbrake and switched off the engine. 'Creepy Cottage is about fifty yards further on.' She shivered as a memory from her childhood flashed into her mind. 'We always said it was haunted. None of us would go too close to it. Not even for a dare and we were brave enough to go into that broken down mausoleum in the churchyard. There were so many stories about the place. I remember Jenny Norris saying that a young boy had climbed in through a window one night and had never been seen again.' She put her hand to her mouth suddenly. 'Oh, Bodkin, you don't think...'

Bodkin shrugged. 'You said it's been abandoned for a long time, Amy. How long, roughly?'

'I honestly don't know when anyone last lived in it. It's been a ruin since I was little. I could ask Mum and Dad. They used to walk in the woods when they were younger, they might know.'

'If you could, that would be very helpful,' Bodkin replied as he opened the door of the car. 'Right, Ferris, you know where you're going. Lead the way.'

The cottage was situated amongst a relatively recent expansion of trees on the right-hand side of an ever narrowing path. Ferris pointed to the collapsed wall as they pushed their way through a thick growth of elder saplings. Over the years, the wood had encroached onto the property and had infiltrated what would once have been a nice sized square of garden. A pair of flaking, once white, fence posts, stood like sentries on either side of an overgrown, stepping stone path. Ferris had just begun to make his way towards the fallen masonry when Bodkin pulled him back by his arm.

'Hang on, Ferris. I want to have a good look around the building before I examine the actual crime scene. Did you check the doors and windows when you were here?'

'No, sir, Chief Inspector Laws just wanted us to concentrate on the area where the body was found. He said you'd give the place a proper once over when you got here.'

Bodkin grunted as he made his way between the rotting gate posts and began to walk along the overgrown path, studying the cottage carefully as he went. Amy followed while Ferris brought up the rear.

The entire side of the cottage was covered in dense growths of ivy and wisteria. Bodkin pulled away a few handfuls of stems to find an empty window frame hidden behind. Reaching out, he pulled away more of the leaves until he had a hole big enough to look through.

Grinning, he turned back to Amy, who was still on the path, reluctant to get any closer to the cottage.

'This might be where Jenny Norris's friend got in.'

'Don't, Bodkin,' Amy said as a shiver ran down her spine. She looked to her side where the comforting figure of Ferris was standing. 'This is as close as I've ever been to this place. We never came into the garden at all. I know it's only old wives' tales and all that, but everything we ever heard about this place was scary.'

Bodkin pulled his head back out of the hole, rubbed his hair to dislodge the strands of ivy and old cobwebs that had clung to him, and returned to the path. 'Well, the vanishing boy isn't inside that room. There are a lot of skeletons in there, but they're just the remains of old leaves that have blown in over the years.' He looked up at the slate roof, which had partially collapsed, then made his way around the building until he came to a flaking, green painted front door that had been made from three wide oak planks. Taking hold of the rusty iron handle, he attempted to force it down as he pushed his shoulder against the door. It didn't budge an inch.

'That handle's so rusty it's never going to twist again,' Bodkin said. He took a step back and kicked at the door with much the same result. 'Ferris!' he called. 'Come on, let's see if we can shift it between us.'

Ferris stepped forward and on the count of three, both men hurled themselves at the door, only to stand back a few seconds later, rubbing sore and probably bruised shoulders. The door, meanwhile, hadn't shifted.

Bodkin winced as he turned to Amy. 'Any ideas?'

'Well, when two hulking men can't force their way in, I think it only leaves one alternative.'

Ferris frowned. 'And that is?'

'Go in through the hole in the ivy that Bodkin made.' She looked at the two men and shrugged. 'Might have spared those shoulders.'

Bodkin rubbed the stubble on his chin, then rubbed his shoulder again. He looked at Ferris and sighed. 'She's not wrong, is she?'

Ferris rolled his eyes heavenward. 'Beauty and brains beat brute force and ignorance every time.' He smiled as he looked at Amy. 'Of course, we could try getting in via the door in the room where the skeleton was found.'

Bodkin blew out his cheeks and let the air out slowly. 'Ferris. Don't tell me that door is unlocked. Where did you find the key?'

'The door is locked, sir, and we didn't find a key. But there are plenty of tools lying around in there. I think we could easily force the lock.'

Bodkin thought for a moment, then shook his head. 'I want to see that door from the other side. There might still be a key in the lock.' He smiled at Amy. 'Meanwhile, I'll follow the lady's advice. I'm going in through that window.' The inspector pointed back along the side of the house. 'Ferris, you take Amy around to the collapsed wall and get in that way. I'll see what I can find inside.' He took a step towards the ivy-clad wall. 'I'll probably need a torch. Some of the roof is down but there are overhanging trees, so I don't know how much light there'll be once I get inside.'

'I brought a torch with me, sir,' Ferris said. 'I left it with a couple of evidence bags by the gateposts.'

'We'll make a detective of you yet, Ferris,' Bodkin said as he stuck up a thumb. 'Well, what are you waiting for? Hurry, or it will get dark before we can have a proper rummage about.'

While Ferris was getting the torch, Bodkin took off his jacket, picked up a piece of broken fencing and attacked the ivy with gusto. A few minutes later, coughing and spitting out a mouthful of years-old dirt, he had formed a hole big enough to be able to clamber through. Amy, standing well back on the path, wished him luck as he took the torch from Ferris and hauled himself through the gap.

'Be careful, Bodkin,' she called, still unable to convince herself that the house was ready to give up its secrets to an intruder.

'Come on, Amy,' Ferris said, making her jump as he put a soft hand on her bare shoulder. 'Let's wait for him in the storeroom.' He looked at her worried face. 'You'll be all right there. There's hardly any wall left upright. You'll feel like you're out in the open air even though you're standing inside the building.'

Amy followed Ferris back along the side of the house, then waited while he climbed over the tree that had fallen onto the end of the building during the storm. Between the branches and leaves, she could make out a pile of rubble strewn over the floor and, in the shadows, a solid-looking door.

Ferris held out his hand and Amy, after offering a quick prayer, clambered over the fallen tree. After balancing unsteadily on a pile of dusty bricks, she jumped down to the floor of the storeroom with her eyes closed.

'It's all right, Amy. They've taken the skeleton away and there aren't any rats scurrying about.'

Amy opened her eyes and looked around. The room was about as big as her own bedroom, some twelve feet by sixteen. At one end was a workbench on which lay assorted dusty tools. On the wall that the door was built into, was a row of hooks that had obviously been used as a coat rack. Only one hook, which held a cobweb strewn waterproof coat, was occupied. Beneath it, on the floor, was a pair of black rubber boots. She turned to face the far wall where she saw a row of cupboards stocked with various bottles of unidentified liquids and a single tin that sported a Paris Green manufacturer's logo and the word POISON emblazoned in red across the bottom half of the label. She knew that the tin contained arsenic and could be bought from numerous places, including the local chemist.

Amy turned again and looked back at the area in front of the collapsed wall. 'Where was the body... I mean skeleton found, Ferris?'

The constable pointed to a clear area in the centre of the room. 'Just there, Amy, face down with the pickaxe stuck in the back of the sku—' He broke off when he saw the look on her face.

Amy closed her eyes to try to picture the scene, then after hearing a scraping noise from the other side of the thick plank door, she called out. 'Bodkin? Is that you?'

She was relieved when she heard a muffled voice emanating from the other side of the door. Suddenly there was a tremendous thud, a loud creak, and the door flew open, leaving Bodkin framed in the doorway with a crowbar in his hand.

'Sorry, couldn't find the key,' he said. He smiled at Amy reassuringly. 'No ghosts. Just lots of spiders, a few mice and a couple of rats.' He paused as he attempted to brush dirt from his filthy shirt and trousers. 'I landed face down when I went through the window. The muck is a foot thick in there.'

Bodkin stepped through the doorway into the storeroom and looked across to Ferris, who was standing by the collapsed wall. 'You'll have to take me through it, Ferris. I left the report in the car like the idiot that I am.'

Ferris spent the next few minutes showing Bodkin where all the pieces of evidence had been found.

'So the handbag was on the floor, not hanging up?'

'No, sir, the bag was over there by the workbench, along with the shoes. The pieces of clothing we found... the skirt, a torn blouse and what remained of her underwear were strewn across the floor.'

'It was definitely a woman then,' Amy said quietly.

Bodkin nodded. 'It appears so, Amy. We won't be a hundred percent sure until we hear from the pathologist, but I don't think there's any doubt after what Ferris found here.'

Amy raised her hand to her forehead. 'Oh course it is... sorry, Bodkin, I've not been concentrating. It's this house. I've always been terrified of it.' Her face saddened as she looked around what was left of the room. 'What a horrible place to die.' She shook her head and sighed. 'I wonder how old she was?'

'The contents of her bag might give us a clue or two,' Bodkin said. 'And I think you might get something from the remains of her clothes, Amy. I know it's not modern fashion but I'm sure you'll be able to glean something from the label or the style of the garments, to give us some idea of whether we're looking at a working-class woman or someone a little more well to do.'

Amy nodded. 'I'll do my best, Bodkin.' She suddenly felt a wave of steely determination sweep over her and her earlier concerns about the house disappeared. Someone was responsible for the death of this woman and she was determined to find out who that person was. She took another long look around the room and noticed a tiny piece of dark-coloured material sticking out from under the fallen bricks. She pointed it out to Bodkin. 'What's that? Just behind Ferris? It looks like a scrap of cloth.'

Bodkin was across the room in a flash. Crouching down, he pulled a dozen bricks away from the heap and dragged out a dust-covered woollen overcoat. 'You missed this, Ferris... mind you, I have to admit that I hadn't noticed it either.' He turned to Amy and nodded as he gave the coat a shake, sending a million flecks of dust into the air. 'Well done, Hawkeye,' he said, before looking back at the pile of bricks. 'I suppose we'd better get a team back up here tomorrow to see if there's anything else of interest under that lot.' He threw the overcoat over his arm and stepped towards the fallen tree. 'Right, let's go back to the station and have a look at the rest of the finds.' He paused. 'I just hope Laws has left his office open or we're going to have to track down a spare set of keys.'

Chapter Three

Back at the police station, they found that the chief inspector's office door was locked. Bodkin banged on it with the heel of his hand and cursed, before apologising to Amy.

'Sorry, it's just that... well... sorry.'

'There has to be a spare key lying around somewhere. Unless Chief Inspector Laws keeps both sets,' Ferris said. 'I'll check the board in the back office.' He turned to Amy to explain 'There's a big board on the wall with a lot of hooks on. It's where the car keys are kept. Officers have to sign them in and out so they don't get lost. There are loads of other keys there, too. They all have a tag on them, so we should be able to find this one easily enough.'

Bodkin began to walk along the long corridor towards his own office. 'Good shout, Ferris. Check there's a spare set for my office while you're there. I might start locking mine at night, see what Laws thinks about that.'

Back at his desk, Bodkin laid the heavy wool overcoat over the back of his chair, then picked up the electric kettle from the top of his filing cabinet and shook it. Pulling a face, he carried it out to the gents toilets where he filled it at the sink, and after taking a look at his grimy face in the wall mirror, he looked heavenward, then carried the kettle back to his office and plugged it in.

'Tea leaves only, I'm afraid, Amy, I'm out of tea bags and the shop can't get hold of any at the moment. They're rarer than rocking horse po... There are none to be had, it seems.'

Amy sat on the chair facing Bodkin's desk and crossed her legs. 'Tea's tea, Bodkin. As long as it's strained. I'm not one of those who likes to leave a mess in the bottom of my cup for the fortune tellers to work on.'

Bodkin tipped three spoons of leaf tea into the pot and placed it back on the top of his filing cabinet next to the already steaming kettle. As he turned back to face Amy, Ferris returned with a single key on a ring.

'Got yours, sir, but I can't find a key to the chief inspector's office anywhere.'

Bodkin sighed. 'Damnation! I can't leave this until Monday and Laws won't be back until then.' He sighed again. 'Looks like I'll have to ring him at home in the morning. That will please the miserable old so and so no end.'

'We could see if Trixie knows anything, sir,' Ferris said. 'She's in and out of Laws' office all the time.'

Bodkin clapped his hands together. 'You're getting better at this job by the day, Ferris. Give her a call. You might have to wait for her to pick up, though. The telephone is in the hall outside her flat. We all share it.'

It was Amy's turn to sigh. Trixie was the station's blonde bombshell come general dogsbody and spent her time typing up case notes or reports for Laws, Bodkin and Chief Superintendent Grayson, the area manager. Amy liked Grayson. He was the man who had given her special investigator status, which allowed her to help Bodkin with some of his cases. He had even given her a police accreditation card, much to the annoyance of Laws. Trixie, on the other hand, had become her sworn enemy and the two couldn't be in the same room without hostilities breaking out.

'Do you have to bring that... creature into it?' she asked, with an exasperated tone in her voice.

Bodkin pulled a face. Trixie lived on the floor below him at Bluecoat House. The small apartment block had been built by the police to house some of their officers. Others, like Ferris, shared rooms above the station itself. Bodkin had never managed to work out how Trixie had wangled herself a flat, but he was sure that Laws was behind it. He wasn't alone in thinking that there was more going on between boss and secretary than there ought to have been. Amy was convinced about it.

Ferris returned as Bodkin was pouring boiling water into the teapot. 'She's on her way over, sir. She has a key to his office.' The detective constable shrugged. 'She didn't say why she has it or why she keeps it at home.'

'Can't you go and fetch it, Ferris?' Amy asked.

'Too late. She's on her way.' He walked up to the front of the office and craned his neck to look over Bodkin's shoulder. 'There wouldn't be a cup going spare, would there, sir?'

'I think I can squeeze another one out of the pot,' Bodkin replied. 'But while I'm pouring it, nip out to the front desk and get that key from Trixie, would you?'

Bodkin poured tea into three cups before sniffing at a bottle of milk suspiciously. Shrugging, he decided to take the risk and topped up the three cups with it. He placed one on a chipped, flower patterned saucer and passed it to Amy, who sniffed at it herself, knowing that Bodkin only bought fresh milk every other day. By the time she'd taken her first sip, Trixie was in the room. Ferris followed her in a few seconds later. He looked at Bodkin and gave a helpless shrug.

Amy's lips formed a thin line as she took in the newcomer.

Trixie had recently topped up her platinum hair dye. Her face was freshly made up with the blackest mascara on her eyelashes, foundation, and a hint of rouge on her cheeks. The thickly applied layer of deep red lipstick provided her with a pair of lips that could out-pout Mae West. She was wearing a white dress that was so tight it fitted like a second skin. She pushed her ample bosom out towards Bodkin as she greeted him.

'No tea for me,' she said, running her hands down her hips. 'I have a hot date.' A shocked look came over her face as she noticed Bodkin's dirty clothes and grime streaked face. 'What have you been up to then? No, don't tell me,' she winked slowly at the inspector. 'I have a vivid imagination. I think I can work it out.'

Amy rolled her eyes at Trixie's performance but pursed her lips and kept quiet.

Trixie looked at Amy out of the corner of her eyes, then took a step towards Bodkin. When she was about three feet away, she dropped the brass key she was holding, but instead of crouching down to pick it up, she turned away from the inspector and bent over to retrieve it; her dress, pulling tight across her bottom as she leaned forward. 'Oops,' she giggled, 'I really am a butterfingers today.'

Bodkin's eyes widened, but after a quick sideways glance towards a glaring Amy, he turned his gaze towards his tea cup. 'We seem to have got to the bottom of the key... I mean, thank you for bringing the key over, Trixie. We know where to find it if we need it again.'

Amy scowled as Trixie simpered.

'Chief Inspector Laws said I could have it any time I wanted it.' She turned away and began to wiggle her way towards the door. 'Shall I open up for you?'

Amy bit the inside of her cheek in an attempt to stop the words that were racing from her brain to her tongue. Bodkin shook his head, cleared his throat, and replied.

'Just leave it with us. Thank you, Trixie. I'll put it in your desk drawer when we've done with it.'

'Oh, don't do that!' Trixie exclaimed. 'Just push it through my letterbox. To say this is a police station, a lot of things go missing.'

Bodkin nodded as he thought about the police issue typewriter that Trixie had on her sideboard. 'You don't know who you can trust these days.' He held out his hand. Trixie wiggled back towards him and dropped the key into his open palm.

'I won't be in later. I have a hot da—'

'You said,' Amy almost spat.

Trixie stared wide eyed at Amy as though she had just noticed her for the first time.

'Hello,' she said, forcing a narrow smile. 'I didn't see you there.' She looked Amy up and down as she sat, legs crossed, on the chair. 'That's a nice dress, or it would have been when it was in style.'

Amy looked down at her floral patterned summer dress. 'It is getting on a bit now, but then I only ever wear it when I'm working in the dress shop.' She looked Trixie carefully up and down, noting every tiny detail. 'That dress looks a teeny bit too tight, Trixie. Didn't they have it in your size?'

Trixie stepped towards Amy and stuck out her bosom. Amy blinked. She had always felt intimidated by Trixie's best assets. Her own bosom was modest in comparison. She knew men could never keep their eyes off that chest for long. She regarded them as tactical weapons and she knew she couldn't match her physically, but when it came to mental agility, it was another matter. Amy was in a different league.

Trixie curled up a red painted lip. 'You think you're so smart, don't you? But come on, admit it, you're just jealous. You know I look a million dollars while you...' she looked Amy up and down again... 'are more like a wrinkly ten bob note.' Trixie tossed her head and turned away with a smug grin on her face.

'I don't think I'm particularly smart, Trixie,' Amy said, ignoring the please don't look she was receiving from Bodkin. 'I just think that if I had a hot date, I'd go out wearing something that left a little bit more to the imagination. I mean, your man would get to see his present before he'd unwrapped it and where's the fun in that?' She paused before going on. 'Oh... and bottoms are designed to be sat on, not waved in the air like a moving target.'

Trixie's mouth opened and closed a few times as she wracked

her brain for a quick response, but when nothing came, she turned, gave Amy the sort of look that would curdle fresh milk, then stomped off towards the door in such a temper that she actually forgot to wiggle.

'Enjoy your hot date,' Amy called as the door slammed shut.

There was silence for a few moments, then Ferris whistled low and long. 'Blimey!' he said. 'Joe Louis and Max Schmeling have got nothing on you two. At least they have boxing gloves on. You two have razor-sharp claws.'

'She starts it every time,' Amy said defensively. She looked up at Bodkin, who was examining his tea cup intently again. 'Doesn't she?'

Bodkin mumbled something about not wanting to get involved, before putting his cup down and tossing the key in the air. 'Come on, let's go and have a look at this evidence.'

They found the two brown paper evidence bags sitting on Laws' highly polished desk. Bodkin tore the larger of the two open and tipped the contents out onto the desktop. Picking the items up one at a time, he examined each one carefully before passing them to Amy.

'We may find that missing heel under the rubble, but I'm not counting on it. She could have broken it before she went into that room, especially if she was struggling with someone.'

Amy passed the shoe to Ferris, who duly dropped it back into the empty evidence bag.

'This is a man's belt,' she said after receiving the leather strip from Bodkin. 'It has a nicely made buckle, but it's too chunky for any woman to wear.' She held it out to its full length. 'She'd have to have a waist the size of Trixie's bottom for it to be of any use to her, anyway.'

She passed the black belt to Ferris and examined the white blouse that Bodkin passed to her. It had been torn down the front. Almost half the pearl buttons were missing. She turned it over and took a long look at the label at the back of the garment. 'Rankins of... what does that say...? Rochester, is it?'

'That's what I thought it said,' Bodkin replied, passing her the badly decomposed skirt.

Amy ran it through her fingers, taking in everything from the cut of the skirt to the label. 'I can't make out what it says. You might need to get a magnifying glass on that,' she said.

Bodkin flicked his head towards the door, and Ferris scurried off to find one. By the time he returned, Amy had checked what was left of the underwear and declared both the camisole and camiknickers were bought from Marks and Spencer.

Ferris waited until Amy had carefully placed the underwear into the brown paper bag before handing her a large magnifying glass. After taking a long look at the label, she passed it over to Bodkin. 'It's a little clearer, but I'd like a second opinion. Does that look like a full moon trademark to you?'

Bodkin took a quick look, then picked up a sheet of paper and a pencil from the desk. After taking another long look, he sketched out what he had seen on the paper. Amy bent over the desk to see what he had drawn and nodded her agreement. 'The picture of a full moon with the words Blue Moon underneath.'

'Does that ring any bells?' Bodkin asked.

Amy shook her head. 'I've never seen it before. They don't have a branch around here. I'll talk to Mum when I get home, but I'll ask Mrs Handsley at the factory on Monday. She's been in the fashion trade for years. I'd be amazed if she can't help us identify the brand.'

Bodkin nodded absentmindedly, then tore open the second bag and pulled out a dull leather handbag with a tarnished buckle holding it together. Bodkin unbuckled the clasp and, once again, tipped the contents onto Laws' desk.

'Right, we have a lipstick, a compact, various other bits of makeup, but no address book or anything that can help identify the owner.' He glanced across at Amy. 'Any thoughts?'

Amy shook her head, 'Not really, it looks like a younger woman's makeup collection though and a young person would be far less likely to carry an address book.' She held out her hand. 'Could I have a look at the bag, please?' She hesitated before taking it from Bodkin. 'Should I wear gloves or something?'

Bodkin shook his head. 'We can easily eliminate your prints, Amy. Don't worry about it.'

Amy took the bag from the inspector and turned it over in her hands. 'There would have been a leather badge of some kind with the manufacturer's logo on it when it was new, or maybe something attached to the clasp, but it's long gone. It could have been lost before the bag got into that room.' She paused as she opened the handbag. 'She might have bought it second hand.... Ah, hang on a minute, there's a slit compartment on the inside...' Amy pushed her fingers into the gap and pulled out a folded sheet of glossy coloured paper. She opened it up and showed it to Bodkin.

'It's a promotional sheet,' she said.

Bodkin took it from her and held it up to read.

THE IMPORTANCE OF BEING EARNEST. A PLAY PERFORMED IN THREE ACTS. By Mr OSCAR WILDE.

STARRING REX LARSON AND THE SPINTON PLAY-HOUSE PLAYERS.

Below was a photo print of the actor in costume, the date of the performance and the price of admission.

'Saturday 19th October 1929. 7.30. PM.' He turned the leaflet over. 'It's been signed.'

Amy leaned forward to look at the signature.

'Signed by the main man himself.'

Bodkin frowned. 'I've never heard of him. You're the movie buff. Do you know who he is?'

Amy shook her head. 'No, but again, I can ask Mum and Dad. They used to go to the Playhouse back in the day.'

Bodkin rubbed his chin, took the handbag from Amy and shoved it back into the evidence bag before folding up the leaflet and sticking it in his trouser pocket.

'Don't forget that's in there when you come to wash those trousers, Bodkin,' Amy said.

'I'll put it in my jacket poc— damn, I left my jacket at the cottage.'

'For a policeman, you're extremely forgetful, Bodkin,' Amy said with a shake of her head.

'Come on,' he replied. 'We can go back to pick it up, then I'll drop you off at home. Your mum and dad must be wondering where you are.'

'I think my dinner might be in the dog… or it would be if we had one,' Amy said, looking at her watch. 'Goodness, it's almost half-past eight. Time flies when you're having fun, doesn't it?'

After ordering Ferris to transfer the brown paper bags and overcoat to the evidence room upstairs and to put Laws' office key in Bodkin's desk drawer, the inspector grabbed the keys to the Morris and led Amy outside. As they walked to the car, Amy looked across the road to see Trixie standing outside the chip shop with a portly, balding man who must have been in his late fifties. She rolled her eyes heavenward and shook her head.

'I'd say that date was lukewarm at best.'

* * *

'So, what did you make of the evidence we've scraped together so far?' Bodkin asked as he returned to the car after picking up his jacket.

Amy pursed her lips. 'As I said earlier, I think we're looking at a younger woman, maybe even a very young lady, a teenager perhaps. The skirt was a straight, lined one, virtually a pencil skirt, and the underwear definitely said young. An older woman… when I say older, I mean someone over thirty, would almost certainly have worn a brassiere of some kind. This lady wore a camisole, so maybe wouldn't have needed much support for her bosom. The knickers are silk Camis, so she was out to impress, or at least look her best if things got a bit more involved later in the evening. Regarding the makeup, it's pretty minimal, so again, I'd say the bag belonged to someone my age, maybe younger. Whoever it was, she was a big fan of Rex Larson. She got him to autograph her promo sheet. I can't see anyone over twenty-five asking for his signature. It really is a young girl thing. They clamour around the actors when they turn up for a press conference.'

'That's all very interesting,' Bodkin said, stroking the stubble on his chin. 'You really are quite remarkable. No one else would have picked up all that from the bits and bobs we found.'

'All part of the service,' Amy said with a grin. 'Now, can we go home? I'm blooming starving.'

As there wasn't anywhere near enough room to turn the car around, Bodkin reversed the car along the narrow track. As he reached the main road, he looked back up the trail towards the cottage.

'Did you notice anything while we were talking in the car?' he asked.

'No. Should I have?'

'There was a figure in the shadow of the trees. Someone was watching us.'

Chapter Four

When Amy walked into the living room with Bodkin in tow, Mrs Rowlings put down her Woman's Own magazine, got to her feet and gave her a hug, smiled and nodded to Bodkin, then went out to the kitchen to put the kettle on.

'You must be starving, our Amy,' she called out as she lit the gas on the hob. 'We had egg and chips tonight. Yours won't take long if you want a heavy meal this late at night. We did wonder where you were, but Dad nipped over to the phone box and rang the police station. The man on the desk said you were out with Bodkin.'

'A sandwich will do for me, Mum. Have we got any ham left?'

Mrs Rowlings' head appeared through the gap between the kitchen door and its frame. 'Yes, we do. I got some from the market on Wednesday.' She looked across to Bodkin, who was flicking through the pages of Mr Rowlings' Evening Post newspaper. 'What about you, Bodkin? I bet you haven't eaten all day as usual.'

Bodkin was about to refuse, but a dig in the ribs from Amy changed his mind. 'If it's no trouble, Mrs R.'

'Of course it's no trouble. Sit yourself down at the table. It will be ready in two shakes.'

'Where's Dad?' Amy asked, throwing a quick glance towards his empty armchair.

'He's up at the Old Bull having a think about things.'

'That sounds ominous,' Amy replied. 'I hope he hasn't had some bad news.'

Mrs Rowlings walked into the living room and looked around as though checking whether she could be overheard. She leaned in towards Amy, her voice dropping to a stage whisper. 'He's been offered a promotion at work.'

'That's wonderful news,' Amy said delightedly.

Bodkin grinned. 'Well done, James.'

'There's going to be a lot of changes at work, mainly because of that Hitler chap. The factory is taking on a government contract.' She dropped her voice again. 'They're going to be making parts for a new aircraft called a...' she paused as she thought... 'Splitfires...? Something like that.' She tapped the side of her nose and winked at Amy. 'It will be a lot more responsibility for him, but he won't have to do any more night shifts.'

Amy looked puzzled. 'He doesn't work night shifts now, Mum.'

'No, but he used to, and they never agreed with him.' She looked up at Bodkin and rubbed her stomach. 'He used to get terrible indigestion. He couldn't eat in the afternoon and he had to be at work for eight for a twelve-hour shift.'

'So, will he have to work night shifts?'

'No, but the factory is moving onto a three shift system. So there will be a night shift.'

'But Dad won't be working it?'

'No.'

Amy looked at Bodkin with a puzzled look on her face, then she shook her head, smiled, and shrugged. She was well used to these confusing conversations with her mother.

'Your dad will be a supervisor on the day shift if he takes the job.'

'Does it mean a pay rise for him?'

'Oh yes, dear. He'll get an extra seventy-five pounds a year. It will pay our mortgage and get us a few extras.'

Amy beamed. 'That's wonderful, Mum, but why is he even having to consider it?'

'It's a lot of responsibility, Amy. He'll be in charge of the whole day shift. The production line will have to run seven days a week, and as your dad is an engineer, it will be his job to make sure the machines keep running. They'll have to produce a certain amount of components per shift and that number will increase as time goes on.' She rubbed her hands together nervously. 'You know what your father's like, Amy. If there's a shortfall, he'll blame himself for it.'

'But they can't blame him—' Amy stopped speaking as she heard the front door open. Mrs Rowlings put her fingers to her lips, made a shushing noise, then disappeared into the kitchen.

James Rowlings hung up his jacket on the peg in the hall and walked slowly into the living room. Amy leaned forward and planted a kiss on his cheek.

'Hello, Dad, how's the whisky at the Old Bull? I bet Stan was pleased to see you. You haven't been up there in ages.'

'I had beer,' Mr Rowlings said. 'I needed a long drink tonight.'

'I hear congr—' Bodkin was cut off when Amy dug him in the ribs again.

'Ah, you know all about it already, I see.' James Rowlings patted Amy on the arm, smiled at Bodkin, then made his way across the room to his favourite armchair. 'It was supposed to be top secret, but I imagine half the town knows about it by now.' He winked at Amy as he sat down.

'I haven't told anyone... only Amy and Bodkin, and they're family... well Bodkin's as close to family as anyone can get.' Mrs Rowlings put the big brown teapot in the middle of the table and ran her hands down the sides of her pinafore. 'And Alice, when she came up to bring us our milk and cheese delivery and I swore her to secrecy, so she'll only tell Miriam.'

Alice was Amy's best friend. Although she wasn't yet twenty, she had been running her family farm since her father died the year before. She was also a single mother.

Mr Rowlings wagged a finger. 'You could get us all shot, Elizabeth. The government haven't announced it yet.' He frowned at his wife, then burst into laughter. 'I'm only pulling your leg, Liz. The news will hit the papers tomorrow.'

'I'll say it again then, seeing that it's common knowledge now.' Bodkin crossed the room and held out his hand to Rowlings. 'Congratulations, James. It's a richly deserved promotion, I'm sure.'

Mr Rowlings took his hand, then slipped into the Scottish brogue he used when he was trying to impress someone from outside the family. He was only one sixteenth Scottish, but he took his heritage seriously, even going as far as donning a kilt at New Year and on Burns Night.

'I have nae accepted the job yet, laddie.'

'Dad!' Amy exclaimed. 'You have to take it. Think of all that extra money. You could buy a car, have a few weekends at the coast... get a telephone...'

'And there we have it, Bodkin,' Mr Rowlings said with a shake of his head. 'There's me thinking my additional responsibilities would be of national importance, but it appears that the prospect of a telephone trumps everything else.'

Amy hurried across the room and dropped to her knees in front of her father. She took both his rough hands in hers and looked up at him with a pleading look on her face.

'Stop that, young lady. You used to look at me like that when you wanted an extra ride on the donkeys at Margate when you were five.' He looked towards Bodkin. 'Do you get the same treatment when she wants something, laddie?'

Bodkin shook his head. 'No, she just won't take no for an answer. She glowers at me until I give in.'

Amy got to her feet and walked over to the table. 'I wish you wouldn't talk about me as though I wasn't here.' Picking up the teapot, she filled four china cups, then added a dash of milk to each.

As she sat down, Mrs Rowlings came into the room carrying a plate of thick cut ham sandwiches. She placed them on the table and gestured for Bodkin to sit.

'Would you like a bit of supper, James?'

Mr Rowlings shook his head. 'I think I had a few chips too many at dinner,' he said, rubbing his stomach. He took the cup and saucer that Amy offered to him and placed it on the small table at the side of his chair. 'Now, where's my paper?'

'Dad!' Amy called out. 'You haven't told us what you're going to do yet.'

Mr Rowlings pursed his lips, then ran a hand across his chin. 'I'm going to accept, of course. I'd be a blooming fool to turn it down.'

'HURRAY!' Amy shouted, jumping up and down on the spot. 'When do we get the telephone put in?'

Mr Rowlings laughed. 'You see what you're getting yourself into, Mr Bodkin?'

Bodkin grinned. 'I wouldn't change her for the world,' he said.

Amy gave him a peck on the cheek, then turned her attention to her father again. 'Well?'

'The factory has to be refitted to enable us to make the components for the new Spitfire. The machines won't be in place until mid-December and we have to test them and gradually build up to full production. I'll help to oversee all that, but I won't be taking up the new post until November at the earliest. The company will want me to be at their beck and call from day one, I would imagine, but there is a bit of a waiting list to get onto the telephone network. We will get some sort of priority, of course, because of the work we'll be doing, but I've been told it will be the New Year before the telephone line can be fitted.'

Amy mentally counted off the weeks, then sat down with a happy smile on her face. 'I'll be able to talk to Alice whenever I want to now.'

Mr Rowlings picked up his paper, opened it up and sighed. 'I'm pleased to see you've got your priorities right.'

After supper, Bodkin wished the Rowlings good night, congratulated James again, then followed Amy to the front door. Despite the late hour, it was a warm night, and the couple stood by the gate with their arms around each other as they talked.

'I hope you're going back to your flat now, Bodkin. You've had a long day.'

'It's only ten. I just want to jot down a few notes about these so-called burglaries while the information is still fresh in my mind. I'll start to work on the new murder case tomorrow.'

'That's twice you've said, so-called burglaries. What do you mean?'

'It's all a bit odd,' the policeman said thoughtfully. 'Someone is breaking into houses and leaving a sort of Valentine's card on the kitchen table for the lady of the house. All the husbands have been on the night shift so far. He must hang around to make sure they've gone to work before he breaks in.'

'Does he steal anything?'

'Not as far as we know. At least no one has reported anything missing. He just forces his way in, leaves the card on the kitchen table, then lets himself out again.'

'And the cards are Valentines?'

'Sort of. They're just blank white cards with a handwritten message saying how beautiful the woman of the house is and how he'd like to whisk her away to somewhere exotic.'

'I bet the men love that,' Amy replied.

'They aren't best pleased. One of them at least has suspicions about his wife's fidelity now.'

'Blimey! Why would anyone do something like that?'

Bodkin shook his head. 'I have no idea, I just wish he'd stop because it's muggins here who has to track him down.'

Amy giggled suddenly. 'Have you got one of those silly newspaper headline names for him yet? Please say you have. I've loved hearing about Back Door Billy and the Notorious Nighttime Knickers Nicker.'

Bodkin cleared his throat. 'We, erm, haven't settled on anything yet as he's only been operating for about a week, and I only got the case on my desk this morning... But... Ferris came up with an idea about Rudolph Valentino, because of the Valentines, but he couldn't find a proper headline so he's still working on it.'

'Valentino... no, I can't think of anything that works either, Bodkin. What have you come up with?'

'Well, because of the love notes, I thought Don Two would be quite good.'

'Don Two?' Amy looked puzzled.

'He's trying to be Don Juan's twin,' Bodkin replied.

Amy laughed, hard. 'Don Two... that's brilliant, Bodkin. Well done!'

Bodkin grinned. 'But then I got a better idea.'

'Better than Don Two? Oh, come on, let's hear it.'

Bodkin stifled a laugh as he began to speak. 'I was just thinking about famous Romeos or wannabe lovers from the literary world when I suddenly had a flash of inspiration.'

'And...?'

Bodkin laughed again. 'Cyrano de Burglar.'

Amy almost doubled over laughing. 'Cyrano... de Burglar... Oh, Bodkin, that's pure genius.'

'I thought it was quite good.'

'Have you told Ferris yet?'

'No, he knows I've got something, but he doesn't know what it is yet.'

'Cyrano de Burglar,' Amy repeated. 'You are clever, Bodkin.'

When the pair had stopped laughing, Bodkin pulled her close and kissed her softly on the lips. 'This makes the longest day worthwhile,' he said softly. His head dropped towards her again for a second kiss.

Amy gave him a quick peck, put both hands on his chest, and

pushed him away. 'That's all you're getting, mister. I've got to be up at the crack of seven-thirty. Brigden's got their new stock of dresses in today. They'll be on the sales rails first thing in the morning, and I don't want to be beaten to a bargain.'

'Heaven forbid,' Bodkin said, blowing her a kiss before turning away and walking to his car. 'Six-thirty tomorrow evening, as usual?'

'It's a date,' Amy said, giving him a quick wave.

Chapter Five

On Saturday morning, Amy came downstairs at seven-thirty to find Mr Rowlings sitting in his armchair, already reading his daily paper whilst sipping his third cup of tea of the morning.

'I might have to give young Bernard a tip this Christmas,' he said after bidding Amy good morning. 'That other lad didn't deliver until getting on for nine.'

Amy sat at the table and poured herself a cup of tea. After taking two quick sips, she closed her eyes and tipped her head back. 'Bliss,' she said.

'What would you like for breakfast, Amy?' Mrs Rowlings called from the kitchen. 'Alice dropped off a tray of fresh eggs with the milk about half an hour ago. She asked if you were up and about yet.'

'I can smell bacon,' Amy said, licking her lips. 'I was only going to have a bit of cereal this morning, but I can't resist that aroma.'

'Bacon and eggs it is,' Mrs Rowlings said, placing a rack of toast on the table and picking up the teapot to refill it. 'So, what were you and Bodkin up to all evening?'

Amy spread a thin layer of butter over a triangle of toast and bit into it hungrily. 'Oh, not much. A dog walker found a skeleton in Creepy Cottage and Bodkin has been given the case.'

Mrs Rowlings almost dropped the teapot.

'A SKELETON! Who did it used to belong to?'

Amy munched on her toast with her head tilted slightly as she thought about how to answer. 'Erm, we don't know who the previous owner was yet, Mum. We do know it's a woman because there was a handbag and some tattered clothes lying about. She was locked in the storeroom at the end of the building.'

Mrs Rowlings recovered her composure and returned to the kitchen as Mr Rowlings looked over the top of his paper. 'How long has it been there? Does Bodkin have any idea?'

'Well,' Amy said, munching more toast and wiping a crumb away from the corner of her mouth. 'It wasn't there much before October the nineteenth, nineteen twenty-nine.'

'How can you be so sure?' Mr Rowlings folded his paper and put it on the table at his side.

'Because we found a leaflet in her bag. It was for a performance at the Playhouse and it had a date on it, so she couldn't really have been in the cottage much before then. It also had a signature on the back. Rex Larson. Can you remember him, Dad? He was starring in the play, The Importance of Being Earnest.'

'I remember the name. He used to come up here with a touring show in the late twenties. We saw him once or twice. We wouldn't have gone to that particular performance though. I've never been a fan of Oscar Wilde.' He held out his hand and took a fresh cup of tea from his wife. 'Wasn't he in one of the scandal sheets in the early thirties, dear? Something to do with young women?'

Amy's ears pricked up as her mother nodded.

'He was in the News of the World three Sundays running. It was a big scandal at the time and it pretty much cost him his marriage and his career. He couldn't get any bookings after those revelations.' She returned to the kitchen and came back carrying Amy's breakfast plate. 'Not that we have that awful newspaper in the house anymore.' She shot a quick glance towards Mr Rowlings and, after picking up her Woman magazine, made herself comfortable on the sofa.

'That's very interesting,' Amy mused as she cut into the bacon and dipped a crispy piece into the yolk of her fried egg. 'He was a bit of a rogue, was he?' She paused as she chewed. 'Oh yes, I knew there was something else I meant to ask.' She looked sideways at her mother. 'Mum, can you remember a fashion label called Blue Moon?'

Amy's mum thought for a few moments before shaking her head. 'Sorry, dear. Is it one of the clues?'

Amy nodded. 'Never mind. I'll ask Georgina Handsley on Monday when I get to work. She'll know if anyone does. She's been mixing with fashion designers for years.' She dipped a piece of toast into the egg yolk and lifted it to her mouth. 'Can you remember when anyone last lived in Creepy Cottage?'

Mr Rowlings picked up his paper again and placed it on his lap, then he took a sip of his tea and furrowed his brow as he thought. 'My aunt told me that there used to be a family living there back in the day. She said the couple had two kids. It can't have been very nice for them, growing up there. No running water and no electricity. I can't remember the name of the family for the life of me, but they were long gone before you were born. Your mum and I used to walk past the cottage when we were courting. That was before the war, so around nineteen thirteen. It was a bit of a ruin, even then. When I came back from France, the place was still unoccupied and it's been that way ever since.' He took another sip of tea. 'So it's been empty for at least thirty years. Possibly a lot longer.'

Mrs Rowlings shivered. 'It always gave me the creeps. I used to cling onto your father's hand for dear life every time we walked past. It always seemed to me as though it was giving out an invisible warning, that there was a presence inside, and not a very nice one.'

Amy nodded in agreement. 'That's exactly how I felt yesterday, Mum. It took me right back to when I used to go into the woods with Alice, Jenny and a few of the other kids. Even the bravest of the boys wouldn't go too close.'

'Wasn't there a story of a young boy climbing in through a window and never coming out again?' Mr Rowlings said, chinking the saucer with his cup as he put it down.

'Jimmy... No Johnny!' Mrs Rowlings suddenly burst out. 'I don't know his surname, but there was a little rhyme the girls sang when we played skipping games. What was it now...?

Little Johnny Braveheart
Climbed in to meet the ghost
But the ghost caught little Johnny
And spread him on his toast.
So stay out of the Witchy Wood
Or you could be the one
To end up on a toasting fork
Just like Little John.'

'MUM!' Amy exclaimed. 'That's awful.' She pondered as she speared the last piece of bacon with her fork. 'If it really happened, it must have been a blooming long time ago for the story to make its way into a skipping rhyme.'

'I don't think the kids chant it anymore. You and Alice never did.' Mrs Rowlings picked up her magazine and opened it at the article she had been reading when Amy first came down.

Amy carried her breakfast dishes through to the kitchen, washed them in the Belfast sink and left them to dry on the drainer. Then she went into the bathroom and had a strip wash before making her way to her bedroom, where she got ready for her trip into town.

Brigden's Nearly New shop resembled an upmarket designer store in London, exuding an air of sophistication. Its shelves and racks showcased a plethora of labelled items, many of which had seen minimal wear. Amy relished her visits to the store, even though the price tags often exceeded her budget. The finest pieces were displayed in well-lit niches, while porcelain mannequins placed strategically around the aisles showed off some of the more reasonably priced items.

Amy's real interest lay with the two bargain rails that were tucked away at the back of the shop. These rails bore items of clothing that, while not in pristine condition, could, for someone with Amy's skills, be easily and quickly repaired.

Some items sported minor labels or tags from London's department stores. If she was lucky, she might discover a summer dress with a torn hem for as little as seven and sixpence, a blouse-skirt combination for fifteen shillings or a stylish out-of-season jacket for twelve and six.

Sharon, the assistant, called to Amy from behind a pile of recently sorted clothes as she walked into the shop.

'Hi, Amy. What are you after today? I put a few lovely summer frocks out this morning.'

'Hi, Sharon.' Amy waved to the dark-haired young woman. Amy had been shopping at Brigden's long before Sharon had started working at the store, and the pair had become good friends since. 'I've got plenty of summer dresses. In fact, I'm thinking about reselling a few of them and trusting to luck again next year.' She walked towards the back of the shop, passing the assistant on the way. 'I'm after a few things for autumn. It's only a few weeks away now.'

Sharon looked up and down the shop to make sure she couldn't be overheard. 'There are a couple of nice skirts on the rails. I fancied the navy one, but it's not my size.' She patted her bottom with one hand. 'Too much on the hips, sadly.'

Amy shook her head. 'You've got a lovely figure, Sharon. Men love the hourglass shape.'

Sharon sighed. 'I think all the sand's run to the bottom.'

'See you at the till, hopefully.' Amy crossed her fingers in front of her face, then turned and walked to the back of the shop.

Most of the items on the first rail were, as Sharon had said, summer dresses and although she found two or three that she would have snatched off the rail a couple of months earlier, she resisted the temptation and made her way to the second row where she immediately found the navy skirt that Sharon had been talking about.

The skirt was just below knee length, had a wide button down waistband and flared from mid hip. Amy took it from the rail, held it up and examined it with a professional eye.

She spotted a line of crooked stitching on the back of the waistband and she could tell that the hem had been lowered, but she reckoned she could do a more than a reasonable job of taking it back up again.

Smiling to herself, she laid the skirt over the crook of her elbow and made her way down the rail to where the blouses were hanging. Straight away, her eyes fell on a white rayon blouse with the faintest of thin blue stripes running through it. Amy had seen one just like it on a mannequin earlier in the year, but it had been way out of her price range. As another shopper appeared at the end of the rail, Amy turned away to keep the blouse out of view, then after offering a silent prayer, she snatched a look at the size on the label.

'Yes!' she almost shouted, then remembering where she was, she muttered an apology to the clearly surprised woman, and laying the blouse on top of the skirt, she made her way to the till where she found Eileen the shop manager, waiting for her.

'Hello, Eileen, I was wondering if you could—'

'What's wrong with them?' the manager asked. She was well used to Amy picking up sometimes minute faults with the garments in an attempt to get a bit of a discount.

'Well,' Amy placed the blouse on the counter and held up the skirt. 'The stitching is wonky on the waistband and someone's done a pretty amateur job of letting down the hem.'

Eileen studied the ten shilling price tag and pursed her lips. 'Repairs will take someone like you half an hour at best.'

'An hour to do a proper job,' Amy said.

'What's wrong with the blouse? It was on a mannequin earlier in the summer.'

Amy held it up. 'It's got more creases in it than Winston Churchill's forehead. You can't just iron those out, not with that fabric it's—'

'Seventeen and six for the two, final offer,' Eileen said firmly. 'I have to make some sort of profit, you know.' She picked up the blouse and held it to the light. 'This is beautiful workmanship... or workwomanship to be more precise. It was priced at a pound when it was on the dummy. You're getting it for next to nothing.'

'It was on the mannequin for nearly two months,' Amy argued. 'It gathered a lot of dust in that time and as I said, the fabric isn't all that easy to launder.'

'I did say it was my final offer, Amy, and I'm not going to change my mind, despite your protestations.'

'All right, you win,' Amy said, reaching into her bag to get her purse. 'I only intended to spend ten shillings today.'

'You've got more than a bargain,' Eileen said. 'Now, while you're here. Can I book you to do a bit more work for me? I've got a few dresses in need of a bit of TLC. You know the thing, frayed hem, loose seams.'

Amy nodded. 'I'm happy to do them, but it might take me longer than usual. I've a feeling I'm going to be rather busy over the next couple of weeks.'

'There's no rush,' Eileen replied. 'I'll drop them off with your mum in the week.'

Swinging her brightly coloured Brigden's bag in her hand, Amy left the shop and made her way to the post office, where she handed over her savings book and a shiny half crown. She usually liked to add five shillings to her account, but she had just spent more than she intended, so the half crown was all that she could spare, after tipping up half her wages to her mother for her keep.

From the post office, Amy walked around the corner to the Sunshine Café where she ordered a cup of coffee and two iced buns. Twenty-five minutes later, with one of the buns wrapped in tissue paper and placed carefully in her bag, she left the café and walked along High Street before turning onto Middle Street and continuing down the hill, past the Roxy cinema and on towards the police station. As she entered the lobby, she found Constable Parlour on the front desk. He beamed as she stepped towards him.

'Hello, Miss... Rowlings, isn't it?'

'The very same,' Amy said, treating the young policeman to a smile. 'Is Inspector Bodkin at home?'

'He is, miss. He's with DC Ferris. I'll just give him a call.'

Parlour lifted the phone, dialled an extension, then spoke into the mouthpiece. A few seconds later, he returned the handset to the cradle, stepped out from behind the desk, walked along the corridor and opened the door to allow Amy to enter.

'He's in his office, miss. I think you know the way.'

The door to Bodkin's office was open, and she found the inspector and Constable Ferris leaning over the desk, studying what appeared to be a couple of scraps of paper.

Amy knocked on the door, then stepped inside as Bodkin waved her in. As she approached the desk, he held up a narrow-waisted jacket that had once been black but was now covered in brick dust.

'The lads found it under the rubble this morning.' He looked down at his desk and pointed to what looked to be two tickets. 'These were in the pocket.'

'Lucky girl,' Amy said, meaningfully. 'You don't always get pockets.'

'We were the lucky ones then,' Bodkin said, still pointing to the desk. 'We have here a bus ticket from Rochester to Mossmoor and a train ticket from Mossmoor to Spinton.'

Amy leaned closer to look at the tickets. 'Can I pick them up?'

Bodkin nodded.

Amy picked up the flimsy bus ticket and examined it. Then, after placing it carefully on the desk, she picked up the train ticket. 'Well, there's a conundrum,' she said after checking the scrap of paper. 'She began her journey in Rochester, but she bought a train ticket in Mossmoor. Why bother breaking your journey there? She could have got the train from Rochester to Gillingham, then straight on to Spinton. It doesn't make a lot of sense unless she was meeting someone.'

'My thoughts exactly,' Bodkin said. 'The bus would have to stop at Gillingham coach station before travelling on to Mossmoor. Then it would terminate at Spinton. I agree with you. It doesn't make a lot of sense.'

Amy narrowed her eyes as she thought. 'There are only what... four or five miles between Rochester and Gillingham? The train only takes ten minutes at most, and there are connections to Spinton via Mossmoor every fifteen minutes, so why would anyone get the bus, only to get off and catch a train through to Spinton unless, as we agreed, she was meeting someone? The other thing I noticed was that both tickets were singles. You would have thought she'd have bought returns. She obviously didn't intend to go back at any prearranged time.'

Bodkin rubbed his hands together. 'I think it's time we had a cup of tea. Ferris, do the honours.'

'I'll make it in the back office,' the constable said. He eyed the yellowing liquid in the bottle on Bodkin's filing cabinet. 'I picked up a fresh pint of milk on the way to work.'

When Ferris had departed, Amy sat on the seat on the opposite side of the desk to Bodkin, put her Brigden's bag on the floor, crossed her legs and smoothed down her dress.

'Did you find anything nice up at Brigden's?' Bodkin asked.

Amy nodded quickly. 'I found a lovely navy skirt and a blouse to die for.' She looked across the desk and smiled at the inspector. 'If you're lucky, I might wear them tonight.'

'I'll look forward to that,' Bodkin replied. 'What are we going to see, anyway? I've driven past the Roxy a dozen times in the last few days and I haven't once noticed the posters.'

'It's The Man in the Iron Mask with Joan Bennett. You know,

the story about the French prince, his double, and the three musketeers?'

'I remember seeing the Douglas Fairbanks' version of that back in the day.' Bodkin thought for a moment. 'That would have been in the cinemas about the same time as Rex Larson was walking the boards. I wonder if they ever bumped into each other?'

'Oh, I have a bit of news about our Rex,' Amy said, leaning towards the desk.

'Okay, let's hear it,' Bodkin replied. 'I haven't had the chance to look into him yet.'

'Well,' Amy said, 'I was talking to Mum and Dad this morning and they remember him quite well. They said he was a decent actor, if somewhat arrogant. Anyway, that's not the point. The thing is, he was involved in quite a large scandal. It virtually ruined his career.'

'A scandal? What sort of scandal?'

'The News of the World ran a story about him that ran for three weeks. It seems he became involved with quite a few young girls. It ended his marriage and he couldn't get a booking for love nor money for quite a time. I don't know if he's managed to revive his career, but he was the talk of the gossip columns back then.'

'How long ago was this, Amy?'

'Dad said the early thirties so...'

'We can check,' Bodkin said. 'I've never spoken to anyone at the News of the World. It's time I rectified that.'

A couple of minutes later, Ferris returned carrying a tray with a teapot, three cups and saucers, a sugar bowl and an unopened bottle of milk.

Amy sat up in her chair and smiled at Ferris. 'Can you make sure the milk is all gone before you go home today? I can visualise it on Monday morning perched on top of that filing cabinet in a race to see which bottle can make its contents go solid first.'

Ferris shuddered as he put the tray on the desk. 'I'll take it up to my room when I clock off. I'll drink it before we go out tonight. It will put a lining on my stomach.'

Bodkin picked up the teapot, swished it around, then poured tea through a metal strainer into the three cups. 'How much are you intending to drink to need a lining on your stomach, Ferris?'

'I like the beer in the Old Bull,' Ferris said. 'I might have one or two extra tonight to celebrate working on my first murder case as a CID officer.'

Bodkin poured milk into the tea, placed a cup on a chipped flower patterned saucer and handed it across the desk to Amy.

'Fair enough, Ferris. You seem to be taking to it like a duck to water. You've impressed me so far this week. I might even buy you an extra pint myself.'

Amy suddenly remembered the iced bun in her bag and leaned forward to retrieve it. 'You'll have to go halves, I'm afraid. I only bought one extra.'

Bodkin and Ferris exchanged glances, then Ferris pulled a penknife from his pocket and, under the watchful eye of his superior, proceeded to divide the bun.

It was gone in no time.

When Bodkin had finished his half, he wiped the back of his hand across his mouth, then took a long sip of tea. After sticking a thumb up to Amy, he picked up the tickets from the desk and slid them carefully into an envelope.

'Do you have anything planned this afternoon?' he asked, looking across the desk.

'I was going to listen to some music, fix the stitching on my new clothes, then have a leisurely bath, but if you've got a better offer, I'm quite willing to consider it.'

'I was thinking of driving up to the Playhouse to see if anyone is still around who might remember that play being performed. I'd be delighted if you could find time to accompany me.'

Chapter Six

The Playhouse Theatre was situated on Main Street, just a few yards away from the Milton Hotel. Edwardian in style, it was designed by Arthur Scatterbrook, a contemporary and close friend of the renowned theatre architect, Frank Matcham. It was erected in the same year as the town hall and the library, at a time when Spinton's industry was expanding. The Playhouse was built to replace the old Majestic Theatre, an eighteenth century building, lit by gas, that had been destroyed in a fire with the loss of some eighty patrons in the winter of nineteen hundred and two.

The Majestic presented music hall acts in the main, but had famously staged a performance of As You Like It, starring the famed actress and socialite, Lily Langtree. Tickets in the late Victorian age had come at a premium because the demand was so high, but by the time the nineteen twenties arrived, much of the clientele had been seduced by the moving pictures that were on show every night of the week at the Roxy cinema.

Boasting a large stalls area, a dress circle and a balcony, the Playhouse could seat some five hundred theatre goers, but by the late nineteen thirties performing to those numbers was just a distant memory.

The foyer of the theatre was a small but decorative area. The walls were covered in deep red flock wallpaper with featured gold painted sconces on the side walls that were lit with electricity.

The booking office was on the wall facing the main doors. On its left was a set of six steps leading down to the auditorium. A second set of steps on the right hand of the mahogany lined reception led up to the dress circle and balcony.

When Amy and Bodkin entered the building, they were greeted by a dark-haired, timid-looking woman of about thirty years of age. She wore a pair of thick tortoiseshell spectacles that were perched on a beak of a nose. Her hair was scraped back over her ears and secured with two rhinestone decorated hair clips. She wore an off white blouse, a brown pencil skirt and flat shoes. She walked towards them, holding a clipboard tightly against her chest as though it was the most valuable thing she owned.

'How may I be of assistance?' she asked, giving Amy a tight smile. When she transferred her gaze to Bodkin, she was unable to hold his eye, and she looked quickly down towards her shoes before giving him a second, nervous look.

Bodkin gave her his best smile, which seemed to make the woman even more anxious.

'I'm Inspector Bodkin of the Spinton police and this,' he held his hand out towards Amy, 'is my associate, Miss Rowlings.' He paused for a moment to let the information sink in. 'And you are?'

'Margo... Margo Ashburner. What do...? I mean... how can...?' Margo's voice tailed off, and she clutched her clipboard even tighter.

'We'd like to speak to anyone who might have worked at, or had any association with, the theatre during the autumn of nineteen twenty-nine,' Bodkin said.

'That's a long time ago,' Margo said, her eyes darting from her shoes to Bodkin and back again.

'Almost ten years,' Bodkin agreed. He nodded in the direction of a round table surrounded by four chrome framed chairs. 'Do you mind if we sit?'

'Please, please do,' Margo stammered as she ushered them across the room.

Bodkin pulled out a chair for Amy, then stood patiently, waiting for Margo to sit. When she finally realised, she sat down quickly, still clutching the clipboard to her chest as though it contained a magical protective property.

Amy, who was sitting next to Margo, reached out and touched her gently on the arm. 'There's no need to be nervous. They're just routine questions.'

Margo flinched as Amy's fingers touched her sleeve, but she looked up and flashed her a thin smile. 'What is it all about?'

'I don't want to go into that at the moment, Mi... is it Miss or Mrs?'

'Miss,' Margo said quickly, looking up from the tabletop for a split second.

'Miss Ashburner... that's a very unusual name. I can't say I've heard it before. Is it local to these parts?' Bodkin's voice softened.

Margo shrugged and said nothing.

Bodkin looked across the table at Amy and slowly shook his head.

'How long have you worked here, Miss Ashburner?'

'About eleven years. I was a volunteer to begin with.'

'And what position do you hold now?'

Margo cleared her throat. 'I'm the assistant to the director, amongst other things.'

'Assistant to the director? Not assistant director?'

'Semantics,' said Margo with more feeling than they'd heard from her up until that point.

'What else do you do?' Bodkin asked. 'You must be quite important to the company.'

'I prompt the actors from the side of the stage. I help out on the front desk.' She looked across to the box office booth. 'I help out with costumes, I type out scripts, I... I do all sorts of things.'

'Head cook and bottle washer,' Bodkin said with a smile.

Margo nodded in her bird like manner and looked at Bodkin from under her eyelids. When she noticed he'd caught her looking, her eyes dropped to the table again.

Bodkin reached into his pocket and pulled out the leaflet they had found in the victim's purse, unfolded it, and laid it on the table. 'Were you working here on this particular night?'

Margo flashed a quick look at it and nodded.

'Were you a member of the cast?'

She shook her head. 'ME? Goodness no. I can't act. I just like to watch others perform.'

'What do you remember about the night? Did you meet Rex Larson?'

Margo nodded again. 'We all met him. He spoke to me when I was making the tea.'

'What was he like?' Amy asked. 'Was he friendly?'

'He was very friendly. He put his arm around me when he realised I was a bit nervous.'

'How old were you back then, Margo?'

'Seventeen.'

Amy shot a quick glance across to Bodkin. 'Where did this happen? You said you were making the tea?'

'In the back. We've got an urn in the changing room.' She held Amy's eye for a moment, then looked away again.

'Was there anyone else present, Margo?'

Margo held onto her clipboard and shook her head.

Amy reached out her hand again and placed it on Margo's sleeve. 'Did anything else happen? Did he—'

'I'm not saying anything!' Margo snapped. She looked from Amy to Bodkin, then back again. 'I'm not saying anything about that,' she added in a quiet voice.

'All right, we don't have to go into that now,' Bodkin said. 'But I do have a few other questions.' He scratched at the stubble on his chin. 'What was your job, then? You said you were a volunteer to start with.'

'I was… A volunteer, I mean. I liked hanging around with the players. It was good fun. They were a lovely bunch.'

'Were any of the players paid as professional actors or were they all amateurs?'

'No one was paid… apart from Rex Larson, of course… Oh, and Caspian.'

'Caspian?' Bodkin smiled encouragingly.

'Caspian Stonehand. He's our director, and lead actor, but he was just an actor in that performance. Rex brought his own artistic director with him.'

'What was his name? Can you remember?' Bodkin pulled his notebook and pen out of his jacket pocket.

'Jeremy, something. I can't remember now. He was a bit younger than Rex, rather effeminate.'

Bodkin looked around the foyer. 'This place must cost a bit to keep running. Who pays all the bills? You can't really make a profit staging one play every couple of months.'

'The council is our landlord, but Caspian runs things. He has his own company. We get a grant from the council; he organises sponsorship from some of the local companies and we quite often hold fundraisers. We had one at the town hall a few weeks ago and it raised over a hundred pounds.' She lifted her head and looked at them proudly. 'We also get to keep all the profits from the productions.'

'It sounds like a thriving concern,' Bodkin said.

'I don't know anything about the finances,' Margo replied. 'Caspian handles all that.'

'Let's get back to the big production. The Importance of Being Earnest. How many characters were there in the play?'

Margo thought for a moment. 'Goodness, it was all such a long time ago… Nine or ten?… no… nine, but we only used eight actors because Stanley Tubshaw played two characters. They only appeared briefly and in different scenes.'

Bodkin jotted down the name in his notebook. 'Is he still a member of the company?'

'Stanley? No, he died at Christmas that year. There was an explosion in the factory he managed. He was killed instantly.'

'How many women were in the company back then?' Bodkin asked.

'The company...? Erm... six, but there were only four cast in the play. Three of them have left now. One though ill health, one has gone a bit gaga... mind you, she is in her eighties. Her name is Christabel Haynes. She played Lady Bracknell. She suited the part so well. She was such an arrogant woman. Thought she was better than the rest of us. Mind you, she did come from good stock so...'

'How many women from back then are still with the company?'

'Two, although Stella only comes in when we put the Christmas panto on for the kids. Imogen Beechwood is still here. She works with a rep company down in Tonbridge for a few months a year, but she helps out here if we're struggling. She's been in a few plays on the radio, you know.' Margo held up a hand and began to count off on her fingers. 'We have five women in the company now. There's Angela Th—'

'We're only interested in those who were with the Spinton Players at the time Rex Larson was here,' Bodkin interrupted.

'Ah, then it's just Stella Mortenson and Imogen Beechwood.'

'Anyone else still around from that time?' Bodkin asked.

'Apart from the ones I've mentioned? No, not among the cast.'

Amy leaned forward. 'What about the crew, the backroom team?'

Margo tilted her head. 'Only me and Jack Draper.'

'Jack Draper.' Bodkin made a note. 'What does he do?'

'He sorts out the lightning, helps make the props, paints the backdrops if we need a new one, that sort of thing.'

'Will he be around any time soon?'

'He'll be here tomorrow,' Margo said. 'We all will. We're having our first read through of Don Juan.'

Amy and Bodkin exchange wide-eyed looks.

'Don Juan?' Bodkin tried to keep a straight face.

'Yes, Caspian's reworked it himself. He's playing the lead, of course. He was made to play that character.'

Bodkin got to his feet, and Amy stood up immediately after.

'Just a couple of things before we go, Miss Ashburner. Going back to Rex Larson. Did you see him with any women or maybe young girls when he was here? Anyone around the same age as you would have been?'

'Oh, there were any number of them hanging around, trying to get his autograph or even a hug off him. He was very obliging like that.'

'I'm sure he was.' Bodkin picked up the leaflet and showed her the signature on the back. 'He signed this for someone. We'd like to know who she was.'

'As I said, there were lots of young girls hanging around. They watched the performance, then hung around by the stage door until he came out.' She beckoned Amy towards her by crooking her finger. 'There were two of them in his dressing room after the show.'

'Two of them?' Bodkin placed his hands on the table and leaned across it.

'Did you see them when they went in, or came out?'

Margo shook her head. 'No, but I know there were two of them. I heard them giggling behind a curtain when I took him the bottle of whisky he'd ordered.' She sniffed and looked away from the inspector. 'Some of their clothes were lying on the floor.'

Before Bodkin could respond. The telephone on the box office desk began to ring. Margo hurried across the room to answer it.

'It's for you, Inspector,' she said. 'Someone called Ferris?'

Bodkin took the handset from Margo and listened intently as Ferris gave him the news. A minute later, he put the phone down and hurried across to where Amy was waiting. 'Time to go,' he said excitedly. 'Ferris thinks we've got a lead on the girl.'

Chapter Seven

'What did Ferris say, Bodkin? How did he manage to track her down?'

'We'll find out when we get back to the station,' Bodkin said, as he started the car, pulled out of the car park and turned onto Main Street. 'He didn't say a lot on the phone.' He paused for a moment, then said. 'What did you make of Margo back there? She was as nervous as a kitten.'

'You're to blame for that, Bodkin,' Amy said with a grin.

'Me? I thought I was very gentle with her.'

'Oh you were, Bodkin, but you exuded power and she just melted. She was so overwhelmed she couldn't bring herself to look at you for more than a second or so at a time. She fancies the pants off you.'

Bodkin shot a glance to his left. 'EH? How do you work that out?'

'Body language, Bodkin. Body language.'

'But... but...' Bodkin stammered. 'A couple of months ago, when we were working on the last case, you said that the women who kept touching their hair or running their hand down their thighs were trying to subconsciously seduce me while I was questioning them.

What Margo was doing was the polar opposite.' He sighed. 'I just don't get it.'

'That's women for you, Bodkin,' Amy said. Turning to face the window, she smiled at the policeman's bemusement. 'We don't make things easy. Where's the fun in that?'

'You could at least give us a fighting chance,' Bodkin replied as he pulled the car across the road and parked outside the police station. 'It's not fair.'

'Life isn't fair,' Amy said as she opened the door of the car and climbed out onto the road. She looked across the top of the car at Bodkin. 'You, of all people, should know that.'

They found Ferris pacing up and down in the corridor outside Bodkin's office. He was holding a buff file in his hand. He raised it in the air as his superior approached.

'I've typed up what I managed to find out, sir.'

Bodkin took the file from the young officer, opened the door to his office and they all trouped inside.

'Shall I put the kettle on?' Ferris asked as Amy sat down.

'Leave it for the moment, Ferris,' Bodkin replied. 'Let's have a look at what you've uncovered first.' He sat down at his desk and opened the file. It contained a single typed sheet of paper.

'Come on, Bodkin,' Amy said impatiently as Bodkin read the contents for a second time.

Bodkin looked up from the file. 'It seems that a Mrs Anthea Honeychurch made several inquiries into the whereabouts of her daughter, Nina, in October and early November nineteen twenty-nine. She contacted the police in Mossmoor.'

'Mossmoor. Not Rochester?' Amy leaned forwards, eager for more information.

Bodkin looked up at Ferris, who was standing almost to attention at the side of his desk.

'Ferris. This is excellent work. Would you like to take us through what you've been up to since we left the office?'

Ferris nodded. 'The first thing I did was to get in touch with the

Rochester police and ask them about any unresolved missing person cases they might have on their records for nineteen twenty-nine. The officer on the desk wasn't all that helpful, to be honest, and he said he'd get his sergeant to ring me back on Monday. Now, I thought I might as well do a bit more digging as we had another forty-eight hours to go before we heard from them, so I rang Mossmoor.' Ferris stuck a hand in his trouser pockets and rattled the change he found there.

Amy waved a finger at him. 'Don't do that, Ferris, it isn't a good look, especially with ladies present.'

Ferris quickly let go of his small change and pulled his hand out of his pocket. 'Oops, sorry, Amy; I was... well I ... sorry.'

'So you got in touch with the Mossmoor police?' Bodkin said impatiently.

'Oh, yes, sir. They don't have a police station as such. Just a couple of police houses. Constable Jay lives in one of them. He hasn't worked there long enough to know anything about what happened ten years ago, but his colleague, Constable Spears, has been there for twenty-odd years, so Jay gave me his number.'

'You're dragging it out now, Ferris,' Bodkin said, giving the constable one of his 'get on with it' looks.

'Yes, sir, sorry, sir... where was I? Oh yes. I was in luck because Constable Spears was the officer who took the calls from Mrs Honeychurch and he'd kept the notes he made in his files.' Ferris paused and pointed to the sheet of paper that Bodkin was still holding. 'It's all on there, sir. Spears made a few inquiries around town, but no one could remember seeing a young girl fitting the description the lady had given, so he just referred her to the Rochester police and told her to report the girl as missing. She rang back once or twice, complaining that the Rochester police were ignoring her and wanted to know if they had sent anyone to Mossmoor to investigate. Spears told her he hadn't seen anyone from Rochester, but he promised her he'd make a few more inquiries himself. He didn't discover anything much, although a conductor said a girl fitting

Nina's description caught his bus on the afternoon of the nineteenth. He remembered her because she was having a bit of trouble with a man who was pestering her. The conductor threatened to throw him off the bus if he didn't stop. Then he got Nina to sit on the front seat with him until they reached the terminus at Mossmoor.'

'Did he give a description of her, or this man?'

'He said that she was young, maybe sixteen, seventeen. She had mousey coloured hair and wore a dark jacket over a skirt and blouse. She was carrying a small overnight case and a handbag. He said that she seemed very excited about something or other. As for the man, all he said was that he was in his thirties, dressed rather scruffily, and was balding prematurely.'

'I wonder what happened to that overnight case,' Bodkin muttered to himself.

The inspector put the file on his desk, then got to his feet and picked up the kettle. Handing it to Ferris along with the teapot, he rested his elbow on the top of the filing cabinet. 'I think we will have that cup of tea after all.' He looked from the big clock on the wall to Amy. 'Spears couldn't provide Ferris with an address for Mrs Honeychurch. But he got a telephone number which, sadly, has been disconnected since. I'll drop you at home after we've had a drink, then I'll get onto the Post Office to see if they still have a record for that telephone number in their files.'

'When are you going to see her, if you get the address?' Amy asked. 'I'm at work on Monday and I'd love to be there when you meet her.'

'If they still have the address, then we can go down tomorrow after you've been to church,' Bodkin said. 'Forget the Spinton Players for now. We can talk to them one evening in the week. They're bound to be rehearsing. Finding Mrs Honeychurch has to be our priority.'

Later that afternoon, after unpicking and re-stitching the waistband of her new skirt, tidying up the hem, and giving both the skirt and her new blouse a good iron, Amy had her weekly bath. Then, wearing her floral patterned dressing gown, and with her hair drying inside a turban made from a towel, she went up to her room and sat in front of her mirror as she filed her nails and plucked the odd stray hair from her eyebrows whilst listening to Billie Holiday singing Strange Fruit and Larry Clinton and his orchestra playing Deep Purple.

At a quarter to five, she went downstairs and ate potted meat sandwiches and a thick slice of homemade lemon cake at the table with her parents, while they discussed the contents of the Evening Post newspaper. A story by the paper's head reporter, Sandy Miles, filled most of the front page under the headline, Bones Found In Witchy Wood. It went on to speculate that the skeleton could be the remains of Mrs Cynthia Brown, the last recorded resident of the premises known locally as The Creepy Cottage. The report also repeated the legend of Johnny, the boy who folklore states went missing after climbing into the cottage through a broken window. At the bottom right of the page was a single column story with the headline, Casanova Caller Leaves Housewives Cold. The article went on to give a few sketchy details about the burglar that Bodkin was now pursuing.

'Bodkin's on both cases,' Amy said proudly. 'He uses a different name for Casanova, though.'

'What does he call him?' Mrs Rowlings said with a shudder. 'He'd better not come around here leaving his Valentine cards.'

'Bodkin is calling him Cyrano de Burglar, but I think you're safe, Mum. So far, he's only targeted night worker's houses and you've got Dad to protect you if he breaks in.'

'You're safe with me here,' Amy's father said, patting his wife's hand.

'Of course, if we had a dog, it would alert us all to the impending danger,' Amy said, looking directly at her father.

'And if we had a dog, someone would have to feed it, walk it, bath it, brush it and get arm ache throwing a ball for it,' Mr Rowlings replied, 'and we all know whose shoulders those tasks would fall on.' He patted his wife's hand again. 'Elizabeth has enough to do looking after us.'

'I wouldn't mind,' Elizabeth replied quietly. 'It would be company for me while I get on with my housework.'

'See!' Amy leapt onto the attack.

'The answer is still no,' Mr Rowlings replied as he picked up the newspaper and retired to his armchair. 'Any more tea in the pot, dear?'

At five-fifteen, Amy went back to her room and sat in front of the mirror to style her flaxen hair and put on her makeup, ready for her night at the pictures. By the time her best friend Alice arrived at five to six, she was ready to go.

Alice was a beautiful young woman and had been Amy's best friend for her entire life. Her hair fell in dark curls around her shoulders and she had the face and figure of a Hollywood starlet. Locals who frequented the picture house compared her looks to the up-and-coming actress Rita Hayworth, and in truth, there was a remarkable resemblance.

Alice checked her appearance in the tall mirror that hung on the wall in Amy's hallway. She was wearing a deep red, knee-length dress with thin straps that showed off her bare shoulders. Her hair was pulled back above the ears and held in place with two matching red hair clips. She carried a black jacket over her arm and wore a pair of black Oxford shoes.

After patting her curls in place, Alice turned to face the stairs to find that Amy was on her way down.

'WOW!' she said as she took in Amy's appearance. 'I love that blouse... and the skirt. Did you get them from Brigden's? You look gorgeous. Bodkin is going to fall head over heels in love with you all over again.'

'Seventeen and six for the two items,' Amy replied. 'It was a bit more than I wanted to spend, but they are worth the extra.'

'They are a bargain,' Alice replied. 'But then, you'd look good in a sack.'

Amy checked herself in the mirror, picked up her handbag and shouted good night to her mum and dad. Out on the lane, she took Alice's arm and the two friends walked towards the bus stop across the road from the Old Bull pub.

'You'll have to come with me one of these Saturdays,' Amy said. 'They have so many lovely things in your size.'

'Saturday morning isn't really a good time for me,' Alice replied. 'By the time I've done mucking out the pigs, feeding the chickens and milking the herd, I smell like I've been sleeping in the sties. I don't get a minute to myself until after lunch.'

'I could hold off until the afternoon,' Amy said. 'But the real bargains will be long gone by then.' She thought for a moment. 'Tell you what. I'll have a look for you next week. I know what size you are and I know what would suit you. Leave it with me and I'll pick something out. What's your budget?'

'I could stretch to fifteen shillings,' Alice said. 'But if you can knock Eileen down and get me a couple of dresses for a pound, I can justify the expense.'

'Done!' Amy said. 'I'm working at the London Connection from Wednesday. I'll nip in during my lunch break and have a word with Sharon. She'll keep her eye out for anything that comes in that might suit.'

Alice patted her bosom with her free hand. 'Just make sure there's plenty of room for these. I'm sure they're getting bigger.'

Amy looked at her own, more modest bosom and sighed. 'Whatever it is you are eating, can you save me some?'

Alice tilted her head to look at Amy. 'You have a lovely figure. I'd swop mine for yours in a heartbeat.' She waved to the bus driver, who was standing on the grass verge, having a cigarette. 'What's brought this on? You're not usually so critical of yourself.'

'Oh, I'm not down, exactly... Look, I had a run in with that minx, Trixie yesterday. She was taunting me again. She knows I'm a little envious of her assets.'

'You won't be in a few years' time when yours are still looking perky and hers are hanging around her waist,' Alice replied.

Amy laughed out loud. 'What a pleasant thought. Thank you, my darling.'

As the four friends left the cinema later that evening, the consensus was that it had been a very enjoyable film, although Bodkin and Ferris said they still preferred the swashbuckling nineteen twenty-nine version that had starred Douglas Fairbanks.

Amy, an avid reader of Photoplay, the magazine that gave out Hollywood's innermost secrets, said that Fairbank's son, Douglas Fairbanks Junior, had been invited to take the lead role by the director, James Whale but the producer, Edward Small had refused to accept Fairbanks Junior and had demanded that Louis Haywood be given the roles of King Louis and his doppelgänger, Phillipe.

'He could have given junior the role of d'Artagnon. It would have been nice to see how he did in his dad's old role,' Bodkin said to the agreement of the others.

As there were still twenty minutes to wait for the bus, the four friends shared two portions of fish and chips as they sat on the bench opposite the bus stop. The evening was still warm, but before they had finished their alfresco meal, the heavy clouds that had formed while they were inside the cinema began to drip their contents onto the streets.

Alice pulled on her jacket, but Amy, who had wanted to show off her new blouse, hadn't brought one with her, so Bodkin, ever the gentleman, took off his rumpled suit jacket and hung it across her shoulders. He was about to throw the newspaper the chips had come wrapped in, into the bin, when he spotted the Casanova headline.

'HA! The Casanova Caller indeed. If the Post is using that name, we know we don't have anyone feeding snippets to Sandy Miles from inside the investigation.'

Amy laughed. 'That's what I was saying to Dad earlier.'

Ferris frowned. 'They might know we haven't decided on a name yet, so they're using their own.'

Amy looked sideways at Bodkin. 'Haven't you told Ferris about Cyrano de Burglar yet?'

Ferris looked puzzled. 'Cyril who?'

'Cyrano de Burglar, Ferris,' Amy repeated. 'Like Cyrano de Bergerac from the book?'

'I haven't read that one,' Ferris admitted. 'Anyway, I thought you wanted to call him Don Two?'

'I left it to Amy to choose, and she liked Cyrano better,' Bodkin said. 'Mind you, Ferris, you might have stumbled onto something. Cyril de Burglar does have more of a colloquial ring to it.'

'Oh, make your minds up, lads,' Amy said with a shake of her head. She pulled Bodkin's jacket over her head as the rain began to get heavier. 'BUS!' she shouted as she spotted the long, green coach turn onto Middle Street at the top of the hill.

The Old Bull snug was busy, as it usually was on a Saturday night. The snug was the room where the girls on a night out sat alongside the groups of wives who nursed half pints of mild or port and lemons while their husbands drank pint after pint in the bar.

Bodkin lifted his arm to hang his coat on the already full coat rack but was given a dig in the ribs by a woman standing near the door with an almost full pint of bitter in her hands. 'Oi! Don't you go soaking my new jacket through with that soggy old rag.'

Bodkin apologised, and after spotting an empty table over by the fireplace, he left Ferris at the bar and led Amy and Alice across the room. When the two women were seated, he hung his jacket over an oval-backed chair before returning to the bar to help Ferris with the drinks.

Ferris took a long pull of his pint and almost half of it disappeared down his throat. 'Ah, that's hit the spot,' he said, wiping the back of his hand across his mouth. 'I'll erm, just get myself another one. I'll join you in a minute.'

'Ferris meant what he said about celebrating, I see,' Amy said as she took her port and lemon from Bodkin and took a quick sip. 'I'll buy him a drink later on, too. He deserves it. He did well, didn't he, Bodkin?'

Bodkin nodded as he sipped his own beer. 'Chief Superintendent Grayson picked the right man when he offered the CID post to Ferris. He'll make inspector himself before too long, mark my words.'

'What if he makes chief inspector, Bodkin? He'll be the one ordering you around.'

Bodkin snorted into his pint. 'I'll be Commissioner by then.'

Amy shook her head. 'Not you, Bodkin. You'd miss the daily grind too much. You'd never swap chasing Back Door Billy or Cyril de Burglar for a desk.'

'So, it's Cyril now, is it?' Bodkin said with a chuckle. 'Fair enough. I quite like it. I'll be hot on his trail again on Monday.' He smiled across the table at Amy. 'You're right, of course. I could never give up on the job. It's in my blood.'

Just then, the door to the snug opened and a uniformed police officer waked in.

'Look out, Mavis, they've tracked you down,' Stan, the landlord called to an elderly lady who was humming an old music hall tune to herself as she sat on a tall, backless stool at the bar.

'He can have me any time he feels like it,' Mavis cackled.

The young constable blushed and tapped Ferris on the shoulder. He turned with his second, half-drunk pint in his hand.

'Hello, Smedley, what brings you here?'

PC Smedley produced a sheet of folded paper from his uniform pocket. 'I was told I'd find Inspector Bodkin here, Ferris. He had a telephone call from the Post Office an hour ago. He left a message on the desk to get it to him as soon as possible, but I haven't been able to track him down. I tried his flat and Trixie told me he'd be in here with you and that... floozy?'

Ferris held out his hand. 'I'll give it to him, thanks, Smedley.'

As the officer left the pub, Ferris ordered another pint, then sipping at it in a more measured manner, he made his way over to the table where Bodkin and the girls were waiting.

'A note for you, sir,' he said, passing the folded paper to Bodkin.

The inspector unfolded the note and read the message before sticking up a thumb to Amy. 'We've got an address for Mrs Honeychurch. Are you still on for a trip to Rochester in the morning?'

Chapter Eight

On Sunday morning, Amy left church with her mother and father by the lychgate exit, to find Bodkin waiting on the pavement. After a quick chat with the Rowlings, he and Amy walked back up the hill by the side of the church to where Bodkin had left his black Morris 8 parked up.

'I'd let you drive,' the policeman said, 'but you'll be on strange roads and they might be busy as we get closer to Rochester. We should try to get you some insurance, really.'

'I've got insurance, Bodkin, didn't I tell you? Uncle Maurice has put me on his policy. I'm quite legal as long as I have a competent driver in the car with me.'

Bodkin handed her the keys. 'That's good enough for me, and for Chief Superintendent Grayson. We were trying to find a way to get you on the police insurance policy.' He waited until they were in the car before he spoke again. 'You should really have a set of L plates on the car, but if anyone asks where they are, we can just say they must have fallen off on the journey. I think there are a few sets lying around at the station for any new drivers that need them. I should have thought about this a while ago. I'll chuck a set on the back seat when I get to work on Monday.'

Amy grinned. 'Just tell anyone nosy enough to ask that you're a copper, Bodkin. They won't ask any more questions after finding that out. Everyone trusts a cop... I'll rephrase that. Most people trust a policeman.'

'Fewer and fewer every year, sadly. And they're probably right not to. There are a lot of rogue coppers about, especially in the Met.' He paused as Amy did her start up checks, then he looked over his shoulder to make sure the road was clear. 'Have you paid your seven and six to book the test yet?'

'Not yet,' Amy said as she pulled out onto the road. 'I was waiting for you to tell me I'm good enough to pass.'

'Oh, you're easily good enough to do what they'll ask. It's not really very difficult at all, but I'd hang on if I were you. If we are dragged into this war, then the department who deals with driving tests might have other things on their minds. Chief Super Grayson is of a like mind. He thinks they might be suspended for the duration of the war.'

Amy shot him a horrified look. 'Does that mean I won't be able to drive legally until the war is over?'

'Not at all. It just means that you won't have to take a test. The law will change to state that you can drive without having passed a competency test. You'll be given a provisional licence which you can exchange for a full one when we've put old Adolph back in his box.'

'Phew!' Amy said as she steered into a sharp bend before straightening up again. 'I hope you know where we're going, Bodkin, because I don't have the foggiest idea.'

Bodkin reached for his roadmap, unfolded it and ran his finger along a couple of B roads before folding it back up and tossing it into the footwell of the car. 'We'll go for the simple route, although it will probably take us a bit longer to get there. Just follow the Gillingham road, then go through the town until we pick up the A2. It's a straight road in from there.'

Forty minutes later, after finding a couple of dead ends, Bodkin reluctantly picked up the map again and directed Amy to St Agnes

Street, which was in a well-to-do area of large Victorian houses. She easily found number twenty-two and parked up outside. Bodkin looked up as they climbed out of the car and pointed to a telephone line that ran from a wooden pole in the street directly to the house.

'Maybe they're back on the network with a different number,' he said as he pushed open the gate. As they walked up the path, they could see a large sign that had been fixed to the wall at the side of the porch. RIVERVIEW GUEST HOUSE. Bodkin looked around and a puzzled look came over his face. 'Riverview? They're having a laugh, aren't they? You might get to see it from the attic room, but all you can see from street level are more houses.'

He stepped into the porch and pushed a white button that had the word PRESS stamped onto it. A couple of long minutes later, the front door opened to reveal a frumpy, grey-haired woman wearing a faded flower print pinafore and a matching headscarf.

'We're full,' she said firmly, looking Amy up and down before turning her attention to Bodkin. 'And even if we weren't, we don't allow that sort of thing under our roof.'

'That sort of thing?' Bodkin looked puzzled.

'You know what I'm talking about... who is this, anyway? Your secretary? One thing's for certain, it isn't your wife. She's not wearing a ring.'

Bodkin fished his warrant card out of his pocket and held it in front of the woman's eyes. 'I'm Inspector Bodkin of the Spinton police and this is my associate, Amy Rowlings.'

'I don't care if you're the Duke of Kent. You're not carrying on in this house.'

Amy bit her lip to stop herself from laughing. She shot a quick glance at Bodkin, who seemed to be getting more frustrated by the minute.

'We aren't looking to rent a room for the afternoon, the evening or the week,' he said firmly. 'We're here as part of an investigation. We're looking for Anthea Honeychurch. Would you be that lady?'

The woman's belligerence dropped a level and her face became less suspicious looking. 'There's no Honeychurch here, dear. Not anymore, at least. She moved out nine years ago. I know that because me and my Gerald bought the house from her.'

Bodkin smiled his best smile. 'And you are?'

'Hilda Frump.'

Bodkin looked down at his feet and composed himself before pulling out his notebook and jotting her name down.

'Have you any idea where she went, Mrs, erm, Frump? Is she still in the area?'

'I know exactly where she went because she left a forwarding address for any post that might arrive. She was quite insistent that I keep it somewhere safe. She said she was expecting some important news.'

Bodkin waited quietly for a few moments, but Hilda didn't take the hint.

'Do you think you could dig it out?'

'Oh, of course, it's not buried. It's in my bureau.' Mrs Frump turned away and hurried through a door on the left-hand side of the hallway. She returned a minute or so later with an unstamped envelope bearing a Rochester address. Bodkin copied the information into his notebook, then thanked the landlady for her invaluable assistance.

'Do you think I can throw this away now? I mean. I've not had a single letter addressed to her all the time I've been here.'

'I'll look after it,' Bodkin said, taking the envelope from the woman's fingers. 'Have a nice afternoon, Mrs Frump.'

'A chance would be a fine thing,' she called after him as he led Amy down the path. 'He's gone to the pub and I'm here on my own to prepare Sunday dinner for six.'

Back in the car, Bodkin consulted his map and after a few minutes tutting as he ran his finger along the streets, he finally found Rosewall Court.

Amy started the car and followed Bodkin's instructions, which took them along the river, past a restaurant and a large pub. Two right turns and a sharp bend later, they arrived at a beautifully designed block of art deco style apartments.

'There's money here, that's for sure,' Bodkin said as he climbed out of the black Morris.

'It does look a bit swish,' Amy said as she dropped the car keys into her bag. 'Don't make your usual assumptions about the well to do, Bodkin. She might be a nice woman and don't forget her daughter is still missing after all these years.'

Bodkin shrugged. 'I take as I find,' he said.

'Of course you do,' Amy muttered, knowing full well how Bodkin regarded the rich.

Flat three was on the ground floor and Bodkin only had to ring once on the buzzer to get a response. After giving his name, he waited patiently until a fifty-year-old with a pleasant smile, grey eyes and white hair, left slightly longer than was the norm for a woman of her age, opened the building's communal front door. She was wearing a smock that was covered in paint drips and she held a wide paintbrush in her right hand.

'I'm so sorry, the automatic control system isn't working at the moment. We're waiting for a man, but he can't come until Tuesday.'

Bodkin produced his warrant card and introduced Amy. 'We're looking for Anthea Honeychurch,' he said.

'Is it to do with Nina?'

Bodkin nodded.

'Then I'm afraid you're slightly too late to be of any help to her. Anthea died of a broken heart in nineteen thirty-one.'

Chapter Nine

'You had better come in,' the woman said, standing aside to allow Amy and Bodkin to enter the foyer.

She led them along the passage and through a door marked with a brass number three. They found themselves in a large room, some twenty feet by sixteen. The walls were littered with artworks, some in sketch form, others in watercolours. The end wall was her work in progress. A surrealist full wall painting in the style of Salvador Dali.

'I'm Winifred Langley. I am... was... Anthea's sister,' she said, offering her paint-smudged hand to them. She nodded towards a two-seater plush red sofa. 'Please sit.'

When Amy and Bodkin were seated, Winifred picked up an open packet of Capstan cigarettes and offered them across the coffee table. Both Amy and Bodkin declined.

'Ah, you don't smoke. How about a glass of whisky, then?' Winifred picked up a decanter and swished the contents around. Once again, Amy and Bodkin declined. 'Oh, you're no fun,' she said as she poured a single measure and carried it over to the open window, where she placed the glass on the windowsill before lighting her cigarette with a silver lighter she produced from her pocket.

Bodkin cleared his throat, but before he got the chance to ask a question, Winifred spoke again.

'It's bad news I take it? Have you found the poor girl at last? It's taken you long enough.'

'We've only been on the case for a couple of days, Mrs Langley,' Bodkin began.

'Miss, it's Miss Langley. I never married. I couldn't face being subservient to a man.' She looked directly at Amy. 'Stay single as long as you can, my dear. There's plenty of time for the drudgery of domestic life when you're older.'

Amy smiled. 'That's my plan.'

'Make sure you stick to it,' Winifred said, before turning her attention to Bodkin again. 'A couple of days, you say, and you've found her already? Goodness me, you're an improvement on the Rochester police, that's for sure.' She took a long draw of her cigarette and blew the smoke out of the open window. 'Where did you find her? I'm assuming there wasn't a lot of her left.'

'I won't go into too many details, Miss Langley,' Bodkin replied. 'It might be rather upsetting, but I can tell you that her remains were found in an abandoned cottage in Spinton on Friday.'

'Spinton? Not Mossmoor, that is interesting.' Winifred flicked ash out of the gap in the window frame. 'What made you look in this cottage after all this time? Did you receive some new evidence?'

'Sadly not,' Bodkin replied. 'The end wall of the cottage was hit by a lightning strike on Friday afternoon. When the storm was over, a man and his dog walked past the building and the dog found it.'

'I hope it didn't steal anything,' Winifred said, coughing as she laughed.

Bodkin ignored the attempt at black humour. 'We found a few items of hers amongst the rubble, and that set us a puzzle. She had two single tickets in her pocket. One a bus ticket from Rochester to Mossmoor, the other a train ticket from there to Spinton. Have you any idea why she might have done that instead of getting the train straight through?'

Winifred took another pull from her cigarette, leaned her head back and blew smoke into the air.

'I have no idea why she would have done that. We've... Anthea always assumed she was taken in Mossmoor. She knew about the ticket because she was with Nina at the bus station in Rochester when she bought it. She told her she was going to stay with a friend from college and would be back on Sunday afternoon.'

Bodkin scratched at the stubble on his chin. 'Did she give her mother her friend's name?'

'I can't remember all the details after all this time, Inspector. Something beginning with M, maybe Margaret, Maggie...'

'Margo?' Amy asked quickly.

'Possibly. I honestly can't remember. All I know is that she attended college in Rochester with Nina. They were both members of an amateur dramatics group.'

'I see,' Bodkin rubbed at his jaw again. 'How old was Nina?'

'Seventeen, she would have been eighteen in the November.'

'There was a performance of The Importance of Being Earnest at the Playhouse in Spinton and she had a leaflet advertising the play in her bag. It had been signed by the lead actor, Rex Larson. Was she a particularly big fan of his?'

Winifred tossed her cigarette end out of the window and wafted the smoke away from her eyes with her hand. 'Rex Larson... she was... what's the word they used back then...? crazy about the man. She had a scrapbook of cuttings from the showbiz columns of the newspaper. She was obsessed.' Winifred took a sip of whisky, then put the glass back on the windowsill. 'She wrote to a few actors via their agents. As I said she was part of an Am Dram group and she really got the bug. The chap who ran the club knew a few people in the business and gave her a couple of names to contact. Larson was the only one who ever replied to her. She became fixated with him after that.'

'Did she ever meet him in person?'

Winifred screwed up her face as she thought. 'No, I don't think so, but she used to go all over Kent to watch him on stage. Anthea used to go with her. They saw him in Maidstone, Dover and Ashford as well as Rochester. I don't think Anthea knew about the Spinton performance, as she'd have definitely gone with Nina.' Winifred paused. 'She was a little overprotective, but Nina was such an outgoing, friendly girl. She saw the good in everyone and I think Anthea suspected it might be rather easy for some man or other to take advantage of her.'

'So she lied to her mother to make sure she could go to the performance on her own,' Bodkin said. 'Was she usually as devious as that?'

'Not that I know, but she was easily influenced. Those college friends of hers might have been behind it all.'

'Did Anthea read the letters that Nina got from Rex Larson?'

'Oh yes, she read all of them. She was home all day and Nina wasn't, so she got to see the postman every time he delivered.'

'Rex may have written to her at a different address though. He could have contacted her at the Am Dram premises or by telephone at one of her friends' houses.'

'It's a possibility, of course it is,' Winifred said, draining her whisky glass and getting herself a refill. 'But to be honest. I don't think she kept much from her mother. I honestly think this was a one-off thing.'

'Was she a good actress?' Bodkin asked.

'Not really. I think she got her kicks by hanging around people who really could act. I saw her in one or two things, but she only ever had bit parts and even then she used to stumble over her lines.' Winifred sipped her whisky and put the glass on the windowsill before picking up her cigarettes and lighting another one.

'Did she have a boyfriend?' Amy asked.

'No, at least no one I heard of. I think she found boys of her own age rather immature.' She glanced at Bodkin and flicked ash out of the window. 'Mind you, in my experience, hardly any of them reach full maturity.'

As Amy choked back a laugh. Bodkin gave her an odd look, then turned his attention back to Winifred.

'A little earlier you said something about the Rochester police. I take it Anthea wasn't satisfied with their investigation.'

'What investigation? They never conducted one. All they ever did was fob her off.'

'I'm not sticking up for them here,' Bodkin replied, 'but they did contact the police in Mossmoor and they couldn't really uncover anything apart from the fact that she made it safely to the bus station. She was only in town for half an hour, according to the timetables.'

'It wasn't that so much,' Winifred said, running the palm of her hand across her forehead. 'It was the way they treated her whenever she rang them or called in at the police station. They were convinced that Nina had run off with some man or other and that was that.' She thought for a moment. 'There was a sergeant... what was his name... Bigger, that was it, Sergeant Bigger. When she dropped in after hearing nothing at all from them for over two months, he warned her that if she didn't stop pestering them, he'd charge her with wasting police time.'

'Oh my goodness,' Amy blurted out. 'How could they treat a heartbroken mother like that?'

'That wasn't the worst of it,' Winifred said. 'A couple of weeks later, she was in town shopping, so she dropped in at the police station. The young man on the desk had obviously been warned because he called the sergeant in from the back office and he literally pushed Anthea out of the door and told her never to come back. The Mossmoor policeman wasn't much better, but at least he was polite when she rang. He said they'd come to a dead end, and it was down to Rochester to pursue any further inquiries.' She took a pull on her cigarette. 'She went into a decline after that. She would sit for hours just looking at Nina's photograph. I tried all sorts to bring her out of her depression, but nothing worked. She wasn't safe on her own in that drafty old house, so I persuaded her to sell up and move in with me. I think I made the wrong call there. She might have been better off staying where she was. At least she would have had her memories.' She flicked ash out of the window. 'She was dead within six months of moving in. She never heard another word from the police. She had an almost religious zeal about meeting the postman at the front door, and every time the telephone rang she thought it might be the police with some news. It never was, of course. They didn't care. I think they'd wound up Nina's case before Anthea was thrown out of the police station. As I said, she died of a broken heart. She hardly ate, and she did nothing all day apart from running to the door if she'd spotted the postman coming down the hill.'

Winifred flicked her cigarette end out of the window and picked up her drink.

'I'm so sorry the police treated her like that,' Bodkin said. 'It was truly unforgivable.'

'I gave him a piece of my mind after the funeral,' Winifred said. 'I'm made of sterner stuff than Anthea, and I told him exactly what I thought of him and his bloody police force at the Riverside parade. His superintendent was there at the time. He didn't look as though he gave a damn, although he showered me with platitudes once I'd explained who I was. He promised me that he'd go over the case notes and that Sergeant Bigger would personally call me to apologise on the force's behalf. He never did. I've heard nothing from them from that day to this.' She picked up her whisky and swirled the amber liquid around in the glass. 'I rang Constable Spears at Mossmoor the day after the funeral to tell him that Anthea was gone. He sort of alluded to some minor evidence that had been passed on to Rochester, but I never found out what it was.'

While listening to Winifred, Bodkin's lips had formed a rigid, straight line. He clenched his fists repeatedly as she detailed her dealings with the police. Amy had never seen him so angry during an investigation. She reached out and put her hand on his arm.

'Do you still have any of Nina's things here?' Bodkin asked after a long pause.

'Oh, yes, but there isn't much. There are some pictures of her, her collection of autographed actors, photographs and a few other bits. I didn't keep her clothes or anything like that. I gave all those to a local charity.'

'Do you still have the correspondence with Rex Larson?' Bodkin asked.

'I assume the letters will be there. I've never read them.' She walked across to the sideboard, opened an end cupboard, and pulled out a shoebox. 'Not much for a whole life, is it?'

Bodkin got to his feet and took the box from her. 'Do you mind if we take this with us? There might be something of use in here. Everything will be returned to you when we've concluded the investigation.' He looked at the box for a moment, then back to Winifred. 'Unlike the Rochester police, I promise that we will keep you informed as to any progress we make. You won't be treated anything like as poorly as your sister.'

Winifred smiled sadly. 'You've done more in two days than they've done in ten years, Inspector Bodkin.' She smiled at Amy, then winked at her. 'Keep a tight hold on this one, my dear. You seem to have found a decent man, and believe me, they are few and far between.' She winked again. 'Just keep reminding him who really wears the trousers.'

Amy stepped forward, gave Winifred a hug and whispered in her ear. 'Don't worry, I intend to.'

Back at the car, Bodkin asked Amy for the keys and they sat for a few minutes going through the contents of the shoe box. Bodkin picked up a small bundle of letters with a scarlet ribbon tied around them, took a sniff at the envelopes, then dropped them back into the box. 'My bedtime reading tonight,' he said. He looked across at Amy, who was quietly studying a six by four-inch photograph of Nina.

The picture looked to have been taken at a performance she had attended. She was smiling, not in the direction of the photographer, but to someone who would have been standing by his or her side. She was a pretty girl with shortish dark hair cut in a late twenties style. A few stray hairs had fallen onto her face and Amy, who suffered with a similar problem, ran her fingers across the photograph as if trying to brush them aside.

'Don't worry, Nina,' she said quietly. 'Bodkin and I will catch the man who hurt you. Sleep softly now.'

Chapter Ten

Bodkin handed the shoebox to Amy and started the engine. After conducting a messy three-point turn in the car park of the apartments, he pushed the accelerator pedal to the floor and screeched out onto the main road.

'Steady, Bodkin,' Amy said. 'I know you're still angry but take it easy. Where are we going, anyway?'

'To the Rochester nick,' Bodkin replied, then he cursed at the driver in front.

'Do you want me to give you the directions from the map?' she asked, leaning forward to pick it up from the footwell.

'We passed it on the way in,' Bodkin replied. 'Thank God for that!' he exclaimed as the car in front pulled across to park outside a closed baker's shop. 'Bloody Sunday drivers.'

'I think you ought to calm down. Either that or pull over and let me drive,' Amy said, staring hard at Bodkin. 'You'll get us both killed driving like this.'

Bodkin grimaced, then nodded slowly. 'Sorry, Amy, I'm just so angry at what the police force... MY police force put that poor woman through.'

Amy stretched across the front seat and patted his arm. 'You won't get your revenge if we don't make it to the police station.' She smiled at him. 'Throttle that anger back from raging, boiling point to just plain seething. We might just make it then.'

Bodkin shot a glance left and blew out his cheeks. 'Temperature falling,' he said. 'Seething level reached.'

After pulling up outside the police station, Bodkin was out of the door in seconds. With two long strides, he crossed the pavement and with one bound; he was on the top step and pushing at the front door.

Amy, meanwhile, calmly walked around the front of the car, leaned in through the driver's door that Bodkin had left swinging open and retrieved the keys from the ignition. Dropping them into her bag, she closed the car door and made her way demurely up the short flight of steps. When she walked into the reception area, she found Bodkin furiously hammering on the large brass bell that was fixed to the counter.

Suddenly, a figure appeared from a doorway behind the front desk. The policeman was chewing a mouthful of pork pie, the rest of it was in his hand. His uniform jacket was undone to the waist and his face was a mask of pure anger.

'OI!' he yelled. 'Hit that sodding bell one more time and you'll be in the cells before you can say, Jack Robinson.'

Bodkin hit the bell twice.

'Right,' the constable spluttered as he spat out tiny pieces of meat, jelly, and crust. 'That does it. You are bloody well nicked.'

'You are bloody well nicked, SIR!' Bodkin replied angrily as he flashed his warrant card. 'Inspector Bodkin, now put that bloody pork pie down, button up your uniform and prepare to apologise as though your mother just caught you dancing around the front room wearing nothing but a Morris dancer's bell-strung garter.'

The policeman tossed the pork pie onto the counter and frantically tried to button up his tunic while repeatedly grunting, 'Yes, sir, sorry, sir.'

Bodkin was in no mood to accept the apology he had demanded.

As the constable was fastening his buttons, he let fly with a string of complaints.

'So, this is how you treat members of the public, is it? The people you are allegedly here to serve. You are a disgrace to the uniform, Constable. I'm seriously considering putting you on a report.'

'Oh, don't do that, sir, I'm sorry, sir, it won't happen again, sir,' the constable gabbled.

'Name?'

'Constable 731 Smith, sir.'

Bodkin pulled out his notepad and jotted down a few words.

'How long have you been on the force?'

'Six years, sir. Please don't put me on a report. Sergeant Bigger will have my guts for garters, sir.'

'I was about to ask about him. Does he live close by?'

'Yes, sir, about two streets away, sir.'

'Is he on the telephone network?'

'No, sir... at least, I don't think so, sir.'

'But you have his address?'

'Forty-two Corporation Avenue, sir.'

Bodkin looked at his watch, checking it against the big clock on the wall. 'Right, Constable Smith. You've got exactly five minutes to get around to his house, drag him out of bed or his armchair, wherever he is, and bring him back here. Do I make myself clear?'

'Yes, sir, but he might be in the Flagon, sir. It's a pub, sir,' he added unnecessarily.

'Is the pub close by?'

'The same street he lives on, sir, about thirty yar—'

Bodkin slammed his fist down on the counter, making both the officer and the half-eaten pork pie jump.

'Five minutes, Smith, or that report goes in first thing in the morning.'

. . .

'Ooh, Bodkin, you are impressive. I've never seen you like this before,' Amy said, taking a pace back to admire him.

'He doesn't deserve to be in that uniform,' Bodkin replied. He reached across the desk, picked up the pork pie and broke a piece off the untouched side. Popping it into his mouth, he offered it to Amy, who shook her head in disgust.

'Ugh, no thanks, I quite like pork but the jelly makes me feel sick.'

Bodkin broke off another large piece, bit into it and tossed the rest of the savoury snack over the counter.

'I prefer Melton pies,' he said.

Two minutes later, a panting Constable Smith reappeared behind the desk.

'He's right behind me, sir. He'll be here in two shakes of... Ah, here he is.'

Amy turned as a squat, round-faced, man came in through the reception door. He was about forty-five years of age, with thinning fair hair and a red drinker's nose. He was wearing his police issue blue shirt and navy serge trousers. He had obviously had a drink or two and wasn't pleased about being unceremoniously dragged out of the pub.

'Who are you?' he asked Amy before noticing Bodkin glaring at him from near the desk.

'Never mind who she is. I'm Inspector Bodkin and I want some answers from you, Bigger.'

The sergeant puffed out his chest and glared back at Bodkin. 'Can't this wait until tomorrow? I'm in a good crib school over there.'

'Can't this wait until tomorrow, sir?' Bodkin said calmly. 'I don't know what it is about this nick, but no one seems to respect rank.'

'Well, can it wait, SIR?'

Bodkin shook his head. 'The matter I'm here about has already waited ten years and I'm not going to let it drag on for one more hour, let alone another day.'

Bigger sighed. 'What matter... sir?'

Bodkin stepped forward and patted Bigger on the shoulder. 'Now you're getting the hang of it, Sergeant.'

Bigger shuffled his feet together and stood straight. 'How can I help you, sir?'

'Well, it's like this, Bigger. I want to hear everything you know about the Nina Honeychurch case from the nineteenth of October nineteen twenty-nine.'

'Christ Almighty!' Bigger exclaimed. 'How am I supposed to remember that far back?'

'Firstly, apologise to the lady for your blasphemy,' Bodkin said firmly, 'and secondly, it's not like you'd forget an unusual name like Honeychurch, is it? Especially after you threatened to arrest her mother for pestering you and then physically throwing her out of that door,' Bodkin pointed to the entrance, 'into the street.'

Bigger turned quickly towards Amy and whispered, 'sorry', then he turned back to Bodkin. 'Honeychurch... ah yes, I do remember now. Missing girl case. Never found.'

'Never bloody looked for in the first place,' Bodkin snarled.

'She was... I mean... look, guv, it was an open and shut case, really. The girl got a bus to Mossmoor to meet a bloke in secret, then they did a runner together, case closed.'

'The girl was seventeen years old, Bigger. You didn't have an investigation at all. You let the copper at Mossmoor ask a few questions of a bus conductor, then you closed the case down.'

'She went off with a bloke, sir. It was obvious to everyone who looked into it. She's probably living in Yorkshire now with half a dozen brats hanging off her ti—'

'It wasn't obvious to the officer in Mossmoor because he sent you his report and asked you to make further enquiries into it, which you didn't.'

'Honestly, Inspector. There was nothing for us to investigate. We get so many missing person cases like that. It's always a young girl and they always run off with a feller their mother didn't like.' He turned to Amy and shrugged. 'It happens all the time.'

'So, this young girl... her name was Nina, by the way, just upped sticks and buggered off to Yorkshire. That's in your final report on the case, is it?'

'Something like that, yes.'

'Did you mention the conductor's evidence that she was being pestered by someone on the bus and that man got off at the terminus at the same time as Nina Honeychurch?'

'Of course it's in there.'

'And you don't think that fact was important enough to follow up?'

'We asked Mossmoor to follow it up.' He looked at Bodkin desperately. 'The chief super signed it off, sir. He said we didn't have the resources to waste time on an open and shut case.' He shrugged towards Bodkin. 'She'll turn up one day with her tail between her legs if she hasn't done already. I haven't heard from that lunat... from her mother since.'

'Since the day you threw her out of that door.' Bodkin grabbed Bigger by the neck of his shirt and hauled him onto his tiptoes. 'That lunatic's daughter will never come home with her tail between her legs because we found her body up in Spinton on Friday. She'd been murdered with a pickaxe. Before that she was almost certainly abused in the most violent manner you can image. Now, what would you say to her mother knowing all that...? Oh, you can't tell her anything, can you, Bigger? Because the poor woman died of a broken heart after being physically abused, ignored and thoroughly let down by you and everyone else at this cesspit of a police station.'

Bodkin pushed him back towards the wall and stared the man down. He crumbled in seconds as the reality of the situation hit home.

'M... murder,' he stuttered. 'Look, Inspector... there was no evidence. Do you think it was the man on the bus? Oh my God, the chief super will have a fit.'

'You'll be lucky to get your pension,' Bodkin spat. 'You... and you...' he spun around to face the still quaking Smith, 'are a disgrace to this institution and if you don't do everything in your power to help me in this investigation, you'll both be down at the dole office by Friday.'

'Of course, we'll help. What do you want me to do? Just say it.'

'I want you to go to your files and bring me everything you've got on the Nina Honeychurch inquiry. And then I want you to go through every single file in the building in case anything has been misplaced. I want records of telephone conversations, of meetings with Mrs Honeychurch. I want everything that you failed to write down back then, put on the record now. I want everything you have to hand sending over to my office in Spinton by lunchtime tomorrow. Everything else I've asked for, including those conversations with her mother and with the officer at Mossmoor, you can send over by post in the week.'

'Yes, sir, I'll make sure it's done,' Bigger said with a pleading look on his face. 'And, er, if I do that, sir, do you think you might overlook the sorry circumstances I find myself in today? I've got a family, sir.'

'Mrs Honeychurch had a family, Bigger. All that's left of it now, though, is an angry sister. A lady to whom your chief super made certain explicit promises. Now, you make sure that by the next time I speak to her, she's had a grovelling personal apology from both you and your boss.'

Bodkin turned on his heel and, after taking Amy by the arm, marched out of the police station.

Chapter Eleven

By the time they were back at the car, Bodkin seemed to have got it all out of his system. Reaching out, he pulled her to him and gave her the sort of kiss that would make Clarke Gable stand back and applaud.

'Blimey!' Amy said, fanning her face when he finally released her. 'We'll have to get you riled up more often.'

Bodkin grinned as he climbed into the passenger seat. When Amy had got herself comfortable, she fired up the engine and pulled the car onto the other side of the road.

'What brought all that on? I bet Sergeant Bigger is feeling a lot smaller right now...'

'It's the injustice of it all,' Bodkin replied. 'We're supposed to help people like Anthea, not make them feel worthless. Anyway, apart from that, I'm hungry and I'm never at my most serene when I'm hungry.'

'We'd better get you back home quickly then, Bodkin. You can have your Sunday dinner at ours to save you having to make a stale bread and cheese sandwich at home.'

Bodkin rubbed his rumbling stomach. 'Are you sure your mum and dad won't mind?'

'They love having you round, you know that, and Mum always makes far too much.'

Bodkin reached down into the footwell to retrieve the road map, but after opening it up, Amy said. 'I'd like to try to find my own way back if that's all right.' Bodkin folded the map up again and tossed it onto the floor. Then, after sliding out of his jacket, he rolled it up and stuck it behind his head. 'Wake me up when we get to the police station, please. I just want to see if anything's come in while we've been down here.'

When Amy chanced a look at him only two minutes later, he was fast asleep and snoring gently.

'We're here, Bodkin,' Amy said, giving him a gentle push.

Bodkin grunted, opened one eye, then quickly closed it again as the dazzling sun reflecting off the bonnet of the car shone into his eyes. A few seconds later, shielding his face with his hand, he opened both eyes, blinked a few times, then sat up straight and pulled his makeshift pillow from behind his head.

'You got us here in one piece, then. Well done.'

'There were one or two hairy moments as I drove out of Gillingham onto that narrow bit. A truck seemed to want to be on both sides of the road, so I couldn't overtake. There was a lot of fist shaking from the driver. I got past him eventually, although he wasn't too happy about it.'

'I hope you were the polite motorist the Highway Code expects you to be,' Bodkin said, stifling a yawn.

'I stuck my hand out of the window and waved to him. Actually, I waved to him three or four times over the following two hundred yards. I think he liked it because he kept beeping his horn.'

Bodkin gave a short laugh, climbed out of the car, put his hands above his head, and stretched.

'There is a gesture you can use for people like that lorry driver,' Bodkin said as he slammed the door and walked around the front of the car to where Amy was waiting. He lifted his hand and folded back his fingers, leaving only the middle digit upright. 'It means thank you. Have a nice day.'

Amy laughed. 'I'm not that naïve, Bodkin. I know what it means.' She straightened her dress and followed Bodkin up the steps to the front door of the station. 'Did you know that the ancient Romans used to call that gesture digitus impudicus? It means the offensive finger.'

'You learn something new every day,' Bodkin replied. 'Keep it in your armoury, though. I think you'll get to use your digitus impudicus a lot more than you might think, when you're on the road on your own.'

Bodkin pushed hard on the door, then held it open for Amy. PC Parlour was in his usual place behind the desk.

'Afternoon, Parlour,' Bodkin said. 'Has anything come in for me?'

'Good afternoon, sir. Hello, miss,' Parlour raised a hand in greeting. 'There have been a couple of calls for you, sir. One from a Superintendent Harmison, from Rochester who seemed rather agitated about something. He's going to ring back tomorrow. There was a call from a lady called…' he looked down at his notes to check the name… 'Mrs Twigley, who rang from a telephone box to report that our Romeo burglar has struck again. She lives on Caldergate just off Middle Street, sir. I got her address.'

'He's called Cyril de Burglar, Parlour. Use that name in the future, but not if the press are involved. Let them use their own title until we catch him.'

'She got a good look at him as it happens, sir.' He studied his notes again. 'It's a bit… well, you'll understand when you hear the description. He seems to be a bit of a pantomime villain.' Parlour cleared his throat. 'The man is about five foot eight. He was wearing a bandana type mask over his mouth and he had a tatty blanket… it looked like the moths had been at it… draped over his shoulders like a cloak. He had one of those tricorn hats on like the highwaymen used to wear, but she thinks it might have been made of cardboard as one side of it was hanging over his ear.'

As Amy began to giggle, Bodkin raised his big right hand onto his forehead.

'For pity's sake,' he said.

'Just a couple more details, sir. He's quite a portly-looking chap. His belly was hanging over his trousers and he has a rather large nose. Mrs Twigley got those details from his shadow that was cast against her toilet wall... the outbuilding, sir.'

'CYRANO!' Amy shouted delightedly before putting her hand in front of her mouth. 'Sorry... but it sounds just like him, doesn't it, Bodkin?'

'An uncanny resemblance,' Bodkin agreed. 'I wonder if that's who he's trying to emulate. The nose could be false, of course.' He looked across the desk to Parlour. 'Let's keep this description to ourselves for a day or so, Parlour, no leaks to the press, please.' He held out his hand towards the constable. 'Okay, give me the address. I'll go and have a word with her.'

'Not until you've had something to eat, you won't,' Amy said firmly. She took hold of Bodkin's arm. 'The poor woman will wonder what's hit her if you question her on an empty stomach.'

When Amy and Bodkin stepped into the hall of Amy's cottage, they were greeted by the sound of a woman's almost hysterical screaming and the guttural laughter of a man. They looked through the gap in the living room doorway to see Mrs Rowlings lying on her back on the sofa with her legs in the air. Mr Rowlings, meanwhile, was dressed only in his vest and a pair of baggy, cream coloured underpants. His wet hair flopped over his eyes as he leaned over his wife, fingers flexed as he tickled her repeatedly.

'James, stop, someone will hear,' Mrs Rowlings gasped before resuming her wild screams.

'HA! Let them hear. I've got you now, my proud beauty.' The tickling and shrieking resumed.

Bodkin covered his mouth with his hand in an attempt to keep in the raucous laugh that he was about to expel. Amy shot him a quick glance with a horrified look on her face as her parents continued to cavort on the sofa.

When Bodkin could hold it in no longer, he let out a strangled half laugh, half cough. The sound caused Mr Rowlings to cease the attack on his wife, and they both froze and looked up at the door with open mouths.

'Mum... Dad...' Amy spluttered. In all the twenty-one years she had spent with them, she had never witnessed anything like it.

'I'll just, er... go and get dressed,' Mr Rowlings grimaced and hurried out into the hallway. 'I've just had my bath, laddie,' he said to Bodkin, as if that explained everything.

Bodkin watched as Rowlings hurried up the stairs, his baggy underpants flapping around the top of his thighs.

By the time they stepped into the living room, Mrs Rowlings had retreated to the kitchen. 'I'll just put the kettle on. Dinner's almost ready. Are you joining us, Mr Bodkin?'

'Yes, he is,' Amy called out, still not quite able to dislodge the scene she had just witnessed from her mind.

'That was worth coming over for,' Bodkin whispered into Amy's ear. 'I wouldn't have missed that for anything.'

'Shut up, Bodkin,' Amy hissed, still staring at the empty sofa.

'I'd like to know if it runs in the family,' Bodkin said, raising his hands in the air behind Amy's back.

'If what runs in the family?' Amy asked absentmindedly.

'Ticklishness,' Bodkin said as he attacked Amy's ribs with his fingers.

Amy's shriek was even louder than her mother's had been.

'Stop it, Bodkin... Get off,' she screamed, giggling like a child at the same time. She turned to face him, backing away. 'Bodkin, no... stop it...'

Bodkin flexed his fingers and took a step forward. 'Here comes the Tickle Monster,' he said menacingly.

'MUUUUUM!' Amy screamed as she hurried into the kitchen, slipping past Mrs Rowlings who was coming the other way, carrying a brown teapot.

'She's always been ticklish,' she said. 'She's worse than me.'

After dinner Bodkin thanked the Rowlings for their hospitality and after a perfunctory kiss at the front door, he climbed into his car and drove to Caldergate to interview Cyril de Burglar's latest victim.

Amy read her library book for an hour, then got the iron out and pressed her freshly washed work clothes. At five-thirty, a now fully dressed Mr Rowlings tuned into radio Luxembourg for the Ovaltiney's Concert Party, a radio show that was meant for younger families but had become such a tradition in the Rowlings' household that they hadn't missed a show since it began in nineteen thirty-four. All three joined in when Harry Hemsley, the show's host, called out one of the catch phrases that had infiltrated the everyday language of the nation. 'What did Horace say, Winnie?'

Because of the late Sunday dinner, they put off their evening tea of ham and cucumber sandwiches until seven, and at eight, Amy gave her still embarrassed parents a kiss on the cheek and went up to her room to catch up on more reading before slipping into bed at nine-thirty.

At seven-fifteen on Monday morning, Amy walked into the loading bay at The Mill, put her clock-in card in the rack and made her way around to the changing room where she found most of the workforce getting changed into their clean pinafores ready to start the week at their machines.

The Mill, the name used locally for Handsley's Garments, was a clothing factory built into what was an eighteen century cotton mill.

The mostly female workforce produced a range of affordable garments for the lower end of the clothing market. The finished items were shipped to a warehouse in London where they were distributed to outlets around the country.

'What a weekend that was,' Amy's friend Carol Sims said as she took off her coat and hung it on the rack.

'Why? What happened?' Amy asked, as she formed a turban out of a headscarf and wrapped it around her head.

'I was up at the Free with Mum on Saturday night again. She had another fall and banged her head. She didn't know what day it was, poor old thing. It's happening all the time now. They have no idea what's wrong with her. She's only sixty, for goodness' sake.'

'Oh, I'm sorry to hear that, Carol. How long did it take before someone got to see her?'

'Hours,' Carol replied. 'I didn't get home until half-past two in the morning. They kept her in. Luckily, they had a bed.' She slipped into her pinafore and tied it at the back. 'I was up there most of yesterday afternoon, too. They let her out at five. The Sister gave her a packet of aspirin and told me to take her home.'

'Things need to change,' Amy said. 'There was talk of a free health service at one time, but I suppose Old Adolph stomping around Europe has put paid to that. Every penny the country has will be put into making weapons now.'

'Never mind Old Adolph,' Beryl Hargreaves, AKA Big Nose Beryl said from the opposite side of the coat racks. 'What about that skellington they found up in the Witchy Wood?' She paused to make sure the room was silent before she went on. 'They say it's the bones of Charity Manson, you know, the alderman's wife who went missing in the summer. Everyone thought she'd run away with that hawker who stood on the market for a few weeks selling bric-à-brac, but it looks like he did 'er in and left the body in Creepy Cottage.'

Amy sighed.

'Beryl, it's always entertaining listening to your fairy tales, but the skel E ton, there's no g in it, that was found, wasn't the remains of Charity Manson. Charity Manson only left Spinton about three weeks ago. She's gone to stay with her mother, who is extremely ill. She'll be back in a few weeks. Anyway, a body wouldn't decompose that quickly.' Amy tied off her pinafore, pulled a packet of mints out of her bag and put them in her pocket. 'As it happens, the skelEton in the cottage has been there for ten years.' She hung her bag on the peg and turned towards the door. 'The police know who the poor woman is, and they have set up a murder inquiry.'

'Who is it, then?' Beryl demanded to know. 'Come on, you're always making out you know more than the rest of us just because you're seeing that copper.'

'I'm not telling you anything, Beryl,' Amy said. 'It would be pointless anyway because by lunchtime, the facts will have been twisted out of all recognition.' She walked to the door and held it open for Carol. 'You're nothing but a windbag, Beryl. No one takes anything you say, seriously.'

As Amy stepped through the door into the corridor, she almost bumped into the factory owner Georgina Handsley, who was walking with her secretary, Clarice, and an official-looking man wearing a pinstriped suit and a bowler hat.

Georgina was a large, tweed-clad woman in her early sixties with pale blue eyes and steel-grey hair pulled back so tightly into a severe, old-fashioned bun that it made her look as if she was continuously surprised. Georgina rarely turned up at her office before nine o'clock, so Amy knew there must be something important happening.

'Good morning, Miss Handsley. Do you think you could find time for a quick word sometime today?'

Georgina looked at her silver wristwatch. 'I'm going to be in an important meeting for most of the day. We have serious matters to discuss.' She looked up at the mezzanine where her office was situated. 'If it won't take long, come up now. I'll see you before the meeting begins. We have to get tea organised before we start to talk, anyway. Meetings always go better with tea.'

Amy followed the group up the stairs to the mezzanine and

waited by the office door as Georgina gave Clarice some instructions. Turning to the bowler hatted man, she smiled. 'Could I ask you to wait here for five minutes, Cedric? Young Miss Rowlings needs a minute of my time. I've asked Clarice to organise a cup of tea.'

Georgina opened the door to her office and Amy followed her in.

'He's from a government department,' she said, nodding towards the door. 'They want us to stop making dresses and start turning out uniforms for our military.'

'Really?' Amy said. 'That will be different.'

'It will be hard work. Those uniforms are heavy duty.' She paused as she stared out of the window and across the factory floor. 'You'll all be better off, of course. The government pays well. You'll get a far bigger bonus than you're paid at the moment. I would think someone with your skills could make another six to eight shillings a week.'

'That will come in handy,' Amy said with a smile.

'You'll have to come back to work here full time, unfortunately. No more days spent in the dress shop.'

'I don't mind,' Amy replied. 'The time will pass quicker on my machine.' She pushed a few stray hairs under her turban. 'When do we switch over?'

'That's what this meeting is about. To be honest, if Mr Hitler decides that Germany is big enough now, and he doesn't need to invade anywhere else, then it might not happen at all. But, if it is to be war, we're going to have to get up to speed with the new system very quickly.'

Georgina pulled out a chair, motioned for Amy to sit, then pulled out her own chair from under her desk. 'Now, what did you want to see me about?'

'Have you ever heard of a clothing company called Blue Moon?'

'Yes, but they went to the wall during the depression. They ceased trading in nineteen thirty-two, I believe. They had a few shops in the big towns. Not here, of course. Spinton wasn't well to do enough. Why do you ask?'

'It's to do with a murder investigation,' Amy said. 'Bodkin... I mean, Inspector Bodkin, is investigating the discovery of a skeleton that was found in an old cottage in the Witchy Wood. There were the remains of a skirt and blouse near the body, and one of the garments had the Blue Moon label. We were... I mean, he was hoping we might be able to get some information from the company about where the item might have been sold. We know who the victim is now, but we'd like to try to piece her life together to see if we can learn more about her.'

'You said we, quite a lot then, Amy. Would this Bodkin be the same Bodkin who investigated the death of my nephew? I know you played a big part in solving that mystery. You and he are stepping out, I believe.'

Amy nodded slowly, wondering where the conversation was heading.

'It must be so exciting, playing the amateur detective role in real life murder investigations. I'm so envious.'

'I like to help if I can,' Amy replied modestly.

'Quite,' Georgina said, looking at her watch again. 'I'd better get on, Amy. Please don't say anything about the production changes, particularly to Beryl Hargreaves. I'd like to keep it quiet until I've signed the contract.' She stood up and waited for Amy to get to her feet before she spoke again. 'I'm sorry I couldn't be of more help with Blue Moon.'

'That's all right,' Amy replied. 'I don't think it matters that much now. We know who the poor girl was.'

'Care to share? Or is it too hush hush at the moment?'

'I can't tell you her name until Bodkin gives the okay, but I can tell you she was a big fan of the actor Rex Larson. She went missing the night he starred at the Playhouse in Spinton. That was back in nineteen twenty-nine, though.'

'The Importance of Being Earnest?' Georgina said. 'I was there that night. I met the entire cast back stage.'

Chapter Twelve

The morning passed slowly for Amy, which was unusual, because time usually flew by for her when she was at her machine. This morning, though, although she had kept up her usual quick pace as she worked towards her bonus, she couldn't stop thinking about what Georgina had said. She had met the cast backstage. Was young Nina there at the time? Margo had said that there were two young girls in Rex's dressing room after the show. Was Nina one of them? Georgina had promised to put some time aside to talk through what she could remember about the night, but Amy hadn't yet been able to let Bodkin know that she would be happy to answer any questions he might have.

At lunch, Amy nipped into the changing room and took Bodkin's card from her bag. The card had the extension number of his office phone printed on the front and the phone number of his apartment block, Bluecoat House, written by hand on the back. After telling Carol she needed to use the lavatory, Amy slipped into the stockroom, where she knew there was a telephone. Luckily, none of the warehouse staff were around, so she picked up the handset and dialled the number. The call was answered by Ferris.

'Hello, Amy, no, he's in with Superintendent Grayson at the moment. They're discussing what happened down in Rochester. He's had a complaint from a chief super down there.'

'But it's not Bodkin's fault that the Rochester police are all incompetent,' Amy said.

'Between you, me and the gatepost, I think he'll be all right. Grayson's a decent sort. He won't take any nonsense from outsiders.'

'I hope you're right, Ferris,' Amy said. 'Can you tell Bodkin that Georgina Handsley was at the Playhouse the night Nina went missing? She's agreed to...' Amy slammed the phone down as she heard footsteps coming towards her. She began to back away towards the door, but then heard the footsteps stop and someone from deep inside the stockroom call out a name. The footsteps then retreated. Amy considered ringing again to explain everything to Ferris but decided against it. She wasn't supposed to use the factory phone unless it was an emergency and even then she should have asked permission.

At five-twenty, Amy switched off her machine and, after waiting for Carol to finish her last garment of the day, walked with her to the changing rooms. 'What did you want with Georgina this morning? I meant to ask you at lunch, but my mind was elsewhere.'

Amy looked around to ensure they couldn't be overheard, then beckoned Carol to come closer. 'She was at the play the same night that young girl... the skeleton... went missing. She's going to help us with the investigation.'

'Ah, that's all. I thought you were going to tell me you'd accepted the job at London Connection full time.'

'I won't be working there much longer. You won't be doing your Saturday shift there either, Carol. There'll be plenty of overtime on your machine and you'll be getting better paid for being on it.'

'Ooh, tell me more,' Carol said, taking Amy's arm and leading her to the time clock.

. . .

At nine-thirty that evening, Amy answered the door to find Bodkin on the step. He looked over her shoulder to the empty hallway, then crooked his finger to beckon her outside, where he looked up at the threatening clouds before pointing at the car.

'Better get inside. It looks like it's going to tip down.'

When they were settled on the front bench seat of the car, Bodkin asked Amy to tell him more about her conversation with Georgina Handsley. When she had gone through it all, he leaned back on the seat and worked something out on his fingers.

'I'll drop in to see her on Wednesday. Are you at the factory or in the shop, then?'

'Shop in the morning, factory in the afternoon.'

'I'll arrange it for after one, then. It means I can buy you lunch and, if you're going to be with me when I question her, you'll get half an hour or so extra, away from your machine.'

'That sounds like a plan,' Amy said. 'Now, how did you get on with Mr Grayson this morning? Ferris said he'd had a call from Rochester.'

'He was fine. He looks after his officers. He's going to take my side in this. He's scheduled a meeting with Harmison in Rochester tomorrow. He'll give him short shrift if he tries to put me on a disciplinary.'

'Did Bigger send the files across?'

'No, he's under orders from Harmison. He gave me a call this afternoon to apologise. The files are ready, apparently, but Harmison won't allow him to send them. Grayson told me that he'd pick them up tomorrow.'

'He can't pull rank, though, can he? They're both chief supers.'

'Ah, but Grayson has the ear of the chief constable,' Bodkin said. 'Grayson has been earmarked for the position when he retires. He'll back him up in any dispute. Especially because Rochester has messed this investigation up so badly.'

Amy smiled and patted Bodkin's arm. 'Good. I hate the thought of you getting into trouble.'

Bodkin shrugged. 'It's not something I worry about. I just do the job the best way I can.'

Amy nodded. 'That just leaves Cyril de Burglar. What did Mrs Twig have to say?'

'Twigley,' Bodkin corrected. 'I met her husband too and I'll tell you what. He's not the sort of man you'd want to meet in a blind alley. Cyril better not make a repeat visit because if Bernard Twigley gets hold of him first, there won't be much left to send to prison.'

Bodkin paused and looked at the rain splattering on the windscreen. 'One thing we do know. He has a car. So he isn't riding into the night on a trusty steed.'

'How do you know he has a car?'

'Mrs Twigley heard him drive away. She ran after him in her nightie. She's not the sort of woman I'd break into a house to leave a note for, but there's no accounting for taste.'

'She's not a young, attractive woman, then?' Amy asked.

'As I said, that's not for me to say. She's no spring chicken, though.'

'So, do you think he could just be choosing houses at random instead of handpicking them?'

'I think it's more likely that he just chose the wrong house. There are two doors side by side at the back of the block. He might have picked the wrong one. I'll nip back over tomorrow to check it out.'

'Right, well, I'd better get back in, Bodkin. I'm up at six for work.' Amy leaned over and kissed the policeman on the lips. 'Good night.'

'Night... oh, hang on. I've got something for you.' Bodkin reached into his pocket and pulled out the photograph of Nina. 'I got Jenkinson the photographer to knock up a few reprints this afternoon. I picked them up this evening.'

Amy took the photograph, then gave Bodkin another kiss. 'Thank you,' she said.

Back in her room, Amy slipped the photograph onto the table at the side of her bed before getting undressed and slipping between the sheets. Picking up the photograph again, she held it up and looked at it with teary eyes for a good five minutes. Then she ran her fingers gently over the picture and put it back on the table. 'Bodkin will get him, Nina, I promise.'

Chapter Thirteen

At one o'clock on the dot, Amy and Josie, the manager of the London Connection fashion shop, walked out of the front door to find Bodkin waiting on the pavement. Josie took him in for a few moments, then tugged at Amy's sleeve.

'Do you know, with a sprucing up and a good shave, he'd be a bit of a dreamboat.'

Amy looked around, but there were no other men in the vicinity. 'Do you mean Bodkin?'

'Your chap, yes. With a decent haircut, a shave and a new suit, he'd be quite a catch.'

Amy shook her head. 'I do my best to smarten him up, Josie, but he could spend an afternoon with the King's personal dresser in Savile Row and by tea time he'd still look like he'd found a pile of ill-fitting clothes in a thrift shop.'

Josie laughed and turned to go back into the shop again. 'Forgot my bag. Honestly, my memory is on the blink.'

Amy gave Bodkin a kiss on the cheek and took his arm. 'Where are you taking me for lunch?'

'I fancied having you all to myself for a while, so I bought us some sandwiches and a couple of bottles of lemonade from the café. We can sit in the car or maybe on the green near The Mill.'

'That sounds lovely,' Amy said as the policeman opened the passenger door of the Morris for her.

Bodkin started up the car and pulled across the road. They had just got to the bus stop opposite the chip shop when he suddenly braked hard.

'What's wrong?' Amy said, after being jerked forward in her seat.

Bodkin pointed across towards the chip shop, where there seemed to be a bit of an altercation in progress.

Amy hurried across the road in Bodkin's wake, eager to see what the commotion was all about. When she reached the pavement, she saw an old man sitting on the bench in front of the shop fending off missiles as a group of five teenage boys wearing the uniform of the local school threw chips at him. In the door of the shop, the owner yelled at the boys.

'Clear off, you lot. Someone's going to have to clean that mess unless that dirty old sod picks them up off the floor.' He waved his arms in the air theatrically. 'Go on, bugger off! I know your faces. You won't be buying fish and chips from this shop again.'

Bodkin was so quick stepping across the pavement that he was on the boys before they realised he was in the vicinity. Grabbing the biggest of the youngsters by the collar of his jacket, he dragged him away from the confused looking old man.

'You heard Tino, he thinks you should bugger off and I agree with him.'

'Who are you to tell us what to do?' the boy said angrily as he struggled to free himself from Bodkin's grip.

'I'm a copper, you lippy little sod. Now, do as I say or you'll find yourselves in my nick in no time.'

The lad stopped struggling and began to straighten his collar as Bodkin let go of it.

'He's only a tramp. What does it matter?'

Bodkin's mouth tightened. 'I want to see you lot on the other side of that road in ten seconds flat,' he growled as the five kids looked at each other.

Deciding that discretion was indeed the better part of valour, the boys shuffled across the road, turning back to hurl insults at the old man, Tino and Bodkin in no particular order.

'And you can move that dirty old tramp along too,' Tino spat as Bodkin walked towards the old man on the bench.

'Hello, Con,' Amy said. 'Are you all right?'

The old man was dressed in little more than rags. He had long, wild, white hair and a beard to match. His brown overcoat was torn, had no buttons, and was held together around his waist with string. He wore two pairs of different coloured trousers, although it was hard to make out what those colours were under the grime. The top pair were torn on the calves and had large holes in the knees. His boots, while still sturdy looking, were covered in dried mud and were tied with thin twine.

He took off his tatty hat, got unsteadily to his feet and doffed it at Amy.

'Cornelius Humphrey Squire, at your service,' he said.

'Never mind all that,' Tino shouted. 'Move him on. He's putting people off their chips.'

Bodkin looked around. 'There doesn't appear to be anyone around to be put off, Tino.'

'No, because that smelly old bleeder is keeping them away.' He gave Bodkin an exasperated look. 'Come on, Inspector, do your job.'

'He's not doing any harm,' Bodkin replied, crouching. Cornelius had sat down again after greeting Amy.

'What are you doing hanging around here, Con?' Bodkin asked. 'You know you only put people's backs up.'

'It's not against the law to sit on a bench, is it?'

'It is if you don't appear to have any visible means of subsistence,' Bodkin replied. 'And you know that as well as I do. You've been lifted for vagrancy enough times.'

Con laughed. 'At least you get a warm bed and a meal in your belly.'

Amy crouched down next to Bodkin but kept upwind of the old man.

'I thought the Salvation Army was helping you, Con.'

'Ah, them...' the old man cackled to himself. 'Too much singing and way too much of the Our Father.'

'They gave you a bath, some clean clothes and a bed, though.' She looked at the rags Con was wearing. 'What happened to the clothes?'

'Swapped 'em for a bowl of soup and a couple of bits of bread.'

'Are you sleeping in the Witchy Wood again?' Amy asked.

Con nodded. 'I like it out in the open. Now the workhouse has gone there isn't anywhere to go, anyway.'

'There's the Salvation Army,' Bodkin said.

'They won't have me anymore. They said I was too much trouble.' He grinned at Bodkin. 'And a heathen,' he added.

'How old are you, Con? You shouldn't be out on the streets at your age,' Amy said with a sad note in her voice.

'I'm ninety... at least I think I am. How long ago was eighteen fifty?'

'If that's when you were born, then ninety is about right,' Bodkin said.

'Come on, just arrest the old sot,' Tino called out, still watching from the doorway.

'Shut it,' Bodkin replied, 'or I'll arrest you for breach of the peace.' He gave the shopkeeper a stern eye.

'I might be a lot of things but I'm no sot. I haven't touched a drop since the end of the war,' the old man said.

'What are you doing here, Con?' Amy asked softly.

'I'm hungry,' Con replied, 'and the fish and chips smell lovely.'

'He was begging,' Tino shouted.

Con bridled. 'I only asked him if he had a piece of fish left over from last night.' His eyes brightened. 'Lend us a penny and I can get some chips.'

'Chips are tuppence a portion,' Bodkin replied.

'So, lend me a penny each. Then I can get some.'

Bodkin shook his head and slipped his hand into his pocket. Amy opened her bag and took out her purse.

'Here's sixpence. Get a fresh piece of fish,' Bodkin said, holding out his hand.

'And here's tuppence for the chips,' Amy added.

'OI!' Tino shouted from the door. 'Don't you go giving him money. He's not coming in here. He's got fleas that can jump six feet.'

Bodkin took the two pennies from Amy, then got to his feet and walked towards the shop.

'Fish and chips please, Tino... heavy on the chips,' he said.

'I'm not serving him,' Tino objected. 'He'll sit there for an hour sucking on the food. He's hardly got any bloody teeth.'

'You're not serving him,' Bodkin reminded the chip shop owner. 'You're serving me. Wrap them in a double newspaper so they don't get cold too quickly and he'll take them off to the park... or somewhere away from here, at least. You'll give him indigestion yelling at him while he's eating.'

Three minutes later, Bodkin handed Con the large serving of fish and chips wrapped in newspaper, along with a bottle of lemonade. 'Right,' he said. 'You'll have to go somewhere else to sit or Tino will end up calling the police and you don't want to be arrested for vagrancy or begging again, do you?'

'Not today. I've got dinner,' Con said, waving the meal in the air. He got to his feet and shuffled off towards the Gillingham road. 'I'll find a nice quiet spot to eat it.'

Amy and Bodkin watched Cornelius shuffle down the hill

towards the junction with the Gillingham road. 'Poor man,' Amy said quietly. 'Why can't people just leave him alone?'

'To be fair, you wouldn't want him sitting outside your shop if you owned one, Amy. He does tend to put customers off. Did you get a whiff of him just then? I doubt he's seen soap in months.' He turned back towards the car. 'Where does he sleep, anyway?'

'He's got an old tarp strung up between two trees in the Witchy Wood,' Amy replied. 'The kids used to torment him something rotten at one time, but I think they've got bored with him now. He never fights back. No one wants to get too close to him anyway, so they just cut the ropes tying his tarp to the tree now and then. They won't go under the tarp, especially not if he's in it. They're wary of getting fleas or nits.'

Bodkin shuddered. 'Ugh!' He looked right and left before crossing the road. 'We'd better hurry up or you'll be late clocking on and you haven't had your sandwiches yet.'

* * *

Georgina Handsley opened the door of her office and waved a hand towards two comfortable looking chairs that had been put in a position in the centre of her office. Pulling out her own chair from under the desk, she waited for them to sit before sitting down herself.

'Tea?' she asked. Amy and Bodkin shook their heads.

'Good,' she said. 'I've had far more than is good for me today.' She placed her hands on her lap. 'Now, this is about the Rex Larson play from ten years ago, isn't it?'

Bodkin nodded. 'I know you probably won't remember the exact details, but anything you can remember might help us.' He paused for a moment, then went on. 'Was it a big crowd that night?'

Georgina's brow furrowed as she thought. 'Not particularly. A few more than normal. Probably because the actor was well known, but then Oscar Wilde is a bit highbrow for some. By a few more than normal, I mean a hundred or so.'

'Were there many young girls there? Sixteen to eighteen.'

'Yes, I think there were. The audience was mainly made up of couples or groups, so they tended to stand out. They were a rather noisy lot, too. Laughing in all the wrong places, shouting out comments to Rex on the stage.'

'Comments?'

'Oh, give us a kiss, Rex, that sort of thing.'

'Was he annoyed by it? I mean, he was trying to put on a performance.'

'No. Not at all, he seemed to welcome it.'

'I believe you went backstage to meet the cast?'

Georgina nodded. 'Although I already knew all the local actors.'

'So, who was there who you hadn't met before?'

'Rex Larson, his agent... what was his name...? Starr... that was it, Fabian Starr.'

'Anyone else?'

'I don't think so, as I said, the rest were the local cast and crew and I got to meet them at most of the performances.'

'What about other audience members? Who else got to go backstage? It's quite an honour to be asked, I believe.'

'It is when you get someone of Rex's standing.' She thought for a few moments. 'The Mayor and his family were there. One or two other local dignitaries. A dozen at most.'

'And how was Rex? Did he appear to be happy to see you all?'

'He was pleasant enough without being too forthcoming. I got the impression he'd rather be somewhere else. That young girl... though she isn't quite so young now... Margo Ashburner was fussing around him, getting him drinks... fawning all over him. I seem to remember there were a couple of young women there too, not more than girls really. They were on the periphery, though. Standing on their own near the dressing rooms.'

Bodkin pulled Nina's picture from his pocket and handed it to her. 'I know it's a long shot after all this time, but can you remember if this young woman was one of them?'

Georgina studied the picture carefully. 'No, I'm sorry, it was a long time ago.' She handed the picture back to Bodkin.

'Did any of the men in attendance, cast, crew or others, seem to be paying particular attention to the two young women?'

'Not that I remember. The cast stood in groups, chatting among themselves. Rex and his agent were the centre of attention... although I remember Caspian trying to get in on the act. There was a press photographer there from the Post and I'm sure Caspian got into a few shots standing next to Rex.'

'Caspian Stonehand. The actor director?'

'He was just an actor back then... not a particularly good one. He was a bit wooden for my tastes. He's improved since then but not by much, though in his own mind he's on a par with Laurence Olivier.'

Bodkin shuffled forward on his seat as Amy sat cross-legged alongside him. 'Did Caspian take any interest in the two girls, or any other of the women?'

'Not that I noticed. Mind you, he could never compete with Rex Larson. To my recollection, the men of the company were standing in a group, the ladies were in a smaller group a few feet away. They didn't seem to mix too well.'

Bodkin got to his feet, and Amy followed suit. 'Thank you, Miss Handsley. You've been very helpful.'

'Are you sure? I don't seem to have told you anything of importance.'

'It all adds to the general picture,' Bodkin said, turning to leave.

'The only man who seemed to be more popular than Rex was his driver.'

Bodkin stopped and turned back to face the factory owner. 'Driver?'

'He was at the stage door when we came out. There were half a dozen young girls hanging around him. There seemed to be something about him they liked. They were all trying to get his attention. I don't know if he had promised to get them an autograph or something.' Georgina paused. 'Mind you, he was a handsome chap in his own right. I might have fancied him myself at their age.' She smiled at Amy. 'The hormones rage in your teens, don't they, my dear?'

Amy looked away quickly.

'Can you tell me anything else about this driver?' Bodkin asked. 'Was he local or did he come with Rex and his agent? Sorry, I don't suppose you'd know that.'

'Oh, he was local. I can even tell you his name. He worked for a car hire company as a chauffeur. We used them a lot when George ran the company. He used to drive some of our more important clients back and forth from the Braithewaite Hotel. We still hire a car from them now and then. They're called Mossmoor Luxury Cars. Their offices are in Mossmoor but the cars are garaged in Spinton. The driver is a local man. He still works for them occasionally, though he runs his own car repair business now. His name is Chester Harvey.'

Chapter Fourteen

Harvey's Motor Repairs traded from a small unit on the industrial estate near the ironworks on the outskirts of the town. When Amy and Bodkin arrived at just after six-thirty, they found the folding double doors at the front of the unit locked and a beautiful gleaming Bentley parked on the road outside. As Bodkin was about to bang on a small window on the corner of the workshop, a welder who was working late in the next unit pointed to a gap between the buildings. 'You'll find him in the back,' he said. 'And tell him I want the fifteen and six he owes me by Friday or I'll weld his doors shut.'

After thanking the man, Bodkin led Amy through the narrow gap between the two sheet iron buildings. Around the back, they found a timber shed with its door hanging open. Inside was a man in his late forties. He was fit looking and still sported a mop of blond hair with just the faintest signs of grey at the temples. He was fastening the fly of a pair of light grey serge trousers as Bodkin stepped into the hut. His white shirt and grey chauffeur's uniform jacket were hung on the backs of two chairs.

'Chester Harvey?' Bodkin asked.

'Who wants to know?' the man replied, pulling a string vest over his head as Amy looked away.

'Inspector Bodkin of the Spinton police. This is my associate, Amy Rowlings.'

Harvey eyed Amy appreciatively. 'She can associate with me any time she likes.'

'I don't think that's likely,' Bodkin said, giving Chester a warning look.

'I'm only joking. Sorry. I've been cooped up in the workshop all day and it's nice to see a pretty face instead of some irate customer who thinks that work on a car should take a maximum of two hours.' He picked up a pair of oil stained overalls from a chair and dropped them on the floor before wiping it down with a greasy-looking towel. 'Have a seat,' he said.

Amy shook her head and stepped forward to stand next to Bodkin. Chester glanced at his watch.

'Look, this will have to be quick. I'm picking clients up at the Braithwaite Hotel in half an hour.'

'This shouldn't take long,' Bodkin said, pulling out his notebook. 'Firstly, how long have you lived in Spinton?'

'This time around. About twenty years.'

'This time around... you moved away, then came back?'

'I was... Look, it's not something I like to talk about, but my mother couldn't look after me. She had a problem with the demon drink. So the welfare stepped in when I was six. We were placed in a workhouse for a time, but after a few months I was sent to a kids' home in Dover. Eventually I was adopted. I moved back here a couple of years after the war ended. My mother was long dead by then.'

'I'm sorry to hear that. It can't have been easy for you.'

'We all have our crosses to bear,' Chester said.

'Even so, I'm sorry you had such a rough start in life.'

Chester fiddled with a ring on his little finger. 'I'm sure something far more important than hearing about my wretched childhood brought you here. Do you think we could get on with it? I am pushed for time.'

'Fair enough,' Bodkin said. 'I'd like to take you back to the nineteenth of October nineteen twenty-nine.'

'I'd happily come too. I was ten years younger then.'

Bodkin tapped his notebook. 'You were on duty that night.'

'If you say so,' Chester replied with a shrug.

'I do say so,' Bodkin said. 'Your duties included ferrying a well know celebrity about. The actor Rex Larson.'

'Ah yes, I remember now, but ferrying him around isn't quite accurate. I picked up him and his agent... I forget his name now... Fabulous something... Anyway, I picked them up at the station around lunchtime and transported them to the Braithwaite. It was a doddle of a job really as they had booked me for the whole day and I spent a lot of it sitting in a café drinking tea. It certainly beat driving a taxi around all day which was my main job.'

'What time did you drop them off?'

'In the daytime? Oh, it would have been around one-ish.'

'And what time did you pick them up again?'

'About four, I think. Larson wanted to do a quick run through of the play with the local actors. They had never rehearsed together, and he wanted to make sure it was all going to turn out all right.'

'What did you do then?'

'I was told I wouldn't be needed again until ten-ish, but I was to hang around in case Larson or his agent... Starr, that was his name, Fabulous Starr, wanted anything bringing in that the Playhouse hadn't thought of providing them with.'

'So, you just hung around in the street, just in case?'

'Pretty much. As I said, it was a doddle of an assignment.'

'What time did he come out after the show?'

'Well after ten-thirty, probably closer to eleven, but I'd been hanging around for nothing as it turned out. Larson said he wouldn't need the car as he'd got a hot date at the George Hotel and that was only a hundred yards further long Main Street.'

'This hot date? Did you get a look at her?'

Chester shook his head. 'Nope, but I think he was meeting her at the George because that's where he headed after leaving the theatre.'

'He went straight there. Didn't he stop to sign a few autographs?'

'Oh yeah, there were four or five young girls with their autograph books or photographs they wanted signing. He sorted them out first.'

'Back to this hot date. Are you sure it wasn't one of the girls waiting by the stage door?'

'If it was, she took a roundabout way of getting to the George. None of them followed him that I can remember.'

Bodkin pulled Nina's picture from his pocket and handed it to Chester. 'Do you remember seeing her waiting by the stage door?'

Harvey took a long look at the picture.

'She's a pretty one, isn't she?'

'Did you see her at the stage door, Mr Harvey?'

'She might have been there, but I can't be sure. There were five of them, all about the same age.'

'Did you talk to these girls while you were waiting?'

'Yeah, I probably did. It was a long wait for me. I would have been bored.'

'Were the girls there all night or did they come out at the end of the play?'

'Two of them were hanging around from about six. I think they were hoping to see Rex Larson arrive, but as I said, he was inside for just after four. Those two didn't go in to watch the play. The other three came out just after the final curtain.' He paused as he thought. 'Yeah, they came out about ten, maybe five past.'

'Did you talk to them?'

'Again, probably. All right, yes, I did, but honestly, Inspector, I'd been sitting there kicking my heels for hours.'

'Did you take Fabian Starr back to the hotel?'

'That's him, Fabian, not Fabulous. No. Apparently he was going for cocktails with a couple of the local bigwigs… they went to the Milton, I think.'

'And were you told to pick him up there later?'

'No, I was told I wouldn't be needed as they were going to make a night of it.'

'Take another look at that photograph, Mr Harvey. Are you sure that young girl didn't go off with either Mr Starr or Mr Larson?'

'Starr was with the Mayor and a couple of his flunkeys. They wandered off while Larson was signing autographs.'

'What time did you go home?'

'Probably ten past eleven. I hung around a bit to make sure the main man didn't change his mind. They're unpredictable, these actors.'

'But he didn't change his mind.'

'Nope, he finished signing the autographs, stood with the group of girls while someone snapped their picture, then he was off. At a right old clip too. Not running, but not far off, he was certainly looking forward to his date.'

'Did you see where the girls went after they had their picture taken?'

'They were all still there when I left. I think they might have been waiting for that local actor. I can't remember his name.'

'Caspian Stonehand?'

Harvey shrugged, 'No idea.' He looked at his watch again. 'Sorry, I'm happy to answer any questions you might have, but I really do have to go soon.'

'I won't keep you much longer,' Bodkin said. He turned to Amy. 'Is there anything you'd like to ask?'

'Yes, I do have a question.' She smiled at Harvey, who smiled back with interest. 'First, you said you were kicking your heels. Were you kicking them in the car, or kicking them on the pavement?'

'I spent a lot of time sitting in the car. I had a novel with me and I read that. I got out to stretch my legs once or twice, but I was in the driver's seat for most of the time.'

'Those young girls. What did you talk to them about? I mean, you would have been what, thirty-five, forty years old? You can't have had much in common.'

'I was pushing forty at the time but I didn't look it. Anyway, young girls like a more mature man. A bit of an uncle figure.'

'Do they?' Amy replied, thinking about her best friend Alice, who had been conducting an affair with a forty-year-old man for over a year. She was barely nineteen when it had begun.

'Everyone knows that,' Harvey said with a grin. 'Don't tell me you've never fantasised about an older man. It's part of growing up for young girls. They like chatting with mature men. They really get off on it.'

'Oh,' Amy replied. 'I think I've missed out on all that.' She flashed Bodkin a look and reddened slightly.

'So what did you talk to them about?'

'I can't remember now. It was such a long time ago.'

'Were they impressed with your uniform or maybe the car? What sort was it, by the way?'

'It was a Daimler Double Six.'

'You seem very sure of that.'

'At the time, the company only had two high end motors. The other was a Lagonda and I only ever got to drive that once.'

'And is that what you talked about with the girls... the car? It can't have been a very stimulating conversation.'

'I honestly can't remember what we talked about. They were impressed with the car, though. They all had a sit on the back seat. They wanted me to take them for a spin, but I couldn't do that in case the clients wanted me for anything.'

'You had all five girls in the back seat?'

'They kept going on about it until I let them climb in. They were only inside for five minutes. They moaned about no one having a camera to take a picture.'

'Wasn't the chap around who took the photograph of them with Rex Larson?'

'No, he came out at the same time as Rex and his agent. I think he worked for the Post. He'd been taking pictures inside the theatre; at least I assume he had.'

'Did anyone else come out from the stage door while you were waiting? Just before Larson... maybe just after?'

Harvey thought. 'There was a young chap about the same age as those girls. He was wearing overalls. I assume he worked there.'

'No one else?'

'A group of women came out. I don't know who they were, though. They didn't hang around. I think they must have had a taxi booked. I honestly can't tell you much about them.'

'You have a very good memory, Mr Harvey, remembering small details like that.' Bodkin pointed to the photograph. 'Now, are you sure you can't remember seeing that young woman?'

Harvey studied the picture again. 'I'm sorry, I can't be certain. She might have been there but I wouldn't swear to it on the bible.'

Bodkin took the photograph back and slipped it into his pocket. 'Right, Mr Harvey, we'll leave you to get on with your evening.'

Harvey pulled his shirt from the back of the chair and slipped it on as Bodkin and Amy turned away. At the door, Bodkin stopped and looked back. 'We may want to talk to you again after we've spoken to Mr Larson and Mr Starr, so I'd like you to think hard about that night in the meantime. If you do remember anything else, no matter how trivial, we'd like to hear about it.'

'So that's why you like to hang around with me,' Bodkin said as they walked in single file towards the gap between the buildings. 'Young women like a mature man. You heard it from an expert.'

Amy snorted. 'If I wanted to hang around with a mature man, I wouldn't waste my time on you, Bodkin. You're one of the most immature people I've ever met.'

Bodkin grinned. 'I'm young at heart, that's the problem.' He pointed to his face. 'Look, I still get teenage acne.'

Amy shook her head. 'You just proved my point.'

'Did you catch him at it?' the welder said as Amy and Bodkin reappeared from the narrow gap between the two units.

'Was there a risk we might have?' Bodkin asked.

'There was a good chance. He's a bit of a ladies' man is our Chester.' He looked Amy up and down. 'You're just his type. He likes them young.'

Chapter Fifteen

'Oh, I know what I meant to ask you,' Amy said as she drove the black Morris back through town. 'Did you find anything of interest in those letters of Nina's?'

Bodkin slapped his forehead. 'I forgot all about those.'

'Well, you've had a lot to be getting on with,' Amy said soothingly. 'Have you got the files from Rochester?'

'I'll have them tomorrow. Chief Super Grayson is reading through them first. I've got to meet him in the morning, first thing.'

'What else is on your list for tomorrow?' Amy asked as she took a sharp bend and straightened up again.

'I'm going to see Mrs Twigley's neighbour to see if she saw anything of Cyril de Burglar the other night. Mrs Twigley said she might not be too helpful, as they don't really get on. The lady in question threatened to report Mr Twigley for ogling her over the fence and making lewd comments while she was hanging her smalls out.'

'You get to meet the nicest people, Bodkin.'

'I can't wait to meet Cyril,' Bodkin replied. 'Especially if he's all dressed up.'

Amy laughed. 'The poor man must have some sort of mental problem.'

'I think he's got a money problem, too. I mean, any self-respecting Cyrano would at least get hold of a proper cloak and hat.'

'He might be saving up for a horse,' Amy replied.

It was Bodkin's turn to laugh.

'Are you going to the police station? I can get the bus from there if you're busy,' Amy said.

'I am, but let's get you home first... hang on, take a quick left. I've got that shoe box in the flat. You can have the first read if you like. See what sexy Rexy had to say.'

Amy nodded eagerly. 'I'll start on them tonight. I want to drop in on Alice first, though. We usually have a catch up in the week.'

'Could we have a catch up tomorrow evening?' Bodkin asked. 'Not at the station, though. I need to spend some time in more pleasant surroundings.'

'If you mean the Old Bull, then I'm not all that keen. I always end up feeling tired at work if I have a drink the night before.'

'Where do you suggest then? I'm happy just to see you. It doesn't matter to me where it is.'

Amy pulled up outside Bodkin's apartment block and turned to face him. 'I'll come here if you like.'

'Here? Are you sure? I mean... what would your dad say?'

'I'm twenty-one, Bodkin. I don't need to ask him for permission. Anyway, he knows you won't take advantage of the situation.'

'I could cook something,' Bodkin said with a doubtful note in his voice. 'It's been a while since I cooked for anyone.'

'How long is a while?'

'Erm... I was living in Maidstone at the time. I did boiled beef and carrots, like in the song.'

Amy pulled a face. 'Get a few bits in and I'll cook for you, Bodkin, but don't expect anything as nice as my mum dishes up. I'm no Marcel Boulestin.'

'Marshall who?'

'I see you're not a big fan of gourmet food. He's a London restaurateur, and he writes cook books, but he also appears regularly on the BBC. He tells people what to cook for posh dinner parties. My mum always listens, but to my knowledge she's never attempted one of his recipes. We're not too keen on Fois Gras in our house.'

'Damn, I was going to get some in for tomorrow night,' Bodkin replied.

'I'll get something bacony from Alice tonight. She's always got a few gammon steaks in the larder. It's handy owning a farm. I'll tell you what, I'll get her to give me some fresh eggs too. You just provide some fresh bread and butter.'

Bodkin rubbed his stomach. 'You're making me hungry.' He opened the door of the car. 'It will give me an excuse to clean up the kitchen, too.'

'Just remember,' Amy said. 'I'm only on cooking duties. You get to do the washing up.'

* * *

'Look what the cat dragged in,' Alice said as Amy pushed open the kitchen door and stepped into her huge farmhouse kitchen.

'Blimey, it's hot in here,' Amy said. 'What's with the fire? It's August, you know, not December.'

'Martha needs some clean things for tomorrow. She's going to Tessa Greenacre's youngest kid's party, and I want her to look nice. You can bet Tessa will have pushed the boat out on her Norma's outfit. I'm making sure they dry off tonight so I can get them ironed.'

'Norma's only a year old, isn't she? Why is she having a party? She can't even walk yet. Let alone run around with the other kids.'

Alice shrugged. 'You know Tessa. Silvia Montford's daughter had a party last month, so she won't want her neighbours thinking she can't afford to have one for Norma.'

'Silvia's youngest is six. There's a big difference.'

Alice held out her palms and shrugged again. 'What can you do? Martha got an invitation so she'll be expected.'

Amy took off her jacket, hung it on the back of a chair and sat down, fanning her face.

'Can't we open the window for a bit? It's stifling,'

Alice walked across the room, flipped up the latches and opened both windows above the big Belfast sink, then she opened the door and held it with a wooden wedge. 'I don't suppose you'll be wanting a cuppa if you're that hot and bothered.'

'It's never too hot for tea,' Amy said. 'And a slice of Miriam's cake if there's any going spare.'

'There's always cake in this house,' Alice replied.

'Oh, while we're on the subject of food. I was going to ask you for a few fresh eggs and a couple of gammon steaks if you have them. If you don't, I'm sort of stuck because I'm cooking for Bodkin tomorrow night at his place, and I promised him gammon and eggs.'

Alice stopped dead, kettle half way to the tap. 'YOU'RE COOKING!'

Amy looked down at her hands. 'Yes, what's wrong with that?'

'You can't cook, that's what's wrong with that,' Alice replied, finally getting the kettle under the tap. 'You can burn cornflakes.'

'I'll ask Mum how to cook them and I'll make some notes before I go.'

Alice shook her head. 'I really hope Bodkin has a robust constitution. He doesn't know what he's letting himself in for.'

Amy sighed. 'I know I'm not a very good cook... alright, I'm pretty hopeless, but it was either that or Bodkin's boiled beef and carrots, which is the only thing he knows how to do.'

'What a pair,' Alice said as she dropped three teaspoons of leaf tea in the smaller of the freshly washed tea pots on the draining board. 'I hope Bodkin is rich because if you two ever do tie the knot, you're going to have to employ a cook or eat out in restaurants every night. That or spend a lot of time in hospital getting over food poisoning.'

'I've offered now, so I have to do it.' Amy thought for a moment. 'Of course, there is a way out of it. If you don't have any gammon steaks, I can't burn them, can I?'

'True,' Alice replied. 'But I bet Bodkin's really looking forward to it now. I bet he'll buy candles tomorrow and a single rose that he'll put in a beautiful little vase that he'll go looking for in the market in his lunch break, and...'

'All right, all right.' Amy blew out her cheeks. As Alice added boiling water to the teapot, she gave her a sly look. 'I, er, I don't suppose you or Miriam could cook the gammon for me so I could just warm it up. I'm all right with the eggs. Even I know how to fry them.'

Alice put the kettle down, frowned, and shook her head as she looked at her best friend. 'I can see a few flaws in that plan. One. Bodkin will be there to watch you cook. Two. I assume Bodkin will be picking you up, so he'll smell the pre-cooked steaks as soon as you get in the car, unless, of course, you're going over there on the bus with the steaks smuggled away in your handbag, and Three... well, see points one and two.'

Amy sighed again. 'It's going to be a disaster, isn't it?'

Alice poured tea into two mugs decorated with a scene from the King's coronation, topped them up with milk, then passed one to Amy.

'Miriam will cook them for you. She's far more impressive in the kitchen than I am. She'll season them properly and they'll be so perfectly done that they'll melt in your mouth. I can nip over with them in the truck so they won't get cold, but... you'll have to come clean with Bodkin.'

Amy nodded. 'I'll confess. At least he'll be eating my eggs.' She looked across the kitchen to the fireguard that was standing in a pool of water in front of the log fire. 'Martha's quite grown up now, isn't she?'

'Yes, she's shooting up. I'll be buying the next size up soon.'

'You won't need to. Those silk bloomers will fit her when she's your age.'

Alice turned around, spotted the underwear on the fireguard next to the baby clothes, and laughed. 'Miriam's going away for the weekend with Michael. They're going to Sheppey on Saturday morning and they aren't coming back until Sunday evening.'

'Ooh, have things moved on with her and Michael then? Packing her best bloomers. She must be hoping for more than a fish and chip supper.'

'Fish and chips are probably all she'll get,' Alice replied. 'But she's ever hopeful.' Michael had taken up with Miriam after his wife of some twenty years had died. He was convinced that she was watching over him and so couldn't bring himself to perform in the bedroom when he was alone with Alice's friend and live-in housekeeper, Miriam.

'So, does this mean you're not coming out on Saturday night?'

Alice shook her head. 'Sorry, I've got to do the good mother thing. Martha's fine with Miriam, but I don't think she's ready for a baby sitter yet and I'm not sure I want to leave anyone else with her.'

'I'd babysit, but I'm the one you'd be going out with, so there's no point.' Amy blew into her tea, then sipped it. 'I'll tell Bodkin tomorrow. His sister, Sal, said she might come up again soon. She got on well with Ferris last time she was here. He can give her a call to see if she's up for it.' Bodkin's sister lived in Dover and helped run a children's and abused women's charity. She had recently become close to Bodkin again after a few years of estrangement.

'So we've sorted out our diaries for the week, and you've been excused kitchen duties...' Alice smirked. 'You in the kitchen? That really takes the biscuit.' She took a long sip of tea, then spat it back into the cup as she first began to giggle, then laugh riotously.

'What?' Amy asked. 'Come on, something's tickled your fancy, out with it.'

Alice banged on the table with the heel of her hand and shook her head as she laughed. 'I was just... thinking about... THAT

COOKERY LESSON!' She began to laugh again as Amy slowly shook her head.

'You just won't let me forget that, will you?'

'THOSE BISCUITS! THEY CAME OUT LOOKING LIKE THE SOLES OF OLD CON'S BOOTS!'

Alice leaned back in her chair and laughed uncontrollably. 'You... had... to tell your mum... you'd dropped them on the way home...' There followed another bout of prolonged laughter as Amy blew out her cheeks and sighed.

'Are you done?' she asked, eventually.

Alice wiped her eyes, spluttered a few more times, then nodded. 'Done,' she said.

Amy watched her friend suspiciously for a few moments before continuing. 'Speaking of Con. I bumped into him today outside Toni's chip shop. Some schoolboys were throwing food at him and Toni was throwing insults.'

'Why can't they leave the poor man alone?' Alice said with a sad look on her face, her laughter all dried up.

'Bodkin sorted them out. We bought him a meal between us. He's ninety, for pity's sake. He shouldn't be sleeping out in the Witchy Wood in all weathers at his age.'

'He sleeps in our barn if it's really bad,' Alice said. 'He steals a few eggs now and then. Miriam says we should watch he doesn't ring the odd chicken's neck, but he's been doing it for years and we haven't lost a bird yet.'

'He's a lovely old soul. He hasn't got an ounce of nastiness in him. I've tried to get the church to help him a few times, but they always make some excuse or other. They won't even let him inside the church. So much for Christian charity.'

'Miriam isn't as hard on him as she tries to make out. I've seen her take a plate of bacon butties over to the barn and leave it just inside the door with a flask of hot tea to see him through the night.'

'Good old Miriam,' Amy said. 'She's one of the good guys.'

'She got him some second-hand clothes from Stan's Emporium

once, but I don't think he ever put them on. He was wearing the same tatty old rags the next time we saw him.'

Amy nodded and reached for the teapot. She poured herself a cup, added milk, and took a sip. 'Stewed,' she said.

She emptied the cup into the sink, then did the same with the teapot before putting the kettle back onto the hob. 'The Sally Army gave him a new set of clothes but he swapped them with another down and out, for a bowl of soup and a couple of chunks of bread in the soup kitchen.'

Alice looked up at the ceiling and sighed. 'I'd love to do something for him, but he's a law unto himself. He doesn't want help. He's happy as he is. He just wants people to leave him alone.'

Amy put more loose tea into the pot and tapped her foot as she waited for the kettle to boil. 'I've been thinking about him all afternoon. I might grab a couple of second-hand blankets from Jim on the market and put them under that old tarp he calls home. He'll have something warm to wrap himself in come winter, at least.'

'If he doesn't sell them back to Jim for the price of a fish supper,' Alice said, tapping her cup on the table. 'Come on, hurry up with that tea.'

While Amy was filling the teapot, Alice went to the larder and came back carrying three quarters of a large cherry cake. Getting a knife from the drawer and two small plates from the cupboard, she cut one generous slice for Amy and a smaller piece for herself. 'I'll wrap the rest in greaseproof paper and you can take it home with you. We've got another one on the top shelf.'

Amy rubbed her hands together as she sat down. Then, after giving her slice of cake a long, lingering look, she picked it up and took a huge bite. 'Miriam, you are the queen of cake makers,' she said, spitting crumbs onto the table.

'How's the skeleton case coming on? Have you managed to dig up anything yet? No pun intended,' Alice asked.

'It's moving on slowly. We questioned a driver today. He was with a crowd of girls outside the stage door on the night young Nina went missing. We met her aunt on Sunday. She's an artist. We're supposed to be meeting all the actors at the Playhouse, but we haven't set a date for that yet.'

'What about Rex Whosit... the actor chap?'

Amy shook her head as she chewed on the cake. 'I honestly don't know when we're going to talk to him. We have no idea where he is. He performs in touring plays, so he could be anywhere.' Amy paused. 'We need to speak to his agent, too. He was with him on the night, but they split up. Rex had a hot date at the George Hotel after the performance and Bodkin thinks it was with one of the young girls that were hanging around inside, but we don't know which one. It could have been Nina.'

'You think he might have whipped her off to Creepy Cottage, had his way then...'

'There's a big problem with that scenario, Alice. How did he know the place existed? He's not from around here.'

Alice smiled. 'I'm sure you'll work it out between you. Are there any other clues you can get your teeth into?'

'There's a shoebox with a pile of letters tied up in ribbon. They were sent to her by Rex. Bodkin's given me the task of reading them. We dropped it off at home on the way over.'

'Ooh, love letters. How delicious. Make sure you let me know if you find anything spicy in them.'

'I can't share information like that with you, Alice. It's evidence in a murder case.'

Alice snorted. 'Like that's ever stopped you before.'

Just then, the telephone rang.

Alice got to her feet and walked smartly into the front room to answer it.

'Hello. You've reached Mollison Farm, Alice speaking.'

Alice paused as she listened for a few moments, then said far more loudly than she needed to. 'Amy, yes, she's still here, Bodkin. She's in my kitchen stuffing her face with cake. She's like a little squirrel going at it... Oh, hang on, she's here.'

Amy gave Alice one of those looks only a best friend can get away with and held out her hand for the telephone.

'What's that, Bodkin? Yes, she is... I know... She's gets so excited when she hears your name. She's looking all doe-eyed, just like the way she looks at pictures of Clark Gable in her magazines.' She took a step back as Amy lunged towards her to try to snatch the phone. 'I know... yes... she is, isn't she...'

'Alice,' Amy pleaded.

'Just a moment, Bodkin. I'll see if she wants to speak to you.' She grinned as she held out the phone, then snatched it away as Amy tried to grab it. 'Yes, it seems she does.'

Amy took the handset, held her hand over the mouthpiece, and nodded towards the door. Her eyes followed Alice as she walked across the lounge. When she got to the door, Amy took her hand away from the mouthpiece and pointed towards the kitchen. *'Go,'* she hissed.

'GOOD NIGHT BODKIN!' Alice shouted, then she walked out of the front room, closing the door behind her.

'Sorry about that, Bodkin,' Amy said. 'Alice is in one of her silly moods. She gets like that now and again.'

'I can just picture you two. You're like a pair of kids when you get together.'

'Yes, yes... all right. What can I do for you, Bodkin? It had better be good. I'm only halfway through the best piece of cake I've tasted this year.'

'Okay, I'll get straight to the point,' Bodkin replied. 'It's Rex Larson. Ferris has tracked him down. He's performing in a play at the Assembly Hall Theatre in Tunbridge Wells this weekend. It's only about forty miles from here. We can be there and back in an afternoon.'

'Ooh, a day out. That will be nice, Bodkin. Can I drive?'

Bodkin laughed. 'I doubt there's any point in trying to stop you. The thing is, you'll have to get your Saturday Brigden's visit done early. Ferris has set up a meeting with him at one o'clock at his hotel.'

'Ferris is becoming indispensable, isn't he? How on earth did he manage to track him down?'

'Via his agent. His number is listed in the London Telephone Directory. He's set up a meeting with him too, but it won't be until the weekend after. He's going up to Scotland for a few days.'

'Are we going to London, then?' Amy said excitedly.

'Yes, but we're going on the train. Even I wouldn't drive in London.'

Chapter Sixteen

That night, in bed, Amy took the lid off the shoebox and emptied the contents onto her eiderdown. Apart from a few photographs of Nina aged from around eight to fifteen, there were signed photographs of two actors that Amy had never heard of and four autographed white cards, but only one name meant anything to her. Caspian Stonehand.

There were seven letters in the bundle. All addressed to Nina Honeychurch at her Rochester address. Four of the letters were from actors' publicists or secretaries replying in a formulaic manner, thanking the sender for her interest and assuring her that her letter would be passed on to the celebrity concerned.

The other three were from Rex.

The oldest of the three was dated the fourth of April nineteen twenty-nine, and it was another formulaic style letter, but read as though the actor had taken a personal interest. The second letter was dated the nineteenth of May and was two pages long. The handwritten paragraphs were mostly filled with details of his on stage triumphs and quotes from some of the reviews he had received from the newspapers. The last two paragraphs were of more interest to Amy as Rex began to ask a few personal questions about Nina. How old was she? Was she still at school? Did she get to theatres, and if so, which ones? Could she send a photograph as he had a wall in his office where he pinned the pictures he received from his fans? Some of them, he told her, were quite risqué.

The first two letters had been signed Yours Sincerely, but the third one ended with Ever Yours, Rex.

Amy read the letter twice to see if she had missed any nuanced references, even holding it up to the light to see if she could see a hidden message scratched in invisible ink. Then she had an epiphany and jotted down the capitalised first letter of every paragraph in the notebook that she kept on her side table.

WILL POST NEXT TO M.

Amy clenched her fist and let out a stifled, 'YES!' Then, leaning back on her pillows, she tried to work out who this M might be. It might be Margo from the Playhouse, but it could easily have been someone from her own neighbourhood, someone from her college or a fellow member of the Am Dram group she was part of. Unable to come to any conclusions, she began to think about where this letter, or letters, might be kept. She couldn't see Nina leaving them in the care of someone else. They would be far too personal for that. She might have had a secret hiding place in her bedroom. Lots of young girls kept diaries hidden away from the prying eyes of siblings or, more importantly, parents.

Beginning to feel tired, she put the letters and photographs back in the box, then leaned over to pick up the lid that had fallen onto the floor. As she picked it up, she noticed a small crease in the paper lining. Holding it closer, she could see that there was a tiny fold in the corner where the lining paper met the cardboard. Grabbing her eyebrow tweezers, she carefully peeled back the liner to find a letter addressed to a care of address in Rochester.

On inspection, she found that it had been addressed to Miss Marylin Beardsley, 21 Boundary Park Road. Rochester. Kent.

Amy opened the envelope with trembling fingers and pulled out a single sheet of paper that had a heart motif drawn in the top corner.

My darling, Nina

I hope this letter gets to you without your annoying pest of a mother reading it. I can't believe she opens your personal mail.

Marylin has said I can use her address to contact you at any time, so this may be the first letter of many. I cannot wait to meet you, hopefully without your mother in tow. Do you think you will be able to find a way to get to the Spinton Playhouse on October 19th? I'd love to see you in the flesh, so to speak.

Thank you so much for the beautiful photograph. I haven't pinned it to my wall with the rest of the fan pictures. It's far too nice for that, so I've put yours in a frame and it sits on my desk where I can look at it whenever I want. And I seem to want to more and more. I am entranced by it and find myself daydreaming about us being together whenever I happen to pick it up. You say you were sixteen when it was taken, so it's very recent. I'd like to see another one with you wearing a little less. I have my own camera, maybe we can arrange that.

Love and kisses,

Rex

Amy got out of bed and paced the floor with the letter in her hand. Should she slip on her coat and run up to the phone box? It was only eleven o'clock. Bodkin might still be at work. You never knew with him. She was sure he slept at his desk occasionally.

After reaching for the door handle twice, she decided against it. She could always leave a message for him on the front desk on her way to work in the morning. Now that the adrenaline had worn off, she was feeling sleep creeping up on her and after placing Nina's photo along with the newly discovered letter in the shoe box. She slipped in between the covers and was asleep within minutes.

At lunchtime the following day, Amy left the shop and walked the short distance to the library, where she copied the route from Spinton to Tunbridge Wells from a fold-out map, then she picked up a well-thumbed volume about the history of Kent. Tunbridge Wells had a very interesting entry.

On leaving the library, Amy walked along the narrow alleyway that ran alongside and strolled across the top of Russell Park before sitting down on a bench near the recently refurbished children's playground to eat her packed lunch. As she ate, she wondered why Bodkin hadn't dropped in to see her in the shop, as he must have received the message as soon as he arrived at work. Then she remembered that he had a meeting scheduled with the Chief Superintendent regarding his actions at the Rochester police station. She crossed her fingers as she chewed the potted meat sandwiches and hoped all had gone well.

She was just thinking about making her way back to the shop when she remembered that she had intended to pick up a couple of second-hand blankets from the market, so checking her watch, she hurriedly put her lunch tin and her flask back in her bag and strode quickly back up the alley and onto the High Street before turning at the crossroads and making her way through the plethora of trading pitches until she came to Jim Stringer's stall. Jim was a short man with broad shoulders, a wide jawline and a boxer's nose. Despite his somewhat scary appearance, he was a friendly sort who always had a cheery word for his potential customers as they perused his goods.

'Hi, Jim. I'd like a couple of warm blankets if you've got any cheap ones. They don't have to be anything special as long as they're clean and not too heavily darned.'

'I'll keep you warm, young Amy,' Jim said with a grin that showed off several missing teeth. 'You won't need blankets. I'm hot stuff me.'

'Much as I hate to turn down such a tempting offer, I think I'll stick with the blankets, thanks, Jim,' Amy replied with a smile. 'They're not for my bed, anyway. I'm buying them for old Con. The nights will be drawing in soon and he's back living under that tarp in the Witchy Wood.'

Jim searched around the back of the stall and came back with two old but useable ex-army blankets. 'These will be just the thing for a cold winter's night,' he said. 'They have a few stains on them, but I'm pretty sure it isn't dried blood.'

Amy shuddered at the thought. 'How much, Jim?'

'They are a shilling each but if you give me two bob, I'll throw the second one in for free.'

Amy looked at him quizzically. 'What the... I mean...'

Jim laughed. 'Just my sales pitch, m'dear. Give me a tanner each for them, seeing as they're for a good cause.'

Amy produced a shilling from her purse and Jim pocketed it before dumping the worn but warm looking blankets into her arms.

Back at the shop, Josie was just opening the front door as Amy arrived. 'Going camping?' she asked.

'Not personally, they're for old Con. He's back under his tarp again.'

'Best place for him,' Josie said. 'I'll never forget finding him in the fitting room that morning.'

Amy carried the blankets through to the staffroom and dropped them on the floor next to the sink, then she hung up her bag, tidied her hair in the mirror and walked back through to the shop to greet the first of the afternoon customers.

At five-thirty, Amy left the shop and wandered down the hill to the police station where she found PC Parlour in his spot behind the front desk.

'Hello, miss. I don't suppose by any chance you dropped in to see me?' He nodded towards the blankets that Amy was carrying. 'Thinking of staying the night?'

Amy dropped the blankets on the bench at the back of the reception area. 'That seat looks a bit hard so I don't think I'll bother after all. Actually, I'm after Bodkin, is he about?'

Parlour shook his head. 'He's out, I'm afraid. He left you a message, though.' He picked up a double folded sheet of paper and passed it across the desk, but before Amy had the chance to open it, Ferris walked in through the front door.

'I saw you walk up the steps as I was coming down the hill. I called in at the shop but it was all locked up.'

'You've been looking for me?'

'I have. I've got a message from Bodkin.'

Amy waited. When he didn't say anything else, she gave him a quizzical look. 'Well.'

'Oh, sorry. He said this message overrides any previous messages you might have had, especially the telephone messages but also the message left behind the desk.'

'All right...' Amy said, holding up the folded paper. 'Is that it? Just that I'm supposed to ignore all previous messages although there was only one message, and I don't even know what that message contains because I haven't opened it yet?'

'There was a second message,' Ferris said. 'He rang me to tell you he'll see you outside the shop at lunchtime. But then he rang me to say he couldn't make it after all.'

'Why didn't he just ring the shop? I was there all day.'

'He didn't have the number with him. He was in Rochester all morning with the Assistant Chief Constable trying to sort out the mess he got himself in.'

'And did he? Sort it out, I mean.'

'Eventually, but I don't think he's going to be made very welcome down there anytime soon.'

'I thought Mr Grayson was going to be with him. He's on his side.'

'He was there. They were all supposed to meet the Chief Constable, who is Grayson's golfing partner, but he had to cancel at the last minute, so the assistant CC stood in and he and Grayson don't see eye to eye on a lot of things. Bodkin had a bit of a rough time, I'm afraid, but... well, he'll tell you about it when he sees you.'

Amy unfolded the single sheet of paper and read it.

Sorry. Busy. See you later.

Amy passed the message to Ferris. 'So, this is what has been cancelled? What on earth is he up to?'

'He's been chasing up the Cyril inquiry over the last hour or so. He's gone to see Mrs Twigstick's neighbour.'

'Twigley,' Amy corrected him.

'Her,' agreed Ferris. 'Before that, he was down at county HQ signing for the files relating to our Creepy Cottage case.'

'But I thought he was picking them up from Rochester?'

'So did he, but they made it all as difficult as possible for him. Tied everything up in red tape. Between you, me and the gatepost, Amy, I think the Rochester chief super is a worried man.'

'So he should be,' Amy said firmly. 'Poor Bodkin's being given the runaround.' She paused as she slid the paper into her bag. 'What time will he be back? I've got something important for him. Didn't he get my message this morning when he got to work?'

'He never got into the building. Grayson was waiting for him on the front step to whisk him down to Rochester. He only had time to write that message and stick it through the letterbox.'

'That explains the brevity,' Amy said. 'Do we have one last message that counteracts all other messages, Ferris?'

'We do,' Ferris replied. 'He says he'll pick you up around seven. He wants to question Caspian Stonehand before you go down to see sexy Rexy tomorrow... his words, not mine.'

'I'm supposed to be cooking him a meal tonight,' Amy said. 'Alice is bringing over the steaks that Miriam is frying up.'

Ferris looked puzzled. 'Alice is... Miriam is... I thought you said you were cooking?'

Amy sighed. 'It got complicated.'

At five past seven, Amy picked up her bag and jacket on the way to answer the front door. She found Bodkin standing on the step; he looked tired.

'Hello, you. I heard you've had a stinker of a day.' She leaned forward and kissed him on the lips.

'It just got a whole lot better,' Bodkin said with a grin. 'Go back in. I'll knock on the door again and it will get better still.'

Amy put her hand on his chest and gently pushed him away. 'Come on, get in the car. I'm cooking dinner tonight, remember?'

Bodkin slapped his forehead with his hand. 'Damn. Sorry, Amy, I forgot all about it. I was supposed to get fresh bread, wasn't I?'

'It's all right, Bodkin. Alice reminded me that I'm hopeless in the kitchen, so Miriam is cooking the gammon for us. Alice was going to drop the hot food off at your flat, but I rang her on the way home. We're eating in style at her big oak table tonight. Caspian is going to have to wait for an hour.'

At eight-fifteen, a fully rejuvenated Bodkin pulled up outside the Playhouse behind an ambulance, which had the back doors open to allow two uniformed men to carry a stretcher inside. Amy got out of the car to find Margo Ashburner standing on the pavement in floods of tears.

'What happened, Margo?' Amy asked, looking from the almost hysterical woman to the ambulance and back again.

'It's Caspian,' Margo blurted out through the tears. 'I found him at the side door. Someone stabbed him in the chest. He's lost so much blood. They don't know if they can save him.'

Chapter Seventeen

As the ambulance was pulling away, Amy put her arm around the still sobbing Margo and led her towards the steps at the front of the theatre. Margo shook her head and pointed to the alley that ran down the side of the building. 'We use the side door on rehearsal nights. It opens into a passageway right next to the stage.'

As Bodkin searched the alley for blood trails or anything that might have been dropped or discarded, Margo led Amy past the stage door, along a corridor to the dressing rooms where a large urn was steaming away. Amy picked up a teapot that was sitting in the sink and held it up.

'Not for me, thanks,' Margo said with a shake of her head. 'I've drunk gallons of the stuff today.'

'Where is everyone?' Amy asked. 'Don't you have rehearsals tonight?'

'They started at six. It was only a read through. Everyone's gone home now.'

'So there were only you and Caspian in the building when the attack took place?'

Margo nodded. 'We were just switching off the lights. I was on my way back here to turn off the urn when there was a loud banging on the side door. I thought it would be one of the cast members who had forgotten something. Caspian shouted that he'd answer it, then there was a lot of yelling and a scream. I ran back along the passage and found him outside covered in blood. I didn't know what to do, I can't stand the sight of blood, not even the fake stuff we use in the plays, so I'm ashamed to say, I left him lying there and ran through to the foyer to telephone for an ambulance.'

'Did you see anyone else out in the alley?'

Margo shook her head. 'I heard the sound of someone running away, then a car driving off.' She looked at Amy with red, teary eyes. 'I know, I'm hopeless, aren't I?'

'You heard it pull away, not start up?'

Margo shook her head. 'No, I heard the squeal of tyres as it pulled off.'

Amy smiled softly at her, then looked up as Bodkin entered the room, followed by Ferris and PC Smedley, who had just arrived on the scene.

'Nothing to see out there apart from the blood spills,' Bodkin said. 'There is a lot of it, so the chances are, his attacker would have got some on their clothing.'

'Margo said she heard the sound of someone running and a car pulling away. She didn't hear it start up, so someone either left the engine running or a getaway driver was waiting.'

Bodkin looked around the dressing room. 'Where is everyone else?'

Amy pointed towards the door. 'They've all gone home, Bodkin. Rehearsal started at six.'

'Of course it did,' Bodkin said. 'That's why I wanted to get here for seven-ish. I'd forgotten all about our dinner date. I rang Caspian at his office this afternoon.'

'That was you, was it?' Margo said. 'I was over there going through some expenses receipts with him. I heard him say he'd be finishing up about eight and he'd be free after that.'

Bodkin frowned. 'What time was this?'

'About three. I was with him until we walked over here; that would have been about a quarter to six. I know that because we'd just finished eating the egg and cress sandwiches I'd made for us. I timed the eggs with the wall clock.'

'He has a kitchen in his office?'

'He uses one of the rooms in his flat as an office.'

'And you're sure this call came in at three?'

Margo nodded her head.

Bodkin scratched at the stubble on his chin. 'Well, in that case, it wasn't me. I rang well before then. It can't have been much after one-thirty, and I merely asked him if he was holding rehearsals this evening. I certainly didn't make arrangements to meet him afterwards.' He pulled a chair from under a square Formica table and sat down. Pulling his notebook out of his pocket, he flipped it open and made a few quick notes before looking back to Margo. 'Who else was at rehearsals tonight?'

Margo picked up her precious clipboard from the table and tapped it. 'There were five actors present. Caspian wanted to run through the one scene that everyone seemed to be struggling with, so he didn't need the full cast to be here.'

'Who were the five?'

Margo read from the sheet of paper on her clipboard.

'Caspian Stonehand, Glenda Thorn, Norman Standish, Imogen Beechwood, she's back for the autumn season, and me, but I was only prompting. I offered to play the character that only had two lines, but Caspian said he wanted a real actress to read his words, so Imogen played two parts.'

'He doesn't sound a very likeable person,' Amy said. 'What does it matter who reads two lines out in a rehearsal? He could have let you do it.'

'He's a professional at all times,' Margo said defensively. 'Everything has to be done properly. He sent me off to get the tea and biscuits.'

Amy bit her lip and said nothing in reply.

Bodkin made more notes, then tapped his pad with the end of his pen. 'And that's the full list. No one else was here, no one else dropped by?'

'Only Jack.'

'Jack?'

'Jack Draper, the props man.'

'Why was he here for a rehearsal? Does he usually show up for them?'

Margo shook her head. 'No, he said he wanted to pick up some drawings he's been working on. He's going to make us a new canvas backdrop for Don Juan.'

'That must be quite an expense,' Amy said. 'A new backdrop for every play.'

'Oh, he paints over old ones. We've got two or three that get revamped.'

'Did he stay for the duration?' Bodkin asked.

Margo shook her head. 'He sat and watched for a while, jotting down notes, but he left about fifteen minutes before Caspian called it a night.'

'He left alone?'

Margo nodded. 'Yes, he was in a bit of a hurry to get home. The silly man left his drawings behind. They're still at the side of the stage.'

Amy and Bodkin exchanged glances.

'How did Caspian and Jack get on?'

'All right, I suppose. He wasn't really Caspian's cup of tea. He's a bit common, you know. He didn't even go to art school.'

'So how did he get the job here if he wasn't up to standard?'

Margo waved the comment away with her hand. 'Oh, I didn't say he wasn't up to standard. He does a reasonable job with the artwork and he's very good with his hands. His wooden props are excellent.' Margo paused for a moment. 'He's been here for years. He was a volunteer to start with, working under Stephen Blatherwick and when Stephen retired... he was getting on and he suffered from terrible arthritis... Jack naturally took over.'

'He doesn't get paid for working here. What does he do for a living?' Bodkin asked.

'Caspian gives him a bit out of the petty cash every week, but it's not enough to live on. He's a cabinetmaker, Inspector. He works for Bennett and Scholes, the furniture people.'

'Does he own a car?'

'No.'

'Does he have a family? A wife, kids?'

'No, he lives alone. He rents the top room of a house in Nelson Street on the old Victorian estate. I think the houses are earmarked for demolition, so he'll have to look for somewhere else soon. I've got the full address in my files.'

'How did he seem this evening? Was he edgy... did he look nervous?'

'I honestly didn't pay much attention to him, to be honest, Mr... I mean Inspector Bodkin. He did seem to be in a bit of a hurry when he left. As though he'd just remembered he should be elsewhere.'

'What about Glenda, Norman and Imogen? What time did they leave?'

'Bang on eight. They were going for a drink together. It's Imogen's birthday.'

'Weren't you invited?' Amy asked.

'Oh yes,' Margo said quickly, 'but alcohol isn't my thing. I feel poorly for days if I so much as sniff it.'

'Was Caspian invited?'

'He was, but he had that appointment to keep... the one that I had assumed was with you, Inspector.'

Bodkin ran his hand through his shaggy mop of hair. 'And you have no idea at all where that meeting was going to be held?'

'As I said, I don't know who he was speaking to.'

Bodkin flipped his notebook shut and pushed it into his pocket. 'Thank you, Margo. Constable Ferris will give you a lift home. I would appreciate it if you could find me Jack's address before you leave.' He turned to the uniformed constable. 'Smedley, I want you to guard that entry. No one comes in or out of it without a good reason. I'll get someone to relieve you later.'

He turned, walked out of the room and along the passageway towards the side entrance. On impulse, he pushed open the stage door and stepped onto the boards. The stage itself was empty except for three chairs and a small round table on which sat an empty wine bottle. At the edge of the stage, front right, was an artist's pad. Bodkin picked it up and flipped it open. The first few pages were taken up with prospective designs for the Don Juan scenery, but on the last page was a scribbled drawing of a heart that had been cut almost in two by a dagger that was dripping blood.

Back outside, Bodkin jotted down Jack Draper's address, then showed Amy the last sketch in the book before handing it to Ferris. 'Put it on my desk when you go back to the station, Ferris. I know you think you're always on duty because you live in a room above, but you've done more than enough for one day. After you drop Margo off, go home and I don't want to see you again before eleven tomorrow. Have a lie in. We don't want you burning yourself out on your first investigation.'

'I was going to nip over to the hospital to see how Mr Stonehand is, sir,' Ferris said.

'I'll do that,' Bodkin replied. 'I want to have a word with the ambulance crew about exactly what they found when they arrived. I...' Bodkin paused as a movement in a car a little further up the road caught his eye. 'What have we got here?' he said as he stepped smartly across the pavement.

Parked up with the lights off, about twenty yards along the road, was a new-looking Mercedes saloon. Bodkin hurried up the street until he was level with the car, then, crouching down, he knocked on the driver's window.

The glass was slowly lowered and the face of a white-haired man with a goatee beard peered out at him.

'You seem to be taking more than a casual interest in what's happening over the road,' Bodkin said.

'I, er, it appears my timing was less than fortunate. I was about to go into the Playhouse when I saw the ambulance arrive. Something serious had obviously taken place, so I thought I'd better stay well back. I didn't want to get in the way of the proceedings.'

'That's very thoughtful of you, sir,' Bodkin said. 'But seeing as I'm in charge of this investigation and you are hanging around the scene of a crime, if you don't mind, I'd like you to give me your name and tell me why you were about to enter the Playhouse?'

'Of course, I don't mind, officer. My name is Fabian Starr. I run a theatrical agency and I was about to drop in on an old friend of mine. Caspian Stonehand.'

Chapter Eighteen

'Would you mind getting out of the car, sir?' Bodkin asked, straightening up and stepping back from the door.

'Am I in trouble?' Starr asked as he slid off his seat.

'For hanging around looking suspicious at the scene of a crime and for admitting that you planned to meet the victim of that crime. Why on earth would you think that, sir?' Bodkin pushed the car door shut and, putting a heavy hand on the agent's shoulder, he led him back towards the Playhouse.

'Ferris, we have a slight change of plan. Could you do the honours at the hospital? I want to have more than a quick word with Mr Starr.' He winked at Amy and flicked his head towards the side entrance. 'I think we'll have a chat on the stage. That seems appropriate, don't you think?'

Amy pushed open the door and led Bodkin and Starr onto the stage. Bodkin pulled one of the chairs away from the table and motioned for the agent to sit. After waiting for Amy to take her seat, he dragged the last chair out and sat down, facing Starr. He pointed to the empty wine bottle. 'I'd like to offer you a drink, but sadly, it's only a prop.' He picked the bottle up and sniffed at it. 'Château de Château 23, a very good year.'

Starr looked at his hands and said nothing. Bodkin leaned back in his chair, nodded almost imperceptibly towards Amy, then focused his full attention on his quarry.

'So, Mr Starr, let's start by asking a simple question. What are you doing here tonight?'

Starr slid his hands onto his knees, then shifted position and clasped them on his lap. 'As I said, I wanted to see my old friend Caspian Stonehand. I haven't had the pleasure of his company for far too long. I thought it was time that we caught up.'

'Hmm.' Bodkin stretched out his legs and crossed them at the ankles. 'This yearning to see your old friend came on all of a sudden, did it?'

'Not really. I've been thinking about him for a while now.'

'But, Mr Starr, you had no plans to drive over to Spinton a couple of days ago when my colleague phoned you to try to set up a meeting. You said you were on your way to Scotland and couldn't possibly see us before the end of next week.' He raised his eyebrows. 'But then, what do we find? Only forty-eight hours later, you turn up on our doorstep.'

'I was driving to Scotland. I decided to pop in on my way up.'

'Pop in? We're nowhere near the A1, Mr Starr. It's hardly popping in, is it? You've come miles out of your way.'

Starr shrugged. 'It's not so far, really.'

'Did you plan on staying over or were you going to drive most of the way back to London to pick up the A1?'

'There are other roads.'

'There are, but if you used them, it would take you a week to get to Scotland.' Bodkin stared hard at Starr. 'Come on, Fabian. You didn't drop by on a whim. Did you call him this afternoon to arrange a meeting?'

Fabian looked at his hands again and shook his head. 'No, honestly, it was just a spur of the moment thing.'

'All right, let's say that's true. How the hell did you know you'd find him at the Playhouse?'

'I didn't come straight here. I went to his apartment block first, but the concierge told me he'd left some time before with Miss Ashburner. I guessed this is where they would be.'

'It would have been so much easier to call him to find out where he would be this evening, wouldn't it?'

'I only made my mind up after I'd set off.'

'There are plenty of telephone boxes between London and here.'

'What can I say? I didn't think. I assumed he'd be at home.'

Bodkin shook his head, then held out his hand, gesturing for Amy to take over the questioning.

'Mr Starr, I'm Amy Rowlings. I assist the police in certain investigations.' She smiled sweetly at him. 'How long have you known Mr Stonehand?'

'Ten years or so.'

'Or so? Where did you meet him? As far as I know, he's always lived in Spinton and you've only been here once before.'

'I met him here, at the Playhouse in nineteen twenty-nine. One of my clients, Rex Larson, was touring the county theatres. He was only performing for one night in Spinton and the film director, Walter Forde, was about to choose the cast for his new comedy movie. The Importance of Being Earnest is a comedy, so we thought it would be a good chance to show off his talents.'

Amy, the film buff, leaned forward. 'Which film would that be?'

'Bed and Breakfast.'

'I've seen that film,' Amy said. 'Rex wasn't in it.'

'No, sadly Mr Forde let us down. He didn't show up at the play. He had already decided to give the role to Richard Cooper.'

'Ah, that was a shame. His big chance gone. He can't have been happy about that.'

'He wasn't happy, of course, but he got over it.'

Amy nodded. 'But on the bright side, you began your long-term friendship with Caspian.'

'I met him that night, yes.'

'Did you think he performed well in the play? Caspian, I mean.'

'He was average, to be honest.'

'So you didn't offer him a contract? You didn't want to represent him?'

'No.'

'Did you spend much time with him that night?'

'Be honest, Mr Starr. We can check,' Bodkin cut in.

'No, not a lot of time. He spent most of it explaining how he would have played Rex's role in the play. I thought he was a bit of a bore, to be honest.'

'But your opinion of him changed after that, obviously, as you've gone out of your way to see him tonight.' Bodkin uncrossed his ankles and straightened up in his chair. 'Just how many times have you seen him in the intervening years?'

'I haven't seen him at all,' Starr almost whispered.

'So why have you driven all this way in the hope of seeing him tonight?' Bodkin scowled at Fabian.

The agent sighed. 'All right. I came here to see if Caspian could refresh my memory about that night. I'm afraid I got rather drunk and can't remember much about it at all. I didn't want to put my foot in it when you questioned me.' He paused. 'My memory isn't what it was.'

'Wouldn't you be better off asking Rex? He's your client, after all.'

'We don't speak anymore and he isn't a client now. I cancelled his contract when he found fame in the Sunday gutter press. He could easily have brought my agency down with him.'

'But you knew where he'd be performing when my colleague rang you.'

'I keep a wary eye on him through my connections. I don't want to inadvertently turn up in the same town, let alone the same venue as him.'

'You say you can't remember anything about your night in Spinton?'

'Very little. I know I woke up in a room at the Milton Hotel with the worst hangover I've had in my life.'

'Were you alone when you woke up?'

Fabian's head dropped. 'Yes, but there was a torn stocking on the floor and my shirt was covered in lipstick.'

Bodkin scratched his head and frowned again.

'What I don't understand is why you think Caspian might have been able to jog you memory?'

'Because he was waiting in the hotel lounge when I finally left the room. He told me I had nothing to worry about as he'd sorted out what he called, my little problem.'

Chapter Nineteen

Bodkin leaned forward in his chair until his face was only a couple of feet away from Starr's. 'What was this, little problem?'

'It was with regard to a woman who had apparently spent time with me in the room I woke up in. There was a disturbance in the night. She had been shouting. The management wasn't happy about it, but Caspian had a word with them and it was all brushed under the carpet.'

'Why was this woman shouting?'

Starr hung his head. 'I still have no idea. I just paid what Caspian asked.'

'Which was?'

'A hundred pounds.'

Bodkin whistled. 'That was one expensive prostitute, Mr Starr.'

Starr looked up quickly. 'She wasn't a prostitute... or at least I don't think she was.' He looked pitifully at Bodkin. 'That's what I wanted to ask Caspian about tonight. I didn't know how much you knew about it all. You might have known more about it than I did.'

'And he didn't explain why it was going to cost you a hundred pounds... what you had done to warrant such a large bill?'

'I think the girl was very young.' Starr got to his feet. 'I can't remember anything about it. Just that Caspian said the management of the Milton had become involved and it was going to cost a hundred pounds to make it all go away.'

'He didn't tell you what the girl was screaming about, then? Or, indeed, how she got into your room in the first place?'

Starr shook his head.

'What can you remember about that night, Mr Starr?'

Fabian looked up at the lighting rig as he pondered. 'I can remember being here at the Playhouse. I remember the performance and sitting backstage with the cast and the local dignitaries.' He paused. 'I remember leaving with the Mayor and a few of his business friends and I remember being in the cocktail bar of the Milton Hotel. There was a jazz band on and a woman singing, but I don't remember anything after about ten-thirty.'

Bodkin scratched at the stubble on his chin as he left Starr to collect his thoughts.

'Were any of the young girls from the Playhouse there?' Amy asked. 'There were two hanging around with Rex backstage and there were five more out by the stage door.'

Starr screwed up his eyes. 'I'm trying to think. Yes, there might have been. There were some young women there. Everyone was very drunk, either on alcohol or other substances.'

'Other substances?'

'Cocaine? Amphetamines? I don't know, I never partake, though Rex was a regular user.' Starr looked from Amy to Bodkin. 'This might sound like a lame excuse, Inspector, but I think my drinks may have been spiked.'

'What makes you say that?' Bodkin asked.

Starr wrung his hands. 'Back then, I was a big drinker. I used to get through a bottle of good scotch a day, more if I was in a crowd. I could take my drink, Inspector. I have never been in the state I was in the next morning, in my entire life.'

'You think you were set up?'

Starr chewed on his bottom lip. 'I'm saying I might have been.

Not quite like you see in the movies where a press photographer bursts into the room to catch the victim in a compromising position, but similar. I think the woman, whoever she was, might have been paid to do a job on me.'

'It's all very convenient this memory lapse, Mr Starr,' Bodkin said. 'There was a woman in your room, perhaps a very young one. She suddenly begins to scream in the middle of the night and has to be rescued by the management, who are then paid off by a third party.' Bodkin narrowed his eyes as he looked at Starr. 'Do you realise how ridiculous you sound? It's far more likely that you went overboard on the drink and got a bit nasty with the girl when you found you couldn't... how shall we put it...' he shot a glance towards Amy... 'rise to the occasion.'

'That couldn't have been it, Inspector. I...' he looked at Amy under his lids... 'it... I have a medical problem and I've had it for over twenty years now. I was wounded in France during the war.' His voice dropped to a whisper. 'I can't perform in that way. It cost me my marriage.'

'What was that? I didn't quite catch it,' Bodkin said.

Starr sat back in his chair and looked at his clasped hands again. 'I'm hardly likely to have become sexually frustrated with the woman when I've been impotent since the end of the war.'

'I'm sorry that had to come out this way, Mr Starr,' Amy said comfortingly.

'It must have been very ha... upsetting,' Bodkin said, relieved to have managed to stop himself from saying hard.

'Let's change the subject, shall we?' Amy said quickly, giving Bodkin a stern look. 'Was Rex at the party?'

'I didn't see him. I think he was going to the George Hotel just down the road. He was... He was supposed to be meeting the two girls he met backstage.'

'Both of them?'

Starr shrugged. 'That's Rex for you. He was always in a state of inebriation, mostly from the cocktail of drugs he used to carry around with him. I think he was running short that day though because I remember him asking our driver if he knew of anywhere he could pick up a supply of whatever it was he needed.'

'The chauffeur you had for the day, Chester Harvey?'

'If that was his name, yes. He didn't seem to think it would be a problem. He told Rex he'd ask around while the play was on.'

Amy crossed her legs and smoothed her skirt down. 'When did you see Rex next?'

'When I was in the lounge at the Milton with Caspian. Rex came in, he was very dishevelled.'

'Dishevelled?' Bodkin repeated. 'Explain what you mean by dishevelled.'

'He was in his shirtsleeves, but his clothes were filthy. His hair... which was his pride and joy, was all over the place. He had bruises on his face and scratches on the backs of his hands. He looked a right mess.'

'Did he offer an explanation for his appearance?'

Starr shook his head. 'No, and I didn't ask for one. I just wanted to get out of there.'

'Where did you go?'

'Back to the Braithewaite to pick up my case, settle the bill, and to get my chequebook to pay Caspian. It was a Sunday, so all the banks were closed.'

'Did Rex and Caspian go with you?'

'Rex did. Caspian said he still had one or two things to tidy up so we could keep the press out of it.'

'So how did you get the cheque to Caspian?'

'I gave it to our driver. He said he'd pass it on to Caspian after he'd taken us to the station.'

'The driver was waiting for you at the Braithewaite, I take it.'

'No, he was waiting outside the Milton when I left with Rex.'

Chapter Twenty

Bodkin and Amy exchanged glances as Fabian Starr squirmed in his chair.

'The pair of you went straight back to London on the train, I take it?' Bodkin asked. 'Did he say anything on the journey about where he got his bruises?'

'We hardly spoke. I was too wrapped up in myself and he was really flat after the effects of whatever he had taken had worn off. He slept most of the way.'

'And you've never spoken about it to this day?'

'Not a word. I was on tenterhooks for weeks, worrying whether I'd wake up one morning to find a reporter on my doorstep, but it never happened. Caspian had been as good as his word.'

'You still seem to hold that man in high regard, and that puzzles me a little,' Amy said. 'After all, he could be a blackmailer. He could have been the one who set you up in the first place. Have you considered that?'

'Of course I have, but don't blackmailers tend to come back for more once they have you on the hook?'

'Not always,' Bodkin said. 'Some just need a pot of cash to kick-start their plans. We know that Caspian wanted his own business. He wanted to be more involved in the running of the Playhouse and that's exactly what he's achieved. He would have had plenty left over after handing out a few pounds to his co-conspirators.'

'The problem is,' Amy said, 'he's not going to spill the beans about what happened any time soon. We don't even know if he'll survive the night.'

'Which makes me wonder whether you were involved in the attack on him tonight, Mr Starr... not physically, but you might well have got someone else to do the deed for you.'

'You have to believe me, Inspector. I only wanted to go over the events of that night with Caspian so I could get my answers ready for when you interviewed me. What good was he to me dead? I needed him to fill the gaps in my memory.'

Bodkin got to his feet and motioned Starr to stand.

'Are you going to arrest me?' he asked nervously.

'Not tonight, Mr Starr, but I'm afraid you aren't travelling on to Scotland, if you ever meant to go there in the first place. I want to know where you are at all times, so I'd like you to drive back to London. But before you go, I want the telephone number at your home address. Every morning at eight o'clock, you'll get a call from us, so we can be sure you're at home. You'll get another one at nine at night, so, if you intend to go out for the evening, to a play or whatever, I suggest you call us just before you leave. Failure to answer our calls will mean you'll get our London colleagues calling on you, and you don't want to have to explain that to the neighbours.'

Starr nodded his head quickly, then pulled out a card from his pocket. 'Here's my home address and telephone number.'

Bodkin took a quick look, stuck it in his pocket and pointed towards the door. 'Off you go then. Have a safe journey.'

When Starr had gone, Bodkin sat down again, took a deep breath and looked across at Amy.

'What do you make of that?'

'I think he's telling the truth... about his sexual problems, at least. As for the rest. Could anyone have made that lot up?' She furrowed her brow. 'Mind you, he is a theatrical agent. He'll have seen any amount of plays and spoken to lots of playwrights.'

'He might just have a very vivid imagination,' Bodkin replied, 'but his story did seem to have a ring of truth about it.'

'Where does that leave us now? We've got to pray that Caspian pulls though, everything seems to revolve around him at the moment.'

Bodkin grunted. 'Even if he does make it, the medical staff won't let us anywhere near him for quite a while yet.'

'Right, let's make ourselves a to do list.' Amy held up a hand and began to count off on her fingers.

'One, we have to catch up with Jack Draper to find out what was so important he had to leave so suddenly and what was the significance of that sketch he left behind. I mean, he could be jealous of Caspian's relationship with a female member of the company... Margo, maybe?'

Bodkin nodded. 'I was thinking along the same lines. From what we've heard from Margo, Caspian treats her abominably. Jack might resent him for that.'

'Two.' Amy pushed down another finger. 'We still have to question Imogen Beechwood. She was in attendance backstage after the play. She might have something she can tell us about Caspian's movements that night. She came out of the theatre after Larson and Starr.'

'She's on my list,' Bodkin said.

'Three. After what Fabian told us tonight, we have even more questions for Rex Larson on Saturday. How on earth did he get into that state, and where had he been all night? I mean, you don't turn up the next morning looking as if you'd just done three rounds in a fairground booth, when you've just had a hot date with two young women in a hotel, although I suppose it depends on what happened in his room.'

Bodkin nodded slowly. 'It's going to be an interesting conversation on Saturday. I'm pretty sure he won't know we have all this information about him.'

'Oh...' Amy reached into her bag. 'Sorry, Bodkin. I meant to give you this, but what with all the excitement tonight, I forgot all about it.'

Amy passed the letter to Bodkin and explained how she had come to find it.

'Armed forces code,' Bodkin said. 'Our soldiers and sailors used to use that code when they were writing home. They weren't supposed to give any clue as to their exact location, especially those who were in places like Gallipoli and Jutland, so they used the same code to let their loved ones know where they were.'

'Alice and I used to use it in the classroom after Mrs Atkinson split us up for whispering in her lesson. We'd write a load of nonsense with capitalised brief paragraphs and pass the notes back and forth via our classmates.' Amy laughed to herself. 'Mrs Atkinson could have worked out our codes in two seconds flat because the only words that made a real sentence read from the top to the bottom of the left-hand side of the page.'

Bodkin smiled. 'Me and my sister Sal did a similar thing when we left messages for each other at home. Dad never worked them out, but then he was drunk most of the time.'

Amy pouted. 'Oh, Bodkin.'

The inspector shrugged. 'It's all in the dark distant past now.' He read Rex's letter again. 'He was a charmer, wasn't he? I bet Nina lapped it up, too. She was little more than a kid and she would have been flattered by his attention.'

'Young girls are usually impressed by older men. We don't all fall for the blatant flattery, of course, but girls mature a lot quicker than boys. They read about love affairs all the time in the books they pick up. Look at any teenage girl's bookshelf... if they are fortunate enough to have one, of course, and you'll find pretty much the same volumes on all of them. Poems by Keats and Shelly, novels like Jane Eyre, Wuthering Heights, Tess of the d'Urbervilles and Pride and Prejudice. All guaranteed to get the heart fluttering.'

'I had no idea,' Bodkin replied. 'Sal had her own small collection of books, but she kept them well hidden from the rest of us.' He brought his hands together and clapped once. 'Do you have a point four?'

Amy nodded, held up her hand, and pulled down another finger.

'Four. Once again, after what we've heard tonight, we have another question or two for our local Romeo, Chester Harvey. He didn't tell us anything about collecting Fabian from the Milton and how he knew he was there in the first place. He didn't mention going in search of cocaine or some other intoxicant for Rex, either.'

Bodkin jotted a few notes. 'It's in my book,' he said, looking up. 'Well, it is now.' He tapped the notebook with the end of his pen. 'Is there a five?'

'Five,' Amy said, pulling down her thumb. 'This is related more to tonight than to ten years ago. I noticed that Margo recovered from her hysteria remarkably quickly this evening. She went from a quivering lump of jelly to a clear spoken, thoughtful witness all in the space of five minutes. Now, that could be down to your calming presence, Bodkin, but I'd say she was laying it on a bit thick when we arrived. Did you notice that she didn't beg to be taken to the hospital to be near him? She didn't mention wanting to visit him once. Not even when Ferris offered to drive over there to see how he was. Had that been me and you were the one in hospital, I'd be demanding I go with him in the car.'

'That's a very good point,' Bodkin said. 'I like number five.' He made a few more notes in his book.

'There is a six,' Amy said, pulling down the first finger of her left hand.

'Caspian seems to be at the centre of everything here. I'd love to know how he found out about the woman's screams in Starr's hotel room in the middle of the night. How he knew he'd be able to, as he said, get everything brushed under the carpet. How did he become so influential all of a sudden? I mean, the Milton isn't like the George is it? We know from the Effie Watkins case what sort of things the George management and staff will tolerate, but it's not like that at the Milton. They have a cultured reputation to keep up.' Amy tapped the next finger but kept it upright. 'I'm wondering if Caspian made his way over to the Milton that night after leaving the Playhouse. What I don't see yet, is who set up this charade to implicate Fabian in a potential scandal. Caspian's the favourite of course, but what gave him the idea? Did he have a plan in place, or was it all done on the spur of the moment? Oh yes, that's the other thing. If Fabian's drinks had been spiked, who did it and who provided the drugs? Could it have been the same person Rex got his new supply from? Another question for Chester Harvey.'

Bodkin shut his notebook and slipped it into his pocket with his pen. 'Time to call it a night, young lady,' he said.

Amy yawned. 'I'm ready for my bed. It's been a long day.' She got to her feet and picked up her bag. 'What's on your schedule tomorrow?'

'I'm going to see our friends at the Evening Post,' he replied. 'Lenny Cartman has been their main photographer for years. He was probably the one who covered the play that night, and if I know Lenny, he'll have kept a record of the event. He'll have copies of his pictures filed away somewhere. If he can dig them out, it might help us. Especially the one he took of the girls and Rex outside the stage door.' Bodkin stuck his finger in his ear, wiggled it about, then pulled it out and studied it. 'If he can find that picture, I'll have a word with his editor to see if he can publish it with a request for anyone recognising themselves in the photograph to make themselves known to the police. One of them might know where Nina went after the show.'

'You see, this is why you're a police inspector and I'm not,' Amy said. 'That's a brilliant idea.'

'We're a team. We bounce off each other,' Bodkin said. 'I honestly wish I had you with me in the office every day. No criminal would be safe.'

Amy laughed and said, 'You've got Ferris now. He's a good stand in.'

Bodkin got to his feet and held out his arms to her. 'He is, but I wouldn't offer him a cuddle.'

'There is something else that's just come to mind,' Amy said as she walked slowly into his arms. 'Rex was in his shirtsleeves when he arrived at the Milton that morning.'

'According to Starr, yes.'

'But it's past the middle of October. It's chilly at night. I can't see Rex running through the streets of Spinton in his shirtsleeves to meet his hot date, can you?'

Bodkin pulled away and looked down into Amy's face as she looked up into his. 'So,' he said. 'The question you're asking is, what happened to his coat?'

Chapter Twenty-One

Bodkin didn't make an appearance at lunchtime on the Friday and as it was an overcast day with regular bouts of drizzly rain, Amy ate her lunch in the staffroom with Jill who was still complaining about having to work on a Saturday when her boyfriend got the day off to spend in the pub.

When the doors reopened for the afternoon, Amy spent almost an hour trying to persuade a woman shaped like a cottage loaf that the tight, body hugging evening dress she had her eye on probably wasn't the best style for her.

'We do have it in a larger size, but it's a different colour completely and it really wouldn't go with your skin tone and hair colour.'

Mrs Hyde was known to the shop staff as Mrs Formaldehyde because of the strong, chemical odour that seemed to materialise whenever they were helping her dress. Amy thought it might have been caused by the overuse of mothballs, but she couldn't be certain. One thing was for sure, she was certainly well preserved for her age.

Bodkin stepped in the shop at four o'clock and, after realising that Amy must be in the back with a customer, had tried to make a quick exit. But it was too late. Josie, the manageress, had spotted him.

'Hello there,' she said, taking his arm. 'Amy will be out in a moment or two. She's just helping a lady put her corset back on.'

Bodkin blushed, as he did every time Josie spoke to him about women's underwear. She seemed to make a point of it. She had once offered him the choice of two pairs of silk bloomers, holding them up in front of his eyes, and he had never recovered from the experience.

'I'll, er... just go... no, sorry, can you give her a message? Tell her I'll pick her up at five-thirty.' He forced a smile. 'Sorry, I have to run. Tell her I've seen Mr Girdle... I mean Girdham, and he's going to run the story in tonight's Evening Post.' Bodkin backed off towards the door. 'Nice to see you,' he said as he turned and fled the shop.

At five-thirty, Amy, Jill and Josie walked out of the front door to find Bodkin standing by his car at the kerb. He raised his hand and waved as Josie called to him from the shop doorway.

'How was Mr Girdle?' she asked, not even attempting to keep a straight face.

Bodkin forced a smile and fixed his attention on Amy. He pulled out his folded newspaper from under his arm and raised it in the air. 'We got the front page,' he said as he cast a nervous glance towards Josie.

Amy handed Bodkin her bag and took the newspaper from him. Unfolding it, she scanned the headline and the photograph of Rex and the five young women.

DO YOU RECOGNISE YOURSELF? The headline asked. ARE YOU IN THIS PICTURE?

Can You Help Find Nina's Killer? The sub heading asked underneath.

'I see Sandy blooming Miles has got the story,' Amy said. She had only met the Post's chief reporter on a couple of occasions, but she didn't like the way he went about building his stories. Many of which were based on hyperbole and downright lies.

'He was always going to be given it,' Bodkin said. 'It might work out well for us this time. I told his editor that the Post would get the exclusive when the case is wrapped up if they help us now.'

Amy read the columns again. 'It's a bit over the top, isn't it? Miles talks as though he's an integral part of the investigation team... and what's all this about him being on hand when the body was discovered?'

Bodkin shrugged. 'Come on, this edition came out at four o'clock I've got three officers manning the phone lines. Let's go and see if we've had any response.'

Amy climbed into the car, and Bodkin drove the short distance to the police station. As he pushed the front doors open, they could hear the ringing of telephones throughout the building. PC Parlour was in his usual place on the front desk. He waved to Amy as he put the phone down.

'Any luck with the public, Parlour?'

The constable had been given the task of collating the responses. PC Smedley and Trixie had also been taking the calls.

'Some are of interest, sir, but we've had a few of the usual nutters on the phone, too. One chap says he doesn't know who the girls are, but if the one in the bottom right of the picture is still single, he'd like to take her out.'

Bodkin closed his eyes and shook his head, but didn't reply. Parlour shuffled through a few sheets of paper, then picked three of them up.

'Tell me about the interesting ones,' Bodkin said eventually.

'Right, sir.' Parlour read the topmost sheet out aloud. 'We've got a Mrs Faye Simpson. She claims to be the girl holding onto Mr Larson's left arm. The one looking at him all lovey-dovey.'

'That's good news. Do we have her telephone number? I'll give her a call back.'

'She called from a phone box, sir. I've got her address, though.'

'Good, what else have you got for me?'

'A Miss Phyllis Shackleton called, sir. She said that she thinks the girl looking over Mr Larson's shoulder, the one with the wide eyes and open mouth, is her friend, Sylvia, but she hasn't seen her since they were in secretarial college together in nineteen twenty-eight.'

Bodkin nodded. 'Anything else? Did anyone recognise the girl holding onto Larson's right arm because we know that to be Nina?'

'Not yet, sir.' He waved a sheet of paper at the inspector. 'I have this, but it's a strange one.'

Bodkin sighed as the words 'a strange one' left Parlour's lips.

'How strange?'

Parlour took a deep breath before speaking.

'Well, sir, the call is from someone called Gretchen. Gretchen Parks, her name might sound German, but she spoke perfect English.'

'What did she have to say?'

'She said the blonde-haired girl with the hair clips behind Nina is her sister, Hildee... it says H I L D E, sir, so maybe Smedley copied it down wrong. It's probably Hilda.'

'It's probably Hilde,' Bodkin said. 'It's a German name.'

'Ah, well, she says it's her sister, sir.'

'Do we have an address for her?' Bodkin asked.

'The sister? No, sir, that's where it got a bit strange.'

'Tell me,' Bodkin said, sighing again.

'Right, well, it seems this Hilda... Hilde married a foreigner, sir. They went to live in the Sodden land and—'

'The where?' Bodkin cut him off.

Parlour reread the typed sheet. 'The Sodden land, sir. I can explain more about it.'

'Please do,' Bodkin replied.

'Well, it's like this. When this Hilde woman got married, they went to live in Czechoslovakia, her husband being a Czech and all that. Anyway, it seems that when Old Adolph invaded the country in March 'thirty-eight, he changed the name of the area he had conquered back to its old name... Sodden land. It's a weird name, isn't it? Do you think it might be a bit marshy there? Whatever the reason, she won't be coming back here anytime soon and we can't contact her at all.'

'SUDETENLAND!' Bodkin raised his voice in frustration. 'Honestly, Parlour, don't you read the newspapers?'

'Only for the football results... oh and the Jane cartoon, of course.'

Bodkin looked towards Amy with disbelief on his face. 'A bit marshy,' he repeated.

Amy held her hand in front of her mouth in an attempt to hold in the laughter that was building up inside. Her eyes were watering. Eventually she managed to blurt out Sodden land, before a series of giggles burst out of her.

Bodkin stuck his tongue in his cheek as he almost joined in, but after a few seconds, he managed to control the urge to laugh. 'Give me the relevant sheets, Parlour.' He pointed at the desk. 'Faye Simpson. Is it a Spinton address?'

Victory Street was situated on the edge of the Victorian housing estate that had been built to accommodate the influx of workers that arrived to fill the many jobs provided by the ironworks, the coal mines and the coking ovens in the mid to late nineteenth century. The Edwardian terraced houses were of better quality than the Victorian slums, but many of them had not been maintained to a very high standard. Number 37 was one such property. The red brick house looked to be a comfortable dwelling from the outside, but once Mrs Simpson opened the door, it was obvious, just from the smell, that the house had a serious issue with damp.

'Hello,' she said as she stood in the open doorway wearing a heavily stained blue pinafore. Her lank hair was tucked behind her ears, and she had strands of mousey brown hair plastered to her forehead. 'Are you from the paper?'

Bodkin shook his head. 'I'm from the police, Mrs Simpson.' He held out his hand towards Amy, 'and this is my associate, Miss Rowlings.'

'I've seen you somewhere before. I never forget a face.' Faye thought for a while with her fingers stuck to her chin. 'I know, you're with the church charity people, aren't you? I've seen you dropping parcels off at the houses on the estate behind us.'

Amy smiled at her. 'I like to do my bit when I can.'

'You never bloody well come anywhere near our street, do you?' She waved her hand towards the house next door. 'We're not all la di da well to do around here, you know. Some of us struggle just as much as those on Ebeneezer Street.'

'I'll have a word with the vicar,' Amy said. 'I'm sure we can organise something.'

'Just the odd bag of sugar and a packet of tea would help,' Mrs Simpson said. She turned her attention to Bodkin.

'I'm not going to invite you in *there*. You'll come out smelling like the drains.' She flicked her head towards the internal door. 'We have running water in this house, but most of it runs down the walls.' She stepped out of the house, shut the front door behind her and opened up a second door at the side. 'Come in here. It's not much better, but this part of the house doesn't smell.'

Faye stepped into the room, which was crammed with leather trunks, suitcases, wicker baskets, and even a few wooden crates. 'My Ken sells them at the Saturday afternoon market. He doesn't make much, but every little helps. He works as a porter at the station in the week.' Bodkin lifted a couple of the labels that were tied to the handles with string as he walked in. All had different names and addresses on them. He shot Amy a look. 'Stolen', he mouthed silently.

Mrs Simpson stopped by the side of a packing case, raised herself onto her tiptoes and slid onto it. 'Ow,' she said. 'Splinters.'

Bodkin pulled out his notebook. 'Mrs Simpson, you called us

today to say that you were one of the girls in the photograph on the front of this evening's Post. Is that correct?'

Faye nodded. 'I rang the Post too. I thought they might pay for an exclusive story, but they weren't really interested. They wanted to hear what I had to say, but they didn't want to pay to listen, so I hung up on them.' She paused and frowned. 'That bloody call cost me fourpence.'

Bodkin gave her a quick smile. 'What was it you wanted to tell them, Mrs Simpson?'

'Call me Faye, please.'

'Faye,' Bodkin repeated.

Faye looked at Bodkin's hands as though he might magically produce his wallet to pay for her story. When he didn't, she pulled a face and began.

'I was just about eighteen back when that picture was taken. I'd not long started a new job in an office in town. I was in the typing pool,' she preened. 'I had prospects back then.'

'Did you go to the theatre a lot?' Bodkin asked.

'Don't look so surprised. I haven't always lived in a dump like this, you know? Mum and Dad rented one of those cottages down by The Mill. You know, the clothing factory? We weren't exactly well to do, but we weren't poor either. I used to go to the pictures on a Saturday night, but I did like a well-acted play too, and when I saw the poster that said Rex Larson was going to be on stage, well, I just had to buy a ticket.' She looked into space as she thought. 'The trouble was none of my friends fancied it. It took me ages to persuade Mum to let me go, and even then it was only because I lied and told her that Ken, who was my boyfriend at the time, was going with me. He wasn't, of course. He wouldn't miss a night in the pub just to go to an arty farty play.'

'You went alone then?' Amy asked. 'That was very brave of you.'

'I wasn't alone for long. I met a few other girls there. Three of them were together. Then there were two other girls who arrived together, but we lost them after the play. I've no idea where they got to.'

'What about Nina, the girl we're interested in?' Bodkin asked.

'The girl with the little case? She tagged along with us. She was nice enough, a bit posh for my tastes, but then I didn't talk to her much. I know she was mad keen on Rex Larson though, every time she did say something, his name cropped up.'

'This is all very interesting, and it's helping us create a picture of that night's events. Thank you, Faye.' Bodkin gave her his best smile. 'Now, what can you tell me about what happened after the play? You were all hanging around by the stage door hoping to get to meet Rex, is that right?'

Faye nodded. 'There was a driver there with a flash car. He was a handsome devil, all spruced up in his uniform. He spent almost an hour trying to persuade us to get in the back seat of the car.'

'Which you eventually did... is that right?'

'Yeah, but we got in all together. That randy old goat only wanted one of us to get in. He didn't seem to care which one.'

'Did he touch any of you?'

'He copped a feel when that girl with the foreign name climbed out. Mind you, she was better developed than the rest of us... what was her name now...?'

'Hilde?' Bodkin asked.

'Bloody hell, I think you're right. It was Hilde. How on earth did you know that?'

'Educated guess,' Bodkin replied. 'So, after you got out of the car, what happened next?'

'We stood around for a while, then the door opened and Rex came out. He looked so handsome. I almost swooned when I saw him. That girl Nina waved at him as though she was greeting a long-lost uncle, then we all pushed our photos and autograph books forwards for him to sign.'

'How did Rex respond to Nina?'

'He pretty much blanked her. She looked devastated, poor thing.'

'Was the Evening Post photographer there by this time?' Amy asked.

'Yep, he followed Rex out. It was his idea to have the group photo.'

'Was Rex reluctant to have the picture taken?'

'Not at all. He was loving the attention. He had his hand up on my arse the whole time.'

'That must have been uncomfortable for you, Faye,' Amy said soothingly.

'What! I bloody loved it. It's not every day a famous, handsome man grabs your arse, is it? I was just happy that he picked mine.'

Bodkin pursed his lips. 'After the picture was taken, what happened then?'

'We all tried to get Rex to kiss us, but only that Nina got one, though it wasn't much of a kiss, not a Hollywood smooch or anything like that. He signed her photo, or whatever it was she was holding out, gave her a quick peck, whispered something in her ear, then was off, like a rat up a drainpipe.'

'Which way did he go?'

'Towards the George, no idea where he was heading, but he was in a hurry.'

'Can you remember what he was wearing?' Amy asked quickly.

'I'll never forget anything about that night. He was wearing a long dark overcoat. It was unbuttoned. Underneath, he had the same shirt on he wore in the play. White, silky stuff it was made of. He had a cravat on too, a lovely blue colour.'

'Did you stay around the stage door area after Rex had gone?' Bodkin asked.

'For a time. That Hilde girl wanted to get Caspian Stonehand's autograph. He looked to have been a handsome chap on stage, so we all agreed to wait with her. That Nina wasn't too keen, though. She stood on the bottom step, holding her little case like she wasn't sure what to do.'

'Then what happened?'

'It all got a bit hectic. The Mayor came out with a lot of his mates. There was a chap with grey hair and a red nose. He looked like a drinker. They had their picture taken in a group, then they toddled off in the same direction as Rex.'

'Did this chap with the grey hair say anything to you, or to Nina?'

Faye shook her head. 'He had a few words with the driver, then he walked after the Mayor and his party.'

Bodkin made a few notes, then narrowed his eyes slightly as he looked back at Faye. 'Did Hilde get Caspian's autograph?'

'Did she ever. She got a smacker on the lips off him too.'

'What about the rest of you?'

'No one was that bothered, to be honest, Mr Bodkin. He wasn't all that good looking without his greasepaint on. Not a patch on Rex. The driver was much better looking.'

'Where did Caspian go when he left?'

'The phone box just past the Lamb and Flag.'

'Were you there when the rest of the cast came out?'

'Yeah, they came out in a group... except... there was one young chap who came out on his own. He was wearing overalls. He didn't hang around... well, not on the steps at least, but when we all began to drift away a few minutes later, I saw him standing on the corner just across from the Lamb and Flag pub. He was smoking a cigarette and just watching us.'

Amy and Bodkin exchanged glances. 'What about the driver? Was he still hanging around too?'

'No, he got back in the car and drove off after the red nosed guy had spoken to him. I can't remember which way he went... Oh, I can! He backed up a bit and turned into that narrow road next to the Lamb and Flag, then he reversed out and drove off the same way everyone else had gone.'

'What happened after that?' Bodkin asked.

'We began to make our way home. I walked to the stop in the marketplace to get the last bus. Hilde and her two friends walked with me part of the way, then they turned off and headed towards the bus station.'

'What about Nina?'

'She walked behind us for a while, but to be honest, I don't know what happened to her. She wasn't with us when we split up to go our separate ways, that's for sure.'

'Anything else you can think of?' Bodkin asked Amy.

She shook her head. 'No, I think we've covered most of what we wanted to ask.'

Bodkin turned towards the door and opened it to let Amy go out first. 'Thank you for that, Mrs Simpson. You've been extremely helpful.'

'Just don't you forget me the next time the church is handing out groceries,' Faye called after Amy. 'Tea is always much nicer with sugar in it.'

Bodkin checked his watch when they got back to the car. 'Oops, sorry, Amy, you must be starving. Do you fancy fish and chips, my treat?'

Amy nodded eagerly. 'I'd love some fish and chips, but do you think Toni will serve us after what happened the other day?'

Chapter Twenty-Two

Saturday morning flew by. After getting up half an hour early, Amy caught the eight-thirty bus to town carrying the two blankets that she had bought for Con.

When Sharon opened the doors at Brigden's bang on nine o'clock, Amy almost ran for the sales rails and after only a five-minute search, found two twelve and six dresses that would suit Alice down to the ground.

The first was a red dress with a deep v cleavage, puff shoulder sleeves and a skirt which flared from the waist. A delicate navy fleck pattern ran through it. The second dress was similar in style but in an olive green colour. Both would show off Alice's beautiful hour-glass figure to perfection.

After taking a quick look for something for herself, Amy, watching the clock, decided to give it a miss this week and took the dresses to the counter where Eileen the manageress was totting up some figures.

Amy dumped the blankets on the desk, then undraped Alice's dresses from her arm and handed them to her.

'If you're looking to trade those in, forget it,' she said, nodding at the blankets. 'They look like they have things living in them.' She peered closer. 'Is that blood?'

Amy picked up the blankets and dropped them at her feet. 'They're for old Con, to help keep him warm in the winter, Eileen.'

'Ah, he's back again, is he? Where has he been this time, prison again?'

Amy nodded. 'Probably, I haven't asked, to be honest. I just know he's back, and he'll need something to keep him warm under that tarp at night.'

'It's kind of you to do it, but let's be honest here. He doesn't help himself, does he?'

'He's ninety. Too old to change.'

'Someone ought to force him to change. His clothes for a start. Have you ever been downwind of him? I reckon someone was buried in that suit of his and he went and robbed the corpse.'

Amy tutted. 'Now, now. No need for that, Eileen, he might whiff a bit, but he's just a harmless old man at the end of the day.'

Eileen decided to change the subject as she shivered. 'It makes me itch just thinking about him.' She picked up the dresses and examined them. 'You won't get much of a discount on these. There's nothing wrong with them.'

'They're for Alice,' Amy said. 'She says she'll give you a pound for the two.'

Eileen looked around the shop. 'Just nipped out, did she?'

'No, she's not here. She asked me to choose for her and said she'd run to a pound for two nice dresses.' She pointed at the clothes. 'And I found two nice dresses.'

'So you're trying to barter for someone who couldn't be bothered to come to the shop themselves? That's not going to work.'

'She's cleaning out the pigs. I could give her a call and she'll drive up in her old truck, but be warned, old Con will probably smell better.'

Eileen pulled a face. 'All right. That's a pound.' She shook her head slowly. 'I'm becoming a soft touch in my old age.'

From Brigden's, Amy skipped her usual visit to the Post Office as well as her morning coffee at the Sunshine Café and instead caught the bus to the second stop on the Gillingham road, where she walked a short distance along the narrow winding lane until she came to the clearing that locals had used as an entrance to the Witchy Wood for generations.

A hundred yards along, she reached a fork in the path. The track to the right led to Creepy Cottage, while the other led deeper into the woods. Amy took the left-hand trail and followed it for a short distance. The track ended in a small clearing where Con had strung up his tarp to form a rough tent between three ash trees.

She found Con sitting on a rotting log a few feet in front of the entrance to his tent, fending off the lumps of bark, branches and sods of earth that were being thrown at him by three boys of around fourteen years of age.

'OI! Danny Partridge, stop that now or I'll have a word with your mother the next time I see her.'

'She won't care,' Danny said, picking up another lump of rotten wood.

'She will if I turn up with a policeman,' Amy said firmly. She looked at the other two boys who she knew from church. 'And as for you, Roland Tandy and you, Peter Swain. You ought to know better. Didn't you learn anything from the sermon last week? The vicar said love thy neighbour, not pelt him with clods of soil.'

'He's not my blood... sorry... he's not my neighbour,' Roland said. 'He's just an old dosser.'

'He's a human being and therefore he deserves respect,' Amy said, walking forwards and sitting on the log next to Con. She immediately regretted it. The smell was overpowering.

Danny flicked his head towards the path. 'We'll come back when she's gone.'

'You will not come back when I've gone,' Amy said, standing up, grateful for the chance to move away from Con. 'I meant what I said. If I hear that you came back to attack this poor, defenceless old man, then the police will be paying you a visit. Mark my words.' She turned towards the other two, who were looking a little less sure of themselves. 'I'll see your parents outside the church tomorrow. Let's see if they have Christian values, shall we? I wouldn't bank on being allowed out for a week or two.'

The boys turned, and muttering to each other, made their way back to the path.

'Smelly old Dosser,' Danny shouted a parting shot.

'Are you hurt, Con?' Amy said, quickly working out which way the light breeze was blowing and making sure to get upwind of the old man.

'Only my pride,' Con said. 'And I haven't got any of that left, so no. I'm not hurt.'

Amy leaned forward and put the blankets on the log next to him. 'These are ex-army blankets, Con, so they'll keep you warm in winter.' She smiled at him as he patted them with his hand. 'Don't you go selling them now. They were a gift from me and I'll be really upset if I find you've given them away for a mug of soup or a bag of chips.'

'I'll look after them, I promise,' Con replied. 'You don't give things away that a pretty girl gave to you.'

For some reason, Amy felt herself blushing. 'You just make sure they're still here come winter.'

'I'll bury them under all my stuff at the back of the tent. They'll be safe there.'

Amy peered into the tent. There was a straw palliasse on the floor and a seat made from a large paint tin with a square of wood nailed on to the top. At the back of the tent was a small mountain of rubbish. Bundles of newspapers, old biscuit tins and empty cardboard boxes. There were also a couple of packing crates and a new-looking hat. The trash was piled floor to ceiling. Amy wondered how many times it had collapsed over the years.

'Why don't you wear the new hat, Con?'

'I'm saving it for my funeral,' the old man said. 'There's a suit somewhere, too. I might need them before too long.'

'You should wear them now, Con. Anyway, I bet you've got years left in you yet.'

'No. It's my funeral suit and my funeral hat. There's even a pair of funeral shoes under that lot. I found them on the steps of a caravan over in Sheppey fifteen years ago or more.' He laughed. 'I'm not even sure they'll still fit. They might pinch a bit, but I don't suppose that will bother me too much.'

The old man gave a cackling laugh, which turned into a coughing fit. When he had recovered, Amy checked her watch.

'I've got to run, now, Con. I'm going with Inspector Bodkin to Royal Tunbridge Wells today and I'm driving.'

'I liked it down there. I had a nice time. The water is good for you. Make sure you have a drink. It'll put hairs on your chest.'

'I don't think I want hairs on my chest, Con,' Amy said with a laugh.

'No…I don't suppose you do.' The old man burst into laughter again. 'It would get in the little 'uns mouths when you're feeding them.'

Amy shook her head to clear the vision that instantly appeared. 'I'll come and see you again soon, Con. If I don't bump into you in town.' She blew him a kiss, which he pretended to catch and rub on his cheek. 'If those boys come back, I want to know.'

'They'll not be back. I think you put the fear of God into them.'

'Well, just in case I haven't, let me know. Failing that, you could drop in at the police station and tell Bodkin. He's a decent sort.'

'They'll arrest me the minute I stick my head around the door,' Con said, and cackled again. 'Don't you worry about me, missy. I've seen off worse than those young toerags in my time and I'm still here to tell the tale.'

. . .

After leaving Con, Amy carried her Brigden's bag in front of her chest as she ducked beneath the low-hanging branches and stepped around the scratchy briars that lined the path. As she got close to the Creepy Cottage, she veered left and made her way through the wood until the trees thinned out and she saw a long line of wooden fencing running along the edge of a meadow. Dropping her bag carefully over the four foot high fence, Amy clambered over it and walked through the fallow field until she reached a small pond. Skirting it, she strolled along a scrub path until some farm buildings appeared almost out of nowhere. When she reached the paddock, she pulled up a handful of long grass and held it over the fence for Alice's huge old Shire horse, Bessie to chew on. Five minutes later, she marched past the new milking parlour, across the yard and up the back steps to the kitchen.

Alice was standing stark naked on the mat in front of the big Belfast sink. At her feet was a pile of foul smelling clothes. She screamed as Amy pushed the door open, then with one hand across her chest and one hand over her pubis, she began to back away towards the bathroom.

'It's only me,' Amy called, laughing. She waved the Brigden's bag in the air. 'I got you a couple of dresses, but you're not going to try them on until you've had a bath. And as for trying to cover yourself up... I've seen you naked almost as many times as I've seen myself. We used to have a bath together every Saturday. Mind you,' she held her nose, 'you didn't smell like that.'

Alice grabbed a towel from the clotheshorse, turned and headed through the parlour door to her relatively new bathroom. 'Make yourself useful, put the kettle on. I'll be out in two shakes. The bath's already run.'

'Can I use your phone?' Amy shouted as Alice's bare backside disappeared from view. 'I want to ring Bodkin to let him know where I am.'

'Feel free,' Alice's voice wafted out from the bathroom. 'But tell him not to be in too much of a hurry. I need fifteen minutes to have a soak.' There was a splashing noise as she climbed into the water. 'I don't know what they put in the pig feed these days but it makes their...' Alice's voice faded away as Amy pushed open the front room door and made her way to the phone.

* * *

'You remember Bodkin's sister, Sal, don't you? The one who runs a family charity in Dover? She's coming over tonight, so Ferris won't be playing gooseberry.'

Miriam, Alice's live-in friend come housekeeper, poured boiling water into the teapot and placed it on the big oak table. 'Of course I remember. Ferris got on well with her, didn't he? Do you think there might be some spark there?'

'You never know with Ferris. One, he's a bloke and two... he's a copper. He's a lot like Bodkin in many ways. Hard to read.'

'What do you think?' Alice came down the stairs wearing the red dress that Amy had bought. 'It might want letting out a bit at the waist. I've been eating too much of Miriam's cake recently. I'm getting fat.'

'There's not an ounce of fat on you,' Amy said, giving Alice an appraising look. 'You look absolutely stunning. You'll have them fighting to get the first dance at the young farmer's ball.'

Alice rolled her eyes heavenward. 'You'll never see me at another one of those. Young farmers indeed. The youngest was Toby Gait-skill, and he's nearly fifty.'

'Let's see the other one then,' Amy said, clapping her hands. 'Bodkin will be here in a minute.'

Bodkin, as it turned out was there in less than ten seconds. Alice had only just left the room when he opened the kitchen door and stepped inside.

'It's a good job you didn't walk in about forty minutes ago,' Amy said. 'You'd have caught Alice in the altogether.'

'My timing has always been lousy,' Bodkin said with a grin. 'I might get to walk in on you in the same state one of these days.'

'Get those thoughts out of your head, Bodkin,' Amy said, putting her teacup on the table and picking up her bag. 'I'm sure you can be arrested for thinking thoughts like that.'

Bodkin held his arms out. 'There are some handcuffs in my coat pocket. I plead guilty.' He looked at the big wall clock. 'I hate to rush you, but we'd better be off. Some of the roads around Tunbridge Wells can get a bit busy at this time of year. We don't want to be late and give Sexy Rexy a reason to slink off.'

Amy hurried across to the door at the bottom of the stairs. 'The fashion show will have to finish later, dear heart. I'm off to Tunbridge Wells with Bodkin, the lecherous.'

'It's Royal isn't it?' Miriam said. 'Royal Tunbridge Wells. I remember it getting the charter in 1908. I was only a kid at the time, but it seemed so distinguished. Imagine Spinton getting the Royal seal?'

'I think there's more chance of nailing blancmange to the wall,' Amy said, blowing Miriam a kiss. 'Good luck with Michael. Make sure those silk bloomers are in your overnight bag.'

'I think Spinton has more chance of being given the Royal seal than I have of getting those out of my case,' Miriam said with a sigh. 'Still, the dinner will be nice.'

Chapter Twenty-Three

'Is there any news on Caspian?' Amy asked as she drove the car past Middle Street and on towards Gillingham.

'No change. I nipped in this morning to have a word with Doctor Spencer, who is looking after him. The prognosis isn't great. He lost a lot of blood in the attack and he has a punctured lung to go with it. It seems the assailant only missed his heart by an inch.'

'Fingers crossed for him,' Amy replied. 'He seems to hold the key to the entire investigation.'

'They're giving him less than a fifty-fifty chance, so we might need help from elsewhere if we're going to crack this case. One thing is obvious, though. He knows something that his attacker is desperate to keep secret. Whether it has anything to do with Nina or not, I'm not sure. He could have been up to anything, really. We know what sort of man he is. He needs to protect the lifestyle he's grown used to.'

Amy nodded and changed the subject. 'What time is Sal arriving? I bet Ferris is excited.'

'Why would he be excited?'

'Well, they did get on rather well the last time she came up.'

'Sal's friendly with everyone. I told Ferris not to read too much into her behaviour.'

'When did you tell him that?'

Bodkin turned his head and looked out of the window. 'Make the turn for the A2. We'll go through Chatham and Rochester, then pick up the A229.'

'Who's driving this thing?' Amy said. 'I've already got a route mapped out in my head.'

'If you're thinking about taking the Capstone Road, forget it. You'll get stuck behind a farm truck before we've gone two miles.' He looked at her seriously. 'I'm not kidding. It might look like a shortcut on the map, but in reality, it will take a good hour longer, maybe more.' He pointed to a signpost. 'It's going to save us a lot of time going by the A2 and the A229. We can't afford to be late.'

'But the A2 takes us west. We want to go south.'

'We'll be on much better roads, Amy, and it's a lot quicker, even though it looks like we're going out of our way.' He picked up his map from the footwell. 'Pull over, I'll show you what I mean.'

Amy said nothing and took the right-hand turn. 'So where do I go from Rochester? I know how to get there from the other day.'

'A229 to Maidstone, then pick up the A26 to Tunbridge Wells.' He pointed to the map. 'Want to take a look?'

Amy shook her head. 'You've travelled these roads a lot more than I have. I just thought I'd be clever and plan a route myself.'

'If we didn't have to be there for one o'clock, I'd happily let you drive me through the beautiful Kent countryside. In fact, the next time I get a day off, we'll take another trip down south and you can choose the route.'

Amy shook her head and flashed a quick smile. 'That will be sometime around February next year, will it? You never take time off.'

'I've got a few days due,' Bodkin said, scratching his head. 'I just need to get this case cleared up first, and Cyril's of course, then there's—'

'As I said, February next year.'

'I'll take a few days after this one is over. Ferris can have Cyril.'

'PAH! There's no way on this earth you'd give that one up, even though it's only small beer compared to some other cases. I know you, Bodkin. You named him so you'll have to be the one to bring him in.'

'Am I that obvious?' Bodkin said with a sigh.

'I can read you like that map,' Amy nodded to the footwell. 'Only I don't need to look at it.' She paused as she read a sign that told her Rochester was only six miles further along the road. 'And don't think you can distract me by talking about the best way to get to Tunbridge Wells. When did you say that to Ferris?'

'This morning,' Bodkin mumbled.

'Honestly, Bodkin, how many times do you need to be told? Sal can make her own mind up about the men she wants in her life. You're not her protector anymore.' She sighed. 'I thought we'd had this conversation.'

Bodkin studied his nails. 'I know but…'

'But nothing, Bodkin. If Sal and Ferris decide they like each other and want the situation to get more serious, it's got nothing to do with you. Ferris is a lovely man. Any girl would be lucky to have him.'

'Ferris as a brother-in-law,' Bodkin moaned. 'Imagine having to put up with all that singing.'

'It would be Sal who had to put up with all that singing, Bodkin. Unless you were thinking of moving in with them.' She gave a sideways glance. 'Anyway, they've only spent a couple of hours in each other's company. I don't think we'll be hearing wedding bells or the pitter patter of tiny feet just yet.' She gave him a wicked grin. 'They've got to get to know each other first.'

'All right, you win. I'll do my best to stay out of it. Ferris is a decent sort and there aren't many men I'd hand pick above him.'

'Listen to yourself, Bodkin,' Amy said in an exasperated voice.

'YOU DON'T HAVE A SAY, IT'S NOT YOUR LIFE, IT'S HERS.'

'That's what I meant,' Bodkin said, studying the road in front intently. 'A229, take the next left.'

'Do you know anything about the history of Tunbridge Wells?' Amy asked as they drove along the A229 towards Maidstone.

'I know it's a spa town, and it's spelt differently to Tonbridge, which isn't a million miles away from it,' Bodkin replied.

'I'll keep it brief. I don't want to risk boring you to sleep with the long version.'

'I'm all ears,' Bodkin replied, settling back in his seat.

'The mineral springs were discovered by a courtier of James the 1st, Dudley North, in the seventeenth century. He declared that the spa had cured him of some malady or other and before long, the place was inundated with the gentry, all wanting to take the waters.'

'Typical of the gentry,' Bodkin said. 'I bet not many peasants got to cure their ailments.'

'Bodkin, you really are obsessed with the well to do, aren't you?'

'Just saying... and it's true. How many working people got to sample the miracle waters?'

'Probably quite a lot of them,' Amy said, 'because it would have been the workers who came into the town to build the houses, lodges, shops and even the church that was required. I bet they gulped down a few gallons of the stuff while they were working on the new buildings.'

'I bet the rich buggers charged them by the pint,' Bodkin answered.

'You're hopeless, Bodkin,' Amy said. 'Here's Maidstone. What road am I looking for now?'

'The A26,' Bodkin replied. 'It will skirt Tonbridge, then take us all the way in.' He looked puzzled for a moment. 'While we're on the history lesson, do you know why a town so close to the Tunbridge Wells spells its name differently? I was given to understand that Tonbridge was the bigger town back in the day, so what gives with the names?'

'I do know the answer to that,' Amy said, as she drove through the outskirts of Maidstone, looking for any sign that mentioned the A26. 'Blame the Post Office. Until 1870 it was called Tunbridge and it was even mentioned in the Doomsday Book, but because there was a lot of confusion surrounding the towns by the letter posting public, the Post Office decided to rename the older town, Tonbridge. The population of the old town weren't impressed and demanded that Tunbridge Wells, being the far newer of the towns, should be the one to have its name changed, but the Post Office wouldn't be moved and it's stayed that way ever since. To make matters worse, Tunbridge Wells received the Royal title in 1908, one of only three towns in the whole of England, to receive the honour. This created even more bad feeling.'

'I can imagine,' Bodkin replied. 'If the council does so much as rename a road these days, the public denounces it. God knows what the Spinton population would do if Mossmoor was given a royal title.'

'Oh, one more thing I found out regarding Tunbridge Wells. It was the place where the first speeding ticket was handed out in 1896. The reckless driver... Arnold something... no, Walter Arnold, was fined a shilling for driving at eight miles an hour in a two miles an hour zone.'

'Blimey!' Bodkin replied. 'How did that work? Even horses travelled faster than that.'

'You haven't heard the best bit,' Amy replied. 'He was caught by a policeman who chased, then overtook him on his bicycle.'

Bodkin laughed heartily. 'The good old British Bobby, eh?'

Amy laughed along. 'You can just picture it, can't you? Oh, I wish I'd seen it.'

'A real live Keystone Cops moment,' Bodkin said, pointing left. 'A26.'

TEN YEARS AFTER

. . .

The Regency guest house was a rundown, three-storey Georgian building that was situated on the street that ran behind the Assembly Rooms theatre. Its peeling front door showed several layers of paint that had been applied by owners or managers of the once thriving business.

They found Rex Larson in the bar, sipping a glass of whisky. A cheap brand, Bodkin noticed as the barman wiped down the bottle and pushed it under the counter. As Amy stepped between the tables to cross the room, she took him in.

Although seated, he looked to be a tall rake of a man. His narrow eyes darted from side to side, giving him the appearance of being suspicious of everything around him. His black hair was obviously dyed, being a good two shades darker than even the darkest natural hair. The few neglected wispy white hairs hanging out of his collar showed the true colour of his thatch. The hair on top of his head seemed to lie strangely. Amy wondered if it was a toupee. His thin face showed off his cheekbones and prominent jaw. His mouth was in stark contrast to the rest of his face. His lips were full, almost feminine, and he reminded her of a goldfish when he pursed them to take a drink from his glass. His jacket had seen better days and while it didn't hang as badly as Bodkin's, it did have the look of an off the peg or even a second-hand suit. His shirt didn't look exactly freshly laundered, either.

He looked up, but didn't get up, as Amy and Bodkin arrived at his table.

'Mr Larson, I'm Inspector Bodkin and this is my associate, Amy Rowlings. I believe you were expecting us.'

'Five more minutes and I'd have been gone,' Rex said sullenly. He took another long sip of his scotch.

'Do you mind if we sit?' Bodkin asked.

Rex shrugged. 'It's a free country.'

Bodkin pulled out a rickety-looking chair for Amy, then sat

down himself on a chair that creaked under his weight. He looked around the shabby bar, the threadbare carpet, the damp patches on the flock wallpaper, the black mould in the corner of the ceiling. 'I hope your room is in a better state than this,' he said.

'I don't spend a lot of time in it. Anyway, I couldn't get into the Swan. They were full.'

'I bet this dump hasn't been full in a hundred years,' Bodkin said. He waved to get the barman's attention. 'Scotch, please, the decent stuff, not that paint stripper you keep under the counter.' He pointed to Rex's glass. 'Make that two.'

'Make mine a double if he's paying,' Rex said, looking over his shoulder.

Amy smiled at the barman. 'I'll just have a glass of lemonade. Have you got any ice?'

The barman shook his head. 'No, but the bottles haven't long come up from the cellar. It's freezing down there on the hottest of days.'

While the barman was preparing the drinks, Bodkin pulled out his notebook and pen. 'Now then, Rex... is it all right if I call you Rex or would you prefer Mr Larson?'

'Seeing as we have never met before and seeing as I honestly can't see us becoming friends, I think Mr Larson would be more appropriate.'

Bodkin waited for the barman to deposit their drinks on the table, then passed him a five-shilling piece. 'I expect change,' he said.

When his change was safely in his pocket, Bodkin tapped his notebook with the end of his pen. 'Rex, I suppose you're wondering why we've come all this way to see you.'

Rex tipped the remains of his whisky into the fresh glass and took a long sip. 'It wasn't to get my autograph. I know that.'

'Much as I can see the appeal in obtaining your signature, Rex, I'd like to see it at the end of a witness statement instead of scrawled across a publicity photograph. No, there is a far more important reason for wanting to speak to you today.'

'If it's about that girl in Folkestone, it was a mistake.' He looked at Amy as though she might lend her sympathies. 'She told me she was sixteen.'

Bodkin looked at him with distaste. Amy opened her mouth to speak, but thinking better of it, took a sip of her lemonade instead. The barman had been right; it was cool.

'How old are you, Rex?'

'I thought we had agreed that I was to be addressed as Mr Lar—'

'HOW OLD ARE YOU, REX?'

'I'm forty.'

'And the rest,' Bodkin sneered. 'I know for a fact that you are nearer fifty.'

Larson looked sullen. 'Then why ask?'

'Because I wanted to see what your second lie would be.'

'My second lie…?'

'Oh yes, the first was when you told us you thought the girl in Folkestone was sixteen. You knew damn well she wasn't. You like 'em young, don't you, Rex… the younger the better.' Bodkin paused as he glared at the actor. 'What's so attractive about them? The teenage spots, the inexperience, the way they melt under your flattery… maybe they just make you feel younger. Which is it?'

'I'm young at heart. That's all it is. I'm like Peter Pan. I never grew up.'

'We're here about someone who wasn't given the chance to grow up, Rex. A seventeen-year-old girl who was murdered and left to rot while her mother suffered agonies, wondering what had happened to her. Were you responsible for all that pain, Rex? Did you kill Nina Honeychurch?'

'You can't pin that on me,' Larson said as his forehead suddenly began to leak sweat. 'I didn't go anywhere near that cottage.'

Bodkin exchanged glances with Amy, then looked back at Larson, his lips tight, forming a thin, straight line.

'Who mentioned a cottage, Mr Larson? Now we have another

important question for you to answer. How did you know where she was left?'

Chapter Twenty-Four

Rex's face crumpled, and he began to sweat profusely. Black dye ran down his temples but oddly, not from his hairline, convincing Amy even more that he was wearing a toupee.

Bodkin leaned back in his chair, picked up his whisky, then put it down again without sampling it. 'Let's take things slowly, shall we, Rex?' He looked at his watch. 'You're not on stage for hours yet. We've got plenty of time to talk this through.'

'The play starts at seven-thirty,' Rex protested, 'and we've got rehearsals. I promised I'd be there for four.'

'That still leaves us three hours,' Bodkin replied. 'Though you probably won't be missed at rehearsals. Not with the role you've been given. I noticed the theatre billboard on the way in. You're hardly top billing these days, Rex. I had to get my binoculars out to read your name. It's right at the bottom. You come underneath the tea lady.'

Rex stiffened. 'I'm between roles at the moment. I'm just helping out here and there, keeping my hand in.'

'You're a has-been, Rex, that's the truth of the matter,' Bodkin said, receiving a kick on the leg under the table from Amy.

'I'm rebuilding my career after a lean time.'

'A lean time? I'd say it was more of a famine,' Bodkin scoffed.

'Work is hard to come by. There are so many actors and so few decent roles. Directors tend to want younger leads these days.' He paused. 'Mind you, when the war comes, they'll be begging me to perform. All the young men will be overseas getting shot at.'

'They want younger looking men. Is that why you try to hide your age with the hair dye?' Bodkin said, getting another kick from Amy, this time a little harder.

Rex took a gulp from his drink, looked surprised at the bit that was left in his glass, then downed it. Bodkin pushed his own whisky across the table towards the actor. Rex snatched it up without a word of thanks.

'Do you think your slump in popularity had anything to do with the newspaper reports? I don't think I'd last long in my job if the powers that be saw headlines like that.'

Rex gulped. 'They were mostly lies. They have to fill their columns with smut and I was the innocent victim.'

'Innocent?' Amy cut in.

'Most of it was lies. Made up tittle tattle. Even the tales that might have held a kernel of truth were blown up out of all proportion.'

'They ran a four page spread on you,' Amy said.

'As I said, they made most of it up.'

'For three weeks running,' Amy continued. 'That's an awful lot of lies, Rex.'

'Those girls were out to ruin me. They were talked into selling their stories to the papers by those scheming scandal sheet reporters. None of it would have stood up under scrutiny in the courts.'

'But you didn't challenge them in court. Why was that? You were libelled after all.'

'I couldn't afford a decent lawyer,' Rex replied. He pulled a dirty-looking handkerchief out of his pocket and mopped his brow, leaving black stains on the linen. 'Then I hoped it would just go away... it would have in time, but then that leech of an agent, Fabian Starr, dumped me and work dried up completely. I had to sell my flat, and because I had to sell it quickly, I lost money on it.' He dabbed at his temples with the handkerchief. 'I couldn't even get minor parts for the panto season. I rang around all the theatres in London but as soon as I mentioned my name they hung up the phone.'

'What did the police have to say about it all?' Bodkin asked in a slightly softer tone.

'There was no proof. It was their word against mine, so they couldn't prosecute.'

'Twelve young women's word against yours,' Bodkin replied. 'You were lucky as hell to get away with it.'

'You seem to know an awful lot about things that happened over six years ago,' Rex said, a bit of his fighting spirit returning.

'That's because I spent an hour on the phone to the News of the World newspaper this morning... at least my colleague did. They were very helpful. They're still very interested in you, Rex. They told my constable that if we finally got you in court, they'd make a five hundred pound donation to the charity of our choice, if they could have the exclusive.' He smiled across the table at Rex. 'Isn't that nice of them?'

Rex put his glass down and began to wring his hands. 'But I didn't do anything wrong.'

'That statement is for the birds,' Bodkin said sternly. 'You should have served time for satisfying your own perverted needs at the expense of those innocent young girls. You've ruined lives, Rex, so please don't expect me to feel sorry for you if yours has taken a downturn.'

Rex began to blubber like a child who has just seen its favourite toy washed away down the river.

'I can't help it. I just feel an attraction. I don't know how old they are. I never ask and they always wanted me to think they were a bit older than they were.' He pointed to his face. 'I can't even attract them anymore. Stress has taken its toll on me. I've aged twenty-five years in the last ten.'

'You haven't stopped trying though, have you, Rex? Not if the stories about Folkestone are true.'

'I told you,' Rex sobbed. 'That was a misunderstanding.'

'Of course it was,' Bodkin said, although he had no idea of what had occurred.

'Is it... going to be in the papers, too? I don't think I'll ever work again if it is.'

'We'll have to see about that,' Bodkin said, winking at Amy. 'It depends if you tell us everything about what happened at the Playhouse in Spinton on October 19th nineteen twenty-nine.'

Rex dried his eyes on his blackened handkerchief, then blew his nose. 'All right,' he said. 'Though my memories of events are very sketchy, I was heavily into certain substances at the time.' He looked under his eyelids at Amy, then down at his whisky glass. 'Where do you want me to start?'

Chapter Twenty-Five

'Let's start at the time we are interested in,' Bodkin said, leaning back in his chair and making it creak alarmingly. He reached into his pocket and pulled out the photograph of Nina. Sliding it across the table, he watched Rex intently. 'Did you ever meet this young lady?'

Rex took a quick look and shook his head. 'I don't think so.'

Bodkin slid the picture closer to the actor. 'Pick it up, Rex, have a proper look.'

Rex reluctantly picked up the photograph. He studied it for a few seconds, then put it down again. 'No, I don't remember meeting her.'

'I bet you met scores of girls of her age at that time.'

Rex nodded.

'You had to fight them off.'

'At times, yes.'

'What about the ones that wrote to you? Do you remember any of them?'

Rex shrugged. 'You know how it is. You get so many letters from fans.'

'I don't know how it is, Rex. I have no idea how it is.' He held out his hand towards Amy. 'But we'd like to know... enlighten us.'

'I'm not boasting, honestly,' Rex said, doing his best to look earnest. 'I used to get twenty letters a week sometimes. Hundreds in a year. I can't remember them all.'

'You used to put their pictures on a wall, didn't you?'

Rex looked suspiciously at Bodkin. 'A few...'

'The risqué ones?' Bodkin said helpfully.

'Some were rather, how shall I say, revealing?'

'And you used to encourage that, didn't you, Rex? You liked to have semi naked pictures of your young fans on your wall.'

Rex narrowed his eyes. 'I don't know where you're going with this but—'

Bodkin leaned across and tapped Nina's photograph. 'Do you remember getting letters from this young woman?'

'No, I don't. I'm not denying that she wrote to me, but I can't remember reading her letter.'

'Letters...plural,' Bodkin said.

'I had a part-time secretary at that time, she worked for Fabian, but she used to look after some of my fan mail.'

'Some of it? You mean the ones that you didn't reply to in person?'

'I answered the odd one when I had a bit of time on my hands.'

'You answered hers,' Bodkin said firmly. 'We've read them.'

Rex suddenly looked like a rabbit in the headlights. 'I, er...' he picked up the photograph again. 'Thinking about it, I do remember her. She was a big fan.' He looked across the table at Amy. 'You know how girls of that age get. They become infatuated.'

'And you led her so far along the garden path you went through the gate and into the hills beyond,' Bodkin replied before Amy could open her mouth.

'I didn't lead anybody on,' he tapped the picture, 'definitely not her.'

'Why not her? She was a very pretty young woman.'

'I'm not saying she isn't... wasn't... I just meant...'

'You used a code when you wrote to her... in one letter, at least,' Amy said.

'I er, I...'

'A code so simple a child could have cracked it. Where did you learn it...? You know, the one that reads top to bottom, the first letter of each paragraph.'

Rex blew out his cheeks. 'In the army. I used to send secret messages home to my girl.'

'How old was she?' Bodkin snarled.

'Now look here...'

'You gave Nina a secret message. Hinting that your next letter would be more personal and it would be delivered to one of her friends at the Amateur Dramatic club.'

Rex licked his dry lips, then cleared his throat. 'I was only flirting.'

'You asked her for another photograph, but you wanted her naked, or mostly naked. We've got all the letters, Rex. We know everything you ever wrote to her.'

Rex groaned and dropped his head into his hands. 'It was only a bit of fun.'

'Not to her, it wasn't,' Amy said. 'Not the way you signed off your letters. They would have seemed full of romantic promises to an inexperienced girl like Nina.'

'What can I say? I'm sorry, but I'm not like that now. I've changed.'

'No self-respecting young woman would write to you these days,' Bodkin snarled. 'Who wants to impress a past it old Lothario whose name only just creeps onto the bottom of the billboard?'

It seemed like Rex was about to argue the point. He opened his mouth, but then closed it again without saying a word.

'Back to Nina,' Amy said, giving Bodkin one of her looks. 'You arranged to meet her, didn't you?'

Rex screwed up his eyes as he thought. 'I might have. Look, I honestly can't remember those letters. I sent lots out saying pretty much the same thing.'

'Nina lied to her mother. She told her she was going to stay overnight with a friend in a small town called Mossmoor. Her mother even waved her off at the bus station in Rochester, thinking she'd be home the following day.'

'That was nothing to do with me.'

'To throw everyone off the scent, she got off the bus at Mossmoor and caught the train to Spinton. She had a little brown case with her. We don't know what was in it, we haven't found it yet.'

Rex lifted his hand towards his hair, but stopped just before his fingers touched his toupee. 'I didn't tell her to lie to her mother. I didn't promise her anything. I didn't even know she was going to turn up on the night. She probably only wanted her picture taken with me.'

'She was wearing her best silk underwear, Rex.'

Rex's hand slid over his mouth. 'She read too much into it.'

'Did you have your camera with you that night?' Bodkin asked. 'You told her you'd like to take a more revealing picture.'

Rex shook his head. 'I don't remember.'

'Finish your drink, Rex, I'll get you another one.' He raised his hand and waved to the barman. 'Same again all round.'

Bodkin looked towards the entrance as a well-dressed man stepped in through the front door. After taking a quick look around, he turned and walked out to the street before the door had had a chance to close. The policeman transferred his gaze to the barman, who shrugged and went back to pouring the drinks.

Amy picked up her fresh glass of lemonade and took a sip before returning her full attention to Rex. 'What do you remember about that night?'

The actor tilted his head. 'I was the star of the—'

'Not the performance, Rex,' Bodkin snapped. 'I'm sure Oscar Wilde would have been applauding you from his grave. We'd like to know what you did before the play, and what you did after you left the stage.'

'Good heavens...' Rex frowned as he thought. 'I got off the train in Spinton at one o'clock, with Fabian Starr. We were driven to a big hotel. I forget the name. It's the only time I've ever been there.'

'The Braithwaite,' Bodkin said, helpfully.

'If you say so. Anyway, I had a couple of drinks at the bar with Fabian... he likes a drink too... then we were picked up by the driver and taken to rehearsals at about four.'

'The same driver who picked you up from the station?'

'Yes.'

'Do you remember his name?'

'Hardly,' Rex scoffed. 'He was just a driver.'

Amy put her hand on Bodkin's, stopping him from asking the next question. 'His name was Chester Harvey.'

'Was it? I honestly can't remember minor details like that.'

Amy nodded in understanding, but then said. 'But you became quite friendly later in the day. You asked him if he could procure your stimulants, as you were running low.'

'Ah, that's right, I did, but that was much later in the day.'

'You got him to hang around just in case you needed anything during and after the performance.'

'Did I? It's possible, I suppose.'

'Did anything out of the ordinary happen during the rehearsal?'

'I remember their main man wasn't very good. Extremely wooden. He was supposed to be a pro, too.'

'Caspian? Caspian Stonehand?'

Rex shrugged. 'Again, if you say so.'

'You don't forget a name like that in a hurry,' Amy said.

'All right, I can remember, mainly because he was so dreadful. They had a young woman in the cast. She was very good.'

'You fancied her, did you? I assume you're talking about Imogen Beechwood. She would have only been seventeen or eighteen at the time.'

Rex shook his head. 'I remember she was very attractive. There was another woman there, too. She looked after me throughout the day. She was one of the staff, though, not a member of the cast.'

'Yes, we heard you took a shine to her. Her name was Margo Ashburner, by the way. She remembers you very well. She told us you couldn't keep your hands to yourself.'

Rex cleared his throat. 'I don't remember doing anything she didn't want me to do. She was begging for it.'

Amy closed her eyes and shook her head slowly. 'She was seventeen. She had no idea what 'it' was. The truth is, you took advantage of her.'

'I didn't... I mean we didn't... I didn't go all the way, if that's what you mean.'

'Only because there were people about,' Bodkin spat. He picked up his drink and put it back down again without taking a sip.

'What about after, Rex?'

'After?'

'After the performance. The Mayor and quite a few local dignitaries came backstage to meet you.'

'That's rather hazy, I'm afraid. I needed a top up. The adrenaline had been pouring through my system when I was on stage and I felt rather drained. My pick-me-ups were in my dressing room. I was pretty desperate for a lift, but Fabian wouldn't allow me as much as five minutes on my own. I can't remember names and faces, but yes, we met a few locals. It's something you have to put up with when you're a celebrity.'

'There were two young girls there too, waiting by your dressing room door. They weren't local dignitaries. They were sixteen, seventeen years old at most.'

Rex made a steeple with his fingers. 'They were old enough, Inspector. I didn't break any laws.'

'So you remember those two, then? They must have been pretty... how shall we put it... eager to please?'

'I had lots of female admirers back then. A lot of them were eager to please.'

'Did you have those two in your dressing room, or did you arrange to meet them later?'

'We had a bit of fun in the dressing room... until we were interrupted by that... what did you say her name was, Margo?'

'You had a hot date that night, Rex, or so you said. Was it with one of those young women, or both of them?'

'You've been listening to Fabian bloody Starr, haven't you?'

'I'm not going to tell you who provided that snippet of information, Mr Larson.' Bodkin narrowed his eyes. 'Just answer the question.'

'You shouldn't listen to that old drunk,' Rex spat. 'He's as bad as me, if not worse. I bet he didn't tell you about his casting couch, did he? I bet he didn't tell you about all the young wannabe actresses he's made to strip for a so-called screen test.'

Amy frowned. 'But Fabian Starr doesn't... can't... perform with women, can he?'

'Is that what he told you?' Rex roared with laughter. 'Ask any young actress on the circuit about Fabian Starr. Not one of the girls got a chance to perform in public until he'd road tested them.'

Chapter Twenty-Six

Bodkin slammed his hand down on the table, making both his whisky glass, and Amy, jump. 'You're sure about this, Mr Larson? Only we have been given evidence that would make the statement you just made, impossible.'

'It's true, ask any of the better looking actresses on his books.'

'I'm not sure they'd admit to it,' Amy said with a shake of her head. 'Are you sure about this? Were you ever present when... when the couch casting took place?'

'No, he wouldn't let me anywhere near that. It was his personal perk.'

'Is this still going on?'

'I would imagine so. I don't speak to the man anymore. You'd have to ask around, but a lot of people knew about it.' He sneered across the table at Amy. 'Especially the actresses.'

Bodkin suddenly got to his feet and called out to the barman. 'Do you have a telephone here?'

'We have, but it doesn't work. The GPO cut us off three months ago for not paying the bill.'

'Where's the nearest phone box... no, forget that.' Bodkin turned and pointed a finger at Rex. 'Move as much as an inch while I'm gone and you're nicked.'

Amy hurried after Bodkin as he headed for the door. 'Where are you going?'

Bodkin held the door open for Amy as he looked up at the buildings across the road. Spotting one with a line running into it from a wooden telegraph pole, he ran across the street and pushed open the florist's door. 'Kent police,' he shouted, causing the young woman behind the till and both her female customer's to hold up their hands as though they were being robbed. 'I need to use your telephone,' he explained, a little less forcefully.

'Parlour? It's Bodkin. Yes, yes, I know where I am... Listen. Do you know who rang Fabian Starr at his home this morning?'

Amy stood by the counter as Bodkin put his hand over the mouthpiece. 'Urgent police business,' he said to the still shocked women. 'Harbottle? Right, he's off duty now isn't he? No, don't bother Ferris, leave him in his room, he deserves a few hours off, you can do it. You have Starr's number there? Give him a call and tell him I want to see him urgently. Use another line. I'll stay on this one.'

He turned to the women again and nodded to the bouquet of chrysanthemums on the counter. 'Nice... erm... flowers... Yes, Parlour... what was that? Starr is out for the day and won't be back until after midnight? Did he leave a number to contact him on...? Damn... Right, listen carefully. I want you to leave Harbottle a note. When he rings Starr in the morning, I want a message passing on. He's to give me a call at the station before ten. If he fails to do so, he'll be in a cell in Paddington nick before he can shout impotent.'

Bodkin put the handset down and faced the three women again. 'Sorry about that. Enjoy the wedding.'

'It's a funeral,' the older of the customers said, but Bodkin was already on his way out of the shop, leaving Amy to apologise for him.

. . .

Rex was still in his seat when they returned to the bar, but the collection of empty glasses sitting on the table in front of him had grown. Bodkin's whisky glass being the latest addition to the cluster.

'Where were we?' Bodkin said as he waited for Amy to sit.

'You were just about to get another round in,' Rex said, waving his glass at Bodkin.

'You'll be lucky,' the policeman replied. He dragged the creaky chair away and pulled another one over from the next table, but heard an even scarier creak when he sat down.

Amy took a sip of her drink and pulled a face. The lemonade was getting a little warm. She put the glass back on the table and faced Rex again. 'You were about to tell us about your hot date.'

Rex ran his fingers around his empty glass. 'It didn't happen. The girls backed out.'

'Let's go back a bit,' Bodkin said. 'Hang on. I'm getting a bit thirsty myself.' He turned towards the bar. 'Have you got anything non-alcoholic?'

'I've got some bottles of Chalybeate water.'

'Give us three,' Bodkin said. 'And don't forget it's the same water we can get for free if we take a walk down to the spring.'

After giving the man one and six, Bodkin handed a bottle to Amy and one to Rex before unscrewing the cap from his and downing it in two long swallows. 'Nothing special,' he said, wiping the back of his hand across his mouth. 'Better than Spinton tap water, though.'

Rex took the top off his bottle and sniffed the contents as though it might contain poison. A second sniff convinced him. Pulling a face, he pushed the bottle towards Bodkin, who lifted it to his lips and took a long drink. 'To the gentry,' he said.

Amy grinned, then gave Bodkin another kick under the table. 'You were asking Rex why the girls didn't show up for the hot date at the George Hotel.'

'So I was,' Bodkin said, putting the bottle down. 'Well?' he said curtly. 'We're still waiting for an answer.'

'I don't know. We'd arranged to meet in the lobby. Chester had told me the George was the best place to go as they never asked questions about what went on in the rooms.'

'You were going to take both of them on? Phew! You must have had some energy back then, Rex.' Bodkin paused. 'Or was it the cocaine you were taking that gave your libido such a boost?'

'Cocaine, opium, you name it, I took it.'

Bodkin picked up his bottle of water and took another long drink. 'Take us back to when you were with the great and the good backstage. You had the girls in your dressing room, but for one reason or another, they sensibly decided to stand you up. Now I want to know what happened when you left the theatre. There were five girls waiting for you on the steps at the stage door.'

Rex furrowed his brow as he thought. 'Yes, that's right. We had a picture taken together, I signed a few autographs, then I shot off to the George.'

Bodkin tapped Nina's picture again. 'You signed a promotional leaflet for her on the steps.'

'If you say so.'

'You gave her a kiss and a cuddle and whispered something in her ear. What did you say to her?'

'I can't remember even giving her a kiss. I—'

'Try harder,' Bodkin interrupted.

'I, er, I might have said something like, you've got a long way to go to get home.'

'You didn't offer to take her to your hotel then?'

'No. As far as I knew, I had an appointment with two other girls.'

Amy glowered at him. 'So, you invite the poor girl... a young seventeen-year-old who had never been outside her hometown on her own before, to what she thinks will be a romantic tryst, only to toss her away like a piece of rubbish, leaving her alone in a strange town where she doesn't know a soul. For all you knew, she hadn't enough money in her purse to get a hotel room for the night.' She shook her head in distaste. 'I had a low opinion of you before I heard this, Mr Larson, but believe me, it's down in the gutter now.'

Larson sat back in his seat. 'I didn't do it intentionally. I was hyped up. I had used up the last of my cocaine supply. I was on a mission to see those girls.' He lowered his head. 'I'm sorry about what happened to her and I suppose I have to take some of the responsibility, but I didn't kill her. Honestly, it wasn't me.'

'You had a quick word with the driver before you left for the George, Rex. What was that about?'

'I asked him to get me a new supply of cocaine, opium, anything he could get his hands on.'

'So, the pair of you agreed to a meeting place for him to hand it over?'

Rex looked at the ceiling. 'I might have... No, I remember now. Chester said that he didn't have the money to buy what I wanted, but he knew someone I could get it from. He said he'd have a word with his contact and then meet me at the George in about an hour.'

'An hour? You must be a bit of an athlete if you thought you could look after two energetic young women inside an hour, less after checking in and the preliminaries.'

'He was going to meet me at reception. He was supposed to get the girl on the desk to ring my room to let me know he had arrived.'

'But that didn't happen, of course, because the girls decided they didn't fancy you that much after all. So, that begs the question, what did you do until Chester turned up?'

'I had a drink in the bar. I was getting really on edge. I knew I'd need more cocaine soon. Booze can help a bit with that.'

'Did you speak to anyone in the bar?'

'I don't think so. Other than the barman, that is. I just kept getting him to refill my glass.'

'Then what? Chester... and you seem to remember his name very clearly now, Mr Larson... Chester turns up with the drugs, with his contact?'

'Just him. He said the contact was worried he was being set up, so he wanted me to go to him.'

'Where did you meet?'

'At the edge of some woods, it was about a five-minute drive, no more than that.'

Amy leaned forward eagerly. 'So, you went to get your drugs?'

Rex nodded. 'It was a trap. A guy met us at the roadside and said he had the cocaine, but I had to go with him to get it. I was in a right state by then, I was sweating like a pig. Shaking like I had the flu.'

'You went with this man. Did he give a name?'

Rex shook his head. 'No, he just asked if I had the money. Then he said there was a party, and I was invited. Well, after the let-down at the George, I was delighted to hear that news.'

'You thought there was a party in the woods?'

'No, I assumed there would be a house, or hut even, I told you, I couldn't think straight.'

'What happened to Chester?'

'I told him to go. I said I'd see him at the hotel in the morning.'

'Which hotel?'

'I don't think I said. I assumed he'd go to the big one. Braithwaite is it?'

'So, he drives off and you follow this man into the woods?'

Rex nodded. 'We'd only walked fifty yards, a hundred at most, then a gang of men came at me from the trees. There must have been four or five of them. They beat the living daylights out of me. I remember dropping into the brambles, but that didn't stop them kicking me.'

'So they robbed you?'

'They took my wallet, my watch, my signet ring, even the St Christopher I wore around my neck. They even took my coat to check the pockets.'

'Then what?'

'They cleared off laughing. I waited a bit for them to get well away, then I tried to find my way back. I've got an awful sense of direction. I didn't get too far before the shock and the withdrawal symptoms struck. I remember falling to the ground and the next thing I knew, the sun was up and I was lying in a pool of my own vomit.'

'What did you do then?'

'I found my way back into town, eventually. I was trying to remember the name of the hotel so I could get a taxi and maybe get Fabian to pay for it when I got there.'

'But you didn't get a taxi. Why not?'

'Because I saw Chester standing next to his car outside the Milton Hotel.'

'Chester? What was he doing there?'

'I think he was about to pick Fabian up.'

'I'm sorry,' Amy said with a frown on her face. 'I don't understand. How did Chester know that Fabian would be there?'

'I assume that Chester was part of the scam that Caspian had dreamed up. You'll have to ask him about that.'

Chapter Twenty-Seven

Bodkin ran his hand over the stubble on his chin as he looked intently at Rex across the table. Amy pursed her lips as she took in the new information.

'Did Caspian actually admit to setting Fabian up?' she asked.

'No, I wasn't really interested in what they were plotting. I just needed to get some drugs into my system.'

'Where were you expecting to get those from? It was a Sunday. The chemists were closed and you couldn't trust Chester's contacts again after what had happened.'

'He rented a room in a small house on a Victorian estate at the time. He shared a bathroom with his landlady and she had all sorts of medication in there, including a half pint bottle of laudanum and a box of Medinal crystals.'

'Medinal? What's that when it's at home?' Bodkin asked.

'It's a barbiturate in salt form. You dissolve it in water. It helps with anxiety.'

Bodkin shook his head. 'You were on first-name terms with a lot of medications back then.'

'They did the trick, made me feel half human until I got home.'

'Did you hear any part of the conversation between Chester and Caspian Stonehand either in the street or in the hotel?'

'Nothing, but then the state I was in I wouldn't have remembered even if I had.'

'Did Fabian talk about his overnight experiences when you got back to the hotel, or when you were on the train home?'

'Again, I don't remember, the Medinal and Laudanum had kicked in by then. I just wanted to sleep.'

Bodkin drained his bottle of spa water and licked his lips. 'It grows on you, this stuff.' He pointed to Amy's bottle. 'You should try it.'

'I'll have it later, maybe on the way back,' Amy said.

Bodkin turned his attention back to Rex. 'I've only got a couple more questions for you, and then we'll be off.' He pretended to read something from his notebook. 'Let's go back to when you were outside the stage door. Who else was around?'

'The girls, Chester, and the photographer from the local paper. That's about it.'

'When you were waiting for the girls at the George, did you wait in the foyer or outside the hotel?'

'To begin with, in the foyer, but I did stand outside for a while. I thought maybe they were too shy to come into the hotel on their own.'

'When you were outside in the entrance lobby, did you see anyone walk by who you recognised?'

'I saw Fabian and the Mayor's party. They had a couple of women with them. I looked close, but they were in their thirties, possibly older.'

'No use to you, then. Were they heading for the Milton Hotel, just down the road?'

'I assume so.'

'Anyone else? You didn't see a young girl with a small brown overnight case, for instance?'

'Nina? No, I'll be honest here. If I'd seen her, I'd have tried to get her into the George with me. I had been badly let down, and I needed some company.'

Amy's lips tightened.

Bodkin leaned on the table and looked hard at Rex. 'How long did you wait before giving up and heading for the bar?'

'Ten minutes. I wondered if the girls got the wrong hotel, so I nipped down to the Milton and had a quick look in the foyer there.'

'Was Fabian about?'

'No, but there was a lot of squealing and shouting coming from the cocktail bar. There was a jazz band on. It sounded pretty full. He was probably in there.'

'You didn't look inside to see if your two... eager to please young ladies were pleasing someone else?'

'No. They weren't in the foyer and that's where I said I'd meet them, so I hurried back to the George in case they'd turned up late.'

'Did you pass anyone on the way?'

'Only that Caspian chap. He was on the other side of the road... oh, and I remember seeing Chester's car drive past. I was hoping his contacts lived close by.'

Bodkin picked up his notebook and pen, then got to his feet. 'That's it, Rex, you can go to your rehearsal, but we will want to speak to you again when we've had a chance to check out your evidence. Just remember this, though. If I find out that you told us even the tiniest insignificant fib, I'll be round to that theatre to arrest you, even if it means hauling you from the stage.'

Rex exhaled visibly. A look of relief swept across his face.

As they were walking away, Amy nudged Bodkin in the ribs and hissed. 'You didn't ask how he knew about the remains being left in the cottage. He brought it up without being prompted. How did he know what we were interviewing him about?'

'I was waiting for the right moment,' Bodkin said quietly. 'Just let him relax for a few more seconds.' He paused as they approached the door. 'Do you want to ask him or shall I do the honours?'

'I'll do it,' Amy said with a quick grin.

'Go for it,' Bodkin replied as he came to a halt only a yard short of the door.

'Oh, there was one more thing, Mr Larson,' Amy said, turning slowly around to face him. 'How did you know that we were going to interview you about the discovery of Nina's body? Inspector Bodkin didn't mention it when he set up the meeting. Also, how did you know about where the body was found? I doubt you get the Spinton Evening Post down here and as far as we are aware, the national press hasn't picked up on the story yet.'

All the colour drained from Rex's face.

'I...'

Amy tilted her head towards him, cupping her hand around her ear.

'Margo Ashburner telephoned the theatre to warn me that she had been questioned.'

'Margo? Why would she do that, Rex? Was she worried about you? Did she think you might need a bit of time to think up an alibi? And why on earth... in fact, how did she know where to find you after all these years?'

'We've been in touch since that night,' Rex replied with more than a bit of a tremor in his voice. 'We were lovers for a time. I told her it was over, but she's never accepted it.'

Chapter Twenty-Eight

Back at the car, Amy started up the engine and pulled out onto the main street that ran through the town. After stopping twice to allow pedestrians to cross, she soon found the signpost for the A26 and looked ahead for the turnoff.

'So, what did you make of that?' Bodkin asked as Amy straightened the car after a sharp bend.

'He was very evasive, obviously. He didn't tell us everything, even after giving us that confession about having a fling with Margo at the end.'

Bodkin pursed his lips. 'Bits of it ring true. It explains his dishevelled state on the night Nina disappeared, but it seemed more than a little convenient, losing his coat in the woods like that. He brought that point up deliberately, yet it seemed to be the most irrelevant part of what happened to him that night.'

'I thought that too, but I didn't want to push him until I'd had the chance to talk to you about it.' She tooted her horn to alert a large brown buzzard that was feasting on a rabbit's corpse in the middle of the road. 'He preyed on innocent young girls, that's a given. The way he treated young Nina was unforgivable... providing what he told us was true, of course. He might well have seen her on the street that night. What if he didn't get beaten up? What if he took Nina to the woods and she tried to fight him off? Maybe Chester helped him. He seemed to be playing Mr Fixit for everyone that night.'

'I'm quite looking forward to my next chat with Chester,' Bodkin said, shifting uncomfortably in his seat.

Amy pursed her lips as she thought. 'Then there's Caspian. He's hardly goody two shoes, is he? The more we find out about him, the more suspicious his behaviour becomes. We've heard that there was a young girl making a lot of noise in Fabian's room that night, but what if it was Nina screaming and the way that Caspian helped solve his little problem, was to bump her off?'

'All very plausible, but we can't really get to the bottom of that until we speak to Caspian himself.' He fidgeted in his seat again. 'Fabian and Caspian may well have concocted the story in the foyer that morning. Did Caspian have a car back then? That's something we have to check on. Although Rex said he saw him walking, he could have parked it up close by.'

'What are you fidgeting for, Bodkin? Have you got ants in your pants or something?'

'I need to... I think that spa water is about to make a reappearance. Perhaps I had one bottle too many. Can you pull over? I'll have to pee in the hedge.'

Amy turned her head back toward the road and watched the buzzard return to its meal as Bodkin seemed to take an age to rid himself of the excess water in his body. Eventually, he turned back to the car, and after spitting on his hands a few times, he wiped them on his handkerchief and in two bounds was back at the open passenger door.

'That's better,' he said. 'I don't think I could have lasted another mile, let alone the twenty odd we still have to go.' He climbed into his seat and slammed the door shut. 'Don't you want to go?'

Amy shook her head quickly. 'I'll find a public lavatory in Maidstone, thanks all the same. It's only a couple of miles away.'

'I wouldn't have lasted,' Bodkin said as Amy pulled away from the verge. 'That stuff goes straight through you.'

'What's the plan now?' Amy asked as she took the turning for Spinton. The journey had passed quickly, even though neither of them had spoken since Rochester. Both had been engaged in their own private thoughts, going over what Rex had told them.

'Where do you want dropping off?' Amy said, as though the car was hers. 'Police station or at Bluecoat House?'

Bodkin checked his watch. 'It's a quarter to five. You haven't eaten all day. We'd better get you home first. Sal should already be at my place. I gave her a key the last time she was here.' He rubbed his stomach. 'With a bit of luck, she might have started to cook dinner.'

'Do you have anything in the larder for her to cook?' Amy asked with a smirk on her face.

'There's a two week old cabbage and a couple of spuds with more roots growing out of them than there would be if they were in the ground,' Bodkin admitted. His face brightened. 'Maybe she brought food with her.'

Amy shook her head. 'You're hopeless, Bodkin. Did I ever tell you that?' She took a left onto Middle Street then a right turn and drove on for a hundred yards before pulling up outside Bodkin's apartment block.

Bodkin leapt out of the car and hurried fifteen yards up the road to look in the small car park. Sal's Ford was parked in Bodkin's spot.

'She's here,' he shouted to Amy, 'do you want to hang on for a sec while I get her? She's bound to want to say hello.'

As Amy slipped out of the car, she noticed a platinum blonde peeking through the curtains of a downstairs window. 'Trixie,' she hissed. 'I'll show you.' Grabbing Bodkin's arm, she turned him to face her, then standing on her tiptoes, she kissed him full on the lips. Bodkin responded by wrapping his arms around her and giving her an even more passionate kiss than the one he had given her outside the police station in Rochester.

Amy clung on for the full forty seconds the kiss had lasted. Then, when he finally pulled his head away, she gasped and said. 'Good grief, Bodkin, I was only proving a point to Trixie. I didn't expect the full on Cary Grant.'

Bodkin grinned and held his arms out. 'Fancy another one?'

Amy pushed him away and fanned her face with her hand. 'I haven't recovered from the last one yet. What brought that on?'

'It must have been the spa water,' Bodkin replied. 'You've still got that bottle in your bag. Can I have it?'

'Not likely,' Amy said mischievously. 'I'm saving that for my wedding night if it works that well.' She grinned at him wickedly. 'Just think, if you win the jackpot prize, you might be there to drink it yourself.'

A few seconds later, the front door opened, and Sal stepped out. She was an attractive woman in her mid-twenties with shoulder length dark hair swept back at her ears. She was pretty much the same height as Amy and wore a pleated skirt and a light blue blouse with a tiny star pattern on it. After giving Bodkin a hug and a peck on the cheek, she grabbed hold of Amy and pulled her into her arms. 'It's so lovely to see you again,' she said. 'I'm sorry Alice won't be coming tonight, but I'm sure we'll have fun.'

'Ferris has had two baths this afternoon in anticipation,' Amy said with a grin.

Bodkin cleared his throat, but Amy gave him a stern look as she wagged her finger at him. 'Don't you dare,' she mouthed.

'I hope he wears the same cologne he wore last time,' Sal said, winking at Amy. 'I went weak at the knees when I was dancing with him.'

'I don't suppose you brought any food with you?' Bodkin asked, quickly changing the subject. 'I haven't had time to get anything in.'

'I've binned everything you did have in,' Sal said. 'Your larder stank. I tell you, the most deprived people in the back streets of Spinton wouldn't have attempted to eat those potatoes, and as for that cabbage…'

'Yes, yes, but did you bring food?' Bodkin asked again.

'I got back from the shops about fifteen minutes ago,' she said.

'Then I'll cook, seeing as you have provided,' Bodkin offered generously.

'Not blooming likely,' Sal said with a look of distaste on her face. 'Anyway. I was too late for the best cuts of beef and the carrots the greengrocer had left, looked like the stuff I've just thrown out. So, it's going to be bangers and mash tonight.'

Bodkin rubbed his hands together. 'Righto, you get started, and I'll give Amy a lift home.'

Amy looked over her shoulder towards Trixie's window before she climbed into the car. The blonde bombshell was still peering between the curtains. Amy smiled sweetly and waved with her fingers, then she put her hand on her breast. Took a deep breath, flashed a glance towards Bodkin, fanned her face, and mouthed, 'PHEW!'

After a rushed Saturday evening bath, Amy sat in her dressing gown with a towel turban on her head while she ate the fish paste sandwiches her mother had made for tea.

'You're running late, our Amy. Don't bolt those sandwiches down, you'll end up with tummy ache.' Mrs Rowlings fussed about with the tea things. 'Alice won't mind waiting while you get ready, and I'm sure Bodkin will understand, seeing as he's the reason you're behind schedule in the first place.'

'Alice isn't coming tonight. She hasn't got a babysitter.'

'Where's Miriam?'

'On the coast with her Michael. They're having a night away.'

'Ooh,' Mrs Rowlings pulled out a chair and sat down quickly. 'Where have they gone? Is it just for the night? Are they back tomorrow? Did she say anything about getting engaged to Michael?'

Amy giggled. 'You know all that I know, Mum. It's up to Miriam if she wants to share any juicy gossip, and we won't get to hear that until she comes back.'

Mrs Rowlings got to her feet again and picked up the teapot. 'I'll get us a refill, shall I? Oh, and tell Alice that I'll babysit Martha any time she likes. I'm surprised she hasn't asked.'

'She doesn't want to put on anyone, Mum, but it is very kind of you to offer. I'll tell her when I see her tomorrow.'

'Has Bodkin's sister arrived? I bet Constable Ferris is looking forward to seeing her.'

'She has, Mum. She's busy cooking for Bodkin.' She smiled as her mother stroked the teapot, holding it at her midriff like a pet cat.

'What?' Mrs Rowlings said.

'Ferris will be delighted to see her again, though I don't think Bodkin is that keen on them being together. He's still very protective of her.'

'Well, I'm not surprised after what he had to go through to keep her safe when they were growing up.' Mrs Rowlings wiped a tear from her eye as she thought about it. 'And his father, a God fearing man too.'

'He hid behind his religion.' Mr Rowlings peered over his copy of the Evening Post. 'Real Christians don't act that way towards their children.'

Amy bit her tongue. She knew many an alleged Christian family in the town where the father ruled with a rod of iron. Bodkin's father had gone further than most with his discipline, even with his young daughter, but she knew he wasn't alone in thinking the way he did.

'Sandy Miles is spouting off in the paper again,' Mr Rowlings said, noticing Amy's struggle to keep her thoughts to herself.

'What's he boasting about this week?' Amy asked.

'It seems the Romeo burglar has struck again. He was almost caught this time. A Mr Winder who works a split shift, not an all-night one, arrived home to find him climbing out of his parlour window, so he gave chase. He almost had him, he got hold of his cloak... well, blanket... what is it Bodkin calls him? It's a much better name?'

'Cyril de Burglar,' Amy said. 'What happened next?'

'He managed to slip out of the blanket and threw it over Mr Winder's head. Then he made his getaway.' He read from the page. 'To say how portly the man is, he has a quick turn of foot.'

Amy laughed. 'Good Old Cyril.'

'You're not glad he escaped, are you, our Amy?' Mrs Rowlings looked shocked.

'Noooo, I want him caught, but I want Bodkin to be the one that brings him to heel. He can't wait to spend a bit more time on the case.'

'That's all right then. I'm sure Bodkin will get him off the streets soon and the women of Spinton can sleep safely at night again.' She turned and walked towards the kitchen. 'That was very good, Amy. Bring him to heel, quick of foot,' she chuckled to herself as she walked through the open doorway.

* * *

When the projector broke down only half an hour into the James Cagney, Humphrey Bogart film, Angels with Dirty Faces and after a further fifteen minutes of slow hand clapping, Bodkin led Amy, Sal and Ferris through the back gate of The Bell Inn and held out his hand, motioning for Amy and Sal to sit at one of the plank tables. They had all seen the movie before, so they weren't too disappointed that the pleasure of watching it for a second time had been cut short.

Bodkin walked up the steps to the back door and reappeared five minutes later with their drinks on a wooden tray. Amy sipped at her port and lemon and made a smacking noise with her lips. 'They know how to serve a drink here. You don't get two slices of fruit at the Old Bull.'

Ferris was sitting next to Sal on the opposite side of the table. They had been in free flowing conversation ever since they had come out of the picture house.

'It's a good job you came this week and not next,' Ferris said. 'I'm singing at the Milton Hotel on Saturday. It's my monthly slot with the house jazz band.'

'But I'd love to hear you sing, Ferris,' Sal replied. 'I'm looking forward to it so much.'

Ferris looked down at the table, then back up at her under his eyelids. 'I'd rather be sitting with you that standing twenty yards away. I like talking to you.'

As Sal put her hand on top of Ferris', Bodkin opened his mouth to speak but was cut off by Amy, who gave him a stern look.

'BODKIN!' she hissed.

Bodkin stuck his tongue in his cheek and remained silent.

'Our famous roving reporter, Sandy Miles, was on the front page of the Post again tonight. Have you seen it?' Amy asked.

Bodkin shook his head. 'What revelation has he come out with this time? Is it to do with Nina?'

'Cyril,' Amy replied. 'He was nearly caught, someone snatched his cloak, and it was only because he's so fleet of foot, despite his portly appearance, that he managed to escape.'

'Ah, I know about that,' Bodkin replied. 'Mr Windup came into the station while we were in Tunbridge Wells.'

'Mr Winder,' Amy corrected him.

'Well, he wound PC Parlour up like a clockwork toy,' Bodkin said. 'He tore strip after strip off him for over half an hour. The man has a thick Welsh accent and Parlour couldn't understand half of what he was saying, so what he wrote down on his pad was pretty much all nonsense.'

'Poor Parlour,' Amy said with a short laugh. 'He does get a bit confused at times.'

'I haven't got over the marshy Sodden lands yet,' Bodkin said, picking up his pint.

Amy spat a mouthful of port and lemon back into her glass. 'That was priceless,' she said.

When they had recovered from their joint fit of laughter, Amy put her hand on his arm and, after shooting a quick look at the happy Sal and Ferris, tried to keep Bodkin's attention on her.

'How will you go about catching Cyril?' she asked.

'We'll either get lucky or he'll get careless. One or the other,' Bodkin said. 'Although I think we could set a trap for him. If we had the manpower and if his crimes were a little more serious than they are.'

'It is pretty serious, breaking into people's houses,' Amy said.

'Of course it is,' Bodkin agreed, 'but he hasn't stolen anything and he hasn't hurt anyone, so according to the powers that be, he isn't our main area of concern. They'd like to see this historic murder case cleared up and there *is* another burglar going about his trade, who *is* stealing and who *has* injured someone during an attempted robbery.' He took a long pull of his pint. 'I haven't seen the details of that yet. The Mossmoor police are still looking into it. They'll pass it on to us soon enough.'

'Hopefully. Last time it took them ten years to talk to Spinton.'

'Maybe they've been taught a cruel lesson,' Bodkin replied as he looked over at Ferris and Sal.

Amy tugged at his sleeve to get his attention. 'How would you go about catching him if you had the manpower?'

Bodkin smiled. 'Have you ever studied the Jack the Ripper case? Properly studied it, I mean?'

'I'm aware of it of course, and I did read up on it at the library. It's a very interesting case. Who do you think he was?'

'I can't make my mind up,' Bodkin replied, 'but I've studied every murder in detail and I've seen all the maps they drew at the time.'

Amy leaned towards him, fully engrossed now. 'Maps?'

Bodkin pulled out his notebook and his pen and drew a square. Inside the square, he drew a series of double lines representing streets. Finally, he marked a few of those streets with small, filled-in circles.

'Criminals usually stick to an area they know well, whether it's a multiple murderer like Jack, or a burglar like Cyril.' He pointed to the centre of the map with his finger and drew an imaginary large circle with it. 'They like to operate in a place where they feel comfortable, a place they know like the backs of their hands. They'll know every bolt hole, every alleyway, every climbable fence. Jack's crimes all took place in less than one square mile. I'd put money on the fact that Cyril's area of opportunity is even smaller than that. My bet is, he lives pretty much in the centre of Spinton, though I'd have to plot his break-ins on a map to be sure. He appears to be an intelligent man... well-read at least, so he might live in the better quality houses down by The Mill. The only thing that draws me back to the centre of Spinton is his get up. A tatty blanket, a cardboard tricorn hat. He's well off enough to be able to afford a car, or he might have the use of one through his job, but he isn't well off enough to actually buy a Cyrano costume although they are available to buy or hire from a number of fancy dress shops down in Gillingham.'

'Blimey! That was quite forensic, Bodkin. You have given this a lot of thought, haven't you?'

Before Bodkin could reply, they heard brakes squeal and a few seconds later, PC Parlour rushed into the pub yard.

'Found you at last, sir. Trixie said you'd be in the Roxy and after that, the Old Bull, but the Roxy was empty and you weren't in the Old... obviously, as you're here.'

'Calm down, Parlour,' Bodkin said, getting to his feet. 'What's so important you need to drag me away from my beer?'

'It's that actor chappie, sir. PC Harbottle took the message but he can't drive so he called me down from my room. Then Trixie thought you were at the Roxy, so it would have been a waste of time ringing around the pubs, so—'

'Spare me the tour of Spinton, Parlour. What's happened?'

'Casper Stonefinger, sir. He died about half an hour ago. We've got two murders on our hands.'

Chapter Twenty-Nine

As Parlour left the pub yard, Bodkin took a last lingering look at his beer, then motioned with his hand for Ferris to get up. 'Come on, Ferris, this isn't a time for sweet talk. There's police work to be done.'

'What are you expecting to do at this time of night?' Amy asked. 'Have you suddenly magicked up a new list of suspects that have to be interviewed before midnight in case they turn into pumpkins?'

'That doesn't even make sense,' Bodkin said, giving her a quizzical look.

Amy shrugged. 'You know what I meant. Anyway, you were only saying earlier today how Ferris deserves a bit of time off.'

Bodkin gave in. 'All right, but I want you in early on Monday, Ferris.' He turned and looked down at his still seated sister. 'And don't think this means you can come home at all hours. I'm on the sofa, remember?'

'BODKIN!' Amy shouted.

Sal gave Bodkin a thin smile. 'It's been many years since I last took advice from you on what time I should come home, G.' She picked up her drink. 'I'm not about to start taking it again anytime soon.'

Bodkin opened and closed his mouth, but no sound came out. He turned back to Ferris. 'Just you make sure you...'

He didn't get to finish the sentence because Amy took hold of his arm and dragged him towards the gate. When they reached the pavement on the other side, she spun around to face him.

'Have a listen to yourself, Bodkin. For pity's sake, man, she isn't sixteen anymore. She's years older than me and yet you seem to think it's all right if I hang around in male company.'

Bodkin visibly deflated. 'Oh God,' he said. 'What have I done?'

Holding his hands up in submission, he walked back into the pub yard and stood in front of the table with his hands clasped together. 'Sal... Ferris, please ignore that outburst. I wasn't thinking straight... the news tonight and... well, I don't suppose that's an excuse for it. I'm truly, truly sorry.' He gave his sister a weak smile. 'Sal, I know you don't need my advice anymore. You coming back into my life after all these years has been the best thing ever to happen to me... apart from meeting Amy, that is. It's just... I suppose it's just hard letting go, but I promise I'll do it. You won't hear anything like that from me ever again.' He turned to Ferris. 'Ferris, mate... I can't apologise enough. I really mean it when I say that Sal couldn't be in safer hands. Take her over to the Milton tonight, spend a bit of that money you make from singing on her. She's worth every penny. Give her the time of her life and if you don't get home until after the cocktail bar shuts at three o'clock, that's fine by me. Dance her toes off.'

As he turned away from his smiling colleague, he found that Sal had got to her feet and was standing at his side. She threw her arms around his neck and kissed him on the cheek. 'G,' she said, using the first letter of his long abandoned Christian name. 'You've been there for me for my whole life, my big brother, my protector, and I love you dearly for it. Never let go. You don't know how much strength it gives me, knowing that you're always at my side.' She leaned back and looked into his face, his eyes glistening with tears. 'Off you go now, big brother. Catch those bad guys. It's what you were born to do.'

Amy, standing by the gate, wiped a few tears from her own eyes as she witnessed the scene. Then, before Bodkin turned away from his sister, she slipped through the gate and walked across to the waiting police car.

Chapter Thirty

They drove to the police station in silence, neither of them wanting to bring his outburst up, but as soon as they walked through the front door into the reception area, Bodkin became businesslike, barking out instructions to anyone in the vicinity. Amy stood back with a look of awe on her face.

'I love it when you get all bossy,' she said. 'You might get to win that bottle of spa water after all.'

Bodkin grinned. 'If I went too easy on them, they'd only take advantage. We have to run a tight ship. The public deserves it.'

'You should stand for the council,' Amy said.

'Perish the thought,' Bodkin replied. 'I'd have everyone locked up inside a week once I got to know how their little money-making schemes worked.'

He was stopped from elaborating on his imaginary mission when PC Harbottle put the handset down and called to him.

'Sir, there's been a development.'

'Stonehand or Honeychurch?'

'Both, possibly, sir, but definitely Stonehand. As you are aware, we've been trying to find Jack Draper for the last couple of days, but no one's seen hide nor hair of him. His employer told us he didn't turn up for work on Friday and his landlady said he hasn't been home since tea time on Thursday either.'

'So, what's the new development?' Bodkin asked.

'A lady was on the blower, sir. She said she thinks she might know where he is.'

'Ring her back,' Bodkin said quickly. 'I'll speak to her.'

'I can't really, sir. She thought there might be a reward. When she was told there wasn't, she lost interest and hung up. She sounded tipsy, sir. I think she was ringing in from a call box, or maybe a pub phone.'

Bodkin sighed. 'Okay, I'll look into that one with the GPO in the morning. Do we have an address for Draper's mother?'

'No, sir. But we know she's somewhere in Dover.'

'How do we know that?'

'Draper's landlady told the officer checking up on him, that his mother often writes to him. She's happy to have a look through his things to see if there is a telephone number among his letters, one he can use in case of emergency, perhaps.'

'The good old British landlady, eh?' Bodkin replied. 'I bet she's already been through them a dozen times already.' He sighed, looked at his watch, then at Amy. 'It's still only eight-thirty. What say we have a wander over to see this helpful landlady? What's her name, Harbottle?'

'Mrs Creasy, sir. Forty-six Nelson Street. That's on the old Victorian estate. I'm surprised anyone still lives there. Those houses have been earmarked for demolition for years.'

The demolition work on Nelson Street had in fact already begun, the last five houses on the right-hand side had been reduced to piles of rubble in which rats, mice, cats and family dogs either searched for prey, or places to hide from their predators.

Number 46 was a smoke stained, once red brick house with dirty sash windows on the ground floor and a broken upstairs window, screened with a thin sheet of plywood that kept out the worst of the weather. The front door was made up of panels, the longer ones at the bottom and the shorter two at the top. The letter box was long gone, leaving just a dark slot for any mail the household received.

Bodkin rapped his usual rat-a-tat-tat on the mullion in the centre of the door. It was opened almost immediately by a scrawny-looking woman in her late fifties. She wore a dirty green pinafore and threadbare slippers. Her stockings bunched around her ankles and the bow she had tied in her headscarf to form a turban had come loose. She frowned as she opened the door, causing her already lined forehead to form even deeper creases. Looking at her, Bodkin thought about how fitting her name was.

'Mrs Creasey?'

'Who's asking?'

Bodkin produced his card. 'I'm Inspector Bodkin and this is my associate, Miss Rowlings.'

'I've seen her about. She's the goody-goody church girl.'

'We've come to ask about your lodger, Jack Draper.'

'I told your constable all I know about him.'

'You offered to go through his things, his letters, belongings.'

'I was only trying to help.'

'It has been noted, Mrs Creasey,' Bodkin said, leaving her unsure whether that was a good or bad thing. 'Have you done that?'

'No, I was going to give him a week or so to come back. He's been a decent tenant, not like that bloke who rents the attic. A right fly by night, he is. If you take my advice, you'll arrest him, not Jack.'

'We might look into his activities at a later date, Mrs Creasey. Now, about Jack's room?'

'Out until all hours he is.'

'Jack?'

'No, Donald Meriweather. He's a salesman but who wants to buy anything at two in the morning, I ask you... Mind you, I think he's nipping over the other side of the estate to see the girls near the station, if you get my drift.'

Bodkin forced a smile. 'Do you think we could see Jack's room?'

Mrs Creasy reluctantly stepped to the side and pointed up the bare, well-worn staircase. 'His room is on the right, first landing.'

'Is it locked?'

'I don't allow locked doors in this establishment. It only encourages men to bring their fancy women back.'

'Thank you, Mrs Creasy,' Bodkin said as he stepped onto the dirty, cracked, tiled floor of the hallway.

'She doesn't need locks on the doors. No one could sneak up that creaky staircase without being heard,' Bodkin said as he stepped onto the landing.

Draper's room was a surprise to both Amy and Bodkin. The place was almost spotless. The bed was made in a military fashion with the folds in the corners running at an almost perfect ninety degrees and the sheet turned down by what Bodkin was sure would be an exact nine inches. There was very little by way of belongings in the room. A photograph of a woman in an Edwardian dress sat on the chest of drawers, the top drawer of which had been left open, along with the door of the single wardrobe. Bodkin reached up and pulled down a battered, brown suitcase, which, when he undid the straps, he found to be empty.

'I don't know if he's done a runner or not,' he said as he opened the wardrobe door a little further and pushed the three shirts and a jacket that were hanging there apart. Neatly folded on the shelves were two pairs of trousers, a pullover, and a thick jumper. On a hook on the back of the door was a winter coat.

'Well, he hasn't taken all his belongings, so he was either in a big hurry or he has plans to come back at some stage.'

'There are three pairs of pants and a couple of pairs of socks in the drawers.'

Bodkin crouched down by the smart, highly polished bedside cupboard and pulled open the small drawer at the top. Inside he found an old bible with Draper's name inscribed on the flyleaf and two photographs of what looked to be himself as a teenager standing alongside a young man wearing a suit. In the cupboard below, he found the treasure. A stack of letters with a Dover street address written in a shaky hand on the top left-hand corner of each letter.

Mrs Emily Draper

The Cliffs Nursing Home

Dover

Kent

Bodkin skimmed through a couple of the letters, then stacked the whole pile together and handed them to Amy to put in her bag.

'Sal's going back to Dover late tomorrow afternoon,' he said. 'I might cadge a lift with her.'

'That means I can't come,' Amy said, giving Bodkin her sad look. 'I'm working at The Mill on Monday.'

'I doubt you'll miss much. He can't be hiding out there. It's a rest home. I'll make a full report on Monday. I'll get the ten o'clock train back. I'll nip over to The Mill at lunchtime if I find out anything interesting.'

As it was still only nine-thirty, Bodkin drove to Long Lane and parked the car outside Amy's cottage. 'I'll get Spencer to give me a lift over to pick it up in the morning,' Bodkin said. 'I'll catch the last bus back to town tonight.'

The Old Bull was busy, as it usually was on a Saturday night. The bar was crammed with men who jostled, heaved, pushed, and even fought for their places at the bar. The snug was much quieter. It was the place where the wives gathered to catch up on the week's gossip, free of the smell of sweat that hung like an invisible cloud over the barroom. Men occasionally nipped into the snug on their way to the lavatory to check on their women or to hand them a few pennies to allow them to buy another drink. The majority, though, were working women who had some sort of control over the small change lying in the creases at the bottom of their purses.

Amy waved to a group of fellow Mill workers as she waited at the bar with Bodkin. After being served, he led her across the room to a pair of tables covered in empty glasses left by the bench seat's previous occupants.

'What's on for tomorrow?' Amy asked as soon as they had cleared the contents of their table, stacking the glasses up on the small round table in the corner.

'Sal's not going home until after six, so I'll be working most of the day. If there's anything relating to our cases on my desk in the morning, I'll come and see you after church. Unless you're doing your charity thing, of course. There are two extra ladies on the lookout for food handouts this week.'

'I'm not on the roster for tomorrow, so I'll probably just go down to see Alice.' Amy took a sip of her drink. 'Not as nice as the Bell.' She took another, longer sip, then put her glass on the table. 'I might drop in on old Con, though. He's having a bit of trouble with the local youth.'

'Trouble?'

'I caught a few of them pelting him with missiles again when I dropped off the blankets I bought him this morning. He claims the boys don't bother him overmuch, but I'm sure they do. It can't be nice being bullied like that.' She picked up her drink again. 'I know the boys in question. I'm so tempted to have a word with their parents. They'll be at church tomorrow.'

'Will the boys be there?'

'Oh, yes, they go every week. They don't seem to learn anything from the sermons, though.' She paused. 'They're not bad lads, but they're easily led by their friends.'

'Tell you what,' Bodkin replied. 'I'll meet you outside the church and we can say hello to their parents. I'll introduce myself and just chat about this and that. I won't even mention Con. Just seeing a copper talking to their mums and dads ought to be enough to warn them off.'

'Would you do that for Con? That's very kind of you, Bodkin.'

'I'm doing it primarily for you, but if it helps the old boy, and it turns two young lads away from criminal activity, then it's time well spent.'

Just then, Pauline Ferguson, who was in a group of women over by the fire, began an impromptu dance while singing Knees Up Mother Brown. Her friends sang along and by the time the song ended, most of the snug had joined in. Delighted with the response, Pauline sang Don't Dilly Dally on the Way. Amy was delighted as she found Bodkin clapping and singing along to the old music hall song. Pauline was in good voice and led the Old Bull snug choir through three more songs before theatrically grabbing at her throat and demanding a free drink from the landlord for 'royally entertaining his customers'. Stan declined, but Bodkin handed her a glass of gin when he went to the bar to get fresh drinks for himself and Amy.

Later, as the pair were walking arm in arm past the telephone box at the top of Long Lane, Amy put her head on his shoulder and snuggled in.

'Thank you for tonight, Bodkin, I really enjoyed the sing song. I love it when you let yourself go a bit.'

'I'm not really a singer,' Bodkin said. 'I join in with the chants at the football, though.'

'Your voice isn't too bad,' Amy replied. 'You can hold a note, you've got quite a strong voice, it must come from shouting, "Stop, police" at the crooks every day.'

'I don't shout it much these days,' Bodkin replied, leading her across the lane. 'The uniform lads get to do that.'

'You're not as good as Ferris, obviously,' Amy continued. 'But you're not bad. I could listen to you while you were singing in the bath.'

'Very few are as good as Ferris,' Bodkin said. 'And I don't sing in the bath. I have to share one with three other people. Not at the same time,' he added.

'Sing me a song, Bodkin,' Amy said, coming to a halt. 'Go on, sing me something. Pretend you live in a big house with a huge echoey bathroom and there isn't another house for miles around, so you can sing as loud as you like.'

Bodkin looked around, hoping to see someone else walking down the lane that he could use as an excuse to get out of it, but apart from them, the lane was empty.

'Go on, Bodkin, sing me something... How about an old music hall song? I'm not expecting a Bing Crosby number.'

Bodkin shrugged and began to walk slowly towards Amy's house. 'I don't know many songs.'

'How about, Daisy Daisy?'

'All right, I know that one.' Bodkin looked over both shoulders, then silently counting himself in, he began to sing.

'Amy, Amy, give me your answer do...'

Amy let go of his arm and walked backwards, swinging her hands as though conducting an orchestra.

'I'm half crazy all for the love of you.

It won't be a stylish marriage,

I can't afford a carriage.

But you'll look sweet, upon the seat

of a bicycle made for two.'

As he hit the last note, the window of the cottage next to Amy's opened and an elderly lady stuck her head out.

'You don't need a bloody bicycle. You've had that car parked outside my house all night.' She paused for breath. 'What are you doing bellowing songs out at this time of night, anyway? You ought to know better, being a copper.'

The head retreated and the window was slammed unceremoniously.

As Amy tried desperately to keep in the giggles that were building up, Bodkin flicked the catch and opened the gate. 'Well, that ruined the moment,' he said. 'I was just about to get down on one knee.'

Amy removed her hand from her mouth to let the laughter escape.

'Oh, Bodkin, Mrs Dormer will live off that story for weeks. It's a good job you didn't, even if you were only messing about.'

Bodkin took her in his arms and kissed her on the lips. 'I'll do it for real one day. You just see if I don't.'

Chapter Thirty-One

Bodkin was as good as his word and as Amy walked out of the church with her parents on Sunday morning, she found him waiting at the top of the gravel and slate path that led to the lychgate. After greeting him with a kiss on the cheek, they chatted together until the parents of the two boys had thanked the vicar for his sermon. Roland and Peter stood anxiously by as Bodkin stepped forward and introduced himself. A couple of minutes later, after handshakes and smiles, he stepped away and nodded towards the boys, who looked at each other with wide eyes before scurrying after their families.

'Thank you, Bodkin, I'm sure that will help. You put the fear of God into those kids without saying a word to them.'

'All in a day's work, miss,' Bodkin touched his forelock. 'Are you going over to see Alice now? I really should catch up with some paperwork. I've got to give Chief Inspector Laws my report at some stage tomorrow.'

'Did Sal enjoy her night out?'

'I assume so. She didn't get in until three. Ferris dropped her off at the front door.'

'Don't tell me you were waiting up for her,' Amy said, horrified.

'I was asleep on the sofa when they got back, but their childish giggling woke me up. I was sleeping with the window open.' He pulled a face. 'I know how your neighbour, Mrs Dormouse, feels now.'

'Dormer,' Amy corrected. 'Was Ferris singing then?'

'His mouth was too busy to sing. Let's just leave it at that.'

Amy clapped. 'Well done, Ferris.'

Bodkin shook his head. 'Those two are the noisiest kissers. It sounded like they were in a custard eating race.'

Amy laughed. 'Oh, Bodkin, I do love your descriptions.'

He checked his watch. 'I'd better get back to the office. I want to give Margo Ashburner another call to see if she's back yet.'

'Let me know if she does come home,' Amy said. 'I'd like to be there when you talk to her. Oh, I meant to ask, did Fabian Starr call?'

'His secretary did... I know... on a Sunday too. It appears that Fabian has a really heavy summer cold. He's taken to his bed, so it will be a few days before we can speak to him.'

'That's rather convenient. I'm surprised you let him get away with that.'

'Oh, I didn't. I told her that if that's the case, a telephone conversation won't be enough. I want him here in person on Saturday, and before lunch, too.'

'What did his secretary say to that?'

'She said she'd have a word with him about the appointment. I told her that if she didn't want to see him dragged out of his flat by two burly policemen, she'd write that date down in his diary in red ink.'

Amy laughed. 'I bet she loved that.'

'She took it seriously, at least. She rang back only two minutes later to say he'd be here as requested. I asked if the agency kept a client album with photographs and contact details. She said they did, so I told her that he would need to bring it with him. I'd like to know which of them he's had on his casting couch.'

Amy walked with Bodkin until he turned off for Middle Street, then she carried on along the Gillingham road until she got to the turnoff for the woods, singing Gershwin's Summertime, as she walked. She soon found herself at the entrance to the Witchy Wood and three or four minutes later, she took the fork in the path and made her way towards Con's makeshift tent. As she approached, two figures came hurtling towards her.

'Roland Tandy, Peter Swain, what have you two been up to?'

'Nothing, Amy,' Roland said with a shocked look on his face. 'It wasn't us. We didn't do anything. We only came to say sorry.'

Amy looked from one boy to the other. 'Come on,' she said. 'Let's have a look.'

'It's nothing to do with us,' Peter said. 'We just found him like that.'

Amy hurried into the clearing with the two boys lagging a few yards behind. At first she couldn't see anything wrong, then she saw the prone figure of Con, lying on his back at the front opening of his tent. His eyes were closed and his long hair was spread over his mouth. She hurried across the clearing and crouched down next to him. The stench was overpowering, but after looking to the side and taking a deep breath, she turned back to him and, using her St John's training, she felt for a pulse. It was there, but it was very weak. After taking another deep breath, she brushed the hair away from his mouth and stroked his cheek. 'Con,' she said. 'Can you hear me, Con?'

The old man's eyelids flickered, but his eyes remained closed. Amy got to her feet and hurried back to the boys. Dipping into her bag, she pulled out her purse and selected four one penny pieces from it. After handing the coins and Bodkin's card with the police station phone number on it to Roland, she gave him instructions.

'Do you know how to use a telephone kiosk?'

'Yes, I've done it once with Mum. We rang Gran in Liverpool.'

'Okay, well, that's the number I want you to ring.' She pointed to the card. 'Ask for Inspector Bodkin... there's his name... look.' She pointed it out. 'Tell him that you're delivering an urgent message from Amy Rowlings. Say I need an ambulance immediately. Tell them where I am and say it's a matter of life and death and that someone is in need of urgent medical attention. Have you got that?'

Both boys nodded.

'Right, lads,' Amy said. 'Do this for Con and it will go a long way towards wiping your slate clean.' She ruffled Roland's hair. 'Get to it.'

Con was still breathing, but very shallowly. Amy looked around for something to use as a pillow and finding a small stack of newspapers tied with string in the piles of rubbish at the back of the tent, she carried it out, lifted his head and slid it underneath, then she turned his head to face her, leaned close and checked for breathing again. He was still alive. She had expected his breath to be foul, but she didn't pick up any sort of odour, even though she knew he had plenty of teeth missing.

Getting to her feet, she paced the floor outside the tent, counting off the seconds. *The boys must have made it to the phone box on the Gillingham road by now.* She crossed her fingers and hoped against hope that Roland had told the truth when he said he knew how to use a telephone kiosk. *If they've spent that money on sweets, I'll throttle the pair of them.*

Ten minutes later, she heard the sound of running feet and the boys rushed into the clearing. 'We did it, Amy,' Roland said. 'Inspector Bodkin said he was coming straight over.'

Amy put a hand on the shoulder of each panting boy. 'You've done well. Thank you for helping me.' She lifted her head as the sound of a roaring engine was heard coming along the track and a couple of minutes later Bodkin appeared, wearing a worried look on his face.

'Is he still alive?' He hurried over and knelt at the old man's side. 'Jesu... Sorry, Amy,' he said, turning his face away. 'How can you stand being so close?'

'I've been sniffing at this,' Amy said, showing Bodkin her compact face powder case. 'You can have a go if you like.'

Bodkin shook his head, took a deep breath, and then leaned over to examine Con. 'He's still with us, but only just.' He looked up at the boys. 'Did you cause this? You haven't been tormenting the poor old bugger again, have you?'

Both boys shook their heads vigorously. 'No, sir, we only came to say sorry. We saw you talking to our parents this morning, so we thought we might try to make up for what we did before.'

Bodkin eyed them with a stern look on his face. 'You'd better be telling the truth or you'll be sorry.' He pointed back along the track. 'Now, go and wait at the fork in the path to show the ambulancemen the way.' He took another look at Con, then turned his face towards the boys again. 'Are you still here?'

'Go easy on them,' Amy said as the lads hurried away. 'They did help me out. I gave them fourpence for the phone calls. They could have spent it on sweets, but they didn't.'

'I'm just letting them know I'm on their case if they have been having a go at him again.' Bodkin sucked the air in and leaned in close to Con again. 'At least his breath doesn't stink,' he said as he lifted his head. Getting to his feet, he craned his neck and looked into the tent. 'I think the best thing we can do with that lot is have a controlled fire. The whole woods could go up if the kids used that lot for kindling.'

Bodkin looked to his left as two stretcher-bearing ambulance men came trotting along the path behind Roland and Peter, then he stood aside to give the emergency team access to the old man.

'He's in a bad way,' the taller of the two said after examining Con. He turned away, pulling a face. 'Christ... we'll have to fumigate the ambulance once we've dropped him off at the hospital. I hope they've got a private room going spare. They can't put him on the ward smelling like that.' He pinched his nose and put his head on Con's chest to listen to his heart. 'Okay, let's get him on the stretcher.' He pulled a pair of gloves from his pocket and his partner did likewise. 'Right, after three, lift.'

They laid Con down and covered him with a blanket. 'That'll need fumigating too,' complained the tall man.

As they lifted the stretcher, Con opened his eyes. They darted here and there until they rested on Amy. Then he mumbled something that no one could pick up. Amy stooped down and put her ear next to his face. 'What was that, Con?'

'Dig out my... funeral suit, please. I think... I'm... going to ... need it.'

Chapter Thirty-Two

'I meant what I said about a controlled fire,' Bodkin said when the ambulance had driven off and the two boys had been sent home. 'There's so much junk in there, it could double the size of Spinton tip.'

Amy stepped into the tent. 'You can't burn it yet. His funeral suit is in here somewhere.'

'His what?' Bodkin followed her under the filthy tarp, shaking his head as he looked at the piles of rubbish.

'His funeral suit. He's got a clean set of clothes and a pair of shoes under this lot somewhere and I'm not going to let you set fire to it.'

'I wasn't going to do it this minute,' Bodkin said defensively. 'He won't be coming back here though, Amy. The welfare people will have to look after him now. I'm not sure how long he's got left, but one thing's for certain, they won't send him back out here to die in the woods.'

Amy plonked Con's new hat into Bodkin's hands. 'I asked him why he didn't wear that the other day and he said it was his funeral hat. Then he explained that he'd got a suit and a pair of good shoes hidden away in here.' She picked up a large brown paper bag, looked into it, then tossed it to the side. 'Handkerchiefs,' she said, 'they look brand new.'

It took almost half an hour to find the rest of what she was looking for. She eventually found the suit and a white shirt rolled up in an oilcloth, the shoes were in a cardboard box along with a spare pair of laces and a tin of boot black.

After passing the items to Bodkin, she stood back and looked at the rest of the small mountain of trash that would have been in anyone else's dustbin years ago. 'I wonder if he's got any clean underwear stashed away,' she said, reaching for a bag in the bottom corner of the pile.

'I wouldn't worry about underwear, Amy,' Bodkin said, carrying the armful of clothes outside. 'He won't need clean pants where he's going.'

As Amy pulled the bag out, something dull and brown with string coloured stitching on its edge caught her eye. Crouching down, she got her fingers underneath the corner, then lifted it. After pushing a few more bags of rubbish to the side, she found a leather handle. Grabbing hold, she pulled it out and held it in the air triumphantly.

'I think we've found Nina's missing case,' she said.

Bodkin dropped Con's clothes on the floor and held out his hands for the case. Sitting it on Con's paint tin seat, he snapped open the catches and lifted the lid.

Inside was a pair of black day shoes, a cream blouse, a navy, calf-length skirt, a pair of heavily mended silk stockings and a set of clean but well-used underwear. There was also a signed photograph of Rex Larson.

Amy looked at the contents with a sad look on her face. 'Oh, Nina,' she said. 'These were the clothes you left home in.'

Bodkin closed the lid of the case, then stuck it under his arm. 'You grab his clothes, Amy. Stick them in the back of my car and I'll drop them off at the hospital before I go to Dover.'

Amy passed her bag to Bodkin, then carefully picked up the pile of clothes. 'Poor Con,' she said quietly.

'I think we're going to have to think the unthinkable now,' Bodkin said as he started up the engine. 'We have to at least consider the possibility that Con killed Nina.'

'Nonsense,' Amy replied. 'He would have been eighty years old. He would still have been a frail old man back then. She'd have managed to fight him off, surely.'

'I agree, but we have to consider it,' Bodkin replied firmly.

'It's your old maxim, isn't it? Everyone's a suspect until they aren't.'

'Exactly,' Bodkin replied. 'And that maxim has stood me in good stead over the years.' He turned onto the narrow lane leading to the Gillingham road. 'Let's just open our minds to it, at least. There is a scenario here where he could have done it.'

'Okay, I'm all ears,' Amy retorted.

'Let's say back then, Con was spending his winters in the cottage... No... hear me out.'

Amy stopped her protest. 'Go on.'

'The cottage wouldn't have been quite as run down as it is today. The roof might not have fallen in yet. It would have been a far better shelter than his make-do tent.' He shot a glance at her as he turned right onto the Gillingham road. 'Is that feasible?'

'Yes, I suppose so. The roof wasn't as bad as it is now when I was a kid.'

'Okay, so...' Bodkin rubbed at the stubble on his chin as he thought.

'He had to get Nina inside there, too. How did he manage that?'

'He could have hit her over the head with a lump of wood or something, then dragged her inside,' Bodkin replied.

Amy shook her head and tutted. 'You're really pushing the possibilities now. What was she doing in the woods on her own in the first place? How did she get there?'

Bodkin sighed. 'She ended up there somehow and old Con managed to get hold of her case and stash it away, out of sight for ten years. Why would he do that?'

'He's a scavenger. We're lucky he found it.'

Bodkin parked the car up at the side of the police station and smiled as he looked across at Amy. 'If you get a chance, could you have a read through Jack's letters this evening? I'd like to know if they will give us a hint or two about his personal life.'

'I'll have a read through them this afternoon.' She put a hand on her rumbling stomach. 'I'm ready for my Sunday lunch. Is Sal cooking for you?'

'I have no idea,' Bodkin said. 'She was snoring her head off when I left for work this morning, so I never got the chance to ask.'

After eating her roast dinner, Amy went up to her room and played a few records as she worked her way through the letters that Mrs Draper had sent to her son. There was nothing particularly interesting in them apart from the regular reports on her physical decline. The last two letters ended with her begging him to come and see her before it was too late. Amy wondered if he had ever replied to her. Reading in between the lines, it didn't appear that he had.

At five, Mrs Rowlings shouted up to let Amy know that Bodkin had arrived. Hurrying down the stairs with the last of Mrs Draper's letters in her hand, she found him standing in the hall, nonchalantly tossing and catching his car keys in his right hand.

'Dover's off,' he said. 'Sal's not going until the morning, so I'll go down with her then. I'll still be back on the afternoon train.'

'Why is she… ah, she's seeing Ferris again tonight, is she?'

Bodkin nodded. 'She is and the pair of them had better eat each other's chops well away from my front door.'

Amy bit her lip. 'But it's all right for us to do it at my front door?'

'That's different,' Bodkin said. 'I'm pretty sure we don't make noises like that. In fact, I know we don't, because Mrs Dormouse would have let us know by now. Honestly, Amy, it sounds like a couple of hounds slurping at a bowl full of leftover gravy.'

Amy snorted. 'I don't think I've ever heard two dogs lapping up gravy... I can imagine it, though.' She waved the letter at him. 'There isn't a lot to report on the contents of Jack's mail, but it's probably a good job you're going to see her soon. She might not have too long to live. Reading between the lines, she's got cancer or something like that. She's almost begging him to visit in the last two letters. The last one only arrived in the week, so it doesn't look like he's been to see her yet.'

'What kind of son is he?' Bodkin replied. 'Then again, it depends what kind of mother she was, I suppose. And what happened to his father?' He scratched his head. 'He's only about thirty, isn't he? She can't be that old herself.'

'Age isn't a factor when it comes to cancer, Bodkin.'

'No, I understand that. I was just thinking aloud.'

'What brings you here, anyway?' Amy said, folding the letter and sticking it in the pocket of her cardigan. 'I hope you're not going to suggest a night in the Old Bull. I've got work in the morning.'

'That, although it would have been a pleasure to take you out, is not the reason I called.' He tossed his keys in the air and caught them. 'This should only take an hour at most. Parlour got in touch with Imogen Beechwood this afternoon. She's happy to talk to us tonight. I said we'd be round for about five-thirty. She lives in an apartment in that newish complex just past the Braithwaite.'

* * *

'Come in, make yourselves at home. Can I offer you tea, or would you prefer something a little stronger?' Imogen Beechwood stepped aside to allow Amy and Bodkin into the hallway.

The apartment was painted white throughout. The hall was dotted with photographs of Imogen in various costumes, some taken on stage, others for promotional reasons. The lounge was similarly decorated with pictures. In the centre of the room was a pair of two-seater, red leather sofas with a beech coffee table separating them. She walked across to a glass fronted drinks cabinet and took out an expensive bottle of brandy. She waved it at them. When they both declined, she put it back in the cabinet and motioned for them to sit. When they were comfortable, she sat down herself on the sofa opposite.

'It's about poor Caspian, isn't it?'

'Amongst other things, but yes, we'd like to ask you a question or two about the other night.'

'I was devastated when I heard the news,' Imogen said, running the back of her hand across her brow theatrically. 'I mean, I only left a few minutes before it happened.'

'Did you notice anything odd during the rehearsal?' Bodkin asked. 'Was Caspian in good spirits, or did he seem worried at all?'

'He was his usual bullish self,' Imogen said. 'He does think a lot of himself and he doesn't treat the staff well at all.'

'How do you mean?'

'Well, take Margo, for instance. The poor girl volunteered to read one of the parts, it was only two lines, for heaven's sake, but you'd think she'd just asked to be given the star role on opening night.'

'He told her she couldn't read, then?'

'He told her to get into the back room and sort the urn out, because that's all she was good for.'

Amy shook her head sadly. 'Did he always speak to her like that?'

'I've never heard him say anything nice to her, not even good evening, or thanks for the tea.'

'That's awful. She worked so hard for him and he didn't even pay her a wage.'

'He didn't even buy her a card for her birthday. It seemed that the harder she tried to please him, the worse he treated her.'

'Was it always like that between them?'

'Initially no. In fact, we used to think they could end up being an item, but it all changed suddenly. I honestly don't know why.'

'When did it change?'

'After Rex's performance. He became cold towards her.'

'How did he treat Jack?'

'All right, really. They were never going to be best friends. Jack isn't on the same level as Caspian intellectually or status wise, but he treats him with a modicum of respect. He always had a nice word for him when he produced a new prop or a new backdrop for the play. He gave him a few bob every Friday out of the petty cash. It wasn't much, but it was more than Margo ever got.'

'And yet she seemed so enamoured with him when we spoke to her,' Bodkin said.

'Oh, she can put on a good act to say she's never trodden the boards,' Imogen said. 'She buttered him up because her life would have been meaningless without the Playhouse.'

'So, nothing out of the ordinary happened at the rehearsal?'

Imogen frowned as she thought. 'Jack was there, sitting on the corner of the stage with his art pad. That wasn't what he usually did. He's got a workshop in the back and hardly ever came out of there unless it was to check some measurement or other.'

'He left just before you, I believe.'

'Jack? Yes, he said he had something urgent to take care of. I think he must have lost track of the time because he suddenly jumped up and disappeared. He left his art pad behind and he never did that. He liked to surprise us with his creations and didn't want us to get a sneak peek at what he had planned.'

'You left a few minutes after?'

'Yes, it was my birthday, so I went out for drinks. I can give you the names of the people I was with if you need them.'

'Thank you,' Bodkin said. 'If you could ring the station with their names, I'll get one of my officers to check them out.' He smiled across at her as she crossed her legs, ran her hands down her thighs and rested them on her bare knees.

Amy bit her lip to stop herself from smiling. Bodkin seemed to have the same effect on most of the women he interviewed.

'How is poor Caspian? I've been down in Sittingbourne for a day or two, so I've been out of the loop.'

'He's dead, I'm afraid,' Bodkin replied bluntly.

'Oh, my goodness!' Imogen exclaimed, taking her hands off her knees and holding them in front of her face. 'He was... murdered!'

Bodkin nodded. He was sure that Imogen's reaction would have been no different had she been standing on stage during the first act of a murder mystery. 'I'm afraid so,' he said. 'Can you think of anyone who would want to harm him?'

Imogen kept her hands in front of her wide-eyed face as she shook her head.

'I'm sorry, but no. He wasn't universally liked as I've already alluded to, but I can't think of anyone who would want to kill him.'

'Not even from way back? How long have you known him?'

'I first met him when I was no more than a girl taking my first steps on the stage. I was only seventeen, and I was at drama school. Caspian gave me small roles in his plays to give me some experience. I was very grateful to him.'

'Where did you attend drama school, Imogen?'

'Gillingham. I used to get the train there and back every day.'

'Did you ever share a stage with anyone from a similar group in Rochester?'

'No, we were a self-contained unit. We had more than enough students for the plays we put on. We never went out of Gillingham at all.'

Bodkin leaned forward and clasped his hands on his lap. 'Do you remember the nineteenth of October nineteen twenty-nine? I believe you shared a stage with a celebrity that night.'

'Ah, Rex Larson. The Importance of Being Rex Larson. Yes, I remember it.'

'How did Rex treat you? Was he courteous or was he a little more hands on?'

'He couldn't have been any more courteous. Mind you, my mother was in the wings or backstage at all times. He had a bit of a reputation around young women.'

'There were a couple of girls hanging around his dressing room that night. Do you remember them?'

'Not really. I was aware of them, but they weren't interested in me. They only had eyes for Rex.'

'When you left, do you remember seeing a group of girls on the steps by the stage door?'

'I think so. Yes, they had to move out of the way as a lot of us came out in a group.'

'Did you speak to any of them? Did anyone ask you for an autograph?'

'No, but then they were only about my age. They were only interested in men.'

'Can you remember seeing a young girl holding a small suitcase?'

Imogen shook her head. 'I'm sorry. I can only remember getting into a taxi with Mum and my aunt.'

'You can't remember seeing a driver standing alongside a big, flashy car?'

'Possibly, but I didn't speak to him. I honestly don't remember what he looked like.'

'That's all right,' Bodkin said as Imogen ran her hand through her dark hair, then recrossed her legs.

'Are you sure I can't get you that drink?'

Bodkin shook his head. 'We've only got a couple more questions now.' He looked at Amy and held out his hand, inviting her to ask a question.

'How did Jack manage to give so much time to the Playhouse for so little reward? He was only a young man, wasn't he? He can't have been earning a lot.'

Imogen clasped her hands on her lap. 'He used to drive taxis part time, to supplement his income. He worked late at night until the early hours of the morning. He must have been tired out when he got to work the next day.'

'What was Caspian Stonehand like back then?' Amy asked. 'Was he always as arrogant as he is... as he was until recently?'

'He was always a bit of an egotist. He honestly thought he'd put on a performance that night. He bored everyone silly trying to explain how he'd have done things differently to Rex. Especially to that agent of his. Fabian... Starr was it?'

'Fabian wasn't interested then?'

'No, he kept looking at his watch all the time Caspian was talking. He wasn't much of an actor back then; he was very wooden.'

'You say Fabian kept looking at his watch. Do you know why? Was he impatient to be elsewhere?'

'I think he wanted a drink. He kept sipping at his hip flask all the way through the backstage pleasantries.'

'Did Fabian ever offer you a contract, Imogen?'

'No, but then my mother would never have allowed me to sign it and he knew it. She knew all about Fabian's reputation.'

'He had a reputation. What sort of reputation?'

'The way he handled the careers of his younger actresses. Mum knew a lot of people in the business.'

'When you left and got into the taxi, did you see any other cast members about? Did anyone try to get a lift with you?'

'No, the Mayor had gone off with Fabian to somewhere. Rex was nowhere to be seen.'

'What about Jack? How would he have got home?'

'He'd have walked. He was renting a room quite close by.'

'And Caspian?'

'Oh, he lived just out of town. He had his own car anyway, so he wouldn't have needed a taxi. He used to park it up on the market place opposite the Milton.'

Chapter Thirty-Three

'Do you think we could drop in to see how Con is doing while we're over this side of town, Bodkin? I'm sure he'll be relieved to know I found his funeral suit.'

'He might not even be conscious.'

'I'm looking on the bright side. He was able to speak to me as he was being loaded into the ambulance.'

'You're a glutton for punishment,' Bodkin said, swinging the car around to take a sharp left. 'I wouldn't want to be stuck in a confined space with him, smelling the way he does.'

'They might have cleaned him up a bit,' Amy said, crossing her fingers.

At the reception desk, Bodkin flashed his warrant card and the nurse on duty told them where they could find Con. He had, as the ambulance men had suggested, been given a small room on his own at the end of a long forty-bed ward.

'I'll just go and find the doctor,' Bodkin said. 'He'll be able to tell me if Con has been attacked or not.'

Carrying Con's clothes, Amy knocked lightly on the door and when there was no response from inside, she pushed down the handle with her elbow and eased the door open with her shoulder.

Con was lying in bed, propped up by a small mountain of pillows. As Amy stepped towards him, she noticed the smell of carbolic soap instead of the years' worth of stale sweat she had been expecting. His hair and beard had been combed and his long, dirty fingernails had been trimmed.

'Hello, Con,' she said quietly, not wanting to wake him if he was asleep.

'Hello, missy,' he replied. His voice was weak, but his eyes were bright. He looked down at his body. 'They sent two nursies to give me a bed bath. They had to leave the room every few minutes, but they got through it in the end.' He gave Amy one of his gap-toothed grins. 'They said they'd never smelled anything like it in their lives.' He lifted an arm with effort and sniffed at his armpit. 'I don't know what they used, but I don't itch as much.'

Amy shuddered, then placed Con's clothes on the chair at the side of his bed.

'They sent all my clothes to the incinerator,' he said before she could speak. 'I'll be running around in my birthday suit when they let me out.'

'I don't think you'll be going back to the woods. Not after this scare, Con.'

'No, they said that. I'm going to be sent to a retirement home, though I don't know where they think I'm going to get the money to pay for that.'

'The welfare people will pay it, Con. They'll have a fund. I'm surprised you haven't been offered a place before now.'

'I was,' Con said. He rolled his head to the side and winked at Amy. 'It was down in Maidstone. I escaped though.'

'What are you like, Con?' Amy said with a little laugh. 'Don't even think about trying to escape from this one. You're in no condition to live outdoors anymore. It's a good job those boys came along when they did.'

'They only wanted to use me as target practice,' Con said with a little cackle.

'They came to say sorry to you,' Amy said. 'They realised they'd done something wrong and wanted to try to put it right.' Amy paused and smiled. 'They did as it happens. If they hadn't been there to help me, things might not have turned out as well as they have.' She patted the back of Con's hand. 'I think that makes up for some of the damage they did previously.'

'Well, they won't be throwing things at me in my posh retirement home, will they?'

'No, they won't. But I have the feeling they'd still like to say sorry to you, so they may pay you a visit when you've settled in. I might even come with them.'

'I'll get the maid to serve us tea.'

'And cakes, don't forget the cakes,' Amy said.

'Did you find my funeral suit?' Con asked suddenly.

'It's here, Con.' Amy pointed to the chair.

Con twisted his neck so he could see them. 'That's good. I wouldn't like to be sent off in the buff.'

Amy laughed. 'I'm sure that won't happen.' She patted his hand again. 'What happened this afternoon, Con? Were you attacked or did you have a fall?'

'I don't know. I remember thinking that it was time to go into town to see if I could scrounge a bit of money for food. I got up and everything started to spin. The next thing I know, I'm on the stretcher, being bundled into an ambulance.'

'Did you have any pains in your chest?'

'I can't remember anything after I stood up. It all went black.'

'Never mind, Con. You're safe now. If anything else happens to you, you're in the best place possible.'

'Could you pass me a drink of water? The nurses said I was to drink a lot. The doctor said I was deflated.'

'Dehydrated,' Amy said, picking up the glass and holding it to his mouth for him to take a drink.

'I knew it was de-something,' he said after taking a few sips.

Amy placed the glass back on the table and then sat on the side of the bed. 'Con,' she said. 'Can you remember finding a small, brown case? It would have been a long time ago.'

Con scratched his head as he thought.

'There's one hidden under my stuff. I was going to use it to put my funeral suit in, but I never got around to it.'

'Where did you find it, Con?'

'From the briars. It was right in the middle. I got scratched to bits, but I got it out.' He cackled again, this time the laugh turned into a fit of coughing.

Amy sat him up straight, patted his back. Then, when he had recovered, she gave him another drink of water.

'It's a good job my clothes were already torn, or they'd have been ruined,' he said, continuing with his story. 'It was right in the middle. You couldn't see it from the path. I only knew it was there because I saw the man throw it in.'

Amy leaned towards him and took both his hands in hers. 'Con, this is very important. Tell me about this man.'

Con furrowed his brow as he concentrated. 'It was in the early hours of the morning, but the moon was up, so there was some light filtering down through the trees. I was out setting my rabbit traps. He was on the track just a bit further down from the old cottage.'

'Can you remember anything about him, Con? What did he look like?'

'My memory isn't what it used to be,' he said. 'But he was in his shirt sleeves. I thought that was odd, as it was quite nippy.'

'Did you see a car?' Amy asked.

'No, just the man. I thought he'd seen me at one point, so I ducked out of sight and made my way back to my tent. I fished the case out of the brambles when the sun came up.'

'This was a long time ago, right? About ten years or so?'

'Passing years don't mean anything when you get to my age. One year melts into another and before you know it, you're lying on your back on the floor looking up at the sky.'

'Did you look inside the case when you got it out of the thorns?'

'Oh, yes, but there was nothing in there that was any use to me. I thought I'd keep it in case anyone came back for it. There might have been a reward.'

Amy got to her feet, then leaned forward and kissed him on the cheek. 'I'll get off now, Con. I don't want to tire you out. I'll pop in to see you again in a few days' time.'

As she was about to leave, she felt the old man grab at her wrist.

'Did you find my funeral suit?' he asked.

Chapter Thirty-Four

'That was all he could give us?' Bodkin looked disappointed.

'He's ninety years old, and he's just had a turn,' Amy said. 'It might even have been a heart attack.'

'It wasn't a heart attack. His heart isn't in top shape, but the doctor thinks he's been suffering from dehydration. He's weak, but to say how he lives his life, I think he's lucky to get as old as he has.'

'He thinks he was deflated,' Amy said. 'They're going to find a place for him in a retirement home. I hope it's got high walls. He escaped from the last one.'

Bodkin laughed. 'He's a character, isn't he? I hope I've got that much spirit when I get to his age.' He paused. 'I don't want to be living under an old tarp in the woods, though.'

Amy leaned across and patted his arm. 'You'll have to tell me what it's like. You'll get there before me.'

'I'll make sure you get a daily report,' he replied. He was silent for a moment as he turned past the phone box at the end of Long Lane. He shot a quick look at the Old Bull as he passed. 'Are you sure about that drink?'

Amy yawned. 'The last couple of days have been so hectic. I

think everything has finally caught up with me. I'm up at six in the morning, don't forget.'

Bodkin performed his usual scruffy three-point turn in the lane and parked the car up outside Amy's cottage.

'I'll catch up with you tomorrow evening,' he said as he looked across at her. 'We really need to get our heads together soon. There are bits of information coming at us from all angles. It's getting rather confusing.'

'I know what you mean, Bodkin. It's like a gigantic jigsaw puzzle at the moment, but we don't have any outer edge pieces to start us off.'

'What we need,' Bodkin leaned across to look her in the face. 'Is one of your excellent Poirot style summaries.'

'I'll get onto it,' Amy replied, as she yawned again. 'But it won't be tonight. I'm going straight up to bed.'

She kissed him on the lips, then turned and opened the passenger side door. 'It's a good job we did that inside the car. Mrs Dormouse is peeking through the curtains. I think we might have been in for another lecture.'

* * *

After lunch at The Mill on Monday, Amy, Carol and half a dozen other machinists were asked to accompany Georgina Handsley to what they thought was an empty warehouse at the back of the factory. Inside they found a row of machines and piles of pre-cut sections of Khaki that would need to be stitched together to make up soldiers' uniforms.

'Go to it, ladies,' Georgina said. 'I want to see how long it takes you to knock out five dozen of these. Don't go too hard at them though, they will have to be checked by someone from the ministry before we get the nod to make them on a permanent basis. You are my best machinists, so I wanted you to have the first go.' Wafting her hand towards the machines, she stuck up both of her thumbs. 'Get to it, ladies.'

The work was hard. The uniform material was heavy and by the time the bell rang at the end of the shift, Amy's arms felt like they had been swinging dumbbells all afternoon. They had, however, managed to turn out six dozen full uniforms. Georgina was delighted and told them that they would be paid an extra bonus for their efforts. When she was asked when the factory would switch to making uniforms full time, Georgina couldn't give an exact date because circumstance may change, but in her opinion the workforce could be starting on the government contract before September was out.

As Amy was saying goodbye to Carol at the phone box opposite the Old Bull, Bodkin drove up in his Morris.

'Loverboy's here,' Carol said, nudging Maggie, who was standing with them. She sighed as the policeman tooted and wound his window down.

'Want a lift?' he asked.

'You can take me anywhere you like,' Carol said, taking a step towards the car.

'Hey, don't forget me,' Maggie added. 'You won't even have to take me home afterwards.'

Laughing, Amy pointed down the lane. 'I'll see you at home in a minute, Bodkin. It's my arms that are aching, not my legs. I can walk that far.'

At the cottage, Amy opened the front door and Bodkin followed her into the hall. 'I'm home, Mum,' she shouted through the open living room door.

'Hello, love,' Mrs Rowlings called back. 'I've got your tea on, it's...' she stopped speaking as she came to the door and spotted Bodkin standing behind her daughter. 'Good evening to you too, Bodkin. Can I tempt you with a fishcake? I've got plenty of mixture and I've got some Parsley sauce to go with it. James isn't keen, but me and Amy love it.'

'If you're sure you have enough,' Bodkin said, walking into the living room. 'I love a nice fishcake.'

'Then I'll give you two,' Mrs Rowlings said. 'They'll be big ones, mind you. They're not like those tiny things they sell at the chip shop.'

'How was Dover?' Amy asked as they sat down at the table. 'You got back in good time.'

'Mrs Draper doesn't have long to go. She's got throat cancer, so it was difficult to make out what she was telling me, but I got what I needed out of her before her nurse threw me out.'

Mrs Rowlings brought in an extra cup and saucer and Amy poured tea for herself and Bodkin.

'I'm all ears,' she said as she picked up her own teacup.

'Firstly, Jack is adopted. He was sent down to Dover to live in a children's home after his mother died. He was five at the time. He was a rebellious type and had quite a few placements, but he couldn't settle at any of them and was always in some sort of trouble. His original surname was Mortenson. Mr and Mrs Draper used to own a coal yard, and they formally adopted Jack when he was fourteen. This was around nineteen twenty-three. He only lived with them for five years. He moved back to Spinton after Bert Draper died. Jack had bonded well with him, but Enid had never really managed to get close, despite her best efforts. According to her, the two of them were out with the horse and cart, delivering coal from dawn to dusk. Jack loved being out with Bert, and he also loved looking after the horse. Mrs Draper tried to get Jack to take on the family business after Bert's passing, but he seemed to lose all interest in it. He sold the horse and began to drink away the money he'd put aside.'

'Fourteen? That's late for an adoption, isn't it?'

'It was the perfect age for Bert. He was getting on and he needed a strong young lad in the business.'

'How old is Mrs Draper?'

'She's got to be in her late fifties, possibly early sixties. Bert was much older.'

'Did she have any idea where he might have gone?'

'None, though I didn't actually tell her why we wanted to speak to him. I just said he might be an important witness. I didn't want her to worry about him.'

'So, did he end up with a police record when he was out of control?'

'A juvenile one, yes. I looked him up at the local nick. His offending stopped when he went to live with the Drapers.'

'He might have a bit of an inheritance coming when Mrs Draper dies.'

'Indeed, there's a small house and money in the bank. Mr Draper was nothing if not thrifty according to his wife.' He paused as Mrs Rowlings came in with two plates loaded with fishcakes and sauce. 'Mrs R, you are a queen amongst cooks.'

Mrs Rowlings blushed and patted her hair into place. 'Oh, I'm just a plain old housewife. My dinners are nothing special.' She walked back out to the kitchen with a beaming smile on her face.

'So, he was a skinflint, in other words. A miser?'

'Close. She's making good use of those savings now, though. That nursing home doesn't come cheap.'

Amy cut into her fishcake. 'We're no better off, really. We still have no idea where he might be.'

'I've asked the local police to check into his records for me. Just to see if there was anyone he was really close to back then, but I'm not holding out much hope. Sal's going to look at the adoption files to see if there is anything to be found there that might give us a clue about his early life in Spinton.'

'That's good of her,' Amy said, after swallowing a mouthful of hot food.

'She could even have his records in her office if it was the charity she works for that handled the case.' Bodkin tucked into his meal and said nothing until his plate was empty.

'There was another reason I called around as early as I did.' He smiled at Mrs Rowlings, who was watching the clock, getting ready to cook her own meal when her husband got home. 'It wasn't just for the superb cooking.' He leaned back in his chair and patted his stomach. 'I thought you might like to know that Margo Ashburner has returned home. One of our beat officers saw a light on in her back room late last night. They've been keeping an eye on the place all weekend.'

'Has anyone called on her yet?'

Bodkin shook his head. 'I thought I'd let her build up a false sense of security. Anyway, as you know, Chief Super Grayson is a very forward thinking man, and he likes female witnesses to be interviewed in the presence of a female officer... or, if there are none available, which there never are because we don't have any at the moment, we might ask a young, accredited private investigator to step in, and you are the only one we know.'

Amy grinned. 'But didn't you interview Mrs Draper on your own?'

'Nope. Sal came with me and her nurse was present all the time. Besides which, she was only adding background information. She wasn't an actual witness.'

Amy got to her feet and downed what was left in her teacup. 'Give me ten minutes. I can't go out investigating in my work clothes.'

Chapter Thirty-Five

Margo's residence was at the end of a row of four red-brick Edwardian houses in the middle of what was classed as a nice street in the area. The houses all had a small front garden partitioned from the pavement by a long wrought-iron fence. Bodkin pushed open the gate and walked the few yards to the porch. Suddenly, the chink of light that had been showing through the front room curtains disappeared.

'She's going to try to make out she's not at home,' Bodkin said as the twitching curtain fell back into place. He rapped out his usual rat-a-tat-tat rhythm on the door, but when Margo failed to answer it, he knocked harder. When that received no response, he crouched down and shouted through the letterbox.

'Margo, we know you're in there. Don't make me kick the front door down. Be sensible.'

Thirty seconds later, a clearly flustered Margo turned a key in the lock and opened the door just enough to be able to look around.

'We've got a few more questions for you now you're back home,' Bodkin said, stepping towards the door.

Margo stood to the side and held the door open to allow Amy

and Bodkin to enter. 'I don't know what more I can tell you,' she said as she closed it quietly behind them.

'It's what you failed to mention that we're interested in,' Bodkin said.

Margo led them into an elegantly furnished lounge which held a glass cocktail cabinet, a long Chesterfield style sofa and two matching chairs sitting on a large oblong of thick pile patterned carpet which ran almost the full length of the room.

Margo was wearing a white, loose fitting, full length Egyptian cotton dress with a red line of hieroglyphics around the neck, waist and cuffs. Picking up a square cushion, she held it to her chest, then sat down in one of the chairs and crossed her legs.

'I thought I'd answered all of your questions,' she said with a look of surprise on her face.

'Have you heard the news about Caspian?' Bodkin asked.

Margo nodded. 'That's why I came back. I thought the Playhouse ought to do something for him. A plaque, a memorial night... something.'

'You don't seem particularly upset by the news.'

'Of course I'm upset. I've worked with him for a long time.'

'But he treated you appallingly,' Amy cut in. 'I wouldn't miss him. He was a bully.'

'That was just his way. He liked to dominate. Whether on stage or in real life.'

'Did he always behave like that towards you or did something trigger it?' Amy asked.

'He... Look, Caspian is... was... Caspian. He was like it with everyone.'

'No, he wasn't, Margo,' Amy replied. 'He used to pay compliments to everyone else if they'd done something to please him, even Jack, and he was just the man who painted backdrops.'

'I didn't go fishing for compliments. I just did my job and got on with things.'

Bodkin looked around the spacious, beautifully furnished

lounge. 'You work as a volunteer. You've never been paid for all the effort you put in. How can you afford to rent a place like this?'

'I don't pay rent. I was left it in my father's will. He and Mum had divorced a few years before he died. She's in Oxford now with her new husband. I got the house and a tidy sum. I don't need to work.'

'Is that where you've been...Oxford?'

Margo nodded.

'But how did you hear about Caspian's death?'

'A friend rang me, Jean. She lives next door.'

'I'll pop in on my way home,' Bodkin said.

A panicked look came across Margo's face. 'No, please don't... I wouldn't like word to get around that the police have been interrogating me.'

'It's hardly an interrogation, Miss Ashburner,' Bodkin replied. 'It's just routine questioning.'

'It feels like an interrogation,' Margo said, clutching her cushion tighter.

'What's your mother's address?' Bodkin asked. 'We might just need to check a detail or two.'

'No, leave her out of this. She'd have a fit if the police turned up at her door.'

'Is she on the telephone network?'

'Yes, but she won't pick the phone up, so it's a waste of time ringing her. She's got a phobia about telephones.'

Bodkin looked puzzled. 'Then why does she have one?'

'It's Denzil's phone. He's her new husband. He runs a business.'

Bodkin pulled out his notebook. 'The phone number will do. We won't have to upset her by sending a uniformed officer around then.'

'I don't want you talking to her at all.'

'Why not, Margo?' Amy asked. 'Is it because you know she'll have to deny that you were there over the weekend?'

Margo hung her head and said nothing.

'Where were you, Margo? Were you with Jack?'

She lifted her head, a puzzled look spread over her face. 'Jack? Why on earth would you think I was with Jack?'

'Because he's gone missing too,' Bodkin replied. 'I admit, we jumped to a conclusion, but it did seem to us to be more than just a coincidence.'

'I haven't seen Jack since he left the Playhouse on Thursday evening.'

'So where did you go, Margo? Are you going to tell us, or do you want us to guess?'

Margo clutched her cushion and looked at him belligerently.

'You went to see Rex, didn't you?' Amy said.

Margo sniffed. 'What if I did?'

'You also called him to warn him that we were asking questions about the death of Nina Honeychurch, didn't you?'

'I thought it was only right and proper to warn him.'

'But you said you had only met him on one occasion. The night of the Oscar Wilde play. Why did you suddenly feel the urge to talk to him?' Bodkin said.

'And, more importantly, how did you know how to get in touch?' Amy put in.

Margo lifted her cushion to her face and buried her head in it.

'Come on, Margo, we know you and Rex were an item for a time. We interviewed him on Saturday morning.'

'I know.' Margo spoke into her cushion, the words muffled.

'What was that? I didn't catch it,' Bodkin said.

'I know you interviewed him on Saturday. I was upstairs in his room when you spoke to him.'

As Bodkin and Amy exchanged glances, Amy held up a finger, pointing to herself.

'Are you still in a relationship with him, Margo?'

Margo shrugged. 'Define relationship. If you mean do I help him out with money and emotional support, then yes. If you mean are we close, physically, then no.' Her eyes misted over. 'I'm too old for Rex.

I've been too old for about ten years, though he did make an exception for me when he had that problem with the newspapers.'

'He made an exception for you?' Amy blew out her cheeks. 'Honestly, Margo, that man is incorrigible. He uses inexperienced young girls, then drops them when he's had what he wants.'

'He didn't drop me,' Margo said defiantly.

'Are you in a relationship? A proper one, I mean?'

'No, but... I've grown used to the idea that Rex has... certain needs that I'm no longer able to fulfil.'

Amy shook her head. 'Margo, you're what... twenty-seven, twenty-eight? You're still an attractive young woman. Most of the men in Spinton would give their eyeteeth to be in your company.'

'None of them are Rex, though. They can't come close. He... he turned a girl into a woman, he...' Her voice tailed off.

'We know you had a sexual relationship with him, Margo. When did it start and when did it end?'

Margo's head dropped. 'We only did it a few times. I couldn't get to see him back then. He was always busy working, or... or...'

'Or seeing other young girls?'

Margo nodded. 'He can't help it. He has a need.'

'He's a swine who uses people,' Amy said with more ferocity than she had expected. She paused for a few moments. 'That night, backstage. He didn't just feel you up, did he? It went much further. Were you caught in the act?'

Margo squeezed hard on the cushion and nodded again. 'Caspian caught us. He was so angry.'

'Why was he angry? You and he were nothing to each other. Why was it of any concern of his?'

'He and I... we... Everyone thought we might become an item. He took me out a few times, met my parents. He... afterwards, he said that I'd humiliated him, that he was about to ask me to marry him.'

'Had he shown you much affection up to then?'

Margo shook her head. 'No, he was always awkward around

women. He was fine on stage, but in real life, he struggled to get his thoughts out. He became tongue tied. I think he was a real romantic inside. He just couldn't show his feelings on the surface.'

'How old was he back then?' Amy asked.

'He was in his late twenties. He wasn't particularly handsome. He had a bit of a nervous tic when he tried to force his feelings to the surface. As I said, he didn't have a problem on stage, he could perform romantic scenes with actresses of any age. Off stage, though, he had to put on a front and it made him appear cold and unfeeling.'

'So,' Bodkin said, cutting in. 'You and Rex were at it? Where? There's nowhere to hide back there?'

'On the table,' Margo said, quietly. 'It was my first time, but to hear Caspian going on afterwards, you'd think I'd been at it with half the men in Spinton. He called me a slut, a whore, all sorts of foul names.' She wiped a tear from her eye. 'It wasn't true. Rex was the first man, or boy, to put a hand on me.' She sniffed. 'It didn't last much longer than a minute. Before I knew what was happening, he was climbing off me and telling Caspian to get out of his way as he wanted to get something from his dressing room.'

'Did they have words about it, Caspian and Rex, that is?'

'No, he didn't say anything to Rex, he just laid into me. I didn't deserve that. Two minutes earlier, I had still been a virgin.'

'Caspian never forgot that night, did he?' Amy said. 'And he's never forgiven you, either. It explains why he treated you the way he did, but I can't understand why you took it for so long. I know you love the Playhouse, but there are other theatrical locations you could have volunteered for. There were acting schools and clubs in Gillingham and Rochester.'

'The Playhouse felt like home to me. I never wanted to be anywhere else.'

'How many times were you with Rex after that night?' Bodkin scratched his head. 'Sexually, I mean. As you've already said, he was a hard man to get hold of.'

'Twice more. Once when he did a one-nighter in Sittingbourne and then one night in his digs in Paddington, after all the trouble with the papers. He'd had to sell his flat, and he was struggling for money. He couldn't pay his rent, so he called me and I got the train to London to see him.'

'How much was he in arrears?'

'It was a horrible place, just a tiny room. It was cheap, but he said he owed twenty pounds.'

'Twenty pounds? No landlord would ever let arrears get that far, especially not on a pound a week room.'

'It was twenty-five shillings. I don't know anything about the exact amount he owed, but I gave him the twenty, then another thirty, to tide him over.'

'This was when? If he'd already been through the mill with the newspapers, sold his flat and spent all the proceeds, this must have been nineteen thirty-three or four?'

'Thirty-four.'

'And you were how old then?'

'Twenty-two?'

'That's a bit old for Rex.'

'His heart wasn't it in, we never got properly going... you know, it was start stop start stop and after five minutes or so, he just gave up, we got dressed and I took him to a restaurant for something to eat.'

'Did he have a car back then?'

'He used to have one before the trouble, but he had to sell it.'

'So he knew how to drive?'

'Oh yes. He used to boast that he could have been a racing driver. He said he'd been talking to the Aston Martin team about having a go at Le Mans in nineteen thirty-three, but that all went by the wayside thanks to the News of the World.'

'Has he tapped you up for money on a regular basis, Miss Ashburner?'

'Now and then, a couple of times a year.'

'Because of his difficulties, I'm surprised he didn't ask you to marry him. It would have afforded him a modicum of respectability and, as a bonus, you were a woman of means. Did he never bring up the idea?'

'I offered to marry him,' Margo replied.

Amy leaned forward. 'How did he react to that?'

Margo looked down at the cushion. 'He laughed.'

'Oh, Margo, I'm so sorry. That must have been so humiliating for you.'

'It's not the fondest memory I have of him.'

'You should have slapped him across the face and told him never to contact you again,' Amy said.

'It wasn't... still isn't, that easy.' She looked directly at Amy. 'Have you ever been in love?'

Amy looked away quickly and didn't reply.

'If you had, you'd know that you can't just walk away. He becomes part of you. He was the man who took my virginity, the only man I'd ever been with that way. He was like a magnet to me. My heart used to flutter every time I thought about what we... about that night in the Playhouse.'

'It's like a Shakespearian tragedy,' Bodkin said. 'I'm sure we both feel very sorry for you. It would have made a good play though, heartbroken young woman and the older man who has no feelings for her at all. You should have got Caspian to write it for you.'

'Bodkin!' Amy hissed.

'Speaking of Caspian. You didn't mention he had a car the last time we spoke.'

'I can't remember the topic ever coming up?'

'He used to park it in the marketplace when he was at the Playhouse. Is that right?'

'Yes. The Playhouse has never had its own car park. The road outside gets busy, so he used to park early to make sure he got a spot.'

'The night Rex performed. When did you leave the Playhouse?'

'I was last to leave. It was my job to lock up and turn out the lights.'

'Was anyone still outside by the stage door when you left?'

'I came out the front so I wouldn't know.'

'But you told us there were several girls by the stage door. How did you know that if you left via the front entrance?'

'I locked the stage door after letting everyone out, then I turned off all the lights and left by the front door.'

'Where did you go then?'

'I walked to the bus stop near the market.'

'Did you see anyone on the way? Did you see Rex hanging out near the George Hotel? Did you see his driver or his car? Did you see anyone from the cast or any of the dignitaries hanging about? More importantly, did you see a young woman with a small brown suitcase?'

'Oh yes, I remember seeing her. She was getting into Caspian's car. I couldn't see her face, but she was definitely carrying a suitcase.'

Chapter Thirty-Six

'Are you sure about that, Margo? A young girl with a small brown case got into Caspian's car?' He took Nina's picture out of his pocket and held it up for her. 'Was it this young woman?'

Margo squinted at the photograph, then shook her head. 'As I said, I didn't see her face.'

'Did you ever talk to Caspian about who she was?'

'No, I assumed he was giving someone a lift to the station. She had a case, after all.'

'Wasn't it a bit late for the station?'

Margo shrugged. 'To be honest, I didn't think anything of it. I was hoping Rex would spot me and take me into the George.'

'You knew the other two girls had let him down, then?'

Margo shook her head. 'No, that's not what I meant. You know how it is when you're daydreaming about someone?' She looked directly at Amy as she spoke.

'So, you didn't see Rex again that night?'

'No, I got to the marketplace, caught my bus and came home.'

Bodkin jotted a few notes down. 'Okay, let's have a chat about Jack now.'

'Jack?'

'Yes, were you aware he had a thing for you?'

'JACK? You're joking.'

'He drew a broken heart on his art pad. A dagger dripping with blood, too.'

'Perhaps he was thinking up designs for the backdrop. Jack has no interest in me. I don't think he's particularly interested in women, anyway. Not that he's effeminate, but he's a man's man, you know. Someone who is much happier in male company?'

'Do you know much about him?'

'Not really, he works as a carpenter... cabinet maker. He's very good with his hands, you should see some of the stage props he makes.'

'You say he has no time for the ladies? Have you ever seen him with one at any time over the last ten years? Men have needs, as you are aware, and Jack will be no different.'

'He's always polite around women at the Playhouse, but he never tries to... you know, get close to any of us. He's never asked anyone out to my knowledge.'

'Do you know anything about him prior to his arriving at the Playhouse? Does he ever talk about his past?'

'The only thing Jack talks about is his props. Honestly, Inspector, none of us really knows him. He gives nothing away about himself. The only thing we ever learned about him is that he was adopted and that he lived in Dover for a time. And we only found that out at Stanley Tubshaw's funeral. Stanley was the actor I told you about. He died the Christmas after Rex appeared in the play. Jack and Stanley got on well and I think Jack had one sherry too many at the wake.'

'He used to drive late night taxis to supplement his income, didn't he?' Bodkin asked.

Margo nodded. 'Yes, he'd pick up his taxi from the driver going off shift, in the marketplace, after rehearsal. I think he worked until the early hours. He was only an apprentice cabinetmaker at the time, so he must have been paid a pittance.'

'Did you see him in the marketplace that night when you were waiting for you bus?'

Margo shook her head.

'You don't have any idea where he might be hiding out?'

Margo shook her head. 'None, I'm afraid.'

Bodkin got to his feet, took one of his cards out of his pocket, and handed it to Margo. 'Call this number if he gets in touch.'

Margo let go of her cushion with one hand to take the card from Bodkin.

'Is that it? Are you done with me?'

'For now,' Bodkin said. 'But don't leave the area again without letting me know.'

'Well, that was a revelation,' Amy said as she smoothed down her dress after climbing into Bodkin's car.

Bodkin frowned. 'We only have her word for it at the moment. She might still be trying to protect Rex.'

Amy nodded. 'I need to get all this straightened out in my head. I'll write out a summary tomorrow after work.' She bit her lip as she thought. 'I suppose I ought to write out two summaries. One for each murder.'

Bodkin stuck up a thumb. 'That's my girl. I'll look forward to reading them. They help to get things straight in my mind too.' He checked his watch. 'I wonder if Chester has finished for the day.' He grinned at Amy. 'It's early yet. Shall we drop in on him?'

The space at the front of Chester's repair shop was empty, so Bodkin pulled his Morris onto it and shut off the engine. Walking to the folding doors of the workshop, he hammered on them with his fist, but the summons received no response.

'Blimey,' said the man in the next unit as he stuck his head out of the window. 'I thought you were trying to break the door down. You nearly gave me a heart attack. I was just having forty winks before I nip down for a couple of pints at the Dragon.'

'Is he round the back?' Bodkin asked.

'Yes, I think so. I haven't seen him go out this evening. I saw him drive his car into his unit an hour or so ago and he doesn't really like to walk anywhere, so you ought to find him back there.'

Bodkin thanked the man and led Amy down the narrow gap between the two units. As he looked in through the half glass front door of the hut, he could see Chester sitting at the table with his back to him. He appeared to be eating as he listened to a dance band playing on the radio. His body jerked, and he swung around to face the door as Bodkin rapped out his rat-a-tat-tat.

'For pity's sake,' he said, putting a hand on his chest as he opened the door. 'Could you knock any louder?'

'If you like,' Bodkin said. 'But I don't see the point. You heard me the first time.'

Chester left the door hanging open and went back to the remains of his dinner. At the back of the hut, was a two ringed electric cooker with a frying pan and a stew pot sitting on a drainer next to a small sink. Hanging on a nail near the sink was a tea towel with the picture of a Rolls-Royce car printed on it.

'You've got all mod cons in here, Chester,' Bodkin said as he followed Amy into the room. 'All you're missing is a lavatory.'

'The units share a communal one.' He pointed to the right, then speared a chunk of potato with his fork. 'It's down that way if you need it.' He pulled a face at Amy. 'I'd hang on if it's you that needs to go. The drains are blocked again.'

Chester got to his feet, walked across the room, and slipped his plate and cutlery into the sink. Putting a hand on his stomach, he pressed and burped twice. 'Sorry about that,' he said, looking at Amy again.

He was dressed in a white, open-necked shirt and dark blue trousers. His suit jacket was hanging on the back of his chair. Picking up a packet of cigarettes, he offered it to Bodkin, then to Amy. When

269

they shook their heads, he put it down on the table again. 'I always like one after dinner, but it can wait.' He pulled out a chair for Amy and motioned for her to sit. 'What can I help you with this time?'

'We're still looking into the murder of Nina Honeychurch,' Bodkin said. 'New information has come to light that leads us to believe that you didn't tell us everything you know about the night she went missing, the last time we spoke.'

'I answered your questions truthfully.' He eyed up the cigarettes again.

'You didn't tell us that you were sent on a drugs hunt.'

'Ah, that. Well, it's not something you'd bring up voluntarily, is it? I'd have told you if you'd asked.'

'Well, now's your chance to remedy that, Mr Harvey,' Bodkin replied. 'Have a cigarette if it will help you remember, but could you stand by the door when you light it up? It's stuffy enough in here as it is.'

'I'll have it later,' Chester said, much to Amy's relief. The hut was warm, and the air was thick with the smell of cabbage.

'We've been talking to Rex Larson, Mr Harvey,' Bodkin said as Chester slipped his hand into his trouser pocket and began to rattle his loose change. 'He tells us a very different story about the events of that night. You see, he told us he packed you off to go looking for drugs. This would be at the time that you told us you'd gone home for the night.'

'As I said, Inspector, it's not something you want to put out there, is it?'

'Put it out there now, Chester.'

Chester tipped his head to the side and stared into space as he thought. 'Rex asked me if I knew where he could get some cocaine or anything else that might help get him through the night. I said I knew a few people and that I'd ask around.'

'You found a supplier, I believe, but not the supply?'

Chester nodded. 'I didn't know those people very well. They thought they might be being set up by the police.'

'So what did you say to allay their fears?'

'I didn't say much at all. They told me to bring Rex to them.'

'Where were they at the time?'

'They were in the Dragon, playing cards.'

'So why didn't you take Rex to the Dragon to meet them?'

'As I said, they thought it might be a trap. They didn't really know me. I only knew them by reputation.'

'So, who were they and what did they say to you?'

Chester shook his head. 'I'm not naming names. I have to live here.'

'It's too late to arrest them over it now, Chester.'

'Nevertheless, I'm not naming names. They still drink in the Dragon. I'm sure you can find them. Just keep my name out of it.'

'You got them to believe that it wasn't a trap, eventually.'

'Yes, I told them I had a rich guy, an actor who was desperate for anything they could get their hands on. I was in my uniform and I took them outside to show them the Daimler. That swung it, but they said they didn't want to come with me to meet Rex. They said they wanted to hand over the drugs somewhere quieter. Rex was a well-known celebrity, and they didn't want to attract attention, so they suggested the entrance to the Witchy Wood and I went back to get Rex.'

'Where was he?'

'In the bar at the George. The two girls stood him up. He wasn't a happy chap, but he cheered up no end when I told him I'd found someone who could get him some cocaine and more, whatever he wanted.'

'So you took him off to the woods?'

Chester nodded. 'Look, I had no idea they were going to do that to him. When I pulled up at the track that leads into the trees, he almost jumped out of the car to greet them. He was shaking like a leaf in a strong wind.'

'He had a chat with them about the drugs, agreed a price, then what?'

'He came around to the driver's side of the car. I wound down the window, and he told me I could go as he had been invited to a party and wouldn't need me. He said he'd find his own way back in the morning.'

'And that was it. He went off with them?'

'I asked him if I'd be getting anything as a thank you. He shoved three quid into my hand. I was delighted with that, so I turned the car around and drove back to town.'

'Not home.'

'No, I'd got three quid in my pocket and I knew where there was a party going on, so I drove back to the Milton. I figured that I'd check on Fabulo... Fabian, to see if he wanted a lift back to the Braithwaite. I'd have been happy to wait for him if it meant another big tip. Anyway, there were a lot of girls at the party, so I thought I might grab myself a drink and see if I could get off with one of them.'

'Wasn't it a rather posh party? You were in a chauffeur's uniform, weren't you?'

'I left my cap and coat in the car at the marketplace. No one questioned me when I walked into the cocktail lounge. The shifts had changed over on reception. There was only one girl behind the counter and she was busy with something, so I just walked in. I can usually talk my way out of anything anyway and I'd have told them I was with Fabian Starr's party, but I was never challenged.'

'Did you find Fabian? Was he still at the party?'

'Oh I found him; he was having a whale of a time. As I walked to the bar, he was sitting on one of those big corner sofas. The table in front of him was almost collapsing under the weight of champagne buckets and cocktail glasses, so I didn't even bother to order a drink at the bar. I just picked a flute up off the table.'

'You said Fabian was having a whale of a time?'

'Was he ever? He had a girl on his knee. She was only a young 'un too. She was bouncing up and down like they were having...' He shot Amy a glance. 'They weren't actually having it off, but she was pretending they were.'

'What time was this, Chester?'

Chester's brow creased as he thought. 'After midnight.'

'Was Fabian drunk? He didn't get to the Milton until after eleven.'

'He was out of it, honestly, Inspector. He had what looked like a triple scotch in his hand. He almost spilled the lot when he twisted himself to the side to kiss another young woman who was leaning in to get his attention.'

'Where was the Mayor?'

'I didn't see him, but he might have been elsewhere in the room. Two of those businessmen who walked across to the Milton with Fabian were there. They'd got hold of a couple of girls too.'

'Did you stay for long?'

'An hour, an hour and a half. I had a dance and a cuddle with a couple of girls, drank another flute or two of free champagne, then I looked at the time and remembered I was on duty in the morning. I tried to have a quick word with Fabian to see if he needed a lift, but he just laughed at me. He'd got a girl on either side of him by then, as well as the one sitting on his lap, so I guessed the answer was no.'

'So you left?'

'I thought I'd try to get a few hours' sleep, but then Caspian came in. He looked to be in a bit of a state. He'd got scratches on his face and on the backs of his hands. I asked him what he'd been up to, and he said he'd had a bit of trouble with some local lads. They'd messed around with him a bit then pushed him into a hedge.'

'This was around one o'clock?' Bodkin asked.

'Maybe one-thirty.'

'Where had he been until that time?'

Chester shrugged. 'I didn't believe the story about the local thugs for a minute. They looked like fingernail scratches to me. I wondered if it had been that girl I'd seen him talking to in the car park when I drove off to find a dealer for Rex.'

Bodkin put both hands on the table as he leaned towards Chester. 'Was it a young girl?' He pulled Nina's photograph from his pocket. 'Was it one of the girls hanging around the stage door?' He held the picture up to Chester. 'Was it her?'

Chester took a long look at the picture, then shook his head. 'I honestly can't say. It was dark. There are no streetlights around the marketplace, but I know he had his rear door open. I remember seeing him chuck something into the back seat as I drove by.'

Chapter Thirty-Seven

'Why didn't you mention this the last time we spoke?' Bodkin said, staring hard at Chester.

'Look, I'd already told you I'd gone home. I didn't want to complicate things for myself. I had agreed to find illegal drugs for a celebrity. I still act as a chauffeur for the same company and I could have been sacked if it had come out, even all these years later.'

'Are you sure it was Caspian?'

'Positive. It was one of those silly little Citroen C3s. There aren't many of those about. Anyway, he had his headlights on, so I'm sure it was him. I'm not so sure about the identity of the person he was talking to. She was on the other side of the car.'

'You're sure he was talking to a woman? It was dark, after all.'

'I'm pretty sure, if it was a man, it was a small one... no, it was a girl, no doubt about it.'

'Okay, that was earlier. What about when he came back? What did he do then?'

'He said we should have a drink together. I told him I was about to leave and I began to walk away. I hadn't even reached the door when he ran after me and asked me if I'd like to make a few pounds for doing very little. I was all ears. So we walked over to the bar and he ordered up a couple of whiskies. We stood there, not saying much, for about ten minutes. He was angry, though. He was grinding his teeth. "Look at the state of Fabian," he said. Then he called him a fat pompous slob who had no idea what real acting talent was, and that he deserved to be taught a lesson. I told him I wasn't going to help him beat the old man up, but he said that's not what he had in mind. He said we'd only have to hang on for half an hour and we could set his plan in motion. I was still unsure about it, but he said I'd get twenty quid if I helped him. That sealed it, really. It would have taken me almost two months to earn that from driving, even with the taxis. Anyway, he went out to the reception for a couple of minutes to chat to the girl on the desk. When he came back, he had a key in his hand. I asked him what it was for and had he booked a room? He said he was borrowing a room, then he said the girl on the counter was his ex-girlfriend, who was now struggling to bring up a child on her own. He'd offered her a couple of quid to let him have the key for the night without logging it in the register.'

'That plan was worked out quickly. It could all have been a waste of time if Fabian had decided to go back to the Braithwaite,' Bodkin said with a puzzled look on his face.

'Inspector, Fabian was totally out of it by then. He'd spilled his drink all over the girl on his lap. She wasn't happy about that and she gave him a few choice words. Not that he heard them. He was sparked out with his head on the back of the sofa. You could hear his snores over the music.'

'Okay, so Fabian is incapacitated, but he told us he could take his drink,' Bodkin said.

'He probably could, but I think he'd had more than alcohol. Caspian wandered across to have a word with the girl who had been sitting on his lap. He started to chat her up. She had been trying to get Fabian to give her a screen test. She was game for anything, I think. She asked Caspian if he'd got a sniff on him as she had run out. She rubbed her finger under her nose to make the point. I assume she meant cocaine. Caspian tapped his pocket and told her that she could make herself a fiver if she was willing to help play a prank on Fabian. For a fiver I think she'd have taken him, me and Fabian to bed. The other two girls were losing interest by then and were smiling and calling out to the men further up the banquette. Caspian beckoned me over and we hauled Fabian to his feet and pretty much dragged him out of the bar. The room Caspian had organised was right at the back of the hotel at the end of a short corridor near a lavatory and cleaners' cupboards. It was probably the cheapest room in the place because it was tiny. It didn't take us too long to get his jacket off and spread him out on the bed. I thought Caspian was going to ask the girl to sleep with Fabian, but he didn't. He just got her to kiss him around his face and neck and leave a few lipstick marks on his collar. As an afterthought, he asked her for one of her silk stockings. When she took it off, he tore a couple of holes in it and threw it on the floor next to Fabian's jacket. Then we all left. It was as simple as that. Caspian handed her some money from his wallet, then he gave her something out of his pocket. She gave him a smacker on the lips, waved us goodnight and off she went.'

'Which left you and Caspian in the lobby of the hotel. What time was this?'

'About two-thirty. The revellers in the cocktail bar had begun to leave the party. It shut at three, I believe.'

Bodkin scratched at his stubbly chin. 'What did you do then? You had to make sure Fabian believed the set up. What if he'd have woken up early and made his way to reception?'

'Caspian said he'd keep an eye on him. He sat in the room with Fabian until it got light, then he took the key back to the girl at reception, went out to the foyer and sat there watching the corridor. It worked a treat. When Fabian came out, Caspian told him about the made up events of the night and Fabian agreed to cough up. He couldn't risk something like that getting into the papers. I think he wanted to go to the reception desk himself to apologise, but Caspian told him that wasn't a good idea, as it had taken him over an hour to persuade the night manager to accept a five pound bribe to forget it ever happened.'

'Where were you while all this was going on?'

'I went out to the car and got my head down for a couple of hours. I didn't sleep for too long. I was awake well before dawn and I just sat there smoking and working out what to spend the money on. At about seven forty-five, Rex came back. He was in a right state. He'd collapsed in the woods and spent the night there. I thought he was going to blame me for what had happened to him, but all he did was beg me to find him something to keep him going until he could get back to London. My landlady kept all sorts in her bathroom so I was able to get him some laudanum and a pack of powder that you mixed with water, it mentioned that it contained barbiturate on the back of the packet, it was called Medi something or other.'

'So Rex didn't blame you for getting him a good hiding?'

'No, I think he was just happy to get the laudanum.'

'Did you ask for money from him?'

'He had some money in his case back at the Braithwaite. I got another fiver.'

'It was a very profitable night for you then, Chester?' Amy said.

Chester winked at her. 'I wish I could get that lucky every Saturday night.'

'What happened when you got them to the Braithwaite?'

'Rex paid me a fiver and Fabian gave me a cheque for a hundred pounds, made out to cash.'

'Caspian was taking a risk, wasn't he? You or anyone else for that matter could have presented that cheque at a bank on Monday morning and walked away with a hundred pounds.'

'I'm an honest man, Inspector. I handed the cheque to Caspian. It was his master plan that got us the money, after all.'

'When did you see him to give him the cheque?'

'He came around to my digs. He was waiting there when I got back from dropping Rex and Fabian off at the station.'

'Have you stayed in touch with Caspian over the years?'

'No, he set himself up in business with his share of the profits. He wasn't interested in the likes of me after that.'

'What did you do with your share, Chester?'

Chester held out his hands in an expansive manner. 'I bought this place.'

'Did you ever hear from either Fabian or Rex Larson after that night?'

'Not a dicky bird. They went back to London, and that was the end of the story.'

'Did you see Rex Larson's name in the News of the World a few years later?'

Chester nodded. 'To be honest, I'm surprised it took them that long to catch up with him. The guy was a complete mess. It was only ever going to be a matter of time before someone took thirty pieces of silver to dob him in.'

Bodkin held out his hand to Amy. 'Is there anything you'd like to ask?'

Amy nodded and turned in her chair to face Chester. 'Do you know Margo Ashburner?'

'I can't say the name rings a bell,' Chester said. 'Should I know her?'

'What about Jack Draper? Do you know him?'

'Jack Draper...? No, I can't say I've ever come across him either.'

'Really?' Amy gave him a puzzled look. 'He used to drive late night taxis. You were a taxi driver too back then.'

'I only ever worked until seven-thirty, though. I didn't have to work long hours like the rest of the lads. I had my chauffeur work to top up my income.'

'You like to bring young girls back here, Chester? Have you always had a taste for them or is it only since you got a little older?'

Chester turned away, but the back of his neck had reddened.

'They're all willing,' he said fiercely. 'I don't bring any underage girls back here. I meet them in the pub, so they're obviously old enough to know what they're doing.'

'It was just a question,' Amy said. 'There's no need to be so defensive.'

'It's the way you people say these things. Trying to make out I might have had something to do with that young kid. Well, let me tell you, I didn't. It was Rex who liked them really young. Fabian was slightly better, but to say how old he was, it wasn't a good look. Then there was Caspian, of course. He's the one you should be talking to, not me.'

'We can't, Chester, as well you know.' Amy pointed to the newspaper that lay on the seat of the chair next to her. 'It's still the main story in the Evening Post. They've been leading with it since Friday.'

Chapter Thirty-Eight

At lunchtime the following day, Amy shared a table with Carol and Maggie in the canteen, as they listened to Big Nose Beryl sitting in judgment on the Caspian Stonehand murder case.

'I've got a spy in the camp,' she said to the four young trainees and the two older women who made up her court. The older ladies were even bigger gossips than Beryl if that was possible, but at least their long tales contained a kernel of truth. Beryl's stories came out of her overly-fertile imagination. 'And she told me everything about what happened that evening.'

Amy pricked up her ears but said nothing.

'It seems that the actor chappie, Capstan Stonehandle, was rehearsing a scene in a play where he and his love rival have an argument and his rival produces a dagger and stabs him.' She paused for effect. 'Well, the thing is, someone swapped the fake dagger for a real one and Capstan took it in the lung.'

Amy rolled her eyes at Beryl's attempt at dark humour, if that's what it was. Capstan was a brand of strong cigarettes.

'Well I never,' Pansy Lorne said, as she took her cup away from her mouth. 'Have the cops arrested the other chap, or was it someone else who switched the daggers?'

Beryl tapped the side of her nose, which wasn't anywhere near as big as her nickname implied. She got the title because she couldn't help sticking it into other people's business. 'I was told the cops are looking for him. He's done a runner.'

'Ooh,' Pansy said. 'A madman hiding out in Spinton, and he's an actor, so he'll be a master of disguise. We women aren't safe in our beds these days. It's bad enough having the Casanova Caller dropping in uninvited while unprotected women are lying in their beds, but now we've got a murderer hiding in our midst.' She shook her head and looked into her cup as if she was reading the tea leaves. 'I don't know what the world is coming to.'

'It's been a long time since I got a Valentine's card,' Sylvia Johns said dreamily. 'Casanova can drop in on me if he likes, but I wouldn't let him out until the next morning, so I hope he has a big dinner to build his strength up.' Sylvia cackled so hard, her false teeth slipped and she almost coughed them out onto the table. 'Scuse me teeth,' she said, pushing them back into her mouth.

'What's this other bloke's name then, Beryl?' Young Samantha Bellamy asked. 'Did they both fancy the same woman, like they did in the play?'

'Who knows?' Beryl said mysteriously. 'There's more in it than meets the eye, that's for sure. These actor types are always a bit strange in my experience.'

Amy wondered how Beryl knew about what actors were like in real life as, apart from the panto, she had never been to the theatre in her life.

'Beryl,' she said as she put the top on her sandwich box. 'The closest you ever got to an actor was when you took your Rosie and Michael to the Punch and Judy show at the fair last summer. How do you know all actors are a bit strange?'

'Stands to reason,' Beryl replied. 'They've always got someone else's words in their heads. That must have an effect. I mean, I bet they don't know who they are half the time. It must give them a split personality.' She looked around her table for support. Pansy nodded her head sagely as Sylvia checked her teeth were in place before speaking.

'You're right, Beryl. The B and B I clean at the weekends had an actor staying with them for a fortnight while Aladdin was on at the Playhouse. Mrs Stay, who owns it, said he would walk around at all hours, having conversations with himself.'

Amy laughed. 'Have you ever thought he might have just been practicing his lines?'

'Whatever he was doing, he should have done it silently. Mrs Stay was going to hit him with her bedpan one night when he wandered down the landing shouting "OH NO HE DIDN'T!" She chucked him out the next day. She said he must have been skittle frantic.'

Amy and Carol looked at each other and shook their heads. Before Sylvia could expand on her story, the bell rang to signal the end of the lunch break.

After tea that night, Amy settled down at the table in the front room where she wouldn't be distracted by the radio, or the conversations her parents would have when Mr Rowlings picked what he considered to be an interesting topic from his evening news. Slipping a sheet of foolscap paper out of the rolltop desk, she picked up her pen and made the list of motives that were used in the Hercules Poirot novels.

Gain. Jealousy. Fear. Revenge. Love. Obsession. Power. Hatred. Desperation. Ambition.

The Nina Honeychurch case.

It's difficult to find a motive, as the murder happened so long ago and apart from Rex Larson, who she had only ever corresponded with before that night, Nina didn't know any of the other suspects. She did speak to Chester Harvey and may have spoken to Caspian Stonehand in the car park before getting into his car. Caspian has now been named by two witnesses.

Rex Larson

The number one suspect from the start, but a few problems have arisen since then.

Rex doesn't have a clear motive, unless, of course, Nina threatened to expose him after rejecting her at the stage door that night. If that was the case, Fear and Desperation and possibly Hatred come into it as motive, though I think the latter is unlikely. Hatred tends to be an emotion that builds up over time and, as we know, Rex had been doing his best to get Nina to meet him. It was only the promise of those two young girls agreeing to go to the George Hotel that got in the way of that tryst. Did Rex see Nina walking past the George that night and feeling let down by the two girls he thought he was going to meet, reverted to his original plan and picked up Nina?

Rex is a despicable man with literally no moral fibre. His testimony, while incredible, was backed up in part by Chester Harvey. Then again, there is no escaping the fact that Rex was in the woods that night. Whether he was beaten up by the drug gang or not, he was in the vicinity of the cottage, and it was probably his coat that was found inside with Nina. He is an utterly unreliable witness. His drug addiction at the time means we can't really trust his statement. He had been in a fight, but we don't have a list of his injuries. Maybe Nina was tougher than he thought she would be.

Margo Ashburner

Comes under Love, Obsession and Jealousy. She openly admits to being obsessed by Rex; the man involved in her first sexual encounter. Could she have been jealous of Nina's fascination with Rex? Margo was on the street at the same time as Nina, but we have no other witness to verify that she walked to the bus stop and went home. She may have colluded with Rex to get rid of Nina.

Obsessed with Rex for over ten years, she has given him money and emotional support even after he laughed at her proposal of marriage. Margo would do anything for Rex. Anything... more about this later.

Chester Harvey

Another libertine who likes younger women. Chester was a taxi driver as well as a chauffeur, so would have known the town like the back of his hand. Chester spoke to Nina and the other girls at the stage door that night and had them all in the back seat of his car. Caspian is the only one, apart from Rex, who could have backed up his parts of Chester's alibi, and he's beyond our reach now. His claim that he saw Caspian in the car park with a woman on a dark night with no street lighting has to be taken with a pinch of salt, although Margo does back up that claim with her testimony, it seems to me like Caspian, the man who cannot reply to the allegations, is an easy target. Chester claims to have been in on the plot to blackmail Fabian Starr and indeed his evidence about what happened in the Milton that night, seems to ring true after listening to Fabian's testimony. I wouldn't trust him as far as I could throw him, but his evidence does seem to add up. If only we could find the woman at the reception desk that night. Sadly, because it all happened a long time ago and hotel staff are notoriously transient, it's unlikely that she'll still be working at the Milton. It might be worth paying them a visit, although no one is ever going to admit to taking a bribe.

Jack Draper

I'll leave his potential involvement in the Stonehand murder until later. What we do know is, he was a part time taxi driver at the time of Nina's murder and he was in the vicinity of the stage door that night, watching from a street corner. Why was he watching? What was so fascinating about those young women? Did he wait until they walked away before following them, hoping to catch one of them on her own? Was he involved in Nina's disappearance? Like Rex, the fact that he didn't have a car is problematic, but taxis run all the time and they would have been numerous at that time of night. He worked part time as a taxi driver himself to subsidise his way through his apprenticeship. Did he go to work after the play that night? Sadly, it's far too long ago to expect any other taxi driver to remember picking him, Rex or, indeed, Nina up. We'll know more when Bodkin finally catches up with him. It will be an interesting interview. Motive unknown. We need to speak to him urgently.

Question. Could a taxi driver have taken Nina? We all trust cabbies. Worth thinking about.

Fabian Starr

A drunk, a devious man who may have lied to us about his sexual problems. Allegedly, Fabian hands out contracts to actresses after they show off their talents on the casting couch. (According to Rex at least. We'll find out more about that on Saturday.) Fabian has no alibi after two-thirty and his claim that he was too drunk to know anything about a young woman shouting for help in his room in the middle of the night is thin, at best. We only have Chester's word that the young girl who went to his room was a plant. Maybe it was Nina. Maybe he took her to a room, then tried to take advantage, so she turned to Caspian to help her escape... more about him later. Fabian and Rex were as thick as thieves at one time. It's possible that their falling out wasn't as serious as either try to make out it was. Fabian did know of Rex's whereabouts, even though he claims not to have spoken to him for years. Motive. Power. He liked to control young women.

Caspian Stonehand

Is right in the middle of all this and we didn't really take him seriously as a murderer until we found out that he owned a car. After that, hints and clues were dropped into our ears thick and fast. He was suddenly seen in the marketplace with a young woman; he tossed something into the back seat, possibly Nina's case. It is possible that he picked her up that night and, being local, he would almost certainly have known where Creepy Cottage was. It is quite possible that others are pointing a finger at him because he can't answer back. According to Rex, Fabian and Chester, he was the man who hatched the plot to blackmail Fabian. Again, we could do with finding the woman on the reception desk and the woman who had allegedly accompanied Fabian to his room. Odds are slim at best. Caspian had it in for Margo, that was for sure, and we finally found out why. Was he so angry after discovering her with Rex that he took it out on another seventeen-year-old? Possibly. He was seen at the marketplace.

He got money to start his business from somewhere and the best part of sixty-five pounds out of that hundred would have gone a long way towards his start-up costs. A motive is hard to find, but that doesn't mean there wasn't one. A crime of passion, maybe, although Caspian, as we have heard, wasn't the most passionate of men.

Imogen Blackwood

Was with her mother and aunt all night. We can definitely rule her out.

Caspian Stonehand Case

Rex Larson

Doesn't appear on the surface to be involved in Caspian's killing, although he has been in touch with Margo for all these years and she would do anything for him. Maybe they colluded to have him killed, if they were concerned about what he'd tell us in his evidence. Fear or Desperation could be the motive.

Margo Ashburner

Although when we first met her, she appeared to be a virtual slave of Caspian's, it soon transpired that her doting on him was an act, as Imogen Blackwood stated in her evidence. She may have been insulted one time too many and lashed out. Although we saw her not long after the attack, she seemed to recover very quickly and we only have her word that the attack took place the way she stated.

If she was his attacker, she would have had blood on her clothing and there was no sign of any. Having said that, she may have been wearing a coat, an overall or some other outer garment that she hid in the theatre before the ambulance arrived. Were she and Jack working together? Is she lying about her relationship with him? She appears to be totally obsessed with Rex and there's a chance that he asked her to get rid of Caspian because he knew too much and the police were asking tricky questions. Motive. Hatred possibly. Obsession. Love. Pretty much the same motives as she would have had if she had been involved in the Nina Honeychurch case.

Jack Draper

Again, we won't know until he's caught, so we can only surmise here. Was Jack in love with Margo? Why did he draw that heart and dagger? Why did he leave so suddenly, just a few minutes before the attack? Why did he run? Why does he have a problem with his adoptive mother? Margo said he's a man's man. What does that mean? Jack doesn't have access to a car as far as we know, and no longer works part time driving taxis as we were told his sole income, apart from the petty cash handouts, is from his work as a cabinetmaker. Was the car heard driving away at speed taking him away from the scene of the crime, or was it just coincidence? Motive. Hatred for the way Caspian used to treat Margo? Love... possibly.

Fabian Starr

Fabian Starr's car pulled up not long after we got to the scene. Had he been there previously and then returned to witness the aftermath? Could Fabian be exacting revenge on Caspian for blackmailing him all those years ago? Or was he worried about what Caspian might come out with under questioning? Motives. Revenge. Desperation.

Chester Harvey

As far as we know has no connection with Caspian other than they were both involved in the blackmail of Fabian. They have lived in the same town since then, though. Spinton isn't a big place compared to other towns, so it's quite possible that they have bumped into each other at times over the years. Once again, Desperation may be the motive if Chester was worried about what Caspian might reveal about the events of that night.

Imogen Blackwood

Has a cast-iron alibi. She was out drinking with friends, and Bodkin has their names and addresses so they can be checked.

What we don't know

How did Margot find out that Caspian had died when she was in Tunbridge Wells?

Where is Jack Draper? He seems to have disappeared off the face of the earth even though he seems to have no way to support himself and has taken few, if any, of his belongings with him. He was almost certainly wearing his overalls that night, and they would have been covered in blood. Has he disposed of them?

What happened to the murder weapon?

Who was the driver of the mystery car on the night of Caspian's death?

Could Rex have actually succeeded in making his drug deal? If so, how did he come by his injuries? Did Nina inflict them on him in a desperate fight for life?

At ten o'clock, Amy picked up the three sheets of foolscap paper and after reading through the notes one last time, she pulled down the roll top, turned out the light and after shouting 'good night' to her parents who were listening to the news on the radio, she made her way upstairs to bed.

Chapter Thirty-Nine

'We've found Jack Draper!'

'Where was he?' Amy asked as she grabbed hold of Bodkin's arm and led him to the front of the shop. Bodkin eyed Josie warily as she waved to him from behind the counter.

'He was holed up in the houses marked for demolition on Ebenezer Street. I don't know why we didn't find him before now. The beat officer has been checking them on a daily basis. Kids like to play in them and they're really not safe.'

'How was he missed then?'

'We don't know. From the officer's report, it doesn't look like he's been there longer than a few hours. He had a pot of fresh cooked stew wrapped in a tea towel, so someone has provided it for him. Whoever it was could have been sheltering him, too.'

Amy stamped her foot. 'Botheration. I wanted to be there when you questioned him, but I'm stuck here until five-thirty.'

Bodkin grinned. 'You can sit in. We won't be questioning him until later this afternoon. He's at the hospital getting his cuts and bruises seen to.'

'Cuts and bruises?'

'He resisted arrest, tried to run, but PC Smedley was his school's hundred yards champion and could run faster. It ended in a brawl and Jack came off worst.'

'I wonder where he's been staying?' Amy mused. 'Do you think Margo could have been putting him up? Her house was never searched.'

'It's a possibility,' Bodkin replied. 'But he must have some friends from work. One of them might have put him up for a night or two.' He stepped back as a customer walked into the shop.

'I'll be with you in a moment, Mrs Culpepper,' Amy said, ushering Bodkin towards the door.

'There was one other thing you might like to think about while you're dressing the great and the good. I received a call from the Dover police this morning regarding our Jack's past record. There were two unresolved attacks on young women in the town a few months before Jack left to come back here. There was also a complaint made against him for an assault on a girl in the children's home he was in. That happened a couple of months before he was adopted by the Drapers.'

'Were they sexual assaults?' Amy whispered.

'No. In the kid's home incident, it was an argument that got out of hand and punches were thrown from both parties. Jack's obviously being the most damaging of them. The two young women in Dover were attacked on different nights as they got off busses in the town centre. There was a description of the attacker given by both women, but they didn't really match. One said the man was in dirty overalls, the other said hers wore a creased suit. One said dark hair, one said fair, so the attacks were never officially linked. The attacks took place after dark and like here, Dover isn't blessed with a lot of street lighting.'

'What if Jack had just finished his coal deliveries? He'd have been wearing dirty overalls and he would have had coal dust in his hair, making it look darker than it was.'

'I like your thinking,' Bodkin said as he took hold of the door handle. 'Make sure you get something to eat before we question him. It could be a long evening.'

Taking Bodkin's advice, Amy left the sandwiches that her mother had packed for her in her bag and at lunchtime walked the few yards around the corner to the Sunshine Café where she ordered a slice of cheese on toast and a pot of tea. The only topic of conversation on the tables around her was whether, by this time next week, the country would be at war with Germany for the second time in just over twenty years. Young men who fought back then could easily be ordered to fight again in this one. It hardly seemed fair.

At five-thirty Amy offered to lock up and when everyone had gone, she sat down in the staff room and ate her cheese and pickle sandwiches with a cup of tea. After carefully checking that all the windows were fastened up, she let herself out of the front door, locked it behind her, and made her way across to Middle Street, then down to the police station. She arrived just before six.

'Perfect timing,' PC Parlour said, as Amy walked into the reception area. 'Inspector Bodkin is just getting everything ready. He's going to interview Mr Draper in his office.' Parlour stepped from behind the counter and opened the door to allow Amy into the station. 'You know the way.'

She found Bodkin sipping tea and flicking through some loose papers in the file on his desk. Ferris was standing at his side with a teacup in his hand. They both looked up as Amy entered. Bodkin beamed at her as Ferris lifted a hand and waved.

'I'm just going through the report you popped through the front door this morning. Well done again. It's nicely summarised.'

'I'll be able to add the missing bits to it later tonight, I hope. Have they let him out of hospital yet?'

'Yes, his injuries were only superficial. PC Smedley's injuries were worse. He got a broken nose when Jack Draper hit him with a half brick.'

'Poor Smedley,' Amy said. 'I hope they can fix it. He's a nice-looking lad.'

'They are going to try to straighten it when the swelling goes down,' Bodkin said. 'He'll be all right, I've had mine fixed twice.' Bodkin motioned to the spare seat he had pulled behind his desk. 'Take the weight off your feet. You've been on them all day.'

Amy sat down as Ferris waved the teapot. She took a quick look at the milk bottle on top of the filing cabinet and shook her head. 'I've just had one, thanks.'

Just then there was the sound of a struggle at the door and PC Smedley, complete with a swollen, twisted nose, pushed a handcuffed man into the room. Once inside, he grabbed the man by the collar and almost dragged him across the floor to the seat by the desk that Amy usually sat on when paying Bodkin a visit. Draper sat down sullenly and snarled at Smedley.

'You'll behave yourself unless you want a trip back to the hospital,' Smedley said, curling up his lip at Draper.

Jack Draper was around five feet ten, with a round face, a wide nose and a mop of tangled, light brown hair. He looked at Smedley belligerently, then turned his head towards the desk.

Bodkin placed his cup on the top of the filing cabinet and sat down next to Amy. He picked up the file from the desk and pretended to study it. After a few moments, he looked across at Draper.

'Hello, Jack, thanks for dropping in.'

Jack glowered back across the desk.

'Why did you run, Jack?' Bodkin asked. 'Today I mean, not last week... although I'll be asking why you did that at some stage.'

'If a copper comes at you, you run,' Draper replied. 'It's just what you do.'

'You do when you're a kid, when you're, say, twelve or thirteen. You don't do it when you're a grown man. Not unless you've got something to hide.'

'I never got out of the habit,' Draper said. He looked at Ferris, who was just finishing his tea. 'Is there one of those going spare?'

'It depends. Let's see how co-operative you are first,' Ferris replied.

Draper sniffed but didn't reply.

Bodkin tossed the file onto the desk. 'You're a bit of a Jack the lad, aren't you?'

Jack said nothing.

'You had quite a record back in the day.'

'I was only a kid. I grew out of it.'

'You did well for a few years, Jack, when you were riding around on your dad's coal wagon, or at least that's how it looked.'

'You leave Bert out of this,' Draper spat, leaning so far forward in his seat that a concerned Smedley dragged him back by his collar.

'You loved that old man, didn't you, Jack? Despite the fact that he was an old miser.' Bodkin paused. 'You didn't take to your new mother quite as well, though. Why was that?'

'We didn't get on. That's all.'

'You don't like women much, do you, Jack?'

Jack frowned. 'What are you getting at?'

'You beat up a girl at the kid's home for a start.'

'She asked for it. She never let up on me.'

'Why didn't she let up on you, Jack? She must have had a reason.'

'She hated me from day one. I didn't do anything to provoke her. Some people just don't get on.' He looked up at Smedley. 'Like me and old flatfoot here. We'll never get on.'

'You got that right,' Smedley muttered.

Amy made a steeple with her fingers. 'I don't understand why you didn't carry on with the coal round after Bert died. It was a thriving business; you could have been set up for life.'

'Who are you to ask questions?' Draper said, as if noticing Amy for the first time.

'Miss Rowlings is assisting us on this investigation,' Bodkin said before Amy could reply. 'You will treat her with the utmost respect.'

'Or what?' Draper sneered.

'Or I'll take you down to the cells and beat some respect into you,' Bodkin scowled.

Draper shrugged. 'Okay, I get the message. Is she your bit of... OI!' he shouted as Smedley cuffed him around the ear. 'You wouldn't dare do that if I didn't have these on.' He raised his hands to show the handcuffs.

'Let's get back to you running away, Jack,' Bodkin said evenly. 'Running away last week, not from PC Smedley. We've already covered that.'

Jack leaned back in his seat, tried to fold his arms but when he realised he couldn't, he dropped his hands into his lap.

'What I don't get, Jack,' Bodkin said, 'is that everyone at the Playhouse thinks you're a quiet, pleasant young man, but you've been anything but this evening. You've been aggressive, surly and utterly unpleasant. Why the change in character? Or is this your true character, and the rest is an act?'

'I treat as I find,' Draper replied.

'I'm just the same, Jack.' Bodkin slammed his hand down on his desk so hard that it made everyone else in the room jump. 'But I'm a bit like that doctor in Jekyll and Hyde. I can change in an instant.' He got to his feet, leaned over the desk and glared at Draper. 'Now, answer the question. Why did you run?'

'Because I thought I might get blamed for it, of course. Why else?'

'Why would you get the blame, Jack? You've never killed anyone before, have you? We'd have had to ask you a few questions, of course, but they would only have been routine. Things like, why did you leave the rehearsal so suddenly and...' Bodkin paused as creases appeared on his brow. 'Why did you leave the rehearsals so suddenly?'

'I realised I had promised to be somewhere else,' Draper replied.

'Where?'

'Someone wants some kitchen cabinets making. Nice ones. I said I'd go to see him and price it up.'

Bodkin produced his notebook in a flash.

'Who, where, what time?'

'It was over Highwater way. I forget the address now. I had to get the bus and they only run at ten to the hour.'

'What about the customer's name? You must remember that. We might be able to trace them through the telephone directory, or even through the council. He'll be on their lists for his rates bill.'

Jack shook his head. 'I'm sorry. It might have been Smith, but I can't be sure.'

'Smith.' Bodkin pursed his lips as he glared at Draper. 'We can check all the Smiths. There won't be too many in Highwater.'

'I only said might have been.'

Bodkin wagged a finger at him. 'I'll give you a piece of advice, Jack. Don't take me for a fool. Many have tried, but none have succeeded.'

Jack held up his hands and nodded in understanding. Bodkin gave him a stern look and then continued the questioning.

'When you left, did you see a car parked up outside on the road? One with someone sitting inside it, perhaps?'

'There were a few cars, there always are. I can't remember seeing anyone waiting.'

Bodkin glanced to the side at Amy and nodded to her.

'How do you get on with Margo Ashburner, Jack?' she asked.

'All right. I get on with everyone at the Playhouse.'

'Caspian used to give you money out of the petty cash, didn't he?'

'Now and then, it was never much though, just a few bob here and there.'

'Do you think you deserved more? I'm surprised you kept going there, to be honest. You're a tradesman. You could have been making decent money if you spent your time, well, making kitchen cabinets to order, in your free time.'

'I like working there. It's a challenge. I don't have anyone looking over my shoulder. I'm just asked to come up with an idea, or a new prop, and they leave me to get on with it.'

'Did you ever have an argument over a prop or a backdrop? Did Caspian always accept what you put forward?'

'Ninety percent of the time. He did offer suggestions now and then.'

'How do you get on with the female members of the cast... staff? Margo, for example. Do you like her? She's a very attractive woman.' Amy smiled across the table as she asked the question.

'She's all right. A bit timid. She lets... she let Caspian walk all over her.'

'What did you think of that, Jack?'

'What do you mean?'

'Was it her fault for letting him bully her, or his fault for doing it?'

'He should have treated her better.'

'Do you know the reason he didn't treat her better?'

'I've heard stories.'

'Who told you those stories?'

'No one, I get to overhear things when I'm at the back of the stage or up in the lighting rig. People forget I'm there. I become invisible.'

'So you liked Margo, but did you fancy her?'

'I wouldn't have said no, but she only had eyes for Caspian, despite the way he treated her. Oh, and that Rex guy, too. I think she'd have run bare-footed over broken glass for him. Every time his name came up, you could see her almost swoon.'

'Did his name come up often?' Amy asked.

'Not often, now and again, especially when he was in the papers.'

'I bet his name was mud around the Playhouse, wasn't it?'

Jack shrugged. 'Caspian seemed pleased. The rest of them just sort of accepted it. It was no big surprise, after all. We all knew what he was like.'

'What about Margo? How did she react when all those lurid stories came out?'

'She stuck up for him, of course, but she knew it was all true. She even went to London to stay with him for a weekend. Caspian gave her a dressing down for that. He said the rehearsals suffered because of her absence.' He frowned. 'I don't know how they suffered. She was never allowed to take part in them. She only ever made the tea or prompted the actors, and any of the others could have done that.'

'Do you know,' Bodkin cut in, 'this is turning into a really nice chat. I think we might have that cup of tea after all.' He turned to Ferris. 'Would you do the honours?'

'None for me, unless you've got some fresh milk,' Amy said, flashing a look at the yellowing bottle on top of the filing cabinet.

'Trixie got fresh in this afternoon. I'll make the tea in the back office.'

Amy suddenly got to her feet. 'If we're going to be late, I'd better let Mum and Dad know. Is it all right if I ring Alice so she can take a message up to them?'

Bodkin picked up the handset and offered it to Amy, but she shook her head. 'I'll use the one in the back office if that's all right. I can help Ferris with the tea at the same time.'

After a quick chat with Alice, Amy sat on the corner of Trixie's desk and accepted a cup of tea on a chipped saucer from Ferris. 'I'm glad you followed me in. I can't fit five cups on the tray.'

Amy took a sip. 'That's a lovely cuppa, Ferris. You'll make some woman a good husband one day.'

'I aim to please,' Ferris replied, loading up the tray.

'How's it going with Sal?' Amy asked, looking over the rim of her teacup.

'It's going well; at least I think it is. It's hard to tell with women.'

Amy laughed. 'We're a mystery, aren't we?'

Ferris nodded quickly. 'She's wonderful, though. I do like her. We have exactly the same sense of humour.'

'That's a good start,' Amy said.

'It's the boss I'm more concerned about.'

Amy sighed. 'Bodkin? What's he been saying now? He promised me he'd leave the pair of you alone.'

'Oh, he is... has... No, it's not that. He...'

Amy took a long sip of tea and raised her eyebrows to encourage him to continue.

'It's the things he says. He's been calling me custard chops all day and I have no idea why.'

Amy spat the tea back into her cup and burst into laughter.

'I see you're in on the joke,' Ferris said. 'Care to explain it?'

Amy shook her head, pulled out a handkerchief from the pocket of her dress, and dabbed her mouth with it. 'I'll leave that to you boys to sort out.'

Back in Bodkin's office, Ferris put the tray down on the desk and Jack reached forward eagerly. 'Three sugars please,' he said to Smedley. He held up his hands. 'Well, I can't do it like this, can I?'

'Are you sure he should have hot tea, sir?' Smedley asked. 'He could use it as a weapon.'

'Have you heard yourself?' Jack said with a laugh. 'Come on, Smedders, I'm not going to waste good tea on the likes of you lot. I'm parched.'

When they were all settled again, Bodkin tapped his notebook with the end of his pen. 'Let's go back a bit, shall we, Jack? I've got a few loose ends that need tidying up from another case you might have been involved in.'

Jack looked at him suspiciously, holding his cup in both hands.

'How far back?'

'October nineteenth, nineteen twenty-nine.'

'Blimey!' Jack exclaimed. 'That's a long time ago. I can hardly remember what I did last month.'

'You'll remember this night, Jack. Everyone we've spoken to does. It was the night that Rex Larson came to town.'

'Ah, him.' He sipped his tea, then nodded towards Ferris. 'Honestly, mate, if you ever leave the police, start up a café, you'll make a fortune.'

'What can you tell us about that night, Jack? How were things back stage?'

'Pretty much the same as normal. The props all worked, the curtains opened and closed and the lighting rig behaved.'

Bodkin gave him a quick smile. 'I mean, after the show. Rex did a quick meet and greet, then disappeared into his dressing room. Who else went in with him?'

Jack studied his teacup. 'Two girls, probably about sixteen or seventeen. They might have been younger, though. It's hard to tell when girls get tarted up.'

'While he was in there with the girls. Did anything unusual happen?'

'No, I don't think so.'

'What sort of mood was Caspian in?'

'As far as I remember, he just bored the pants off that theatrical agent. The guy with the funny name.'

'Fabian Starr.'

'That's the feller.'

'What about Margo? What was she up to?'

Jack thought for a few moments. 'Look, I can't really remember that much about it. I was standing with the b list actors sipping at a glass of beer.'

'Did she seem upset at all, agitated?'

'She's always looked agitated, but yes, now I think about it, she was hanging around Rex's dressing room door. She had a bottle of decent scotch in her hands. She kept putting her ear to the door. I think she was listening out for him to call.'

'When you left, you went out via the stage door?'

'We always did. Still do.'

'Who was hanging about out there?'

Jack blew out his cheeks. 'Strewth... I don't know.... There were a few autograph hunters, a couple of taxis. Rex's driver and his Daimler... I can't think of anyone else.'

'Did you know the taxi drivers, Jack? After all, you were one yourself. Were they from the company you worked for?'

'No, I didn't recognise them, but then I only worked from eleven to around two or three in the morning. They could just have been evening shift drivers, or even private hire. I didn't take much notice of them.'

'Did you recognise Rex's driver? He drove the taxis too.'

'No, I might have seen him around town, but he wasn't anyone I knew well enough to speak to.'

'The young autograph hunters. Did you speak to them?'

'No, I had my overalls and a flat cap on. I wasn't anyone they'd be interested in.'

'What did you do when you got through the crowd?'

'I wouldn't say there was a crowd. Half a dozen at most.'

'Okay, but where did you go then?'

Jack tipped his head as he thought. 'I was on shift at eleven, so I must've walked down to the marketplace to pick up my taxi.'

'Did you always pick it up at the marketplace?'

Jack nodded. 'Yep. I took the car of whichever driver was finishing at eleven.'

'Were you always on time to make the changeover?'

'Within five minutes, yes. Sometimes I had to wait for them to get back if they'd just had a fare.'

'Jack, we have a witness that says you were standing on the corner near the Playhouse for quite some time. What were you doing?'

'I can't remember doing that. I'm always on time for my... hang on... I might have stopped for a ciggie. I don't like smoking when I'm walking. I like to enjoy the experience, I didn't smoke that many, probably only five a day, so I used to take my time and savour it.'

'You were watching the girls at the stage door.'

'You have to look somewhere.'

Bodkin nodded. 'Fair enough. Then what did you do, after you'd savoured your ciggie?'

'I took a walk over to the marketplace. It isn't far.'

'Did you follow the group of girls from the stage door?'

'For part of the way, then I crossed the street.'

'You have to pass the George and the Milton to get to the marketplace, don't you?'

'Yes.'

'Did you see anyone outside the George? Rex, for instance?'

Jack shook his head. 'No, but I was on the other side of the road by then.'

'You didn't see Fabian Starr and his friends go into the Milton?'

'Nope.'

'What about Margo? Did you see her?'

'No, but she was always last out. She locks up.'

'What about Rex's driver? Did you see him drive by?'

'I can't say that I did.'

'And Caspian? Did you see him?'

'Yes. While I was waiting for my changeover.'

'Where was he?'

'He was standing next to one of those silly little Citroen C3 cars. You don't see many of those about. I was on the corner opposite the bus stop. I always waited there. He was on the other side of the market.'

'Was he with anyone?'

'He was with a short woman. He chucked something of hers in the back seat. It might have been a case. I remember thinking, that's typical, taking a fare out of a cabbie's mouth.'

'Think carefully, Jack. Was it one of the girls from the stage door?'

'It might have been, one of them had a case. She might have been walking to the marketplace to get a cab. I was on the other side of the road, as I said, and there was traffic, so I didn't see where she went. I wouldn't swear on it, Inspector, but it could well have been her.'

Chapter Forty

'Did your taxi turn up soon after?' Bodkin asked.

'Yes, I think so. I didn't have to wait too long, anyway.'

'Were you busy that night? Did you get many fares?'

'It was probably a normal night. I always got a lot early on, then it eased off in the early hours. I was kept busy though on the whole.'

'Did you have a break during your shift?'

'No, it was only four hours maximum, so I didn't need one. There are no cafés open at that time of night, anyway.'

'Do you know the Witchy Wood?'

'Of course.'

'Do you know where the old house called the Creepy Cottage is?'

'I've walked past it a time or two. I think everyone in the town knows where it is.'

'Did you drop off a fare anywhere near the wood that night?'

'No... no, I don't think I did.'

'Did you keep your overalls on when you drove?'

'No, I used to take them off and put them in the boot.'

'That's interesting, so had you been wearing a coat under your overalls all night? You must have been very hot in the theatre.'

'I always drove in shirtsleeves. The taxi had a heater. It wasn't great, but it did the job.'

Bodkin stuck up his thumbs. 'Even when the snow was on the ground? You never wore a coat?'

'I used to wear one in winter, of course, but this was October. It wasn't too cold.'

'Did you pick up any female customers that night?'

'I honestly can't remember. Women don't tend to go out alone late at night so I wouldn't have thought so. My passengers were almost always men. I made good money from them, as they were mainly drunk when they left the clubs and late bars, so I could add a few coppers onto the fare.' He put his cup on the desk. 'Is there another one going?'

'Not yet, Jack. Let's move it on a bit. You are stating as a fact that you didn't get any female fares late at night.'

'Hang on, I didn't say I never got them. I just can't remember any that night. I used to get the odd street girl coming or going after seeing a client, but not many respectable women.'

'Did you ever try out the services of the street girls, Jack? You know… a free fare for a good time in the back of the cab?'

Jack's face twisted. 'What do you think I am? I wouldn't go near the dirty scum. They disgust me.'

'You don't like prostitutes then, Jack?' Amy asked quietly. 'Is it just prostitutes, or all women?'

Jack jabbed a finger at her. 'Don't you try to put words in my mouth. You're just like the rest of them, aren't you? You think you're bloody royalty sitting over there with his lordship.' He leaned forward, his face a mask of anger. 'Well, you're not. You're just another two bob tart.'

Smedley hauled Jack back into his seat and wrapped an arm around his neck. 'Just say the word, sir.'

'I think you answered Miss Rowlings' question quite succinctly. Now answer the obvious follow up one. Why do you hate women,

Jack? We've been told you prefer male company, but that outburst told us a lot more about your character.'

'I'm not one of them, if that's what you mean,' Jack said angrily. 'I don't like that sort.'

Bodkin took a deep breath. 'You don't like women, Jack. You even despised your mother. You say you're not a homosexual and I believe you. But that just leaves us with the other option. The one that tells us that you like to control women, have power over them. We looked at your room, Jack. Most men of your age would have a picture of a girl to look at now and then. Maybe a pin up photo or something from a magazine... You get my drift? But not you. You have a photograph of yourself as a teenager alongside a twenty something man with his arm around you. The only picture of a woman you have is of a lady dressed in early Edwardian clothes. Was that your actual mother, Jack? The one that died and left you to fend for yourself. Is that why you hate women so much?'

Jack stuck out his chin but said nothing.

'You see, Jack,' Bodkin leaned forward, 'I think there's a distinct possibility that you did see Nina Honeychurch that night. As you told us, there aren't that many women walking the streets when you begin your shift. Especially young, pretty girls who are lost or who have nowhere to go. I think it might have been you who was talking to her in the marketplace. I think it might have been you that chucked her case into the back seat and drove off with her, to do whatever it was that you had decided to do. The problem is, you can't afford a hotel, and being a woman, she didn't deserve a soft bed, anyway, so where can you take her? Then you have a brainwave... the cottage in the woods. No one will disturb you there. You can take your time and give the good-for-nothing woman what she deserves.' Bodkin leaned back in his chair. 'How does that sound, Jack? Does it ring any bells?'

Jack's mouth opened and closed, but no sound came out. Eventually he regained his composure, and he leaned back in his chair, struggling to ease out of PC Smedley's grip. 'That's a load of old tosh. You're trying to fit me up and I'm not going to say another word until I see my brief.'

'Your brief?' Laughter erupted from Bodkin. 'That's the biggest laugh I've had in days. Jack has a solicitor.' He pushed his notebook and pen across the desk. 'Jot down his telephone number and I'll give him a call.'

Jack didn't take up the offer. Instead, he glared across the table at Bodkin. 'You can't keep me here. I know my rights.'

'My brief! I haven't got over that yet. This isn't a Hollywood film, Jack. You don't have a lawyer and could never afford to have one on your wage. As for knowing your rights, that's an even bigger laugh. You don't know anything about the law.' A faint smile came across his face. 'But fortunately, I do and I'm telling you now, Jack, if I suspect you of having committed a serious crime, I can keep you here as long as I like.' He looked up at the constable standing to the side of Jack. 'Smedley, you know that key you have in your pocket? The one that fits the lock on the cell that's been put aside for Jack? Just chuck it in the kitchen drawer when you get home tonight. You won't be needing it for a while.'

Bodkin was silent as he let his statement sink in. Jack suddenly became more amenable. 'I'm sorry about what I said to you,' he said to Amy, giving her only the slightest of glances. 'I let my emotions get the better of me at times.' His gaze turned towards Bodkin. 'I know you're just trying to wind me up like a clockwork monkey, but I'm not going to crash those cymbals. I had nothing to do with that girl's death. I didn't go anywhere near the Witchy Wood that night, let alone Creepy Cottage. I'm innocent, honestly. You have to believe me.'

Bodkin clapped his hands together. 'That's better. Now that we're all friends again, I think we should have another cup of tea to mark the occasion.' He pointed to the tray on the desk. 'Smedley, you do the honours this time.'

'But, sir, what about...'

'Ferris can watch our friend here,' Bodkin replied. 'You're going to behave yourself, aren't you, Jack?'

Bodkin and Amy shared a couple of whispered conversations while Smedley was away making the tea. Bodkin looking across at Jack now and then as though Amy was telling him something he hadn't noticed, when, in fact, what they were discussing was what Bodkin might have for his supper when the questioning was complete.

When Smedley came back, he placed the tray containing four cups on the desk, then went back to his place at Jack's side.

'Only four cups?' Ferris queried.

'I didn't want one this time,' Smedley replied. 'I'll be running to the lavvy all night if I have any more.'

Draper sniggered as Ferris tipped the three spoonsful of sugar into the suspect's tea. Picking the cup from the tray, he passed it to Jack, who lifted it in both hands and took a tentative sip.

'Christ,' he said, pulling a face. 'Don't employ him in your café if you start one up. You'll go bust inside a week.' He handed the cup back to Ferris. 'That's probably the worst cup of tea I've had in my life.'

Amy picked hers up with trepidation and after taking the smallest of sips, she too pulled a face and put the teacup quickly back onto the tray. 'Ugh,' she said with a shudder.

Bodkin decided to skip the tea.

'Now we'll see how good your recent memories are, Jack. Take us back to last Thursday. You were on the stage instead of in your workshop, which was unusual. Why did you decide to take your art pad to the stage to sketch out your designs? It would have been noisy, what with the rehearsals going on.'

'I just fancied a change, that's all. I wanted to show Caspian my new backdrop design too. I knew I had to go early and I might not have had the chance if I'd stayed in the workshop.'

'Did you get to show him your design?' Bodkin opened his drawer and pulled out a brown paper bag. Inside was Jack's pad.

Bodkin pulled it out and flicked through the pages until he found a sheet with the outline of an old-fashioned coaching inn sketched on it. 'Was this it?'

Jack nodded as Bodkin showed him the drawing.

'But what about this one, Jack?' He flipped the page and showed him the heart and dagger sketch. 'Where did this fit in?'

'I was doodling,' Jack replied.

'It's pretty detailed for a doodle. That heart is nicely shaded and the blood dripping from the dagger looks almost real.'

Jack's face lost a little of its colour.

'Are you sure you weren't imagining what Caspian's heart would look like when you caught up with him outside?'

'No... it was nothing like that. I...'

'It's not even a broken heart, Jack. Broken hearts are what teenagers draw when they've been dumped by the person they thought was the love of their lives. There's a great big dagger here, and it's dripping blood. Now, I don't know what that says about your mental state. I'm not a psychiatrist after all, but I think Sigmund Freud might have read something into it. He thinks all men fancy their mothers. I don't think I did. What about you, Jack?'

'Sod off. I was only a kid when she died on me.'

'Fair enough,' Bodkin said. 'I think it's a load of old bunkum, too.' He reached for his tea, then thought better of it and pulled his hand back quickly.

'All right then. You'd done with your doodling, then what?'

'I suddenly noticed the time. I would have to run to catch my bus.'

'Did you catch it?'

'No, I saw it go down towards the marketplace as I came out onto the street.'

'So what did you do then?'

'I walked home. I don't live far away. I rent a room on Nelson Street.'

'Did you see anyone hanging around? A suspicious-looking character lurking in the shadows with a knife, perhaps?'

'No.'

Amy put her hand on Bodkin's arm, then smiled sweetly across the table at Jack.

'Where are your overalls, Jack?'

Jack looked back as though he had been slapped.

Amy continued, not waiting for an answer. 'Only you were wearing them that night, but they weren't in your room. We searched it.'

'Answer the lady, Jack,' Bodkin said firmly. 'Did you have to destroy them because they were covered in blood?'

'They're at work. I left them at work.'

'They aren't at work, Jack. You haven't been near the place since you did a runner.'

'I don't know where they are, then. I must have left them behind when I was in hiding.'

'Ah, that will be it,' Bodkin said, smiling at everyone in the room in turn. 'Where were you hiding? It must have been a good place. We couldn't find you until today.'

'I was in the demolitions in a cellar.'

'No, you were not. Our beat officers were told to check the site on a daily basis.'

'Well, they didn't do too good a job. That's where I was.'

Bodkin sniffed the air.

'You don't smell, Jack. It's been quite warm and you are telling us you've been wearing the same clothes since you took off your overalls last Thursday. That's a week. You should be smelling like a sewer by now.'

'One of the demolitions had a tap still working. I washed under that.'

'Where did the fresh food come from, Jack?' Amy asked. 'Please don't say from the market. You can't buy a pot of stew wrapped in a tea towel in the market.'

'And there was no sign of a fire anywhere,' Smedley put in. 'So how did you cook it?'

Jack began to fidget in his seat.

'I've got friends at work. One of them helped me out with a bit of food.'

Bodkin slid his notebook back across the desk. 'Name and address?'

'I'm not dropping anyone in it,' Jack said sullenly.

'Come on, Jack. Be a pal.' Bodkin checked his watch. 'We're going to be here all night at this rate. Give us a name. Who helped you? I'm not having any of this friend from work nonsense. Was it Margo Ashburner?'

'Margo? No. Why would she help me?'

'I don't know, Jack,' Bodkin replied. 'But I do know we'll be searching those houses again for your overalls tomorrow and we'll be going to see your boss and we'll be asking all your workmates whether any of them helped you. I don't think your boss will take our intrusion too well, especially when he finds out you're in the nick, facing a murder charge. I doubt you'll have a job to go back to even if you are released soon. Which, if I'm honest, I can't really see happening.'

'This isn't fair,' Jack shouted. 'I'm being set up.'

'Life isn't fair, Jack,' Bodkin said with a sad note in his voice. 'It wasn't fair to Nina Honeychurch, and it wasn't fair to Caspian Stonehand... unless they got what was coming, of course.' He paused as he looked intently at the cabinetmaker. 'Well, Jack, did they deserve to die?'

'I don't know! Does anyone deserve to die? Did Bert deserve to die? Did my real mother deserve to die? Why are you asking me?'

'Your adopted mother is dying, Jack,' Amy said softly. 'She asked you to come and see her in her letters. She begged you, in fact, but you haven't been.'

'She's one of those who deserves all she gets,' Jack said tersely.

'I honestly can't work out why you hate her so much. Did she beat you, starve you, send you to bed without a cup of milk? What did she do to make you despise her so much? It's obvious that she has feelings for you.'

'HA!' Jack pushed himself back into his chair.

'Did she try too hard, Jack?' Amy asked. 'Did she try to replace your birth mother, the one who deserted you when she died?'

Jack got to his feet suddenly, taking Smedley by surprise. 'Charge me with something or let me go. I don't have to sit here listening to this.'

'Oh, but you do have to listen, Jack, and then you have to reply. That's how conversations work,' Bodkin said, nodding to Smedley, who put his hands on Jack's shoulders and forced him onto the seat again. 'We can all sit here and have a nice friendly chat, or I can get Smedley and his mate Parlour to ask you a few questions in private. The choice is yours.'

Jack let out an enormous sigh and wriggled about on his chair until he was comfortable.

'Jack,' Bodkin said when he saw that he had settled down. 'All we've found out from you so far is that you don't like women and you can draw a decent picture of a dripping dagger. We need to know a lot more than that before we allow you to go home.' He looked at Amy, then back at Jack. 'So do me a favour. I don't want to clutter our cells up more than I have to. I'd much rather Mrs Creasey had the pleasure of your company tonight.'

'I've answered your questions. I haven't done anything wrong.'

'Where did you stay over the weekend, Jack? And don't give me any cock and bull story about hiding in the part demolished houses. We know that's a lie.'

Jack opened his mouth to reply, then shut it again.

'Have you spoken to anyone since last Thursday?' Amy asked. 'If you were really so well hidden, you wouldn't have been able to communicate with anyone.'

'I haven't spoken to anyone.'

'So, how did you know that Caspian had died?'

The colour drained from Jack's face again.

'I must have overheard people talking about it.'

'While you were in the cellar of a partly demolished house? Who was talking about Caspian's death... the rats?'

'Look, I... I don't know, I heard it somewhere.'

'Or from someone,' Bodkin said. 'I'm going to be honest with you here, Jack. No one and I mean, no one would have gone out of their way to visit you in the cellar of a house that could fall down any minute, just to tell you that Caspian had died, yet that's the only way you could have known.' Bodkin got to his feet. 'I'm done with messing around. There's no way you would look as clean and smell as fresh as you do if you had been living in a vermin infested cellar, washing under a cold tap.' He paused. 'Stand up, please.'

Jack got reluctantly to his feet.

'Jack Draper, I'm arresting you on suspicion of the murder of Caspian Stonehand. You do not have to say anything, but anything you say may be used in evidence against you. Do you understand?'

Jack's mouth fell open. 'You can't do this. I've done nothing.'

'Take him away, Smedley,' Bodkin said, wafting his hand as though he was shooing away an insect.

Amy watched as Smedley dragged a loudly protesting Jack Draper from the room. When his screamed insults became as faint as the buzzing from the electric light overhead, she picked up her summary file from the table, then picked up her bag. 'I'll finish this off tonight, Bodkin, though I don't know how much we actually learned from him.'

'We may not have got much, but he will have learned something. He'll know that he isn't going to be let out anytime soon. He'll also realise that if he doesn't come up with a reasonable explanation as to who's been sheltering him and what he really knows about Caspian's death, then he's going to be up before the beak and remanded to prison.'

Amy stepped out from the back of the desk and took a few steps towards the office door. 'I can get the bus home, Bodkin. Don't worry about giving me a lift. You must have lots to do.'

'I'll be with you in two shakes of a donkey's tail,' Bodkin said, picking up the phone. He checked his notepad, then dialled. 'I'm just going to send Sexy Rexy a message via Margo Ashburner.... Hello, Miss Ashburner, it's Inspector Bodkin again... yes, I'm sorry to interrupt your meal, but it is important. I'd like you to get in touch with Rex Larson. Tell him to present himself at the police station in Spinton not one minute later than ten o'clock on Saturday morning.' He paused as he listened to Margo. 'Yes, I know it's short notice but let's be honest, he's got nothing better to do, except maybe rot his liver with cheap whisky... I don't care how he gets here, there are buses and trains that run direct. You can even drive over and get him yourself if you like, but just think on this, and make sure he understands. If he isn't here by the stipulated time, then Tunbridge Wells police will drag him out of his hotel and escort him up here in handcuffs... Yes, you can come with him if you must... ten o'clock on Saturday. I look forward to seeing you both.' Bodkin put the phone down and grinned at Amy.

'Rex and Fabian here at the same time, that will be interesting,' she said.

'They'll be in the same room at the same time,' Bodkin said, tapping his pocket to check his car keys were still there. 'They'll be like two starving rats in a cage. I can't wait to see them fight it out.'

Chapter Forty-One

On Friday morning, Amy got an extra hour's lie in as she was working at the shop and didn't start work until nine, instead of the seven-thirty start she usually had at The Mill. After eating a bowl of cornflakes and pouring her second cup of tea, she picked up the summaries she had worked on the night before and skim read them. She hadn't been able to add much to Jack Draper's entry other than his testimony that he had seen Caspian Stonehand with a girl that could have been Nina on the night she went missing. On her second summary, she noted that he had been evasive and added a line to the end of the page under the important questions section asking who told Jack about Caspian's death.

At one, Bodkin took her for a surprise lunch at the Sunshine Café where she had egg and cress sandwiches, a pot of tea and a slice of Maderia cake. Bodkin ate two rounds of ham sandwiches and two pieces of the Maderia with his coffees. They discussed the murder cases in low voices as they were eating.

'Have you heard back from Margo?' Amy asked.

'I have as it happens. She's bringing him in tomorrow morning.'

'Does she have a car? It's not something we ever asked her.'

'No, she doesn't. He's coming up this evening on the train. He's staying over at her place.'

'Ooh, that will get the neighbours talking.'

'I hope none of them have young daughters,' Bodkin said, chewing a little more heavily on his sandwich.

Amy picked up her own sandwich and held it in front of her mouth without biting into it. 'What about Jack? Has he decided to play ball?'

'Not yet, but he will. I'd put money on it. He asked whether he's allowed to have visitors today and when I asked, 'anyone special?' he shook his head and said he'd like to make a private phone call. I've refused so far, but I might let him do that later on today, to see if anything crawls out of the woodwork.'

'Is Fabian still coming? It looks like he was telling the truth about his night at the Milton.'

'I still want him over here. I want to see how Rex reacts when he walks into my office and finds Fabian sitting there.'

Amy washed her mouthful of egg and cress down with a long sip of tea. 'I'm giving Brigden's a miss tomorrow. I wouldn't miss this for anything.'

Bodkin finished his sandwich and wiped his mouth on a napkin. 'What have you got planned this evening?'

Amy tipped her head as she thought about it. 'I might nip down to see Alice. What about you?'

'It's Friday. Cyril usually makes an appearance on a Friday. At least he has done for the last two weeks. I'm hoping he fancies a night out on his trusty steed, or in it, seeing as it's a car.'

'You'll catch him soon, Bodkin. He's making too many mistakes.'

'They're usually the hardest to catch. They tend to be lucky. Cyril has been incredibly lucky so far.'

'He has,' Amy agreed. 'He's lucky Mr Windup didn't knock his block off. His blanket cloak saved him.'

'It would be nice to get that case wound up at the same time as the two murders. We're so close to solving those. I can feel it in my water.'

'Bones,' Amy said. 'I always say, feel it in my bones.'

'Well, wherever it is, we're close to finding out who the murderers are.'

'Do you think it was two different people, then?' Amy asked.

'I have an open mind about that.'

'What do your waters say?'

Bodkin got to his feet. 'My waters say I shouldn't have had that second cup of coffee. I need to nip out the back.'

As they left the café to walk around the corner to the shop, Amy slipped her arm through Bodkin's. 'I know what I meant to ask. Have you heard back from Sal about Jack's adoption? Did she find anything?'

'She's going to give us a call in the morning. She's over in Hythe today seeing how the O'Toole's are settling in.'

'Kathleen and the kids are in Hythe? That's a lovely place. I hope they'll be happy there. I meant to ask Sal how they were getting on, but events got in the way.'

Amy and Sal had helped Kathleen O'Toole and her two boys escape from a bully of a man through Sal's family charity. They had moved down to Dover in secret a few weeks earlier.

'Is Sal coming up again tomorrow? It's Ferris's night on stage at the Milton.'

'Yes, she said she'd be here about five.'

'I hope you've got something better in the larder than you had last week,' Amy said as they approached the shop door.

Bodkin choked and stopped dead. 'I'd forgotten all about it.' He gave Amy a quick kiss on the lips, turned and hurried off towards the marketplace.

'He's in a hurry,' Josie said as she put the key in the lock to open the shop door. 'That wasn't much of a goodbye kiss.'

'He's got food on his mind,' Amy replied. 'I do hope it's not boiled beef and carrots.'

* * *

At eight-thirty on Saturday morning, Amy folded her updated summary sheets and slipped them into her bag, before shouting a hasty goodbye to her parents and walking out of the front door. Her excitement was so intense, she had to force herself to stop running to the bus stop where she knew she'd have a ten-minute wait.

At the police station, she found PC Parlour on the desk.

'Hello, Miss,' he called cheerily as Amy came into the reception area. 'Inspector Bodkin asked me to send you straight through when you arrived. He's got a message for you from the hospital.'

'Oh, no,' Amy said as she tapped her foot impatiently waiting for Parlour to open the door to allow her access to the main part of the building. 'Not Con, please, not Con.'

'What's happened? Is Con all right?' Amy blurted out as she entered Bodkin's office.

'He was when he asked the nurse to get in touch with you about half an hour ago. She didn't know how, obviously, so she rang here.'

'What does he want? Did she say?'

Bodkin shook his head. 'He wouldn't tell her. He just said it was something important.'

Amy checked the clock on the wall of the office. 'What time does the fun begin?'

'I told them to be here by ten. I won't let them meet until then, so you've got an hour or so.' He put down the file he was reading and shouted for Smedley.

'Give Miss Rowlings a lift to the hospital, will you? Park up and wait for her. She shouldn't be too long.'

When Amy pushed Con's door open some fifteen minutes later, she found him sitting in an armchair by the window.

'You look so much better, Con. Have they taken you outside yet? It's a lovely day.'

'I can sit outside tomorrow for an hour but I'll have to do it in my pyjamas in case I try to escape,' Con said, cackling as the words came out.

'You behave yourself,' Amy said. 'I mean it, Con. You might not be so lucky next time.'

Con shrugged. 'But I might.'

Amy sighed and looked at her watch. 'I'm sorry, Con, I can't stay long. I've got a busy morning. What did you want me for?'

'Did I want you?'

Amy closed her eyes, then looked at the old man with a sad look on her face. 'You sent me a message. The nurse rang the police station and asked them to get in touch with me.'

'Did you find my funeral suit?'

Amy looked at the ceiling and sighed again. 'Was that it, Con? The nurse said it was important.' Amy checked the small cupboard at the side of his bed, but there was only an empty fruit bowl and a rolled up bandage in there. Crossing her fingers and silently praying that the hospital staff hadn't destroyed the clothes, she opened the built-in wardrobe door. 'Here's your funeral suit hanging up. It looks like someone has pressed it for you.'

Con stuck up a thumb. 'I wouldn't want to lose that.'

'It's safe,' Amy said. 'Look, I'd love to stay and chat, but I've got to be getting back. There are some important things happening this morning.' She blew him a kiss and turned for the door.

'There was a car that night,' he said. 'It was parked up near the house. I remembered when I was having breakfast this morning.'

Amy stopped dead in her tracks. Turning on her heel, she hurried back towards him. 'Can you remember anything else about it?'

'It was a posh one, very shiny, the moon reflected on it.'

'Was it a short car or a long car? Think carefully.'

'It was a long one with lots of windows.'

'Was it black?'

'Can't remember; it must've cost a fortune though, all those windows.'

Amy smiled encouragingly. 'What about the man who threw the case into the briars, Con? Can you remember anything else about him? You said he was in shirtsleeves.'

Con tilted his head as he thought. 'It was the same colour as his trousers, I know that.'

Amy clenched her fists in excitement. 'What colour? Can you remember the colour? Could it have been grey? Might it have been a light coloured jacket and not a shirt?'

'Might have been,' Con replied. 'It had lots of shiny buttons on it.'

Chapter Forty-Two

When Amy returned to the police station at nine-fifteen, she found the place a hive of activity. PC Parlour was on the front desk trying to control half a dozen irate women, all wanting to know why the Casanova Caller hadn't been arrested yet. There had apparently been another break in during the night. This time on the well-to-do estate that had been built at the turn of the century just past The Mill. At the back of the small crowd of women, Sandy Miles, the reporter from the Evening Post, made notes on his pad while shouting the odd question at the clearly flustered Parlour.

Inside the station, Ferris hurried between Bodkin's and Chief Inspector Laws' offices, carrying messages and files. Chief Superintendent Grayson was also in attendance, which was unusual for him on a Saturday.

'What on earth is going on?' Amy asked.

'Panic stations,' Bodkin replied. 'Laws wants to charge Jack Draper with the murder of Caspian Stonehand and he wants to...'

'Bodkin!'

The inspector looked towards the door as the broad shouldered, saggy faced Chief Inspector bellowed at him.

'Sir?'

Laws walked into the room and handed a thick wad of files to Bodkin.

'It's an open and shut case. Sign it off now.'

'Which case are you referring to, sir?'

'The ten-year-old murder... What's her name... HornyCrutch?'

'Nina Honeychurch,' Bodkin replied.

'Her... sort it out, Bodkin. Chief Super Grayson isn't happy. He's under pressure from the chief constable's office. They want the two investigations tied up with a red ribbon and filed away with the rest of the closed cases.'

'But we don't know who did it yet, sir. I've got two candidates dropping in this morning, one in the cells and another one within reach. It won't be long now; I can feel it in my—'

Laws lifted an index finger.

'Bodkin. We all know you like to drain every last drop of evidence from the bottle, but you aren't going to get any more out of this one and you don't need to.' He paused and frowned as he noticed Amy standing near the desk, nodded curtly towards her, then went on. 'Read those witness statements, man. It's as plain as the nose on your face who the culprit is and the best thing about it is, he's already dead, so we won't have to bother hanging him. We won't have the expense of a trial either.'

'It's not as open and shut as it might look, sir. We think that—'

'Who's we? You and Ferris, or you and Hercules Marple here?' He waved a hand towards Amy.

'Me, Ferris and Miss Rowlings, sir.'

'Well, you're all barking up the wrong tree like pack of...' Law's voice tailed off... 'mad dogs,' he finished lamely.

'Sir, I'm due to question two suspects, in about half an hour or so. I'm sure things will be much clearer by the time I've done with them.'

Laws laid his hand on the pile of files he'd dropped on Bodkin's desk. 'I want this tied up, typed up and on my desk, no later than five o'clock this afternoon. I shouldn't even be here, man. It's Saturday.'

He took a deep breath. 'Oh, and charge that Draper fellow with the Stonehand murder while you're at it. He's only been arrested on suspicion, hasn't he?'

'Yes, sir but.'

'No if, no buts, man. Charge him with murder and let's get it to court.' He turned away and walked towards the door. 'Then get back to the cases you've been ignoring. Have you seen that mob at the front desk demanding to know what we're doing about this Casanova character? The press is here too, Bodkin. I'll leave it to you to give them some answers.'

Laws nodded to Amy, muttered, 'a pleasure,' then stormed out of the room.

'Blimey!' Amy said. 'Five o'clock. We'd better get our skates on, Bodkin.'

Bodkin picked up the stack of files that Laws had dropped onto his desk, opened up a drawer and dropped them in. 'Filed under closed cases,' he said with a wink. 'Now, let's get a cup of tea before Fabian and Rex get here.'

Amy had just finished her tea when there was a sharp knock on the door and PC Smedley, with the bruises from his injury spreading to below both eyes, led Fabian Starr into the office. He was dressed in a brown checked suit, a fawn coloured trilby and was carrying a briefcase.

Bodkin offered him a seat on the opposite side of his desk and sat down next to Amy.

'Are you feeling better, Mr Starr? Nasty things those summer colds, I hope you sweated it out quickly.'

Starr muttered something that Amy didn't catch, then said. 'What exactly is it you want from me? I thought I'd answered all your questions.'

'All?' Bodkin replied. 'Not all, Mr Starr. There is no end to them. I think more up all the time.'

Fabian took a deep breath and forced a smile. 'Okay, go ahead.'

'Did you bring the client file, you know, the one with all the aspiring young actresses in it?'

Starr opened his briefcase and passed a thick photo album to Bodkin.

Bodkin took it, flipped it open at a random page, and twisted the album around so it faced Starr. 'Did you ever find her any well-paying parts on stage or screen?'

Starr nodded. 'Yes, she's done well. She's a good actress.'

'That's good to hear, Fabian,' Bodkin replied. 'How old is she?'

'Twenty two, twenty-three.'

Bodkin read the notes at the side of the photograph. 'She was sixteen when you signed her up?'

'Yes, she was very good, even then.'

'Did she audition on your casting couch, Fabian?'

'I... what... I have no idea what you ate talking about.'

Bodkin flipped to another page. 'What about her?' He showed the picture to Starr, then flipped to another page. 'Or her? What about her? She only looks to be about fourteen.'

'She was sixteen,' Starr said, loosening his collar. 'They are all old enough.'

'Old enough for what, Fabian? To act? I didn't think there was an age limit on that.' Bodkin took another look at the photograph. 'Or did you mean old enough to have sex?'

Fabian's face turned scarlet, his brow suddenly swimming in sweat.

'I really don't know what you're talking about.'

'Your casting couch, Fabian. That's what I'm talking about. Is it comfy? I hope it is. It gets used a lot, doesn't it?'

Fabian shook his head quickly. 'Who's been telling lies about me? I bet it was that bloody Rex Larson.'

'I'm not at liberty to say. But I will be keeping this.' Bodkin shut the book and tapped it with his finger. 'And I'll be making a few telephone calls, too. Just to see what the girls themselves have to say.'

'It's not illegal. I haven't broken any laws.'

'You lied to us during a murder investigation. You gave false evidence, Fabian. You told us you were impotent.'

Fabian's head dropped. 'I am,' he said. 'I didn't lie. No one would admit to something like that.'

'But... the casting couch. What good is that if you can't take part?'

'I watched,' Starr said quietly. He looked at Amy as if she might show a little sympathy. 'I took pictures. The auditions were set up for a few actors I wanted to entice onto my books.' He clasped his hands as if he was about to pray. 'I couldn't get the bigger names. I needed some bigger names.'

'So you got these young girls, not much more than kids, to have sex with grown men? Did you promise them the stars? Parts in plays and big Hollywood productions.? All you have to do is let a well-known actor have sex with you.' Bodkin slammed his hand down on the book. 'You make me sick, Fabian. You're every bit as bad as Rex Larson. You take advantage of young girls just like he does.'

'It's how I got him... Rex, that is. He was in the office one day. I'd been trying to get him to sign up for weeks. I showed him that book, or the one I was using back then at least, and he spotted someone he fancied, then someone else. Before long, it was a regular thing. Girls came to the agency, had a screen test, then the prettier ones went on to meet one of their favourite actors in the...'

'Flesh?' Bodkin finished for him.

Fabian put his palms on the desk, took them off again, then once again clasped them together.

'How old were the girls, Rex... auditioned?'

'All about sixteen or seventeen, I kept the younger ones in a separate file. He never got to see that one.'

As Bodkin was about to reply, there was a rap on the door and PC Smedley opened it to reveal Rex and Margo standing behind him in the doorway.

Fabian immediately got to his feet. 'What's he doing here?'

Rex scowled at the agent. 'You... I told you what I'd do if I ever saw your face again.' He rushed towards Starr, swinging his arms around like a windmill.

Ferris was around the desk in a flash and positioned himself between the portly Starr and the scrawny fist pumping Rex. Smedley was only a second behind him and before Amy could get out of her seat to allow Bodkin to get by, both men had been restrained.

Bodkin clapped his hands twice as he stepped out from behind his desk. 'Now, now, children. This really is dreadful behaviour.'

'Why is he here? What are you setting me up with?' Rex demanded to know.

'You don't need setting up Rex,' Bodkin said. 'You do that very well without my help.' He looked around his office as Margo tried desperately to get between Smedley and Rex. 'Do you know? I think this was a bad idea. This place isn't near big enough for us all to sit comfortably in. Perhaps we should go somewhere with a bit more room.' He put his finger on his lips and tilted his head slightly as he thought. 'I know. Let's go to the Playhouse. We can all sit around on the stage. That would be much more appropriate.' Bodkin squeezed past the jumble of figures in the centre of his office and walked towards the door. 'Come on, you lot. I've got an audition of my own, planned.'

Chapter Forty-Three

Just then, the phone rang.

Bodkin turned back, but as he did, Rex and Starr began to push and shove again. He took hold of Rex's arm and pulled him towards the door. 'Get that, Smedley.'

Smedley walked behind the desk and picked up the phone. 'It's your sister, sir. She says she has some information for you.'

Bodkin forced Rex's arm up his back and pushed him against the wall.

'Can you take the call, please, Amy? Just jot down the details and I'll have a look at them when I have time.'

Amy took the handset from Smedley and sat down in Bodkin's chair.

'Hi, Sal, it's Amy... Yes, I'm fine thanks, how are the O'Toole's? Have they settled in?'

'We found them a nice house in Hythe, Amy. The kids are doing well but they miss their friends, obviously. They don't understand why they can't write to them, but it really isn't safe. We don't want that bully of a man to find out where they are, and it only takes one slip and he'll find them.'

'I think Bodkin might have sorted that Marty character out once and for all,' Amy replied, 'but it's better to err on the side of caution.'

'They'll be fine. The kids are really enjoying being by the coast. They've spent all the school holidays on the beach.'

'Bless them,' Amy replied. 'Danny said they'd never been to the seaside before.'

'He'll be the champion sand castle builder one day.'

Amy looked across the room and saw Bodkin hand Rex over to Smedley. 'What was it you wanted to tell Bodkin, Sal?'

'Oh yes, it's about those adoptions. There have only been two involving children from Spinton. We have Jack Mortenson, who became Jack Draper, and we have another case, from eighteen eighty-eight, which is probably too far back to be of any interest to him.'

'I might as well jot it all down, Sal. Go ahead.'

Sal gave Amy the details of what she had discovered. Both boys had been sent to the same children's home twenty years apart. 'The second child's name was Winstanley. John Winstanley.'

Amy frowned as she thought. 'I'm sure I've heard that surname recently.'

After giving Amy a set of dates and the names of the adoptive parents, Sal changed the subject. 'Are we still hitting the Milton to hear Ferris sing?'

'We wouldn't miss it, Sal. Alice is coming tonight too, though no doubt she'll complain about feeling like a gooseberry, but she'll enjoy it, she always does.'

'I really can't understand why she's still single,' Sal said. 'She looks like one of those Hollywood starlets. You'd think some bloke or other would have offered to marry her, young baby or not.'

'She's very particular, Sal.' Amy replied. 'She's had offers, but none of them were exactly what she wanted and Alice will never settle for second best, or second hand.'

'Good for her,' Sal replied. 'Now, before I go, I want to ask you something.'

'Go ahead,' Amy lifted her index finger to Bodkin and mouthed 'ten seconds.'

'What's all this about Custard Chops?'

Amy burst out laughing. 'Sorry Sal, you'll have to ask Bodkin about that.'

'Oh, I will, have no fear. It just seems a strange nickname to give someone.'

'It's better than the alternative, believe me,' Amy replied.

'The alternative?'

'Gravy Bowl,' Amy replied and then, laughing again, she said goodbye.

Fifteen minutes later, Rex and Margo walked onto the stage as Ferris finished setting out a row of five chairs in a semicircle, leaving a swinging arm length's gap between them. Opposite the five chairs, Ferris set out two more seats for Bodkin and Amy. Rex sat down first, but Fabian, who had just walked onto the stage with Smedley, waited for Margo to sit before taking his place next to her. He would have to twist his head and lean forward to see Rex, and vice versa. Amy and Bodkin were the last to join them on the stage. As Bodkin was about to sit, he noticed PC Spencer, who had driven Jack Draper over in the police van, standing in the wings, and walked back across the stage to talk to him.

'Before we left, I asked Ferris to call Chester Harvey and order him to meet us here within half an hour. When he arrives, bring him straight through to the stage. Let Johnstone sit with Draper in the back of the van. Tell Johnstone not to bring him into the building until I'm ready for him.'

Amy sat down, opened her bag, and pulled out her summaries and the notes she had made from Sal's telephone call. Margo watched her with suspicious eyes, wondering what their relevance was. Ferris and Smedley took up their positions on either side of the half ring of seats.

'Isn't this nice?' Bodkin said, looking around the stage. 'I bet it brings back some memories, eh, Rex?'

Rex put his tongue between his teeth and said nothing.

'I bet it's nice for you, Margo, having Rex back on your beloved stage after all these years.'

Margo fidgeted about on her chair, then smoothed her dress down. She reached for Rex's hand, but he pulled it away as her fingertips brushed it.

'I still can't understand why you ordered us to come up here in the first place,' Rex snapped, giving Margo a scowl. 'Whatever the reason, can we get on with it?'

'Do they have a stand in for you tonight if you don't make it back to the Assembly Hall?' Bodkin asked.

'The run has finished, but I'm hoping to get a part in their next production. Casting starts today.'

'I wouldn't worry, Rex,' Bodkin said. 'It will more than likely only be a walk on part, anyway.'

Rex got to his feet with an angry look on his face. 'I didn't come here to be insulted.'

'No, you came here because I ordered you to. Now, SIT DOWN!'

Rex glared at Bodkin for a few seconds, then did as he was told.

'If you have something else to ask me, why not do it in your office, why bring us here...?' he spread his arms... 'and why do I have to breathe the same air as him?' Rex jabbed a finger at Fabian.

'I thought I'd explained all that,' Bodkin said brightly. 'We needed more room. Anyway, I like it here. It creates an atmosphere, don't you think?'

'For the first time in years, I agree with Larson,' Fabian said angrily. 'Can we get this over with? My reputation will be tainted forever if it gets out that I've been spending time with that perverted...'

'Talk about the pot calling the kettle black,' Rex yelled.

'You should be in jail. Young girls aren't safe around you,' Starr retorted.

'You're the one who can't be trusted around young girls. Putting them on a plate just to get another actor on your books.'

'You were one of them,' Fabian leaned forwards and pointed an accusing finger. 'You had more than your fair share… and I still think you went after some of my child stars.'

'Say that in public and I'll have you in court faster than you can say libel.'

Bodkin turned to Amy and treated her to a big grin. 'Starving rats in a cage.'

'They're both disgusting,' Amy whispered back.

Just then, PC Spencer stepped onto the stage from the wings. 'Mr Harvey has arrived, sir,' he announced.

Chester looked confused as he noticed the seated figures of Fabian, Margo, and Rex. 'This is a little theatrical, isn't it?'

'Very good. I like that one,' Bodkin said. He pointed to the seat next to Fabian. 'Please, join us.'

Chester sat down, crossed his legs, and reached into his pocket for his cigarettes. 'Does anyone mind if I smoke?' After being greeted by silence, he lit one, leaned back, and blew smoke into the air. 'What's all this about, then?' he asked.

'This,' Bodkin said, getting to his feet, 'is all about a conspiracy. A conspiracy to frame a dead man for a murder he didn't commit. It's also an opportunity to discover who killed that man to ensure his silence and to find out who took the life of a seventeen-year-old girl who thought she was in town to spend a romantic evening with her actor hero.'

'You won't have to dig too deep to find out who did that.' Fabian said, flicking his head in the direction of Rex.

'Shut your mouth, you fat old lecher,' Margo spat before Rex could respond.

'Don't you play the innocent, either,' Fabian said. He looked at Bodkin but held out a hand towards Margo. 'Ask her who tried to get everyone to say they'd seen Caspian in the marketplace with that poor young girl. Then ask who ordered her to do that.'

Bodkin smiled at Margo. 'Miss Ashburner?'

'Fabian wasn't even in the marketplace that night, but Caspian was.' She shot a quick look at Chester. 'That's right, isn't it?'

Chester took a long draw of his cigarette and blew smoke across the room. 'That's right.'

Margo nodded, smugly. 'You see, you can't trust a word this man says.' She gave Fabian a hard stare.

'You called me. My secretary will confirm it.' Starr replied.

'That was for something else and you know it,' Margo said.

Bodkin sat down again and looked inquiringly at Margo. 'Why did you call him?'

Margo looked nonplussed for a moment, but quickly recovered her composure. 'I wanted to ask him if there was anything he could do for Rex. He tries so hard to find work, it's a genuine tragedy that his talent is going to waste having to play such small roles.'

Bodkin chuckled to himself 'A tragedy.' He looked from Margo to Chester. 'I do love all these theatre references.' After smiling at Amy, he focussed on Fabian again. 'Well, Mr Starr?'

'She did actually ask me about finding some work for Rex,' Starr said. 'But the first thing she mentioned was to do with Caspian. She wanted me to change my statement to say I could remember seeing him in the marketplace with the girl before I walked into the Milton.'

'Nonsense! I was just trying to help Rex get a foothold in the business again,' Margo said huffily.

Bodkin leaned back in his chair. 'Would you like to change your evidence, Fabian? Or are you sticking to your story?'

'I'm changing nothing. My statement stands.'

'What about you, Rex? Do you want to change anything you've told us?'

'No, why would I?'

'So, you didn't tell Margo to ask other witnesses to shift the blame to Caspian, seeing as he was dead and wouldn't be able to contradict anything he was accused of doing.'

'No.' Rex said emphatically.

'Hmmm,' Bodkin mused. 'And yet the reports of Caspian being seen with Nina only ever saw the light of day after his death. Four out of the five suddenly remembered seeing him there.'

'Four out of five? You mean three out of four, surely,' Fabian said.

Bodkin shook his head. 'No, I mean exactly what I said. There is another witness. Chester knows who it is, don't you, Chester?'

Chester cleared his throat but didn't reply.

'You know, because you were helping him when he was in hiding.'

'That's preposterous,' Chester said.

'Really, then why was Jack the lad so desperate to speak to you after being arrested? When he was refused visitors, he asked to make a single telephone call. We got the GPO switchboard to trace the call.' Bodkin nudged Amy. 'Can you make a wild guess as to who he called, out of all the people listed in the telephone directory?'

'Chester?'

'CORRECT! Give the lady a coconut.'

'So what?' Chester protested. 'He called me. It doesn't prove I was colluding with him.'

'It proves that you lied when you told us you didn't know him.'

'A white lie. I didn't think it mattered that much at the time.'

'All right. Let's let that one go for a moment. Are you still saying that Margo didn't contact you after Caspian's death to persuade you to link Caspian with Nina?'

Chester bit his lip. 'I'm saying nothing.'

'I urge you to reconsider, Mr Harvey. I'm going to ask you one more time. Did she or didn't she ask you to fabricate a statement that would put Caspian in the frame for murder?'

'Yes.'

'That's a lie,' Margo shouted.

'You know it's the truth.' Fabian said. 'You'll do anything to help that creep.'

'Back to you, Chester. Why did you agree to the request? Didn't you question why she would ask such a thing of you?'

'I assumed it would mean people stopped thinking of Rex as a suspect.'

Bodkin nodded. 'Correct. She was wrong, of course, but she had to do her best for him.'

Rex shook his head. 'I was nowhere near that girl. She was at the stage door the last time I saw her. I didn't try to point the finger at anyone else. Why would I when I was nowhere near the marketplace myself that night?'

'You were directly over the road from it,' Bodkin replied. 'And there were plenty of taxis about.'

Rex leaned forward with his hands on his knees. 'Chester's evidence will back me up. We met in the George after Caspian was seen with the gi... with Nina.'

'You both also agree that you were in the woods that night. A few yards away from where Nina's body was discovered.'

'But I didn't know that cottage even existed at the time!' Rex exclaimed.

'No, Margo mentioned it to you when she telephoned to say she had been questioned about the murder, didn't she?'

Rex nodded.

'I only wanted to warn him about what you'd want to talk to him about,' Margo said defensively.

'You seem to be in this up to your neck, Margo,' Bodkin said, staring at her. 'Are you still saying you didn't contact Mr Starr and Mr Harvey regarding shifting the blame to Caspian?'

'No,' Margo whispered.

'What was that Margo, I don't think any of us heard what you said.'

'I said I'm not denying it. I did it to try to help Rex.'

'Why would he need help if he was innocent?'

'I just thought…'

'Did Rex ask you to do it? Whose idea was it?'

'Mine, I thought it would help.'

'It wasn't going to help young Nina, was it, Margo? And it wasn't going to help the reputation of an innocent, recently deceased man, was it?'

Margo shot a glance at Rex, then hung her head.

'You've just made things worse,' Rex hissed.

'Back to you, Mr Harvey,' Bodkin said, twisting in his seat to look at him. 'Tell us about Jack Draper. Why did he waste his only telephone call on you?'

'I don't know why he chose me, but he asked if I'd help him with his alibi.'

'And did he tell you why he needed an alibi? Did he tell you he was under arrest, suspected of murder?'

'Yes, and I told him I couldn't help him.'

'I still don't understand why he chose you,' Bodkin said, with a puzzled frown on his face. 'What did he ask you to do? The phone call only lasted a couple of minutes.'

'He wanted me to say I saw him going into his digs at the time the murder was taking place.'

'But why choose you? I still don't get it.'

Chester shrugged. 'He knows I have a car. He wanted me to say I saw him as I drove by.'

Bodkin shook his head. 'Come on, Chester. You'll have to do better than that.'

Chester stared earnestly at Bodkin. 'Look, if he killed someone, he's hardly likely to explain himself to me. I'm not his confessor.'

Bodkin got to his feet. 'Shall we ask him why he called you?' He turned to face the wings. 'Spencer, bring him in. It's time he joined in the fun.'

A few minutes later, with the inspector waiting at the door at the side of the stage, a handcuffed Jack Draper was bundled up the short flight of stairs. As he reached the top step, Bodkin brought him to a halt.

'Jack Draper. You were arrested on the suspicion of murder. Chester gave you up, Jack. I am now charging you with the murder of Caspian Stonehand.'

Jack's face fell. He shook his head slowly from side to side before looking past Bodkin towards the seated figures on the stage. Suddenly he lurched forwards his face contorted with rage.

'You stinking swine, Chester. I'm not going to hang for the likes of you. I'll tell them the truth.' He turned his face towards Bodkin, who was desperately trying to hold him back. 'He did it. He killed Caspian! I saw him.'

Chapter Forty-Four

If Chester was shocked by Jack's rant, he didn't show it. Choosing a cigarette, he lit it and blew smoke towards the newcomer. 'Has the hot sun gone to your head, Jack? You've gone doolally.'

Bodkin led Jack across to the empty chair on the end of the semi-circle but pulled it a bit further away from Chester before telling the handcuffed man to sit down. 'Smedley, just stand between these two, will you? We don't want to get real blood all over the stage. I'm sure that fake stuff they use is hard enough to clean up as it is.'

Amy, who had been quietly making notes on the back of her summary sheets until this point, leaned in to whisper, 'Con,' to Bodkin whilst pointing to her notes. Bodkin leaned forward and read the few lines she was pointing to.

'That is interesting,' he said, loud enough for the assembled guests to hear.

'Then there's this.' Amy handed Bodkin the notes she'd taken from Sal's telephone call earlier.

'Curiouser and Curiouser.' Bodkin looked at each suspect in turn. 'That's from Alice in Wonderland, by the way. It's a good line for a copper, although my favourite quote from the book is...' he paused, then snapped, 'OFF WITH THEIR HEADS!'

Margo jerked backwards in her seat as Bodkin's voice echoed around the stage.

'But enough of Alice. She was off her nut on drugs... a bit like you were back in the day, Rex.' Bodkin smiled warmly at the actor and handed the sheets back to Amy, as Fabian smirked. 'Now, where were we?'

'We were just about to get to the bottom of how well Chester knows Jack,' Amy said. She looked across at the driver, then down at her notes. 'It turns out he knows Jack very well and has done, for over twenty years. You see, they both spent time in the same children's home in Dover, albeit a good few years apart.'

Amy's words seemed to knock Chester's confidence a little. He reached for his cigarettes but came up with an empty packet. 'Anyone got a ciggie they can spare?'

Smedley looked at Bodkin and held up a finger. When Bodkin nodded, he reached into his pocket and pulled out a pack of Player's Navy Cut. He handed it to Chester, who opened the pack, selected a cigarette, lit it with a match, then put the pack into his own pocket. 'I'll see you right later,' he told an angry-looking constable.

'It was a very austere place according to this.' Amy tapped her notes with her pen. 'It was a very strict regime, wasn't it, Jack?'

Jack nodded. 'You had to be tough to survive St Mary's.'

'You were given the bare minimum of food and you were expected to work from the age of seven?'

Jack nodded again. 'Kids were better off in a workhouse.'

'Were you beaten a lot, Jack?'

'Most days,' Jack said with a shrug. 'They didn't need much of an excuse to whip you with the birch. You got used to it, though.'

'Did things get any easier as you got older?'

'A little. We were allowed a visitor once a month, and the food got a little better. We got fresh meat instead of scrag end soup.'

'Who visited you, Jack?'

'Mostly a local vicar's wife. I think she felt sorry for me as I'd had a lot of placements but had always messed up somehow and got sent back to St Mary's.'

'You got into trouble quite a lot, didn't you?'

Jack shrugged again. 'I couldn't settle anywhere.'

'Until the Draper's found you. Your original name was Mortenson, wasn't it?'

Jack nodded. 'I don't know what they've got to do with any of this, though. I was happy with them and I was never in trouble.'

'That's what it says here,' Amy said, smiling reassuringly at Jack. 'You used to get a special visitor now and again, didn't you?'

Jack turned to Chester. 'He used to come to visit.'

'Just you. How come he visited you?'

'The home superintendent used to like the idea of old boys dropping in to show us that there could be a reasonable life ahead if we knuckled down and worked hard. I was cleaning the front steps one Sunday afternoon when Chester arrived and we got chatting. We both had a similar background. Mother dying early, being sent away from our hometown. He used to get in trouble too in his younger days, so when he heard my story, we sort of clicked.'

'How old were you then, Jack?'

'Thirteen or so.'

'How often would he come?'

'Every three months. He used to take me out for Sunday afternoons. We used to go to Dover castle. Chester used to make up stories about knights and damsels in distress.'

'Did you like the stories?'

'Some of them were quite good.'

'How old was Chester when he was visiting you?'

'I've no idea, I thought he was in his mid-twenties but I've since found out he was a fair bit older. He looked very young, but I knew he had fought in the war.'

'You liked him so much you still have a picture of the pair of you in your room.'

Jack nodded. 'I was almost fourteen when that was taken.'

'The picture of the Edwardian lady. Is that your birth mother?'
'Yes, she died when I was five.'
'Did Chester's visits go on for months, years?'
'I first met him in nineteen-nineteen. He came every three months until I was adopted in the summer of nineteen-twenty.'
'Did he ever visit you at the Draper's?'
'He used to call in now and then, but she never liked him.'
'She?'
'My adopted mother.'
'What about Bert?'
'Bert got on with him. They used to have a beer together.'
'What about after Bert's death? Did he still come?'
'No, he knew she wouldn't like it, so he used to write.'
'He used to write to you about Spinton? What was he doing then?'
'Driving taxis. He got me a job with the same company he worked for when I moved back here. I was only young still, so they wouldn't give me a full-time job. They needed drivers for the early hours and single men were happier doing those shifts than married ones.'
'You didn't earn enough to live on, did you?'
'No, I was only twenty, so I got an apprenticeship as a carpenter, cabinetmaker. It was going to take me five years to qualify, so the taxi work was handy.'
Amy made a few notes. 'So, you had a friend up here? That was nice for you. Did you used to hang around together? Go to the pub, that sort of thing?'
'I was never really interested in the pub. Anyway, I was always too busy. I had two jobs. I had to be at work for seven in the morning and I didn't finish on the taxis until two, two-thirty, most nights.'
'I'm amazed you could stay awake to drive.'
'Oh, I used to get my head down after I had dinner and set the alarm for ten. I had to pick up my cab at eleven.'
'You didn't see much of Chester, then?'

'We weren't in each other's pockets, though we'd meet up on Saturday afternoons to watch the football sometimes.'

'You were still friends, then?'

'Yes... at least I thought we were... then he goes and gets me involved in this mess.'

'You say you saw Chester kill Caspian? I've got a few questions about that, but first off, how did you get involved?'

'He came around to my work one evening and said he needed an urgent favour. He said he'd helped me out enough in the past and now it was my turn to pay him back.'

'Rubbish,' Chester shouted. 'Don't listen to this. He's trying to lay the blame elsewhere. He killed Caspian.'

'I'd appreciate it if you kept quiet for a while, Chester,' Bodkin said sternly. 'You'll get your chance to tell your side of the story.'

Chester reached for Spencer's cigarettes and lit one.

Amy waited patiently until Chester became quiet, then returned to questioning Jack.

'What was the favour, Jack?'

'He said he wanted me to act as a getaway driver for him.'

'Wow! What did you think of that?' Amy asked.

'I asked him if he was going to rob a bank or something, but he just laughed at that and told me not to worry. I wouldn't be in any danger of getting caught.'

'Did he say what he had planned?'

'No. He just asked me when the next rehearsals were to take place at the Playhouse.'

'That would be the Thursday night. What did he ask you to do exactly?'

'He said I was to leave a few minutes early and meet him on the street. When Caspian came out, I was to keep the engine running and get us out of there quickly when he returned.'

'Lies!' Chester spat. 'You're not taking any of this seriously, are you?'

'How did he know that Caspian would be alone, Jack?'

'I told him. Caspian was always second last out. It was Margo's job to lock the stage door after Caspian left, then she'd leave by the front entrance. It happened every time. All Chester had to do was to wait for the rest of the cast to leave, and he'd have Caspian on his own.'

'Did he say why he wanted to see him?'

'Not exactly. I assumed he wanted to talk to him about him being questioned by the police. He told me that Caspian had seen something that might be misinterpreted ten years after the event.'

'So, you're saying that Chester felt Caspian might tell the police something incriminating about him?'

'That's the impression I got. I didn't know what it was at the time, but then afterwards he told me to lie if I was ever questioned about the night Rex appeared at the Playhouse. He said I was to say that I'd seen Caspian in the marketplace with a young girl carrying a suitcase.'

'I see.' Amy jotted down some more notes, then turned over her second sheet of the summaries and looked up with poised pen.

'Okay, let's get to the actual night of the murder,' Amy said. 'What happened?'

'I went into rehearsals as usual, but I had a drawing I wanted Caspian to look at. It was a basic design for the next play, but when I got on stage, he was busy rehearsing the others and he wasn't in the best of moods, so I sat on the stage and added a bit to my idea, then I just began to doodle.'

'You drew a broken heart and a dripping dagger.'

'I know, but that was to give me inspiration for the Don Juan backdrop. It wasn't anything to do with what happened afterwards.'

'It's a rather large coincidence,' Bodkin put in.

Jack shrugged. 'What can I say? That's what it was.'

'You left early Jack. Imogen said you were in a hurry to get out.'

'I had just realised what time it was. Caspian would be calling a halt before nine and it was a quarter to.'

'So you left... by the stage door?'

Jack nodded.

'Were you wearing your overalls?'

'I always did.'

'Was Chester waiting outside?'

'He was parked up the road in his Ford. He stayed where he was, even when I waved, so I walked up towards him.'

'Then what?'

'Chester moved across to the passenger seat and I got into the driver's side. When we saw Imogen and the rest of the cast leave, he told me to pull forward, so I did. When I got to the Playhouse, I parked and kept the engine running while he jumped out and ran towards the stage door.'

'Where he met Caspian?'

'He was only there a few moments before Caspian came out. I craned my neck to see, thinking there might be an argument, but then Chester pulled out a knife and stabbed him in the chest.'

'LIAR!' Chester jumped up from his seat and threw himself towards Jack, but Smedley was quick to spot the danger and, hurling himself at Chester, he forced him back into his chair.

'Now, you stay there and behave, or I'll get you in a neck hold. I'll take my fags back too.'

The second of the threats seemed to get through to Chester and he slumped back in the chair. 'All right, get off me,' he grunted.

'Is it all right with you if we continue now?' Bodkin gave Chester a glare. When he didn't reply, Bodkin smiled. 'Good. I find these things tend to drag out when we get continual interruptions. Carry on, Amy.'

'Thank you,' Amy said before looking back at Jack. 'What happened after that?'

'He ran back to the car, the door was still open, he jumped in and I heard a scream as we drove away. I assumed it was Margo discovering what had happened.'

'Where did you drive to?'

'His workshop, eventually. But we took a detour past the ironworks. He made me stop at the old, abandoned brickworks and he threw the knife into the rubble, then he got back in and he told me to drive carefully so as not to attract attention. We ended up back at his workshop about ten minutes later. He wouldn't get out of the car to begin with because the bloke in the next unit was standing out front having a fag. So I parked up in front and he gave me the keys to the folding doors. I opened up, drove the car in, then shut the door behind us.'

'What did Chester do then?'

'Took off his overalls, they were covered in blood. He chucked them in an oil drum around the back of the unit, poured some petrol in, and set them alight. He told me to clean up the seat in the car as there was a fair bit of blood on it. I got it all over my own overalls, so he chucked them in the oil drum too.'

'And after that?'

'He said it would be better if I went away for a while until things had calmed down, but I had nowhere to go. My mother was in hospital and I couldn't stay in her house as she'd rented it out.'

'Where did you stay then?'

'To start with in his workshop. Then he said it would be better if I hid in the demolitions while he found somewhere better for me. He said I was being hunted, and it was best all round if I wasn't found until he could work out an alibi for the pair of us.'

'He brought food to the demolitions for you?'

'No, he gave me the stew the next day, just before I left. He said I'd have to make it last a day or two.'

'I didn't do—'

Bodkin held up a hand to silence Chester. 'I won't tell you again.'

Amy tapped at her notes again. 'PC Spencer. You found Jack Draper in the partly demolished houses. He had a stew pot wrapped in a tea towel. Did the tea towel have the picture of a car on it?'

Spencer nodded.

'Well, that's your denial up in smoke, Chester. I saw that tea towel in your hut when we came to question you.'

Chester grimaced. 'All right, I helped him hide, and I fed him, but that's the sort of thing I do for people like Jack. We go back a long way.'

'What a hero,' Bodkin said. 'Let's have the truth now, Chester.'

'I burned his overalls. They were covered in blood,' Chester said smoothly. 'I found him on the street near his digs. He told me he was in trouble and I said I'd help him, soft hearted fool that I am.'

'Good old Chester to the rescue,' Bodkin replied.

'I can show you where he threw the knife,' Jack said. 'And if you check his car, there is still a bloodstain on the front seat. I couldn't get it all off.'

'That was from your overalls,' Chester said. He shook his head sadly. 'This is the way you treat me, after everything I've done for you.'

Bodkin scratched at the stubble on his chin. 'There might still be recoverable prints from the knife.'

'There was blood on his boots,' Jack said suddenly. 'He didn't burn those. They'll still be in his lockup.'

'Chester,' Bodkin said, getting to his feet. 'I want the keys to your car and your workshop.'

Chapter Forty-Five

After initially refusing to give them up, Chester, under pressure from Smedley, eventually handed them over and Bodkin passed the keys to the garage unit to Spencer.

'You and Johnstone get over to his lock up. Check the workshop and the shack that he lives in at the back. I want you to bring back every pair of boots or shoes you can find. Also, there's an oil drum around the back. Check to see if there's anything remaining of what was set alight. Ferris, Smedley, just make sure this lot don't try to escape while I nip out to have a look at Chester's car.'

Ten minutes later, Bodkin returned. Standing just behind Amy's chair, he focussed his attention on Harvey. 'That's a pretty big bloodstain, Chester,' he said.

'It's an oil stain,' Chester replied. 'An oil can spilled when I was transporting it.'

Bodkin sighed. 'It will only take a short while to test it and I've already put the wheels in motion. If my officers come back with some blood stained boots, I'd say you're up the creek without a canoe let alone a paddle.'

Bodkin pocketed Chester's car keys and sat down again next to Amy. 'Please continue,' he said.

Amy gave him a quick smile before focusing her attention on Chester again.

'You two are responsible for the failure of Margo's little scheme to get Rex off the hook. Although the narrative about Caspian being in the marketplace with Nina was never really going to fly, the pair of you shot it down before the story had a chance to flap its wings.'

Chester shot a glance at Jack. Both looked puzzled.

'You used exactly the same words when you told us about seeing Nina get into Caspian's car.' She flicked back through her notes and began to read. 'It was one of those silly little Citroen C3s. There aren't many of those about.' Amy raised her eyebrows. 'What are the chances of both of you coming up with exactly the same sentence without so much as a comma's difference?'

'You bloody fool,' Chester spat. 'You haven't got the brains you were born with.'

Jack glowered but said nothing.

Amy tutted at Harvey. 'That's hardly fair, Chester. You accuse Jack of being a careless fool, but you gave him the very distinctive tea towel that was hanging on a nail in your kitchen the evening we came around to visit you.'

Chester pursed his lips, then opened his mouth to speak, but thought better of it.

'Inspector Bodkin is correct, Chester. You are up the creek. When we're finished up here, he's going to take Jack to the old brickworks, and rest assured, they will find the murder weapon. It hasn't rained since the night of the murder, so any fingerprints on that knife will be easy to find.'

Chester looked at the tips of his fingers as though blaming them for leaving the evidence behind, then clasped his hands together on his lap.

'I'd like to move on a bit now. Well, go back really, to the night Nina went missing.' She held out a hand in the direction of Fabian. 'We're quite happy with a lot of your evidence, especially regarding the plan to blackmail Mr Starr, but some of what you had to say doesn't quite ring true.' Amy waited to see if Chester would respond. When he didn't, she continued. 'Caspian could never have persuaded the receptionist to give him a spare room key, and the idea that she was an ex-girlfriend who was willing to help him is laughable. Likewise, Caspian wouldn't have had the nerve to offer money and drugs to the girl on Fabian's knee to join the blackmail plan. We know that Caspian used to get tongue tied around women unless he was on stage. There is no way on earth that he would walk up to a total stranger and offer her money to engage in criminal activity. Likewise, he wouldn't have been capable of persuading young Nina Honeychurch to get into his car.' She paused and narrowed her eyes as she looked at Chester. 'You, on the other hand, find it easy to persuade girls to give you what you want. You still do to a degree... No, it was *your* ex-girlfriend who was persuaded to hand over a room key, and it was you who talked the young woman into joining the plot to blackmail Fabian. We're quite willing to accept the fact that it was Caspian's idea to begin with. He was more than a little annoyed with Fabian for not offering him a contract, but there's no way on God's earth he would have talked the two women into joining in.'

Chester bit his lip, his eyes darting from Amy to Bodkin, who was sitting with his arms folded, watching the proceedings.

'Going back a little. Jack told us that Caspian had seen something that might be misinterpreted. I think what Caspian saw was Nina getting into your car. You picked her up, didn't you? It wasn't in the marketplace, because Margo or Jack, one of them at least, would have seen you. When did you see her, Chester? Was she still hanging around when you got back from dropping Rex off with the drug dealers or had you spotted her heading towards the railway station when you went to meet them at the Dragon? It's only across the road from there, after all. Caspian was seen at the telephone kiosk, so he would have walked back through town later than everyone else. Did he spot you picking her up on his way to the Milton?'

Chester stuck out his jaw but said nothing.

'That's why you killed him, wasn't it, Chester? Because he had seen you with Nina. You thought you were safe after all these years. You and he had done a bit of blackmailing together. Nina's body lay undiscovered. You thought you'd got away with it, but then we have the worst summer storm in living memory. A wall collapses and the poor girl's remains were found. Not only that, but the police were asking awkward questions at the Playhouse. You couldn't trust him not to spill the beans, could you, Chester? You had to silence him for good.'

'Come on, Chester, admit it,' Bodkin said. 'You'll at least stand a chance of skipping the noose if you cooperate.'

Chester curled up his lip. 'Cooperate? You're joking. You can't trust a copper.' He took another cigarette from the pack and lit it with shaking hands.

'You picked Nina up that night, you took her to the cottage in the woods and you killed her,' Amy said firmly.

'That's nonsense. You have no proof I was ever there. Why would I take her to that dump? It could have collapsed at any moment. No one ever went near the place because of that.'

'Your real name isn't Chester Harvey, is it?' Amy said, tapping her pen on her notes. 'The Harveys changed your name when they adopted you, because they wanted you to have a completely fresh start. Your birth name was John Winstanley.'

'What if it was? What's that got to do with anything?'

Amy pursed her lips as she considered her reply. 'I thought that it might not have any significance to begin with, but the name Winstanley reminded me of something I'd heard or read recently. Then I remembered. When Nina's body was found, the Evening Post ran the story, and they named the cottage's last known resident... Cynthia Winstanley. She was an alcoholic who couldn't look after her son in that tip of a house. There was no electricity back then, of course, but she didn't even have the luxury of running water. She couldn't look after her son, so the welfare people put them both in the workhouse where she died very soon after. Her son, being only seven at the time, was sent off to a children's home in Devon where they knew he'd be given the disciplined upbringing they thought, in their wisdom, he needed.'

Chester hung his head and looked down at his feet.

'The reason they didn't send you to a home in or around Spinton was two-fold. One, there was only one place suitable for a child of your tender years and that had a reputation of being too easy going. The second reason, however, was far more important. They figured that you wouldn't be able to find your way back to the cottage from all the way down there. They were fed up with you absconding and having to drag you kicking and screaming from that wreck of a house.'

She paused, then began to chant the old skipping rhyme.
'Little Johnny Braveheart
Climbed in to meet the ghost
But the ghost caught little Johnny
And spread him on his toast.
So stay out of the Witchy Wood
Or you could be the one
To end up on a toasting fork
Just like Little John.'

When she finished the rhyme, she spoke to Chester with a sad note in her voice.

'That was you, wasn't it, Chester? You were Little John. You knew that cottage like the back of your hand. You knew there was a storeroom with no windows and a door you could lock. You knew that no one went near the place, so you could do what you wanted with her and no one would hear the screams. You killed Nina Honeychurch, and you killed Caspian Stonehand because he was the only person that knew you had taken her.'

Chester stood up suddenly. 'All right, I'll admit to killing Caspian, and I'll admit to taking that girl to the cottage, but I'm not going to hang for something I didn't do while the person who did walks away scot-free.'

Amy watched open-mouthed as Chester held out his arm and pointed an accusing finger at Rex.

'He killed Nina. She was alive when I left.'

Chapter Forty-Six

Rex leapt to his feet as Margo almost fell off her chair in her haste to get close to him.

'It's not true,' he wailed. 'I don't know anything about this cottage or about what happened to that girl. You have to believe me, Inspector.'

'That girl still has a name. It's Nina and you would be wise to remember that in future, Mr Larson.' Bodkin glared at the actor. 'Now, sit down. You'll get your chance to give us your side of the story.'

'Rex,' Margo wept. 'I believe you.'

Chester stayed on his feet for a good thirty seconds before lowering his accusing finger and getting slowly back onto his seat.

Rex, after shooing the sobbing Margo away, sat down himself and dropped his head into his hands. 'It wasn't me,' he muttered to himself.

'That's quite a revelation, Chester,' Amy said. 'Would you like to explain it to us?'

Chester took a deep breath, then began to speak, his voice husky. 'I'll admit that I picked Nina up outside the station. The trains had all stopped for the night, except the odd coal train and I was a little concerned for her, as that's where all the street girls hang out, along with their customers. I saw her walking towards the station as I came out of the Dragon after meeting the men who were going to sort out Rex's drugs. I didn't think much about it at the time, but on the way back from dropping Rex off, I thought about her. I figured she'd be much safer with me than she would be hanging around with the prossies all night, so I drove back. She was sitting on a bench outside the station.'

'What did you say to persuade her to get into the car?' Amy asked. 'Was she reluctant?'

'She was to start with. I explained what sort of area she was in and she began to get nervous, but she still wouldn't get in the car.' Chester looked up at the ceiling for a moment. 'Look, she was a pretty girl. I fancied her, so I made up a story. I told her that I'd just dropped Rex off at a party and he'd sent me back to see if I could find her, as he wanted her to join him.'

'Did she believe you?'

'Not to start with, but she was shivering with the cold and it was getting chillier by the minute, so eventually she agreed to get in. She asked where we were going, and I told her the party was at a house in the Witchy Wood. If she was worried about me, that worry dissipated when a drunken bloke hammered on the side of the car and asked if he could have her next. She begged me to drive off after that.'

'Why take her to the woods, Chester? Why not a hotel?'

'It was only ever going to be a quickie. I didn't intend spending the night with her.'

'What were you going to do after you'd had your way with her, then?' Amy asked.

'I hadn't thought of that. All I could think about was having her. She really was very attractive.'

'She was little more than a kid,' Bodkin spat.

'She was old enough. It wasn't against the law.'

Amy put her hand on Bodkin's arm to quieten him, then

returned her gaze to Chester. 'So, you drive into the woods, then what?'

'I was just going to park up and get into the back with her, but then I thought about the cottage. No one would come across us in there. I had a torch in the glove box so I would have been able to find my way around easily enough.'

'How did you get her to go into the cottage with you? I mean, it was a partly collapsed dump, even back then.'

'She got out of the car because I told her that I knew where we would find Rex. She didn't argue, she just followed me. You can't see the cottage from the track.'

'And when she did see the cottage?'

'I told her that there was something I'd hidden inside and that I needed to get it for Rex.'

'Didn't she ask what it was and why it was hidden?'

'She did, sort of. I got her to wait by the front door. I told her that I'd stashed some cocaine inside and Rex wanted it.'

'Then what?'

'I went in with the torch, then shouted out as though I'd been hurt and asked her to help me.'

'You really are despicable.'

Chester shrugged. 'I was extremely worked up by this time. As I said she was...'

'Yes, we got that, loud and clear,' Bodkin replied.

'She had to walk through the front room to get to the kitchen and that's where I was waiting. I aimed the torch beam towards her so she could find her way. I was lying down on the floor near the door to the storeroom. I told her the cocaine was in a box just inside the door and asked if she could get it for me. I even handed her the torch.'

Amy shut her eyes. 'Dear God.'

'I didn't do anything to her. The next thing I know there's a crash and a bang and Rex is in the room. He'd seen me drive by as we entered the woods and he'd followed us.'

Bodkin flashed a look towards Rex, who still had his head in his hands.

'Don't listen to this, please, it isn't true,' he wailed.

'Shhh,' Bodkin put his finger to his lips to silence him.

'Did Rex say anything? What happened then?' Amy asked.

'He was wild-eyed. He was as high as a kite. He grinned at me like that man who plays the werewolf in the movies. Then he said he'd bought enough stuff to last him a month. To be honest, it looked like he'd taken half of it. He'd been sick down the front of his shirt and his sleeve was almost hanging off.'

'Then what happened?' Amy asked.

'He said she was his, that he should have taken her to the George instead of messing about with the other two girls. It was only right as she had come all this way to sleep with him.'

'Did Nina say anything?'

'She tried to sidle past him to get out, but he got hold of her arm and dragged her through the door into the storeroom. I protested about that, as I wanted her myself, but he said it had been ages since he'd had a virgin, and he wasn't about to pass this chance up.'

'You did nothing to stop him?'

Chester shook his head. 'I told him I'd brought her here, so it was only fair that I should get the first go, but he just grinned and said he'd give me twenty-five quid if I got lost. So I got lost.'

'Just how lost did you get?'

'I didn't go far. I waited near the car for him. I thought he might want a lift back to town, and then he'd give me the money.'

'How long did you wait?'

'Not long. I heard her doing a lot of screaming and him doing a lot of shouting and I thought I'd be better off out of it, so I drove to the Milton where I hoped there might be a girl or two available. I was ready for a drink, anyway.'

Bodkin took a deep breath. 'And that's where you met Caspian and hatched the plot to blackmail Fabian?'

Chester nodded.

'I knew Rex was in a state, but I honestly didn't think he'd go that far.'

'That far?'

'Yeah, to kill her. I thought he'd just have his way with her and as he was her big hero, they'd kiss and make up.'

'How did you find out they hadn't?' Amy asked.

'Listen, I'm not an uncaring man. I felt a bit concerned about her, the state he was in and everything, so while Caspian was sitting in the room with the unconscious Fabian, I drove back to the cottage.'

'Did you see Rex?'

'No, I've no idea where he was. Everything was very quiet.'

'Maybe they'd walked out of the woods and got a taxi... to the George so they could do it in comfort,' Bodkin said. 'Is that what you were thinking?'

'I was hoping that was the case, but of course he hadn't. I went in to see if anyone was still around and that's when I saw her lying on the floor with a pick blade in her head. Her clothes were spread out on the floor along with Rex's coat.' Chester bowed his head and shook it slowly. 'It was awful.'

'But you closed the door and locked it behind you?' Amy said. 'Where did you get the key?'

'It was kept on a nail on the wall just outside the door when I was young. It was still hanging there.'

'Did you lock the front door too?'

Chester nodded.

'Where was the key to the front door?'

'Where it always was, under the plant pot.'

'THIS IS A PACK OF LIES!' Rex screamed, getting to his feet again.

'REX!' Bodkin yelled. 'I won't tell you again. I'll get to you in a minute.'

Amy scratched her head. 'You just left the poor girl there to rot.'

Chester held his hands up in a gesture of submission. 'I wasn't thinking straight. I was in shock. I threw the keys into the well in the back garden, then I ran for the car and drove back to town.'

'You didn't see Rex on the way?' Amy asked.

'There was no sign of him. The next time I saw Rex was the next morning when he found me outside the Milton. I told him what I'd seen and asked why he'd done it. He said he'd just lost it when she wouldn't do as he asked.'

'Noooo, nooooo,' Rex sobbed.

'Then what? Did you tell him you'd locked her in and thrown the keys away?'

'No, I told him the price for my silence had just gone up and the twenty-five quid he'd originally offered me wasn't going to be anywhere near enough. He offered me fifty quid. I said I wanted two hundred and if he agreed, I'd go back to the cottage after I'd dropped him and Fabian off at the station and tidy things up.'

'Wow! You were loaded then, Chester. You had money from the drug deal, money from the blackmail scam, and now three or four years' wages just for keeping quiet. You must have thought all your Christmases had come at once.'

'And birthdays,' Chester said. 'But it came at a cost. I think about seeing that poor girl dead like that most nights. I have to live with it.'

'Quite,' Amy said.

'What about you, Rex,' Bodkin said. 'How's your conscience?'

'I don't have one... I...'

'That's something we can agree on,' Bodkin said. He looked down at Amy's notes, then nudged her with his shoulder. 'Go on then, finish it.'

Amy folded her papers in half and stuck them into her bag, then she smoothed down her skirt and looked hard at Chester.

'There are a few things I don't quite get, Chester.' She held up a hand and pushed one finger down.

'One. Why did you throw Nina's case into the briar before you knew she was dead? Surely she would have needed it later had she lived.'

'I didn't notice it until I went back to the cottage. It was still in the back seat. I couldn't put it in the room with her as I'd thrown the keys away, so I threw it into the brambles. I didn't think it would be found for years.'

'Ah, but the thing is, the moon was up and you were seen. It was nearer one o'clock in the morning than three o'clock, which is when you said you left Caspian at the Milton. The witness was laying traps for rabbits. He said it was no later than one-thirty.'

'Then the witness was wrong... You're making this up, there was no witness.'

'A man wearing a matching grey shirt and trousers. It might have been a jacket because it had a row of shiny buttons on it. The car was a posh one. Sleek, long with lots of windows,' Amy recited.

Chester looked nonplussed.

'Two,' Amy said, pushing a second finger down. 'In your original evidence, you said that Rex came back in a state. That he was in dire need of drugs... anything to take the edge off, so you took him to the house you were staying at and stole some of your landlady's medication. Laudanum and barbiturates, I think you said... So, my question is, why would he be in such a desperate need if, as you have just told us, he'd just bought enough drugs to last a fortnight, although it looked like he'd taken half of them? Please don't try to tell us your second statement is true, because Rex told us you had found him something to keep him going until he got back to London. His statement was identical to your original one.'

Amy pushed down a third finger.

'You say you looked in and saw Nina on the floor with the blade of a pick in her head, her clothes strewn around the floor and Rex's coat lying next to them?'

'That's right, that's exactly what I saw.'

'But you told us that when Rex came into the cottage, he had been sick down his shirt and one sleeve was hanging off. He obviously wasn't wearing his coat. Or are you saying he was carrying it?'

'It was... he...'

'The only reason you know about her clothes being torn off her and the coat lying on the floor was because it was you who raped and killed her. The information about the pick was never mentioned in the press. Only someone who was there at the time would have known about it.'

'But I saw her after. She... Rex...'

Bodkin got to his feet. 'Stand up please, Chester.'

Chester remained seated, looking like a rabbit in the headlights.

'Get him to his feet, Smedley.'

PC Smedley hauled a babbling Chester to his feet and pulled an arm up his back.

Bodkin cleared his throat, then spoke. 'Chester Harvey, I am arresting you for the murders of Caspian Stonehand and Nina Honeychurch. You do not have to say anything, but anything you do say may be used in evidence against you.'

Bodkin patted Amy on the shoulder, then turned back to Smedley. 'Cuff him,' he said.

Margo suddenly threw herself at Rex, who, still in shock, allowed her to smother him in kisses. When he finally pushed her away, he had a smug grin on his face.

'I suppose this means the rest of us can go now,' he said.

Bodkin shook his head. 'Not at all, Mr Larson. I haven't finished yet.'

He turned to face Jack.

'Jack Draper, I am arresting you for conspiracy to commit murder and for aiding and abetting a murderer.'

Jack hung his head as Ferris put his hand on his shoulder.

'We're going to need more officers, I think,' Bodkin said. 'Where the hell are Johnstone and Spencer?'

He turned to face Rex and Margo.

'Margo Ashburner, I am arresting you for bearing false witness in a murder inquiry and for attempting to pervert the course of justice. Please sit down.'

A clearly shocked Margo collapsed onto her seat. 'Oh dear, oh dear, what will mother say?'

Bodkin shook his head as he looked away from her and focussed on Rex.

'Rex, Larson, you can wipe that smug look off your face or I'll do it for you.'

Rex nodded quickly. 'Can I go now?'

'I'm sorry, Rex, but no, you can't. You see, this morning, just before you arrived. I telephoned the Folkestone police and asked them whether they had anything they wanted to talk to you about. When they told me they'd never heard of you, I asked them if they had any recent sexual abuse cases that hadn't yet been resolved. The officer mentioned that they had just the one. A fourteen-year-old girl had made allegations against a middle-aged man with black hair who had assaulted her on the seafront. He told me that they hadn't been able to trace the man.' Bodkin grinned at Rex. 'But they've traced him now, Rex. Your guilty conscience got the better of you the day we met at your hotel. You admitted committing a serious crime before you were even asked about it. They're sending someone over to question you this afternoon. You can wait for him in one of my cells.'

Bodkin looked up as PC Spencer hurried onto the stage.

'We found the boots, sir, lots of blood drips on them.'

'Well done, Spencer,' Bodkin said. 'Which van did you drive over in earlier? I hope it was the big one. It's going to be pretty full going back.'

'WHAT ABOUT HIM?' Rex roared, pointing at Fabian. 'He's getting off scot-free.'

'There's nothing to charge him with, sadly,' Bodkin replied. 'He hasn't broken any law that I know about.' He pushed a thumb towards the exit door. 'Off you go, Fabian.'

Fabian hurried across the stage. He had almost reached the door when Bodkin spoke again. 'There is the matter of the News of the World, mind you. I promised them a story and I think the one about a theatrical agent and his casting couch will go down well with their readers as they eat their bacon and eggs on a Sunday morning.'

Later, in Bodkin's office, Amy sat next to the inspector as they looked across the desk towards the hangdog figure of Chester Harvey.

'Just the little details to tidy up, Chester. Now you've admitted to the two murders.' Bodkin put his pen down on the witness statement sheet. 'The first thing I'd like to know is, how did Rex's coat find its way into that storeroom?'

'He got it wrong about it being taken off him by the drug dealers. I told you how he was sweating and shaking in the car as we drove over to meet them. Well, he took his overcoat off to try to cool down a little. It was still in the back seat when Nina got into the car. She was shaking and shivering for a different reason. She was cold, so I suggested she put the coat on. She was still wearing it when we went into the cottage.'

'Why the pick? Why kill her with that, of all things?'

'She attacked me with it,' Chester said. 'When we'd done... when I'd finished, I was pulling my trousers up and she came at me with it. She must have found it lying on the floor.' He looked across at Bodkin with tears running down his face. 'I didn't take her there to kill her. I was hoping she'd forget the whole thing afterwards. I was even going to buy her breakfast and give her the train fare home.'

'That was very thoughtful of you. I'm sure she would have been pleased to know you were such a caring man,' Bodkin snarled. 'Now, back to the pick.'

'She came at me, but she could hardly lift it, let along aim it properly. After she missed at the first attempt, she had another go, but she slipped and fell over. I just... I don't know why, I snatched it from her and while she was on her hands and knees, I... hit her with it. I didn't mean to do it, but she was screaming and yelling like a mad thing. I realised there was no way I was ever going to calm her down.'

Chester wiped his tears away with the back of his hand, then looked across at Amy. 'Was there really a witness?'

'Oh, yes, that was all true,' Amy said. 'But he wasn't sure of the time. I just threw that in to see how you would react.'

Bodkin pushed a sheet of paper across the desk, then handed Chester a pen. 'Sign your confession statement, please.'

Chapter Forty-Seven

That night, the projectionist at the Roxy managed to keep the film running and the five friends came out of the movie house raving about James Cagney's performance in Angels With Dirty Faces, the film that they had seen less than half of the week before.

On the way to the Milton Hotel where Ferris was due to perform at nine o'clock, Sal laughed hysterically at Ferris's James Cagney impressions. Amy and Bodkin were not so impressed.

'Do me a favour, Ferris,' Bodkin said, grimacing. 'Stick to singing. Don't use that in your act.'

In the cocktail lounge at the Milton, Amy sat between Alice and Bodkin, with Ferris and Sal on the opposite side of the table. When Ferris was announced by the compere, Sal jumped to her feet and applauded madly. Ferris walked onto the stage to a smattering of handclaps and took the microphone from the compere before having a quick word with the jazz band.

'My first song tonight is dedicated to the lovely lady at the back of the room wearing the green dress.' He then began to sing, I Get A Kick Out Of You, from the Cole Porter musical, Anything Goes.

Sal was transfixed by Ferris's voice from the moment he started singing. 'Oh my goodness,' she said, grabbing Bodkin's hand across the table. 'Isn't he wonderful?'

Bodkin pulled his hand away as he shook his head. 'Remarkable,' he said, picking up his whisky glass. 'Please don't start on the impressions.'

Amy laughed and gave him a nudge. 'Shh,' she admonished.

Alice, wearing the red dress that Amy had picked out for her at Brigden's and who always enjoyed hearing Ferris sing, tapped her foot and sang along before giving Amy a sideways glance. 'I still feel like a gooseberry,' she said.

Amy picked up her fruit stacked glass of Pimm's and handed it to Alice. 'Take a sip of that. There's lots of fruit in it, but it could be made better by adding a gooseberry.'

Alice laughed, handed the drink back and picked up her own glass of port and lemon. 'Here's to you and Bodkin, well done on catching the murderer.'

Amy grinned as she turned to face Bodkin, who acknowledged Alice's toast with a smile.

'I was thinking about earlier today when I was getting ready this evening,' Amy said. 'Do you know, Bodkin, I don't think I've ever met five nastier, more despicable people in my life, let alone together in one room.'

Bodkin sipped his scotch and nodded slowly. 'Not one of them had a morsel of kindness in them. They were all out for what they could get, even Margo, though all she ever wanted was Rex.'

'Did the Folkestone police turn up?'

'Yep, he's in their custody now. They're going to let me know when they charge him. He'll be looking at jail time for certain.'

'Not before time either,' Amy said. 'Disgusting man.'

During the break between songs, Sal spun around in her chair and stared at Bodkin for a few moments. Her smile looked a little tight, but her eyes were shining. 'Don't think you've got away with Custard Chops, my darling brother. I want a full explanation when Ferris has finished his act.'

Amy looked from Sal to Bodkin and back, then suddenly burst out laughing. Sal frowned, but Amy couldn't stop. Eventually she grabbed Alice's hand, and the pair hurried away to the ladies' toilets, both giggling like schoolgirls.

When they returned to the table, having managed to contain their laughter, Amy picked up her drink and held it out towards the inspector. 'You do make me laugh, Bodkin. Some of your little quips have me in hysterics.'

Bodkin chinked his glass on Amy's. 'All part of the service,' he said.

Amy sipped her Pimm's. 'Do you know, I can't imagine life without Pimm's now.'

Bodkin snorted. 'Thank goodness we only come here once a month. My wallet couldn't take it if they started selling it at the Old Bull.'

'Meanie,' Amy said, taking a long sip. 'I wonder if Cyril's out and about tonight.'

'There's a good chance,' Bodkin said. 'Apart from a couple of shoplifters and someone caught urinating in public, I don't have a lot else on my desk. I could do with bringing him in. I might even get a gold star on my homework from Laws.'

'Enjoy the rest,' Amy said. 'We both know that come Monday your desk will be collapsing under the weight of new cases.'

Bodkin sighed. 'I know.'

Amy laughed again. 'Don't give me that, Bodkin. You wouldn't have it any other way, and you know it.'

After church the next morning, the Rowlings family walked out of the lychgate entrance to find Bodkin leaning on his Morris car with what Amy immediately recognised as an 'I've got news' look on his face. After swapping pleasantries with Mr and Mrs Rowlings, he took Amy by the arm and led her up the street, away from the crowd pouring out from the Sunday service.

'Come on, Bodkin. Out with it, I can always tell when you've got something to tell me.'

Bodkin grinned. 'We've got Cyril, only he's not Cyril. He's Don.'

As a puzzled look came across Amy's face. Bodkin grinned again.

'He was caught last night climbing out of a window on Norman Street. He didn't actually make it out of the window because his cloak got caught on the latch and he got stuck.'

Amy began to giggle. She put her hand to her mouth.

'The window was a sash type and when his cloak caught; it was pulled down onto his back, trapping him.'

'Oh no...'

'There were two women living in the house he'd chosen, a mother and daughter. And while the younger lady ran outside, slipped a tin bucket on his head and started hitting it with a broken spade handle, the older one pulled down his trousers and smacked his backside with an ancient, steel-bladed fish slice.'

Amy almost collapsed laughing. 'Oh no,' she gasped. 'Poor Cyril.'

'An unfortunate end,' he said.

When Amy had recovered somewhat, she wiped the tears from her face with the back of her hand and asked. 'So why isn't he called Cyril anymore?'

'Because his name is Donald Meriweather. Mrs Creasey was right about her salesman lodger. He was the Casanova Caller, but since his name is Donald, I've reverted back to calling him Don Two.'

'Oh, I bet she loves it, doesn't she? She'll dine out on that for the rest of her life.'

'She asked if there was a reward when I took her blankets... Cyr... Don's makeshift cloaks, around this morning. He'd nicked them out of her cupboard.'

'Poor Don,' Amy said, laughing again. 'Imagine the indignity of it. What a tragic end to his heroic story. I hope she doesn't cook with that fish slice again.'

Epilogue

At 11.15 that morning, Amy stood along with Alice, Miriam and the farm lads who had been working that day, in the farm kitchen to listen to the Prime Minister, Neville Chamberlain's radio announcement.

I am speaking to you from the cabinet room at 10 Downing Street. This morning the British ambassador in Berlin handed the German government a final note stating that unless we heard from them by eleven o'clock that they were prepared at once to withdraw their troops from Poland, a state of war would exist between us. I have to tell you now that no such undertaking has been received, and that consequently, this country is at war with Germany.

THE END

Acknowledgments

Maureen Vincent-Northam for her expertise, friendship and immeasurable patience.

Paul Lautman for his meticulous eye for detail.

My late wife Doreen, who loved a murder mystery. I wish she was still here to read them. I would love to know what she thought of Amy and Bodkin.

Nikki East for once again designing such a wonderful cover.

Sumaira Wilson for all she does at SpellBound Books.

Also by T. A. Belshaw

AMY ROWLINGS MYSTERIES

Murder At The Mill
Death At The Lychgate
The Murder Awards
Murder on The Medway

Printed in Great Britain
by Amazon